In the dream, she was standing by the freeway watching the traffic rush by, and then, far in the distance, she had seen her mother's car. There didn't seem to be anything different about that car—in fact, in the dream it had looked just like all the other cars on the freeway. But still, somehow, she had known that that particular car was her mother's. And then, as the car passed her, she saw her mother turn and look at her. The odd thing was that the woman in the car, whom she *knew* was her mother, didn't look like her mother at all. While her mother's hair was sort of drab brown the woman in the car in her dream had long black hair that fell around her shoulders, and deep blue eyes that seemed to penetrate right into Cassie's soul.

Her mother's eyes had been brown, like Cassie's own.

And then, in the dream, her mother had said something.

Cassie couldn't quite make out the words, but a second later her mother had begun laughing, and the car had suddenly shot forward. A second after that, it veered sharply to the left, smashed headlong into the concrete supports of an overpass, and burst into flames. It was then that Cassie had awakened, sweating and shaking, her ears still ringing with the sound of the explosion, her vision still filled by the sight of her mother's face—the stranger's face—as, flames consuming her, she stared at Cassie and uttered a single word: "Good-bye." Then she had started laughing as if she didn't care that she was leaving Cassie alone in the world.

It had been the very next night that the dream had repeated itself—this time in horrible reality. . . .

BANTAM BOOKS

BY JOHN SAUL

The Unwanted

JOHN SAUL

BANTAM BOOKS
NEW YORK • TORONTO • LONDON • SYDNEY • AUCKLAND

THE UNWANTED

A Bantam Book / August 1987

ISBN 0-553-26657-8

Published simultaneously in the United States and Canada

Bantam Books are published by Bantam Books, a division of Bantam Doubleday Dell
Publishing Group, Inc. Its trademark, consisting of the words "Bantam Books" and the
portrayal of a rooster, is Registered in U.S. Patent and Trademark Office and in other
countries. Marca Registrada. Bantam Books, 1540 Broadway, New York, New York 10036.

PRINTED IN THE UNITED STATES OF AMERICA

OPM   28   27   26   25   24   23

For my father,
the best father
in the whole world.

The
Unwanted

Prologue

The sun was high in the cloudless blue sky, and had it not been for the faint trace of a breeze drifting in from the sea, the stiflingly humid heat of the August afternoon would have been unbearable. The beach was all but deserted. Only far away—much farther than she was allowed to go—could the little girl see the barely visible figures of the big children playing at the water's edge. Once—and it didn't matter how long ago it had been, for in her two-year-old world every day was forever and each week an eternity long forgotten—she had tottered toward the distant figures, her tiny hands reaching out as if she could touch them at any moment. But long before she had gotten close enough even to see them very well, she had felt the stinging slap of her mother's hand and heard the horrible word.

"*No!*"

Even before the first scream of pain burst from her, she had felt herself being jerked around and dragged back in the direction from which she had come, the rough sand scraping the skin from her knees as a stream of unintelligible sound rained down on her from her mother's looming face above. Though she didn't know what all the words meant, the message was clear.

She had done something wrong. When they got back to the blanket, her mother would spank her, and then she would have to sit on the blanket even long after she had forgotten just why she was there or what she had done.

1

Today she watched the children playing in the distance for a while, but made no move to abandon her bucket and shovel and try to escape down the beach toward them. Though she no longer remembered exactly what would happen if she did, she knew going that way hurt, and she didn't want to hurt.

She began digging in the sand with her shovel. In a little while there was a hole beside her, with water seeping into it as if by magic. She tried to splash the water out of the hole, but each time more water came in, and it always seemed to be just as deep.

She tried digging the hole deeper, but that didn't work either. It kept filling up with water, and then the sides would cave in, and pretty soon the hole would be wider but almost all filled up again.

Then she noticed that if she dug into the sand at the bottom of the hole, and scooped up whole handfuls of the mixture of sand and water, she could dribble it out onto her legs in neat rounded drops that looked like tiny little gray pancakes.

And if she dribbled more on top of that, it looked like a whole stack of little pancakes.

Chuckling and clucking softly to herself, she began covering her legs with dribbles of sand, building towers of it on top of her knees and ankles, then covering her toes as well.

After a while she noticed that if she held very still, the gray sand would turn white. And if she waited for it to turn white, then wiggled her toes, it would crumble away into the beach again.

Over and over she repeated the game. Then another idea came into her head.

She packed her bucket full with wet sand from the bottom of the hole, then patted the sand next to the hole flat. Turning the bucket upside down on the flat space, she lifted the bucket away and found a neat round pile of sand with a flat top.

Scrunching around onto her knees, she began dribbling wet sand from the hole over the top of the mound, letting it run down over the edges like frosting on a cake. Then she began dribbling it into towers, turning it into a castle. When she was done, she picked up her shovel and began carefully digging a moat around the castle. But when the moat was about six inches deep, it began to fill up with water and its sides began to cave in.

The little girl watched in fascination as her sand castle crumbled away.

When it was gone, she started another one.

The sun drifted slowly across the sky, but the little girl didn't notice.

She was surrounded now by the ruins of five sand castles, and was starting to build another one when she felt something brush against her.

It was a kitten, its tail sticking straight up in the air, its gray fur matted with sand.

It mewed softly, then sat down in the sand, staring up at her with large, curious yellow eyes.

The little girl reached out to touch the kitten, but it backed quickly away.

"Kitty," the little girl said softly. Then, again: "Kitty."

Her sand castles forgotten, she pulled herself to her feet and took an uncertain step toward the kitten.

It was then that she saw the little boy standing a few yards away, frowning deeply as he stared at her.

She looked back at him, then grinned and plumped back down onto the sand.

The little boy giggled and came closer.

The kitten, three feet away now, sat back down on the sand and wrapped its tail around its legs.

As the sun continued its slow course across the sky, the two children sat in the sand looking at each other, giggling happily as each of them mimicked the other's movements, with the kitten sitting a few feet away, watching them both.

Then, mewing softly, the kitten stood up, stretched elaborately, and darted away across the beach.

"Kitty!" the little boy exclaimed. Pushing himself to his feet, he started after the tiny cat, the little girl apparently forgotten.

The girl sat where she was for a few seconds, then turned around and stared solemnly at the blanket on which her mother was sitting.

Her mother was looking the other way, talking to a man the little girl didn't recognize.

The little girl scrambled to her feet and started after the

boy and the kitten—her bucket and shovel, as well as her sand castles, completely forgotten.

She had to hurry to catch up with the little boy, but she knew that if she called to him, her mother might hear and stop her, so she stumbled along as fast as she could, tumbling down every few steps, then scrambling back to her feet and hurrying forward once again. Every few steps she felt her shorts slipping down over her bottom and reached down to pull them up again, but when the little boy kept getting farther and farther ahead, she finally abandoned the shorts altogether, leaving them in a heap on the sand.

The slope of the beach got steeper, and the little girl found her feet sliding out from under her with almost every step. But there was dune grass here, and she could use that to pull herself along. When she finally got to the top of the slope, the little boy was standing by himself, the thumb of his right hand poked securely into his mouth while his eyes—wide set and round—stared at the kitten. The kitten was sitting next to what the girl knew was the Bad Place.

She wasn't sure why it was the Bad Place, but dimly she remembered her mother bringing her here once and pointing to the place, then spanking her while she repeated the Word.

"No! No, no, no! Do you understand?"

Between the Word and the angry sound of her mother's voice and the stinging on her bottom, she understood.

She stopped uncertainly, and instinctively looked back. But all she could see was grass.

After a moment the little boy saw her, and his thumb suddenly popped out of his mouth. He pointed at the kitten and giggled happily. Then he started walking toward the Bad Place, holding his own shorts up with his left hand as his right thumb went back into his mouth.

The little girl hesitated, then followed.

The slope dropped away, and in a few seconds the little girl caught up with the little boy. He stopped walking and turned to stare at her, but didn't say anything. Instead his eyes watched her gravely.

She reached out and put her hand in his. Then, following the skittering kitten, the two of them started toward the Bad Place.

Suddenly there was no more of the warm dry sand that felt so good between her toes.

Instead there was an icky sticky feeling, and she could feel something cold oozing around her feet. She stopped and looked down.

Mud.

Thick and black, it squished around her feet, and there was an odor about it that made her wrinkle her nose and make a face. But the kitten didn't seem to notice it at all, and neither did the little boy.

The little girl took another step, pulling her foot loose from the muck and wiping it carefully on her other leg before putting it back down into the ooze.

But there was a path into the Bad Place, and if there was a path, it must be all right.

Now there was tall grass on both sides of her, and it almost felt as though she was in a jungle.

And there were sounds all around her, sounds she had never heard before.

At first she didn't know whether she should be frightened or not.

Then she remembered the sounds she'd heard in her room on the nights when the "monsters" had come for her, and she'd started screaming until her daddy had come in and turned on the lights and told her that there weren't any monsters.

But she knew there *were* monsters, and as she walked along in the Bad Place, holding on to the little boy's hand, she knew that the monsters were all around her, even if she couldn't see them.

It was the monsters that were making the sounds.

She had a crawly feeling in her tummy now, and her skin felt all tingly.

And in her chest, her heart was beginning to thump loudly.

If the monsters heard her heart, they would know where she was and come after her.

A tiny whimper of fear escaped her lips, and her eyes burned with tears.

She wanted to call to her mother—wanted her mother to

come and get her, although she was afraid of what would happen to her if her mother found her in the Bad Place.

She tugged at the little boy's hand and he stopped. His thumb still in his mouth, he gazed at her uncomprehendingly.

"M-monster—" the little girl managed to say. "There!" She pointed at the jungle that was all around them, but the little boy shook his head.

"Kitty."

Then, pulling at her arm, he toddled along the path toward the kitten that they never seemed to be able to catch up with.

She didn't know how far into the Bad Place they had gone, but she was crying now, her heart pounding so hard she knew the monsters had to hear her soon.

They were all around her, making low moaning sounds, and she could hear them rustling softly as they searched for her.

Her crying got worse, and she let go of the little boy's hand and started running as fast as she could, trying to catch up with the kitty. But the muck seemed to grab her feet, slowing her down, and the harder she tried to run, the slower she seemed to go.

Just like in the middle of the night, when she had to run away from the monsters but couldn't. . . .

The jungle was reaching out for her, trying to trap her in its writhing green arms, trying to wrap her in a web and pin her down so the monsters could come and eat her. . . .

It wasn't grass and vines around her now. It was snakes, coiling up and striking out at her, hissing angrily as she fled past them.

And then, so suddenly the little girl didn't realize it was happening, the jungle opened up to one side and there was a big sandy place that looked just like the beach down by the water.

She was safe!

She was out of the Bad Place, and there was sand, and she was safe!

The kitten was still a few yards away, but it had stopped again and was sitting in the path, watching her. The child's heart was pounding a little less now, and she stumbled out onto the sand, out of the sucking muck, away from the terrors of the jungle that had threatened to suffocate her.

The sand gave way beneath her feet.

She screamed now, a full-throated howl of terror that echoed around her and made even the jungle monsters fall silent.

She screamed again, then tried to pull her legs free from the sand that was suddenly knee deep.

Knee deep and cold and oozing like the mud in the jungle.

The little boy tottered out of the jungle and stopped, staring at her.

She screamed again, then lost her balance and fell into the cold, wet quicksand.

The little boy took a step toward her, then another.

First his right foot then his left sank into the bottomless depth of the sand.

The little girl knew why it was the Bad Place now.

It was the place where all the monsters of her nightmares lived, and as she thrashed in the quicksand, she could feel them coming closer, creeping out of the jungle, coming to get her.

She could hear her heart pounding, and her screams grew even louder, but even in her panic she knew her daddy wouldn't come for her.

She wasn't in her room, and it wasn't night, and her daddy couldn't hear her.

Even her mother couldn't hear her.

This time the monsters were going to get her.

She knew they were going to get her, because always before, when they had come for her in the night, her daddy had been there.

But now it wasn't night, and her daddy was nowhere near, and there was nothing but the monsters.

The monsters and the little boy.

He was coming closer to her now, but she knew the monsters were going to get him too. And even as she watched—his image blurred through the tears that streamed from her eyes—he stumbled in the sand and fell.

The quicksand closed over him for a moment, then his head reappeared and his screams were added to her own.

And the monsters grew ever closer. . . .

Night came suddenly, a cold dark night that closed around the child, cutting off her screams, blocking out the sound of the monsters as well as the light.

Her chest felt as though it was going to burst, and she struggled against the chill weight of the darkness, struggled to breathe against the watery night.

Now she couldn't even scream anymore, couldn't fight the monsters anymore, couldn't escape the black abyss of the Bad Place. . . .

She opened her eyes, a scream welling in her throat.

The blackness was gone.

Hands were touching her.

Warm hands.

But not her daddy's hands.

She blinked, the scream dying in her throat.

Warmth was all around her, and she felt herself being held close to the softness of a body.

When she looked up, there was a face above her.

Not her mother's face.

A face she had never seen before, but a woman's face.

And then she heard the voice, a low, crooning voice.

"You are mine now. You've come to me, and now you will belong to me. Forevermore you will belong to me."

Chapter 1

Cassie Winslow stood quietly in the heat of the April afternoon, doing her best to focus her mind on the casket suspended over the open grave. The machinery that would lower it into the ground in a few more minutes was only partially concealed by the flowers that her mother's friends had sent, and even the largest bouquet—the one from her father—looked tiny in its position of honor on top of the coffin. There was a numbness in Cassie's mind—the same numbness that had settled over her three days ago when the police had arrived at the little apartment in North Hollywood she and her mother had shared to tell her that her mother wouldn't be coming home. Now, no matter how often she reminded herself that it was her mother they were about to bury, she couldn't bring herself to accept the idea. Indeed, she half expected to feel her mother's elbow nudging her ribs and hear her mother's voice admonishing her to stand up straight and pay attention.

I'm almost sixteen! Why can't she leave me alone?

She felt herself flush guiltily at the thought, and glanced around to see if anyone was staring at her. But who would there be to stare? Except for the minister and herself, the only other person who had come to the funeral was the lawyer who had arrived the day after her mother had died to tell her that he was taking care of everything; the day after the funeral—tomorrow—she would be flying to Boston, where her father would pick her up.

Pick her up in Boston! If her father really cared about her, why hadn't he come out for the funeral?

But Cassie knew the answer to that—her father was too busy taking care of his new family to bother about the one he'd dumped almost the minute she was born. So why would he fly all the way to California just for a funeral? As if she were still alive, her mother's voice rang in Cassie's ears: *"He's no good! None of them is any good—your father, your step-father—none of them! In the end they always run out on you. Never trust a man, Cassie! Never trust any of them!"*

Cassie decided her mother had been right, for her step-father, who had always made such a big deal about how much he loved her, hadn't shown up at the funeral either. In fact she hadn't heard from him since the day he'd walked out of the apartment almost five years ago.

It had been almost that long since she'd heard anything from her father.

The minister's voice droned on, uttering the words of prayers Cassie hadn't heard since the last time she'd gone to church—about ten years ago, she thought, before her mother had gotten mad at the minister. Her attention drifted away from the gravesite, and she looked out over the broad expanse of the San Fernando Valley. Her home had been here for so long that she couldn't remember anything else. It was a clear day, and on the far side of the Valley, the barren mountains were etched sharply against a deep blue sky. It was the kind of day when everyone always said, "This is why I came to California. Isn't it great?" By tomorrow the smog would close in again and the mountains would disappear behind the brown stinging morass that would choke the Valley all summer long.

As the machine began whirring softly, and the coffin was slowly lowered into the ground, Cassie Winslow wondered if they had smog on Cape Cod.

Then the funeral was over and the lawyer was leading her down the hill to put her into the limousine the funeral home had provided. As they drove out of the huge cemetery that seemed to roll over mile after mile of carefully watered green hills, Cassie wondered if she would ever come back here again.

She knew that a lot of people went to cemeteries to visit their dead parents, but somehow she didn't think she would.

For as long as she could remember, she'd always had a fantasy that perhaps her mother wasn't really her mother at all. Sometimes, late at night in the dark security of her bedroom, she'd let herself dream of another woman—a woman she saw only in her mind—who never yelled at her, never corrected her, never soured her with bitter words. Never—

She shut the thought out of her mind, unwilling even to remember the other things her mother had done to her.

She concentrated once more on the woman in the fantasy. This woman—the woman she wished were her mother—always understood her, even when she didn't understand herself.

But that wasn't the woman they had just buried, and in the deepest place within her heart, Cassie knew she would never return here. But would she ever find that other woman, the woman who existed only in her dreams, who would truly be her mother?

Eric Cavanaugh watched the ball hurtle toward him, tensed his grip on the bat, squinted slightly into the afternoon sun, then swung.

Crack!

The wood connected with the horsehide of the baseball, and Eric swore softly as he felt the bat itself splitting in his hands. Then, as the ball arced off toward right field, he dropped the bat and began sprinting toward first base. If the bat hadn't splintered, it would have been a home run for sure. As it was, he'd still get a base out of it, unless Jeff Maynard managed to snag it.

There was little chance that Jeff would make the catch. That was the reason Eric had hit it to him in the first place. He rounded first easily and, fifteen feet before he got to second base, he plunged headfirst into a slide and felt his uniform tear away at the shoulder.

"You're gonna break your neck doing that someday," he heard Kevin Smythe say, and knew from the second baseman's tone that he'd made it. Safe! Grinning, he got to his feet, and began scraping mud from his torn jersey. But then, as his eyes swept the field, his smile faded.

Beyond the fence, parked by the curb on Bay Street, was the old white pickup truck with CAVANAUGH FISH emblazoned in cobalt blue on its side. Leaning against the truck was his father, his arms folded over his chest, his head shaking slowly as he muttered something to the coach, who nodded in apparent agreement from his place just inside the fence.

Eric's heart sank. Why couldn't his father have shown up half an hour before, when he'd put the ball over the left field fence? But that was the way it always seemed to happen: if he was going to make a mistake, his father was going to see it, and over dinner tonight Ed Cavanaugh would want to talk about it. Since this mistake had come on the baseball diamond, it meant that after dinner he and his father would be back here on the high school diamond, going through batting practice until the light got so bad neither of them could see. Even then Ed would insist on "just a couple more," so Eric wouldn't be able to get to his homework until after eight o'clock.

Unless his father got drunk. That was always a possibility. But when his father was drunk, things were always even worse than when his father was sober.

The coach's whistle signaled an end to the practice session, and Eric, after waiting for Jeff Maynard to catch up with him, started toward the locker room, wondering if he should skip the four-thirty student council meeting. If he weren't the president of the council, he wouldn't even be thinking twice about it. The council, he knew, didn't really mean anything at all. Being on it just gave him one more opportunity to have his picture in the yearbook, and gave his father one more thing to brag about when he was out getting drunk. But Eric *was* the president, and if he didn't go, his dad would be sure to hear about it. Coach Simms would make sure of that. Then there would be a long speech about "living up to what I expect of you" to go with the extra batting practice.

"That woulda been another homer if the bat hadn't busted," Jeff observed as he caught up. "How come you always hit those to me? You know I can't catch 'em."

Eric's grin came back, and his blue eyes sparkled with quick good humor. "You don't care if you catch 'em or not. If

I hit 'em to you, I know I'm gonna get a base, and I know you're not gonna worry about it."

Jeff shrugged his indifference, but his eyes clouded slightly. "Your dad saw what happened," he said quietly. "You gonna get in trouble?"

"I always do, don't I?" Eric replied. He tried to make his voice sound as if his father's wrath didn't mean any more to him than a missed fly ball meant to Jeff. Except that Jeff had been his best friend almost as long as he could remember, and Jeff always seemed to know what was going on in his head, no matter what he said out loud. Now, he proved it once again.

"Wanta cut the council meeting? If we did, we could get the trig assignment out of the way before you've gotta be home. Or we could cut the trig, too, and go down to the beach," he added hopefully.

Eric thought about it, then shook his head as he pulled open the heavy locker-room door and stepped inside. "Can't. If I don't get an A on the test next week, I won't get an A in the course. And you know what that means."

Jeff rolled his eyes. "How would I know? And you don't either, since you've never gotten anything *but* A's. Besides, your dad won't kill you, will he?"

"I don't—" Eric began, but was immediately cut off by the coach yelling at him from the equipment cage next to the showers.

"That's two bats this week, Cavanaugh! One more and you start paying for them! Got that?"

"I didn't mean—"

Simms's voice grew louder, and his words seemed to echo the lecture Eric heard from his father so often: "I don't care about what you meant. All I care about is what you do!"

Eric felt a sudden surge of anger flood up through his body, and struggled against it. Getting mad would only make things worse. What the hell was the big deal about a broken bat anyway? Except it wasn't just the bat—it was everything. And it had been that way as long as he could remember. No matter what he did, it never seemed to be good enough—not for his father, not for his teachers, not for anyone. Always they seemed to think he wasn't trying hard enough, that he ought to do better. But he was already doing the best he could. What more did they want?

Once again Jeff Maynard seemed to read his mind. "Forget it," he heard his best friend say so softly that he knew no one else could hear. "If you say anything else, he'll tell your dad you mouthed off and make you run laps. Then you'll miss the meeting and flunk the test too! 'Course," Jeff couldn't resist adding, "it might be fun to watch Mr. Perfect fall on his face just once!" Then, as Eric swung around to punch him on the arm, Jeff darted off and disappeared around the corner toward his locker.

Eric glanced at the big clock on the wall, and realized he only had ten minutes to get to the council meeting. He began stripping off his stained jersey, shoving it into his book bag for his mother to wash that night.

He would mend it himself.

It was five-thirty when Eric finally left Memorial High and started home. The streets of False Harbor were nearly empty, since the summer season wouldn't start for another six weeks and most of the small fishing fleet was out to sea. The summer shops along Bay Street were still boarded up, and the town wore the strangely deserted look it took on every winter after the summer people were gone and the seasonal shopkeepers had closed their stores, heading south to bask in the sun and sell the same merchandise to the Florida vacationers that they sold on Cape Cod all summer. Though the town had an oddly forlorn appearance, the off-season was still Eric's favorite time of year. It was only then that he could go off by himself sometimes, hiking across the dunes and combing the beach, alone with the pounding sea and the stormy winter skies.

Then there was the marsh, flooded at high tide, that had given the town its name by making the harbor appear much larger and more easily accessible than it actually was. In the summer the dredged channel, which provided the only opening to the deeper harbor inland of the marsh, was choked with pleasure boats, and when the air took on the stillness of August, the acrid exhaust of their engines hung over the reeds like a poisonous haze. But in winter, with a northern wind howling, the marsh held a special magic for Eric, and he would sit for hours, his back to the village while gulls screamed and wheeled overhead. Once or twice he'd talked Jeff Maynard into exploring the marsh with him, but Jeff had only shivered in the cold for a few minutes, then suggested that they go bowling at the little six-lane alley on Providence Street, where at least it was warm. But that was all right with Eric—he didn't have the opportunity to go to the marsh very often, and when he did, he preferred to be alone.

Today there was no time for a hike out to the marsh, but as Eric strode along Bay Street, his book bag slung over his right shoulder, he considered stopping at the wharf. A gull had built the first nest of the season on one of the pilings, and Eric had already checked it twice for eggs. So far there were none. Still, you could never tell.

When he reached Wharf Street and glanced up at the clock that stood atop an iron tower at the entrance to the marina, he changed his mind. If he wasn't home by six, there would be hell to pay. So he turned left, starting toward the old common two blocks away.

It was only there, in the center of the town, that False Harbor began to look lived-in again, for it was in the long central strip—four blocks wide and eighteen long—stretching from the marsh at the western end of town to the rolling expanse of dunes that marked the far eastern boundary, that the year-round population lived. The residents of False Harbor had left both Cape Drive and Bay Street to the summer people. Indeed, once you left Bay Street there wasn't much to set False Harbor apart from any other small New England village. It was built around a rectangular common that hadn't seen a sheep grazing in more than a century, and the owners of the buildings facing the common had resisted the temptation to turn the village center into anything that might be called *quaint* by the tourist guides.

Yet quaint was exactly what it was, for many of the buildings were more than two centuries old. Once they had been private homes, but most had long since been converted into stores, remodeled by former owners in the days when Victorian architecture had been modern. The brick town hall still dominated the acre facing Commonwealth Avenue, which was bounded on the east by the common and on the west by High Street. Next to it stood the stone Carnegie library, which had replaced the town stables in the early twentieth century.

Eric turned away from the town hall as he emerged from Wharf Street, cutting diagonally to the point where Commonwealth picked up again after having been broken for a block by the square. Then, changing his mind, he veered south again, toward Ocean Street and the old Congregational Church which occupied its own acre between the common and Cambridge Street.

The church had always been Eric's favorite building in False Harbor, though if anyone had asked him why, he would not have been able to say. A tall, narrow structure, its severe white clapboard side walls were broken at regular intervals by stained-glass windows which had only replaced the original flashing two hundred years after the church had been built and a hundred fifty years after the last of its puritan founders had been put to rest in the adjoining graveyard. Its steeply pitched slate roof was surmounted by a tall steeple in which the original bell still hung, though it was rung now only on Sundays and holidays. Eric paused again in front of the church, wondering if he dared take enough time to slip inside and watch the ancient clock in the vestibule strike six. Just as he'd made up his mind to risk it, a horn sounded. He turned to see his father's white truck idling at the curb. From the driver's seat Ed Cavanaugh was waving impatiently.

Eric felt his stomach begin to knot up with a familiar tension as he hurried across the lawn and slid into the truck next to his father.

"Got time to waste hanging out in there?" Ed Cavanaugh growled as he shoved the truck into gear, then let out the clutch.

Eric said nothing. He looked straight ahead. He could feel his father's eyes boring into him.

"Seems to me you could be spending your time a little more productively than standing around watching an old clock strike," Ed Cavanaugh went on. His voice was dangerously soft, a certain sign to Eric that his father was angry.

"I wasn't going to be there more than a couple of minutes—" he began, but got no further.

"Unless you want to end up in the gutter, I don't think you've got a couple of minutes to waste," the elder Cavanaugh replied. He glanced at the road as he turned into Cambridge Street, then shifted his attention back to his son. "And you can damn well look at me when I talk to you," he added.

Eric felt the knot in his stomach tighten, but he was determined not to let his expression betray his fear. Obediently he turned to face his father.

"You think I'm too hard on you, don't you?" Ed Cavanaugh asked, his voice edged with an acid whine. He was breathing harder now, and the heavy reek of whiskey on his breath made Eric shrink back slightly. When the boy made no reply, Ed shook his head. "Well, I'm not. All I want's for you to do your best. And you can't do that by dawdling your afternoons away."

Like you can dawdle yours away in a bar? Eric thought, but didn't dare voice the thought. "I was on my way home, and I just decided to stop at the church for a minute," he ventured. "That's all."

"Should have been home studying," Ed groused. "And it seems to me you and I better spend a couple hours on the diamond after supper. At sixteen you should be able to hold a bat right."

"It was an accident," Eric groaned. He'd hoped that if nothing else, at least the drinks his father had consumed had made him forget about that afternoon's baseball practice. "I know how to hold a bat. You taught me yourself, didn't you?"

Ed Cavanaugh's eyes narrowed with suspicion, and his jaw tightened. "You getting fresh with your old man, Eric?"

"But you did teach me," Eric insisted. "And I'm not getting fresh. You didn't see the rest of the practice, did you? I hit a home run, and I pitched three strikeouts in a row. How come you couldn't have seen that?"

"It wouldn't matter if I had," Cavanaugh replied. "Home runs and strikeouts are what I expect of you. What I don't expect are broken bats and pop flies that any idiot except Jeff Maynard could catch. And I don't expect sass either!"

"Jeff's not an idiot," Eric protested. "He just doesn't car

as much about baseball as you do. If he'd wanted to catch that fly, he could have."

"If he could have, he should have," Ed said tersely. He swung the truck right into Alder Street and halfway down the block pulled it up in front of the shabby two-story clapboard house he'd bought when he and Laura arrived in False Harbor the year Eric had been born. Back then he'd only thought of the house as something temporary, a place for them to live while he built up a fleet of commercial fishing boats. But the business hadn't worked out at all. Ed Cavanaugh's "fleet" still consisted of nothing more than the same fifty-foot trawler he'd started with seventeen years before. He'd long since given up any hope of moving into one of the larger houses in the west end of the village. Besides, he told himself whenever he still bothered to think about it, it wasn't really his fault the fishing hadn't panned out, any more than it was his fault that the house, like the boat, had gotten more and more run down over the years. But where the boat only needed a coat of paint, the house needed a new roof as well, and the garden that had once run neatly along the front of the house was overrun with weeds.

Of course, if he'd had a wife who gave him at least a little bit of support, it all would have been different. The house would look great and the business would be booming. Well, it didn't matter anymore. In fact nothing mattered much anymore.

He glanced over at Eric once more, and found a point of focus for the anger that was suddenly threatening to boil over inside him.

Eric, he decided, wasn't much better than Laura. Everything came too easy for the boy, and the rotten kid didn't appreciate it. Besides, the little know-it-all wasn't quite the hot shit he thought he was.

Oh, Eric was smart—Ed knew the kid was a lot smarter than Laura, if not himself, and he was almost as well coordinated as he himself had been at the same age. Almost, but not quite.

Nobody—but nobody—had been as good an athlete as Big Ed Cavanaugh. And if things had just turned out different—if he'd just gotten even one decent break—he'd have played in the big leagues. But, of course, he'd never gotten a decent break.

Eric, on the other hand, always seemed to get the breaks. And all it had done for him, as far as Ed was concerned, was to make him cocky.

That meant he had a duty to take the kid down a peg or two.

And he knew how to do it too. Just keep pushing at the kid. Never let him think he was doing enough.

Swinging himself down from the cab of his truck, Ed glanced around the yard, looking for some extra chores to add to Eric's list of weekend duties. Then he glanced at the house next door, and the rage he was feeling toward his son shifted again.

How come, he wondered, the Winslows' house always looked so much better than his own? But, of course, he knew the answer: Keith Winslow—who wasn't any better than any-one else, except he always got all the breaks—had somehow managed to snag himself a decent wife. And that made all the difference in the world. If *he'd* been married to Rosemary Winslow, things would be different for *him* too. Not only did she keep the house looking good, but she made a decent living as well.

And that let Keith spend his time lounging around on a boat that never did any real fishing at all. Just took a bunch of rich people from Boston and New York out for sport every now and then.

Ed's gaze drifted to the upstairs front window of the Winslows' house as he thought about what Rosemary Winslow was doing right now. But he figured he knew, since Keith had gotten home from a four-day cruise just this morning.

He wondered what Rosemary did all those nights when Keith was gone. Sometimes, when he could see that she'd put the kid to bed, he'd thought maybe he ought to go over and keep her company for a while. Of course, so far he hadn't actually done it, but that didn't mean he never would. And if Laura didn't like it, that would be just too damned bad.

Suddenly he became conscious of his son's eyes on him, and he turned to see Eric staring at him, almost as if the boy

had been reading his thoughts. "You got a problem?" he
demanded. Then his mouth twisted into an ugly leer. "You're
thinkin' about Winslow's daughter, huh? The one that's comin'
from California tomorrow?" Eric, quickly shaking his head,
turned away and started up the driveway toward the back
door, but Ed merely raised his voice. "Well, you can forget
about her, boy! I don't want you gettin' in trouble with any
trashy little slut from California. You hear me?"

Once more Eric said nothing, but his shoulders hunched
defensively, as if he could physically deflect his father's words.

A moment later, with a last glance at the Winslows'
house, Ed followed his son up the drive. There was going to
be trouble tonight. He could feel it coming. Either Eric or
Laura was going to smart off, and he'd have to teach them a
lesson. But that was all right. He'd had a lousy day anyway.
He always felt better after he'd let off some steam.

From her regular post by the kitchen sink Laura Cavanaugh watched her husband and son come up the drive, and
knew immediately that there was trouble. Ed's face—always
florid—was redder than usual, and Eric wore the expression
of strained placidity that she had learned a long time ago to
recognize as repressed anger.

What was it about this time? she wondered. Well, she
would find out soon enough. She opened the oven door to
give the spareribs a final basting, then pulled the salad out of
the refrigerator and took it into the dining room, where the
table was already set for dinner. She heard the screen door
slam, and went back to the kitchen just as Ed and Eric came
in from the service porch. Eric gave her a quick kiss on the
cheek, and a moment later she heard him taking the stairs
two at a time as he went up to his room. Ed dropped his
lunch box on the counter, then started washing his hands at
the kitchen sink. The muscles on his back rippled under his
blue denim shirt.

Fifteen years ago she would have gone to him, slipped
her arms around him and hugged him. But she knew what
would happen if she tried that now. He would stiffen, then
twist away from her, his eyes flashing with anger. Then,
acting as if nothing had happened, he'd ask why dinner was

late, and before she could reply, he would settle into the breakfast nook and bury himself in the newspaper.

Unless Eric came back down.

If Eric came downstairs, Ed would put the paper aside and start rehashing every minute of Eric's day with him. What had happened? Who had he had lunch with? How were his classes going? What had he done after school? What was he doing in the evening? Was he seeing Lisa Chambers?

And Eric, looking to Laura like a trapped animal, would do his best to give his father satisfactory answers. Except, as Laura was all too well aware, there were no satisfactory answers.

Now Ed turned away from the sink, dried his hands on one of the dish towels, then shoved his bulk into the breakfast nook. His eyes met hers, and his brows knit into a scowl. "Something wrong?" he asked.

Laura opened her mouth, then changed her mind, closed it and shook her head.

For a second she thought Ed was going to stand up again, but he merely reached out and pulled the newspaper over to the place in front of him. Breathing a silent sigh of relief, Laura turned back to the sink.

I should leave him, she told herself. I should take Eric and get out.

But, of course, she wouldn't. There was no place for her to go. She was trapped, and there was no way out.

Besides, none of what had gone wrong for her family was Ed's fault. She knew that—Ed reminded her of it almost every day, one way or another.

Everything that went wrong was her fault. Somehow, some way, she'd failed Ed. And having failed him, she couldn't walk out on him.

But why did he always have to take it out on Eric too?

She'd tried to talk about it with him a few times, when he seemed to be in a particularly good mood, but he'd always insisted that he wasn't being hard on the boy, that he was only giving Eric the guidance that a father owed to a son.

But Laura was certain there was more to it than that. Though Ed maintained that all he wanted was the best for Eric, Laura always had the distinct feeling that it was something else, that it wasn't just the normal desire of a man to see his son succeed.

It was as if her husband wanted to punish Eric. But she had never been able to discover the reason why.

Almost surreptitiously she found herself studying her husband. His hair—dark brown when she had first met him—was iron gray now, and the athlete's body that had been his pride then had thickened over the last twenty years. His hands—the large hands that had once made her feel so safe when they held hers—were callused now, and the veins on their backs stood out, even under the thick mat of hair that started at his fingers and ran all the way up to his elbows. His face had been ruggedly handsome when he was in his twenties, but the years of drinking had blurred those sharp features, and there was a puffy looseness in the skin under his eyes.

So different from Eric, whose lithe body would never attain the mass of his father's, and whose hands always struck Laura as being the hands of an artist or a musician. Not, of course, that Eric had ever tried any such thing, although Laura knew that sometimes, when he was by himself, Eric liked to draw. Several times she had found sketches in his room. Once she'd even thought about showing them to Ed.

She had quickly changed her mind, knowing how her husband felt about art: "Sissy way to make a living," she remembered his saying as he'd sat in front of the television, drinking a beer while she watched a documentary about the life of Andrew Wyeth. "And even most of the good ones wind up starving." So she'd put Eric's sketches back in the drawer where she'd found them, and never mentioned them at all.

Eric's face, too, was different from Ed's. Where Ed's handsomeness—while he'd still had it—had always been rugged, Eric's face was sensitive, his blue eyes ringed with long black lashes, and his delicately chiseled features framed by an unruly mass of curly black hair which, when he was small, had been the bane of his existence. Even today Laura found it difficult to pass her son without running her hand through his hair.

Indeed, she sometimes wondered if it was Eric's looks alone that make Ed ride him so hard. Perhaps, she sometimes thought, if Eric had looked more like his dad, Ed wouldn't have needed to mold him quite so strictly.

Suddenly her husband's angry voice intruded on her reverie.

"It's ten after six, Laura. Can't you ever have dinner ready on time?"

Laura jumped at his voice, then hurriedly bent to open the oven. "I'll start serving right away," she promised. "H-how was your day? Did everything go all right? Did you get the engine fixed?"

Ed glared at her, his attention already drifting back to the sports page open in front of him. "If it went badly, I'd tell you, right? And no, I didn't get the engine fixed. I had to spend most of the afternoon with the wholesaler, trying to soften him up to give me a decent price on the catch."

Which means you sat in the Whaler's Inn, drinking all afternoon, Laura thought as she began placing the ribs onto the three plates on the counter.

Silently she carried the plates into the dining room. Then, just as she was about to call upstairs to Eric, he appeared in the doorway that separated the dining room from the kitchen.

"Mom?" he asked, his voice low enough so that Laura knew he didn't want his father to hear. "Can you talk to Dad? He wants me to go practice batting with him tonight, but I have to study."

Laura stood still. Her eyes met her son's. She could read the fear in them, and the shame he was feeling at asking for her help. She hesitated, then almost in spite of herself, shook her head.

"I can't," she said quietly. "If he's made up his mind, I can't change it. You know that."

For a moment something flickered in Eric's eyes, then it was gone. "Yeah," he said finally. "Yeah, I know. Well, don't worry, Mom. It'll be all right—I'll figure something out."

A moment later Ed Cavanaugh came in and took his place at the head of the table. He waited silently until his wife and son had seated themselves. His eyes surveyed the dinner in front of him, then came to rest on them.

"I guess I can't complain," he said, his voice oozing with a stinging slime of vicious sarcasm. "A crappy house, a lazy son, and a wife who can't cook. What more could anyone want?"

Eric's eyes flashed with anger as his mother winced at the lash of the words, but neither of them answered him, each silently hoping that when Ed started shouting, the neighbors wouldn't hear him. But of course, they would—they always did—and though none of them ever said much, Laura and Eric always knew what they were thinking.

Eric always did his best simply to act as if nothing had happened, but for Laura the pitiful looks she always got from the neighbors—particularly from Rosemary Winslow—were almost as painful as her husband's blows.

Chapter 2

"If you don't get started, you won't make it," Rosemary Winslow said, her eyes flicking to the clock on the wall. It was already after nine, but Keith didn't seem the least bit worried. As she watched, he poured himself another cup of coffee and neatly folded *The Boston Globe* to the sports page. "Keith! Didn't you hear me? This is not a fishing trip—you're picking up your own daughter, and you can't be late!"

"I won't be late," Keith replied, setting the paper aside. "It's Saturday—there won't be that much traffic." He heard the sound of a screen door slamming next door, and glanced out the window to see Ed Cavanaugh starting down his driveway, his eyes bleary, his footsteps dragging. He gestured toward the window with his head, at the same time grinning wickedly at his wife. "Bet Laura doesn't nag *him* the way you nag me."

Rosemary's eyes darkened as she remembered the sounds that had erupted from the Cavanaughs' house late the night before. Though Ed's yelling hadn't been punctuated with any of Laura's quickly stifled screams of pain, Rosemary was still certain the man had been slapping his family around again. Perhaps last night she should have given in to Keith's desire to call the police. "It's not funny," she said, "and I wish you wouldn't make jokes about it."

From her place next to her father Jennifer, who had mercifully slept through the Cavanaughs' argument, looked up from the little rivers of maple syrup she was dredging through the scrambled eggs on her plate. "What's not funny?" she demanded, her large eight-year-old's eyes searching her parents' faces.

"The way Mr. Cavanaugh treats his family," Keith replied, his bantering tone suddenly gone. "And your mother's right. I shouldn't make jokes about it."

"Oh," Jennifer replied, immediately losing interest. Then, once more taking up an argument she'd lost earlier that morning but saw no point in abandoning, she turned to her mother. "How come I can't go to Boston with Daddy to pick up Cassie?"

"I already told you, sweetheart," Rosemary replied. She reached out to ruffle the red curls that capped Jennifer's freckled face. "Cassie just lost her mother, and she won't be feeling very good. We just think it would be easier for her if she didn't have to deal with anyone but your daddy right away. Besides, you and I have a lot to do. We have to go shopping, then finish the bedroom. We want it to be ready for Cassie, don't we?"

Jennifer's face darkened and her lower lip quivered petulantly. "That was supposed to be my room," she reminded her mother. "You promised me—"

"I know what I promised." Rosemary sighed, wondering how to explain to an eight-year-old that promises sometimes had to be broken. "But that was before we knew Cassie was coming to live with us. And didn't you decide it would be nicer to have a big sister than a bigger room?"

Jennifer hesitated, then decided not to answer the question at all. "But what if she doesn't like me?"

"Of course she'll like you, Punkin," Keith told her. "What's not to like? Just because you talk all the time, tend to be a little sassy, and kick and scream when you don't get your way? What's not to like?"

"I do not!" Jennifer protested. She was trying very hard to look indignant, but instead she dissolved into the giggles that always came over her when her father teased her. "And my name's not Punkin, either. It's Jennifer."

"Right, Punkin," Keith said. He slid off his chair just in time to avoid his younger daughter's fist as she aimed it at his side. "Stop worrying—Cassie will like you."

Jennifer's giggles faded away, and suddenly her expression became serious. "If she'll like me, how come she never came to visit me? Doesn't she like you?"

For a split second Keith's eyes met his wife's. Jennifer, they both realized, had just asked the question neither of them was willing to deal with.

Neither Rosemary nor Jennifer had ever met Cassie, and Keith himself hadn't seen her for more years than he liked to admit. The last time he'd gone to California to see his daughter—until then an annual pilgrimage—the trip had turned into a disaster. His first wife, Diana, had been divorced for the second time by then, and she seemed to blame the failure of her second marriage—as well as her first—squarely on Keith.

"I don't want to see you," she'd told Keith on the phone. "I don't suppose I can stop you from seeing Cassie, but I don't have to see you myself."

"But why?" Keith had demanded. "What did I do?"

"Tommy left me," she'd said bitterly. "He left me because I couldn't trust him, couldn't let myself depend on him. And that's your fault. Thanks to you, I can't trust anybody."

Immediately Keith had understood what had happened. Once more Diana's insane jealousy had destroyed her marriage. It wasn't, he knew, that she hadn't been able to trust or depend on him. Somewhere, deep inside her, there was a demon who whispered to her every minute of every day, telling her that people didn't like her, that they looked down on her, that she wasn't good enough.

But the worst of what the demon whispered was that her husband was cheating on her.

And though it was untrue—Keith had never betrayed her, had never even contemplated doing so—Diana had believed the demon within her. She had begun questioning his every move. When he wasn't with her, she sat alone at home, imagining him in the arms of another woman. Eventually, she'd come to the conclusion that a baby was the answer to their problems, and Keith had finally agreed with her. It had occurred to him that Diana's jealousy might be rooted in her deep-seated conviction that Keith didn't truly need her. A baby might change that, giving Diana both the self-esteem of being a mother and a new focus for her energies.

And so they had conceived Cassie.

But Diana's jealousy had only worsened, until finally, unable to deal with it any longer, Keith had left.

Diana had never forgiven him. When the divorce had finally come, he'd given up his rights to partial custody of Cassie rather than subject the child to what Diana swore would be an unending fight through the courts. As soon as she'd won, Diana had taken Cassie to California.

Each year Keith had gone by himself to Los Angeles for a week, checked into a hotel, and spent as much time with his daughter as Diana would allow.

But on that last trip Cassie had barely spoken to him, and toward the end of the week Keith had finally discovered that Diana had convinced the child, too, that the loss of her stepfather was her father's fault.

One week a year, Keith had decided, was not enough to repair the sundered relationship. The following year, when Diana had told him that Cassie didn't want to see him, he and Rosemary had decided it would be better for Cassie, if not for Keith, to stay out of the situation entirely.

Then, four days ago, Diana had gone out after work for dinner with some friends, but never made it home.

It had been three o'clock in the morning when Rosemary had sleepily answered the phone, to be told her husband's first wife was dead.

Cassie, not knowing what else to do, had given the police her father's phone number, but Rosemary had learned the next day that Cassie had also warned them not to be surprised if Keith hung up on them. Her exact words were, "He hung up on my mom and me a long time ago." When Rosemary had repeated them to Keith, he'd winced with a pain that was almost physical.

Had it been any other time, Keith would have been on a plane to Los Angeles immediately, but when Rosemary was finally able to reach him, he was two days out of False Harbor, with no one else on the boat who was capable of skippering it alone. And so, through a series of tense radio-telephone calls, arrangements had been made for Cassie to fly to Boston, where he would meet her and bring her to False Harbor to live with him and his second family.

As for Jennifer's question, he had no simple answer for it.

As far as he knew, no, Cassie did not like him.

On the other hand, she hadn't seen him for five years, and hadn't lived with him since she was two.

But he was still her father. He still loved her, and now that she needed him, he would be there.

"She'll like me," he finally told Jennifer. "She'll like us all."

Then, after kissing his younger daughter and giving his wife a hug, he left the house and hurried out to the car. Five minutes later he was out of False Harbor and on the highway to Boston.

Cassie felt a gentle tap on her shoulder, and glanced up from the book in her lap to see a stewardess leaning over the two vacant seats between her and the aisle. She reached up and pulled one earphone of her Walkman away from her head.

"Your seat belt," the stewardess said, pointing to the sign that glowed on the bulkhead three rows ahead. "We're making our final approach. We'll be landing in five minutes."

Cassie nodded silently, removed the headset, and dropped both it and the Walkman, along with her unread book, back into the big leather tote bag that had been her mother's. The previous night, when she'd decided to take it with her, she had thought that the bag might make her feel better, might give her at least a tenuous connection with her mother. But every time she looked at it, her eyes flooded with tears, and already she was wishing she'd left it behind with everything else in their little apartment in North Hollywood, to be packed for shipment by the movers who would arrive the next day. She looked resolutely away from the bag as she fastened the seat belt, and her gaze drifted out the window to the city that lay below.

All through the five hours of the flight, she had entertained the impossible hope that she might recognize Boston, but deep inside had known she wouldn't. Now she discovered she'd been right. As the plane soared out over Massachusetts Bay, then banked into the final turn before gliding over Boston harbor to touch down on the runway at Logan

Airport, Cassie searched the landscape below for something—anything—that looked familiar. But there was nothing, and as the plane sank lower and lower, until finally only the buildings along the waterfront were still visible, she turned away from the window. Why, after all, should anything look familiar? She hadn't been here since she was barely two years old. How could she remember it? Besides, if it hadn't been for the accident, she wouldn't even be trying to remember it. For a split second she felt a flash of anger toward her mother, then resolutely put the feeling aside. The accident, she told herself one more time, was only that—an accident. But still the thought remained. Twice since her mother had died, Cassie had awakened in the dark, her body trembling and damp with a cold sweat, for the dream she'd first had the night before her mother died had come back.

In the dream she was standing by the freeway watching the traffic rush by, and then, far in the distance, she had seen her mother's car. In the dream it looked just like all the other cars on the freeway, there didn't seem to be anything different about it. But still, somehow she had known that that particular car was her mother's. And then, as the car passed her, she saw her mother turn and look at her. The odd thing was that the woman in the car, whom she *knew* was her mother, didn't look like her mother at all. While her mother's hair was a sort of drab brown—at least at the roots—the woman in the car in her dream had long black hair which fell around her shoulders, and deep blue eyes which seemed to penetrate right into Cassie's soul.

Her mother's eyes had been brown, like Cassie's own.

And then, in the dream, her mother had said something.

Cassie couldn't quite make out the words, but a second later her mother had begun laughing, and the car suddenly shot forward. A second after that it veered sharply to the left, smashed headlong into the concrete supports of an overpass, and burst into flames. Cassie had awakened then, sweating and shaking, her ears still ringing with the sound of the explosion, her vision still filled by the sight of her mother's face—the stranger's face—flame consuming her as she stared at Cassie and uttered a single word: "Good-bye."

Then she'd started laughing, a high-pitched screeching

laugh, as if she didn't care that she was leaving Cassie alone in the world.

But the strangest part of the dream was that the woman in the car—the woman Cassie was still certain had been her mother—was a stranger.

It didn't make sense. Had her mother killed herself, or had Cassie herself, in some unknown way, caused the accident? And yet she knew she couldn't have caused it, for she hadn't even really seen it, except in the dream.

The very next night the dream repeated itself—this time in horrible reality. And Cassie's feeling that she might somehow have caused the accident still persisted.

She felt a slight bump as the plane touched down. She tightened her grip on the armrests as the engines reversed, fighting the ground winds, and the plane slowed to a stop. A few minutes later it was parked at the gate and the jetway was swinging slowly around to link up with the door. Beyond that door, waiting for her, was the man who had abandoned her when she was only a baby, and eventually even stopped visiting her.

Why couldn't she have stayed in Los Angeles? At least there she would have had her friends around her.

As the other passengers streamed up the aisle past her, Cassie stayed in her seat putting off as long as she could the moment when she would have to get off the plane and face her father.

What if he didn't even recognize her? Would she have to go up to him and say, "I'm Cassie?" No, that wouldn't happen. There wouldn't be anyone else left on the plane, so he would *have* to know who she was. Finally, when the last person had disappeared from the aisle in front of her, she released the seat belt, pulled her coat down from the overhead compartment, and picked up her tote bag. She passed the stewardess at the door, saying nothing when the woman wished her a nice day, then moved slowly down the jetway. A few seconds later she stepped into the terminal and looked around.

The last of the passengers was drifting away, and a few people sat in chairs, baggage at their feet, waiting for the next leg of the flight.

But no one at all was waiting for her.

Her first instinct was to turn around and hurry back into

the airplane, but she knew she couldn't do that. Suddenly she felt embarrassed, as if everyone in the airport were watching her. What should she do?

Maybe she had misunderstood, and her father was going to meet her at the baggage area. But no, she distinctly remembered his telling her that he would meet her at the gate and she needed only to pack enough for a few days. Everything else would be shipped, and what she didn't have room to pack in a bag small enough to carry on, they could buy. She wasn't to worry about checking luggage. That, in fact, was the other reason she had chosen her mother's tote bag. It was big enough to carry a lot of things, but had a shoulder strap.

She looked around once more. He had to be there. He *had* to! He couldn't make her fly all the way across the country and then just not show up. Or could he?

She remembered how her mother used to talk about her father: "I could never trust him. Every time I turned around, he was gone, and I could never be sure he'd ever come home again. And then one day he didn't. There wasn't any warning, any sign that anything was wrong. He just didn't come home one day, and the next thing I knew, he was divorcing me! And he did the same thing to you, Cassie! Just stopped coming to see you, and stopped writing to you! Just like that. In a way, it's lucky for you you're finding out what kind of man he is now, before he can hurt you any more."

But he wouldn't do that, Cassie told herself. I just talked to him last night. He promised he'd be here.

But he wasn't.

A few yards away a bank of telephones lined one wall of the terminal area. Cassie started toward it, fishing at the bottom of the tote bag for some loose change. She would call him and find out what had gone wrong.

When she'd let the phone ring twenty times, she hung up. She slumped down on the floor, staring up at the phone, her eyes flooding with tears. What if the same thing had happened to him that had happened to her mother? What if he was on his way to Boston, and there had been another accident?

What if he was dead?

Then, as if from a great distance, she heard her name

being called. She looked up, and there he was, hurrying toward her.

"Cassie? Cass!"

She stood up and started to take a step toward him, but then he was there, his arms around her. She stiffened for a moment before she let herself relax slightly.

"I'm sorry, baby," Keith whispered in her ear. "I would have been here in plenty of time, except for the tunnel. It's my own fault—I should have left a little earlier."

Cassie pulled back and tipped her head up to look at him. "I—I was afraid something had happened. I was afraid—"

"Shh," Keith purred, pulling her to him again. "You're safe, and I'm safe, and nothing's going to happen to either of us."

Taking the heavy tote bag from her, he led her out of the terminal.

Neither Keith nor Cassie spoke much on the long drive from Boston down to Cape Cod, for Keith was reluctant to press his daughter to talk until she felt like it, and Cassie was, for the moment, content to sit curled against the door, staring out the window at the passing scenery, still hoping for a feeling of familiarity to come over her.

But none did.

Instead she had a growing sense that here, in the part of the country where she was born, everything was too small. As they left Boston, and suddenly the urban area ended—replaced by gently rolling hills covered with forests which had a miniature look to them—she suddenly realized that she had no idea which direction they were going.

At home she'd always known which direction was which, just by the positions of the two mountain ranges that bounded the San Fernando Valley on the north and the south. But here, no matter which way she looked, there were no mountains.

Cassie began to have a feeling that the countryside was closing in around her. She tried to get over it by concentrating on the forests, but they, too, had a different feeling to them. Her only previous experience with forests had been in the Sierras, or among the redwoods of northern California, where enormous trees, widely spaced and primeval, dominated the woods with their splendor. Here even the trees seemed small and crowded together, and looked to her as if they were fighting to survive. Then, finally, they turned off the main highway and began winding along a narrow road, passing through one small town after another. Suddenly things began to look more familiar.

It wasn't memory, she decided, or the feeling that she'd been here before. Instead she recognized the towns from pictures she'd seen in magazines, from movies she'd been to, and from television shows she'd watched. Small towns with well-kept yards, which seemed to begin quite suddenly, emerging from the surrounding woodland with no warning, then as suddenly disappearing again. Not at all like the towns she was used to, where you couldn't really tell where one ended and the next one began. In California, when you went out into the desert, the towns always seemed to start slowly, with a lone house or two sitting back from the road, surrounded by wrecked cars. Then, a little farther on, there would be a junkyard, or a gas station, and then more houses, until eventually you would find yourself in a town, not quite certain when you had gotten there.

Here, in New England, you knew. First you were in the woods, then you were in the middle of a town, then you were in the woods again.

"Are all the towns like this?" she asked her father.

Keith, startled out of a reverie, glanced over at her. "Like what?"

"I don't know. So . . . well, all the towns seem separate, as if they're all by themselves. At home everything runs together."

Keith smiled. "I noticed the same thing when I used to go out there. I could never tell the difference between North Hollywood and Studio City and Van Nuys and Sherman Oaks. I could never see how anyone could stand it."

For the first time since her mother had died, Cassie found herself giggling. "That's because there isn't any difference," she said. "They're all the same. The whole Valley's all the same." Her smile faded. "Is that how come you stopped coming to visit me? Because you didn't like the Valley?"

Keith said nothing for a moment, then shook his head. "I

wouldn't have cared where you lived. I just thought— Well, it doesn't matter now."

Now it was Cassie who fell silent. *He doesn't want to talk about Mother*, she thought. Her mind drifted back to the last time she'd seen him, right after Tommy had moved out. She'd wanted to talk to him then, wanted to ask him what had happened when she was little and he'd left her mother. But she'd been afraid to. Her mother had told her often enough that all he'd do was lie to her and that she shouldn't believe a word he said. So she hadn't said anything at all that day. And then she'd never seen her father again.

"You could have written to me," she said finally.

Keith looked at her once again. She was facing straight ahead, her eyes apparently fixed on the highway, but he could see they were glistening with tears. "I did write to you, honey," he said quietly. "I wrote to you every month. And I sent you Christmas presents, and birthday presents too. But I never heard anything back." Keith waited, but Cassie said nothing. "Your mother never gave them to you, did she?" he finally asked.

Cassie hesitated, then shook her head.

For the rest of the trip to False Harbor, neither of them said anything.

Eric Cavanaugh was mowing the front lawn when he saw the Winslows' station wagon pull into the farthest of the twin driveways that separated his house from the Winslows'. He waved, and was about to call out a greeting, when the passenger door opened and a girl got out.

She looked about the same age as he was. Her face was pale, and her dark brown hair, pulled back in a ponytail, made her skin seem even whiter than it was. She was wearing a pair of red jeans, with sneakers of the same color, and had on a white blouse. As he watched, she opened the back door of the station wagon and pulled out a brown raincoat and a bulging leather bag. Though Eric couldn't see anything about her that looked much different from all the other girls he knew, he had a distinct feeling that there was something odd about her. Then he heard Mr. Winslow speaking to him.

"I want you to meet someone, Eric. This is my daughter, Cassie. She's just arrived from California to live with us.

Cassie, this is Eric Cavanaugh. The proverbial boy next door,"
he added, winking at Eric.

Cassie smiled shyly and held out her hand, but Eric
didn't take it. Without meaning to, he frowned slightly, still
trying to place her in his mind. As their eyes met, he took an
involuntary step backward. Then, remembering his manners,
he recovered himself and managed a crooked grin. "H-hi," he
stammered. "I'm sorry about your mother. . . ." Cassie's face
turned even more pale, and as she turned and hurried toward
the house, Eric wished he'd thought of something else to say.
But his mind had suddenly gone blank, for as he'd looked at
Cassie, something had happened to him.

It was as if their minds had met, as if an instant connection had been made. Something within her had reached out,
and something within him had responded. As he went back
to his lawn mowing, the strange feeling inside him grew
stronger.

She was someone he'd been searching for, though he
had been unaware that he was even searching. He knew her,
knew how she felt, knew what she was thinking. For some
reason he didn't understand, he was certain that it had been
the same for her.

And in that instant, he had known something else—that
Cassie Winslow didn't truly care that her mother had died.

But that's stupid, Eric told himself. *I've never seen her
before, and I don't know anything about her at all.*

Chapter 3

She looks so much older than I thought she would, Rosemary Winslow thought as the front door opened and Cassie stepped inside. But, of course, why wouldn't she? After all, the last pictures Keith had brought back had been taken when Cassie was only eleven. The child in those pictures, the little girl with the large—almost haunted—dark brown eyes which had stared out from beneath thick bangs, was gone. The girl who stood before Rosemary was now almost grown up. Nearly as tall as Rosemary herself, Cassie held herself erect, her long chestnut hair drawn back to expose a pale face that seemed more mature than her fifteen years. But the girl's eyes still seemed to have the same haunted look that Rosemary remembered so vividly from the last set of snapshots.

"I'm Rosemary," she said, offering Cassie a smile and stepping forward, ready to hug the girl. "I'm so very sorry about what's happened. If there's anything I can do . . ."

Cassie hesitated—Rosemary could almost feel the girl shrinking away from her. Then she offered Rosemary her hand. "I'm Cassie," she said softly. "It . . . it was good of you to take me in."

Good of us? Rosemary repeated in her own mind. What a strange thing to say—what else could she have thought might happen?

"I've been wanting to meet you for so long," Rosemary said out loud. "I even tried to convince your father to take Jennifer and me along the last time he went to visit you, but

37

Jennifer was only three, and in the end it just didn't seem like it would be fair." She turned and glanced up the stairs. "Jen? Don't you want to come down and meet your sister?"

Jennifer suddenly appeared at the top of the stairs, looking shyly down at Cassie. Very slowly she started down the steps. "My name's Jennifer Elizabeth," she said, offering her hand to Cassie. "But you can call me Jen, or Jenny. Just don't call me Punkin. Daddy calls me that, and I hate it. Did he call you by a dumb name when you were little?"

Cassie stared at the little girl, who was a tiny feminine version of her father. Her reddish curls seemed to go in every direction, and her sparkling green eyes peered out of a square face with a jaw that gave her a stubborn look. But though her voice had been serious when she spoke, Cassie still saw a happy gleam in Jennifer's eyes.

"I don't remember what he called me," she said. "I was only a baby when he went away." She turned to her father. "Did you have a nickname for me?"

Keith spoke without thinking. "Same as Jen's. Punkin." Then, seeing the hurt in both his daughters' eyes, he wished he could take the words back. "I guess I don't have any imagination, do I?" he offered, trying to ease the moment.

"Jenny, why don't you take Cassie upstairs and show her her room?" Rosemary said hurriedly, then turned to Cassie. "Did you really manage to get everything into that one little bag, or are there some suitcases in the car?"

Cassie shook her head. "This is all I brought. Daddy said I shouldn't bring anything else—"

"And you paid attention to him?" Rosemary replied with an exaggerated gasp. "I told him no girl your age could put everything in one bag, and that he shouldn't have asked you to."

"It's all right," Cassie replied. "I don't really have much anyway. All I needed was a few extra clothes."

"Well, all right," Rosemary said doubtfully. "But if you find out you forgot anything, just let me know, and we'll go do some shopping."

Jennifer, who was already halfway up the stairs, whirled around. "Come *on*," she urged. "Don't you even want to see the room?"

Cassie hurried up the stairs after Jennifer, then followed

her down the hall to a large room in the southeast corner of the house. As she stepped through the door, she stopped short. The room had obviously just been done over, but whoever had planned it must have thought she was still ten years old. The walls were papered with what looked like characters out of *Alice in Wonderland*, and the curtains were made out of material that matched the paper. Against one wall there was an ornate brass bed, covered with a blue quilt with white ruffles. In addition to the bed there was a wooden desk, a bureau, and a rocking chair, all of it painted white. The rocking chair had a cushion on its seat, upholstered in the same blue as the quilt on the bed.

"Don't you just love it?" Jennifer asked excitedly. "*Alice in Wonderland* is my favorite book in the whole world."

Cassie suddenly understood. "This is your room, isn't it?"

Jennifer hesitated, then slowly nodded. "It's always been my room. Mom and I just finished decorating it, and I was going to move back into it today. But then when we found out that you were coming, we decided I should stay in the other room and you should have this one, because this one is bigger."

"That's dumb," Cassie announced. "Let's go see the other room."

Jennifer's eyes clouded over with doubt. "I shouldn't show it to you. Mom says I shouldn't let anyone in my room unless I've cleaned it, and I didn't even pick it up today."

"Well, that's dumb too," Cassie decided. "I never cleaned my room at home, and I had anyone in it I wanted. Let's go see it."

Reluctantly Jennifer led Cassie back into the hall, then across to the other side of the house. "It's kinda small," she said before she opened the door. "Daddy says there didn't used to be a bathroom up here, and when they put one in a long time ago, they took half of this room for it." She pushed the door open and let Cassie step inside.

This, she knew as soon as she crossed the threshold, was the room that would be hers.

Had it not been for the space lost to the bathroom, the bedroom would have been large and L-shaped, with two windows on each wall. As it was, the room was perfectly rectangular, but no more than eight feet wide, with its fifteen-foot length giving it more of the feeling of a hall than a room. Just inside the door—to the left—a closet had been built. The floors were pine, and as Cassie moved slowly down the length of the room toward the single window at the far end, the planks creaked under her feet.

And yet despite its odd proportions and creaking floor, or maybe even because of them, the room felt right to her. Its relationship to the rest of the house seemed to her to reflect her own relationship to her father's family.

Not quite connected, not quite fitting in.

Set apart.

In her mind's eye she emptied the room of Jennifer's toys and filled it with her own things. She covered the pink wallpaper with forest-green paint, and trimmed the window sashes in white enamel. Suddenly the room took on a cozy feeling, as if it were wrapping itself around her, protecting her. As Jennifer had said, the room wasn't nearly as large as the other one, but it wasn't really small either. It was just oddly shaped. As Cassie examined it more carefully, she realized she could divide the space in half, with her bed in the part closest to the door. The rest of the room would be set aside as a private place, a place shut off to everyone else but her.

She came finally to the window and looked out. Below her was the backyard, its lawn neatly cut, and beyond that, separated from the yard by a black wrought-iron fence, was a small cemetery. "What's that?" she asked, and Jennifer came over to stand beside her.

"It's the graveyard," the little girl said solemnly. "It's the oldest one in False Harbor, and everyone in it's been dead a real long time. Practically nobody ever gets buried there anymore—it's almost all full."

Cassie grinned mischievously at the little girl. "Are there any ghosts in there?"

Jennifer's eyes rolled scornfully upward. "There's no such thing as ghosts. Everyone knows that!"

"But it's still fun to think about," Cassie replied. "I mean, wouldn't it be neat to think maybe there are still people down there who've been there for hundreds of years, and sometimes, when it's real dark, they get up and wander around the town?"

Jennifer frowned. "Why would they want to do that?"

Cassie shrugged, and let her imagination begin to flow. "Lots of reasons. Maybe they just want to see the houses they lived in, or keep an eye on their descendants." Her voice dropped slightly. "Or maybe there are people in the graveyard who weren't supposed to die, and they're still there, waiting for revenge."

Jennifer's eyes narrowed, but when she spoke, her voice quavered just the tiniest bit. "Now, *that's* dumb!" she declared in conscious imitation of Cassie's earlier pronouncements. "All you're doing is trying to scare me, and you can't. I'm not a baby."

"But it could be true," Cassie insisted, her gaze returning to the graveyard once more. "Nobody knows what happens to us after we die. Maybe we just die, but maybe we don't. Maybe we keep on living, in different bodies."

Jennifer frowned. "You mean like re—reincar—whatever that word is?"

"Reincarnation," Cassie said. "Maybe—" She fell silent as she noticed a slight movement out of the corner of her eye. Peering out the window, she looked to the left and saw Eric Cavanaugh leaning into the power mower, pushing it through the thick grass in his backyard. She frowned slightly, remembering his odd reaction when he'd been introduced to her. For a second he'd almost seemed afraid of her.

She watched him for a few moments, and then, as if he could feel her eyes on him, he turned, squinted against the sun as he tipped his face up, and hesitantly waved. Another moment went by before Cassie waved back.

Abandoning the window, she looked at the room once more, then her eyes fell on Jennifer, who was watching her warily. "I told you it was small," the little girl said cautiously. "You don't like it, do you?"

"Yes, I do," Cassie said. "In fact I like it a lot better than the other room, and I think we ought to trade."

Jennifer's eyes lit with sudden excitement. "Really?"

Cassie nodded. "Why don't you go down and tell your mother, and if she says it's all right, we'll just start moving your stuff back into your room, okay?"

Jennifer squealed with delight, and darted out of the room. A second later Cassie heard her pounding down the stairs. Then, alone in the room, she let herself feel it once more.

As before, it felt right.

This house wasn't hers, and the people she lived with weren't hers. Not really. But this room, for some reason she couldn't quite understand, truly felt as though it belonged to her, and she was meant to have it. Here she would feel comfortable, feel safe.

When Rosemary appeared in the doorway a few minutes later, Cassie was still by the window, sitting on its ledge.

"Cassie?" Rosemary asked. For a moment the girl didn't move. "Cassie, is something wrong? Is there anything I can do?"

Cassie looked at her then, and fleetingly Rosemary had the impression that the girl was somewhere else, somewhere far removed from the little bedroom. Then something in Cassie's eyes changed, and she smiled.

"No. I just think I should have this room, and Jennifer should have the other one. Is it all right?"

For a moment Rosemary was tempted to argue, tempted to point out that surely Cassie would need the extra space much more than Jennifer. But as her eyes met Cassie's, she changed her mind. For in Cassie's eyes she saw something that suddenly worried her.

Keith's stubbornness, like Jennifer's, was in his jaw, and was nothing more than a physical feature. But Cassie's was reflected in her eyes, and that, Rosemary knew, was something else entirely. Cassie's stubbornness was in her spirit, and Rosemary was suddenly quite certain that once this girl made up her mind about something, it would be very difficult to change it.

"If that's what you want," she said at last, "I don't see any reason why you shouldn't have it."

But as she left the room a moment later, Rosemary had the strange feeling that although Cassie's voice had betrayed nothing, the two of them had just had their first confrontation, and Cassie had won.

That's ridiculous, she told herself. All she did was make a very nice gesture toward Jennifer, and I should accept it at face vlaue.

But for some reason she couldn't. And as she went back

down the stairs, she realized why. All through their conversation she'd had the unsettling feeling that she wasn't truly talking to Cassie at all, but to someone else, some persona Cassie had devised to present to the world. Beneath that persona, Rosemary thought, there was someone else—the real Cassie.

Of that person, she was certain, nothing at all had been exposed.

Eric finished his yard work at six-thirty, put the tools back into the garage, swung its lopsided door shut, and started across the driveway toward the back door. At least the lawn looked all right, and he'd gotten most of the weeds out of the garden. But the Cavanaughs' house still didn't look nearly as nice as the Winslows' house next door, and Eric knew exactly why: paint.

If he could only talk his father into buying a few gallons of white paint, Eric knew he could make their house look a lot better than it did. But he also knew it was hopeless, for he'd asked his father about it last year. Ed had only glowered darkly at him and told him he should keep his mind on his schoolwork and not worry about the house. "Besides," he had added, "I don't have money to waste just to put on a show for the neighbors. Only reason to paint a house is to sell it, and I don't plan to sell this place."

But there was another reason why his father wouldn't buy paint, and Eric knew all too well what it was: most of Ed Cavanaugh's money was spent on liquor.

It had happened again today. His father had left right after breakfast, having announced that he was going down to the pier to finish the repair job on the *Big Ed*. But when lunchtime came around and his father hadn't come home, both Eric and his mother had known where Ed was, though neither of them had said anything. Then, half an hour ago, the truck had pulled into the driveway. When his father climbed down from the driver's seat, Eric immediately knew that he was drunk. His step was unsteady, and his eyes held the bright glaze of anger that meant he was looking for a fight. Eric had looked away as quickly as he could, concentrating on clipping the edge of the lawn next to the sidewalk. But he hadn't been quick enough.

"You staring at something, boy?" Ed had growled. "Well, let me tell you something—anyone works as hard as I do deserves a little relaxation, and if I stop off for a coupla beers with my friends, that's my business. Got it?"

Eric had nodded mutely, not daring to challenge his father, but sure in his own mind that it had been a lot more than a couple of beers his father had shared with his friends. Maybe it started that way, but after the second beer Ed would have switched to a shot of whiskey with a beer chaser, and bought the same thing for anyone willing to listen to him talk while they drank his booze. Only when there was no one left willing to listen, would his father have finally come home. Eric kept his mouth shut and his eyes on his work, and after a few seconds which seemed to stretch out into eternity, his father had shambled down the driveway and into the house.

Now, unable to put off going inside any longer, Eric pulled the screen door open and went into the service porch. He could hear his father's voice from the kitchen beyond. Though he couldn't see him, Eric knew Ed was sitting in the breakfast nook, a half-empty glass of bourbon in front of him, his glazed eyes fixed dangerously on his wife.

"Some reason why supper's late again?" Ed Cavanaugh was saying, his voice slurring slightly, his words edged with bitter sarcasm. "You been doing something useful again, like sitting on your ass watching TV all day? Seems to me if I can work all day, the least you could do is have my meals ready when I get home."

"I'm sorry, Ed," Laura replied, her voice barely audible. "But I'm fixing you a roast, and it's just taking a little longer than I expected."

Eric moved into the kitchen. The oven door was open, and his mother bent down in front of it, tapping the meat thermometer with a wooden spoon. As Eric watched, she removed the roast from the oven and set it on the counter.

"Smells good, Mom," Eric offered, hoping to deflect his father's anger.

"It should," Ed growled. "The price they get for that crap, and all it is is gristle."

"Aw, come on, Dad," Eric protested when he saw his mother's eyes start to flood with tears. "Mom cooks great—"

Suddenly Ed was out of the breakfast nook, his bulk

planted in front of his son, his eyes blazing with fury. "What the hell do you know about it?" he demanded. "You an expert on cooking too?" His right hand rose threateningly.

"Ed, don't!" Laura protested. "Eric didn't do anything."

But it was too late. Ed's arm flashed downward and his open palm smashed against Eric's left cheek, twisting his head around. Eric staggered, stunned by the blow. Then, as his own eyes flooded with tears of pain, he rushed out of the kitchen and up the stairs toward his room.

"And don't come back down till you can show some respect!" he heard his father shouting after him.

Eric lay on his bed, still seething from the blow his father had dealt him nearly three hours before. The stinging on his cheek had diminished, but in his head the rage he felt only grew stronger.

I'm going to kill him, he thought. *Someday he's going to hit me once too often, and I'm just going to kill him.* Staring at the shadows that played over the ceiling of his room, wishing the anger would subside so sleep would come, he found himself beginning to fantasize about how he could do it.

How he could actually kill his father.

The boat would be the easiest way. There were all kinds of things he could do to the boat, and nobody would ever know what had really happened. If it sank, no one would even think twice about it. His father took such crummy care of the *Big Ed*, it was a miracle it hadn't sunk already.

Except that deep in his heart, Eric knew he would never do it. He might dream about it, might even figure out exactly how it could be done, but when it came to actually doing it, he knew he wouldn't.

Because in the end his father was still his father.

He tossed restlessly on the bed and punched at the pillow. If only he could understand why his father was always mad at him. It wasn't as if he didn't try to please him—he did. But for some reason nothing he said or did was ever good enough.

His mother always told him it wasn't his fault, that he should just try to ignore it when his father got drunk and started beating up on him. But how could he when no matter how hard he tried, it always seemed to turn out wrong?

The rage and frustration grew. Eric tossed and turned, twisting the bed covers. If he didn't do something, he was going to start ripping the bed apart.

He got up and went to the window. Outside, beyond the suddenly confining walls of the house, the night was calm and peaceful. The first of the tree frogs were beginning to chirp softly to each other, and in the distance he could just make out the sounds of a low surf washing the beach.

Maybe he should go out—just go for a walk—until he was calm enough to sleep. He started to pull on a heavy sweater, then stopped, aware that he could not leave the house.

Often on nights like this when his father was drunk and angry, he came into Eric's room late, his fury still not expended. If Eric wasn't there, it would enrage Ed more, and he'd turn on the only other person in the house.

His mother.

Better to take the beatings himself than have to watch his mother's silent suffering as she nursed her bruises in the morning.

Trapped in his room, he stared out across the driveway to the Winslows' house, where the window to Jennifer's room stood open.

That, too, was sometimes the subject of his fantasies. Some nights he lay awake for hours, wondering what it would be like to live there, where no angry words ever erupted in the night and everyone seemed to love each other.

Suddenly there was a flicker of movement in the window across the driveway, and a face appeared. But it wasn't Jennifer's face.

It was Cassie's.

His eyes met hers, and for a long moment they simply looked at each other. As the moment stretched on, Eric slowly began to feel his anger draining away. It was as if in the look that passed between them, Cassie had somehow understood the feelings he was experiencing, had let him know that she understood.

At last Cassie smiled slightly and nodded, then disappeared from the window.

Long after she was gone, Eric stayed at the window, trying to figure out what had happened. After several minutes had passed, he felt something else.

Somewhere in the night something was watching him.

His gaze shifted then, to scan the little graveyard that lay behind his yard as well as the Winslows'. At first he could see nothing but the shadows of the trees and the tombstones, but then, slowly emerging from the night, a shape took form. It was indistinct at first, but as he concentrated on it, he suddenly knew what it was.

Miranda.

The strange woman who lived alone outside the village. But what was she doing here in the middle of the night, watching his house?

And then, as the dark figure moved slightly and became clearer, he realized that it wasn't his house Miranda was watching.

It was the house next door.

Like himself, Miranda was watching the room in which Cassie Winslow now lived.

Cassie awoke in the blackness of the hours before dawn, her heart thumping, her skin damp with a cold sweat that made her shiver. For a moment she didn't know where she was. Then, as she listened to the unfamiliar sound of surf pounding in the distance, the dream began to fade away, and she remembered where she was.

She was in False Harbor, and this was where she lived now. In the room next to her, her stepsister was asleep, and down the hall her father was in bed with her stepmother.

Then why did she feel so alone?

It was the dream, of course.

It had come to her again in the night. Again she had seen the strange woman who should have been her mother but was not.

Again, as Cassie watched in horror, the car burst into flames, and Cassie, vaguely aware that she was in a dream, had expected to wake up, as she had each time the nightmare had come to her.

This time, though she wanted to turn and run, she stood where she was, watching the car burn.

This time there had been no laughter shrieking from the woman's lips, no sound of screams, no noise at all. The flames had risen from the car in an eerie silence, and then, just as Cassie was about to turn away, the stranger had suddenly emerged from the car.

Clad in black, the figure had stood perfectly still, untouched by the flames that raged around her. Slowly, she raised one hand. Her lips moved and a single word drifted over the crowded freeway, came directly to Cassie's ears over the faceless mass of people streaming by in their cars.

"Cassandra . . ."

The word hung in the air for a moment. Then the woman turned, and as soundlessly as she had emerged, stepped back into the flames.

Instinctively Cassie had started toward her, wanting to pull her back from the flames, wanting to save her.

The silence of the dream was shattered then by the blaring of a horn and the screaming of tires skidding on pavement.

Cassie looked up just in time to see a truck bearing down on her, the enormous grill of its radiator only inches from her face.

As the truck smashed into her she woke up, her own scream of terror choked in her throat.

Her heartbeat began to slow, and her shivering stopped. Now the room seemed to close in on her, and she found it hard to breathe. Slipping out of bed, she crossed to the window at the far end of the narrow room and lifted it open. As she was about to go back to bed, a movement in the darkness outside caught her eye.

She looked down into the cemetery on the other side of the back fence. At first she saw nothing. Then she sensed the movement again, and a dark figure came into view. Clad in black, perfectly silent, a woman stood in the shadows cast by the headstones.

Time seemed to suspend itself.

And then the figure raised one hand. Once more Cassie heard a single word drift almost inaudibly above the pounding of the surf from the beach a few blocks away.

"Cassandra . . ."

Cassie remained where she was, her eyes closed as she

strained to recapture the sound of her name, but now there was only the pulsing drone of the surf. And when she re-opened her eyes a few seconds later and looked once more into the graveyard, she saw nothing.

The strange figure that had stepped out of the shadows was gone.

She went back to her bed and pulled the covers close around her. For a long time she lay still, wondering if perhaps she'd only imagined it all.

Perhaps she hadn't even left the bed, and had only dreamed that she'd seen the woman in the graveyard.

But the woman in the graveyard had been the woman in her dream. But she didn't really exist.

Did she?

Chapter 4

"Can't I go with you?" Jennifer Winslow begged. The little girl was gazing at Cassie with the wistful expression that never failed to soften her father, though her mother usually ignored it. "Please?" With Cassie, the look seemed to work.

"All I'm going to do is look around the town," Cassie replied. "Don't you think it might be kind of boring?"

Jennifer shook her head vehemently, and pushed her empty breakfast plate aside. "I like to go for walks. And I know all the neatest places too." She turned to her father. "Can I show Cassie the boat? Please? We won't touch anything!"

Keith glanced questioningly at Rosemary, then shrugged. "Why not? In fact, maybe we should all go for a cruise this afternoon. We can run over to Hyannis if the weather holds."

"And if you get all the yard work done," Rosemary added pointedly. "I believe Jennifer was going to help you with that."

Jennifer's eager smile faded. "Do I have to?" she asked plaintively.

"Why don't Jennifer and I go for a walk, and then we can both help Dad?" Cassie suggested. Her eyes fixed on Rosemary, and a small smile played around the corners of her mouth. "We won't be gone very long. I promise."

Rosemary hesitated, feeling vaguely uncomfortable, as if she'd just been manipulated. And yet what Cassie had suggested made perfect sense. Still, she felt a certain reluctance

50

as she nodded her assent. She said nothing until the girls had shrugged into their jackets—Cassie nearly lost in one she had borrowed from her father—then sat down opposite her husband. "Do you get the feeling we've just been worked around?" she asked, carefully keeping her voice light.

Keith glanced up from his paper. "Worked around? All they wanted to do was go for a walk. I'm just glad that Jen wanted to go with Cassie, and Cassie didn't object to her tagging along."

"Jennifer knew perfectly well she was supposed to help you this morning," Rosemary pointed out.

Keith snapped the newspaper impatiently. "There'll be plenty of other mornings, and there isn't that much work to do in the yard. Let them have a good time. Considering what Cassie's been through—"

"It's not that," Rosemary objected, suddenly wishing she'd never brought the subject up, but determined to have her say. "It's just that I had a feeling both girls were trying to manipulate me."

Now Keith set the paper aside entirely. "Oh, come on, Rosemary. Jennifer's always trying to work her way around both of us. All Cassie did was suggest a compromise."

"Then why did I suddenly feel as though I'd lost control of my own daughter?" Rosemary blurted out. "Why do I feel as if everything has changed?"

Keith was silent for a moment, then reached out to cover Rosemary's hand with his own. "Because it has, sweetheart," he said gently. "I know you weren't planning on having to deal with a teenager for another few years, but sometimes things don't work out the way we want them to. Let's not start getting ourselves worked up over nothing, all right? Cassie's only been here a few hours. Let's just get used to it." He grinned. "Or are you planning on turning into a wicked stepmother on her very first day?"

"I don't know what I'm planning." Rosemary sighed. Slipping her hand out from under Keith's, she got up and started clearing away the breakfast dishes. "It's just a feeling I have, that's all. I would have thought Cassie would want the nicer room, but she didn't. And I've never yet met a teenaged girl who wanted a younger sister tagging around after her. It just doesn't seem . . . well, I guess she just isn't reacting to things the way I would have thought she would."

"But she's reacting fine," Keith replied. "And don't forget that she's a stranger here. She's just trying to feel her way along and fit in. But give her a week or so, and I'll bet you find you have a perfectly normal teenager on your hands. Then we'll both have something to complain about."

Rosemary forced a smile she didn't feel, and began scraping the leftovers into the disposal. Of course Keith was right. What had just happened was nothing out of the ordinary. She should count herself lucky that Jennifer and Cassie were accepting each other so readily.

Then why did she feel so uneasy about Cassie?

It's just that it's something new, she reminded herself. And if I'm feeling uneasy, how must Cassie be feeling?

Terrified, she silently answered herself. She's lost her mother, and she's been jerked out of the only home she ever knew.

She finished the dishes, then went upstairs to straighten up the master bedroom. Jennifer's door, as usual, stood open to reveal the mess in which the little girl always left her room.

Cassie's door was closed.

Rosemary stared at it for a moment, knowing she should go about her business, remembering how much she herself at Cassie's age had resented it when her own mother violated her privacy. I won't do anything, she told herself. I won't touch anything, and I won't go in. I'll just take a look. Guiltily, she put her hand on the doorknob, twisted it, then pushed the door open a crack. Feeling like a spy in her own home, Rosemary peered into the room.

The bed was perfectly made, and the few clothes Cassie had brought with her were neatly hung in the closet. On the small dresser, her comb and hairbrush were laid out, and behind them stood a silver picture frame.

The frame was empty.

Frowning slightly, Rosemary stepped into the room and approached the dresser. Then, instinctively, her eyes went to the wastebasket that stood on the floor next to the dresser. Scattered on its bottom were the fragments of a picture.

Ignore it, Rosemary told herself, but knew she couldn't.

Almost against her will she fished the pieces of the photograph out of the wastebasket and carefully fit them back together.

A chill passed through Rosemary as she realized what she was looking at. Cassie had destroyed her own mother's portrait.

Cassie walked slowly beside Jennifer, studying the village with fascination. Everything about it was completely different from what she'd been used to. Everywhere, enormous maple and elm trees were just beginning to come into leaf. Their branches stretched out, meeting and intermingling overhead to form a canopy over the street. Even now, with the last traces of winter still in the air, she could picture them in summer, when their full foliage would create cool green tunnels of shade.

There were no fences between the yards, and all the houses looked to Cassie as if they were at least a hundred years old. Most of them were two or three stories high, surrounded by neat borders of tulips and daffodils which were already sprouting. Even now, in early spring, the grass was lush and green.

Then they came to the square, and Cassie looked about her curiously. There was a drugstore and a market, but they, too, looked nothing like the enormous stores surrounded with huge parking lots that she was accustomed to. Here instead were small wooden buildings looking out on the sidewalk, with diagonal parking spaces marked in the streets they faced. She could also see a little bookstore, three clothing stores, and some antique shops. Jennifer was dragging her toward one of them.

"This is Mom's store," the little girl said excitedly when they were in front of a window displaying a Queen Anne dining room set. "Isn't it neat?"

To Cassie the shop didn't look much different from the other antique stores on the block, but she dutifully squinted in through the window, scanning the contents of the store as Jennifer continued, "It's open every day during the summer, and sometimes Mom lets me help out if I'm real careful not to break things. That's in the summer, though. This time of year hardly anybody comes out here."

As Jennifer chattered on, Cassie turned away from the shop, and surveyed the rest of the square with disappointment. "Is—is this all there is?" she asked finally, and Jennifer giggled next to her.

"Except for the stores down on Bay Street," she explained. "But only the summer people go to them."

"But where do you shop?" Cassie asked. "Isn't there a mall?"

Jennifer shook her head. "Sometimes we go to Providence, or Boston. We don't even have McDonald's in False Harbor."

Cassie looked curiously at the little girl. "But . . . what do all the kids do here?"

Jennifer shrugged, unconcerned. "There's lots to do. All summer long we can go to the beach, and in the winter you can go ice skating on the pond out by the school," she explained. Then, as a figure turned the corner onto the square a block away, she fell silent, and a moment later tugged at Cassie's hand. "Come on," she said in a whisper. "Let's go somewhere else."

Startled, Cassie looked down to see Jennifer watching the approaching figure, her small face creased in worry. "What's wrong, Jen? Who's that?"

"It's Miranda," Jennifer breathed. "Let's go somewhere else. Please?"

Cassie felt the little girl tug at her arm, but she stayed where she was, transfixed by the approaching figure. As the woman drew closer, Cassie began to feel a chill of déjà vu pass over her.

Silently, the woman drew closer. She was dressed all in black, and her skirt nearly touched the ground. She was pushing a shopping cart, and in the cart were several shopping bags that looked as though they were filled with old clothes. She moved slowly along the sidewalk, pausing every few steps to stare into the shop windows.

Every now and then her lips moved as if she were speaking, but no sound came out.

"Come *on*," Cassie heard Jennifer urging her. The little girl had started to cry, and was now tugging at her arm hard. Cassie finally gave in and let Jen pull her across the street and into the square.

But she turned back to look at the strange woman once again. The woman was moving steadily along the sidewalk now. At first Cassie didn't think she was even aware of being watched. Then, when she was directly across the street, she stopped abruptly and turned to face Cassie.

Her eyes met Cassie's and held them for a moment. Then she nodded and turned away. Moving more slowly than before, the black-clad figure continued down the street, pushing her shopping cart ahead of her.

Cassie, her heart pounding now, felt another chill as the odd figure turned the corner at the end of the block and disappeared.

In that single moment when their eyes had met, Cassie recognized the woman in black.

It was the woman she had seen in her dreams ever since the night her mother died.

The woman who had been driving her mother's car.

The woman who was a stranger, but who—in the dream—had also been her mother.

The woman she had seen in the graveyard last night, who had spoken her name.

But it didn't make any sense—how could she have dreamed about that woman? She'd never seen her before, had she? Again Cassie became aware of Jennifer jerking at her arm. She looked down to find the little girl staring up at her worriedly, her face streaked with tears.

"Did she look at you?" Jennifer asked, her voice sounding surprisingly younger than before.

Cassie hesitated, then nodded.

Jennifer's eyes widened with apparent fear. "Don't let her do that," she said. "Don't ever let her do that again."

Cassie frowned, puzzled. "Don't let her look at me?" she asked. "Why not?"

"Because she's a witch," Jennifer breathed, then glanced around as if she was afraid the woman might still be watching them. "She's a witch, and she can put a hex on you just by looking at you."

Cassie stared at the little girl in disbelief. "A witch?" she repeated at last. "Who told you that?"

"I . . . I don't know," Jennifer said uncertainly. Then, seeing that Cassie didn't believe her, her eyes darkened. "It's true," she stated. "All the kids know she's a witch. She lives out by the beach, and she's real mean, and you have to stay away from her. And don't ever let her look at you."

"But, Jen, there isn't any such thing as a witch. It's just a story, that's all. You're not really afraid of her, are you?"

Jennifer's head bobbed up and down. "Everybody's afraid of her. She acts real crazy, and all she ever does is stay in her house, except when she pushes her grocery cart around."

"She's just a bag lady," Cassie protested, despite the eerie feeling that had passed through her when the woman's eyes had met hers. "They're all over the place. We even had them at home. They used to wander up and down Ventura Boulevard all day, and sleep in the park, if the cops would let them. They're just a little crazy, that's all."

But Jennifer shook her head. "Miranda's different. Wendy Maynard's mom told her that Miranda's mother was just like her, and that all the kids were just as scared of her as we are of Miranda. And her mother lived in the same house she lives in, and nobody ever goes out there."

Cassie stared at the little girl. It was just childish nonsense—it had to be! And yet Miranda was the woman she'd seen in her dreams—she was almost positive of it now. But how was it possible?

Her heart beat faster as she realized that she had to know more about the strange woman in black—had to find out the truth about her.

She was frightened now—very frightened. But at the same time, she was fascinated. "Do you know where she lives?" she asked Jennifer, and the little girl, after hesitating a moment, slowly nodded.

"Will you show me?"

Instantly Jennifer shook her head. "I won't go anywhere near her house," she said. "And if you do, I'm going to tell Mom and Dad!"

"But has she ever actually done anything to anyone?" Cassie pressed. "I mean, anything really bad?"

"I . . . I don't know," Jennifer replied. "For a long time she wasn't even around here. When I was a little girl, she was locked up somewhere. In an insane asylum."

"Well, then, what's there to be afraid of? If she was dangerous, they wouldn't have let her out, would they?"

But Jennifer wasn't to be dissuaded. "I don't know," she said stubbornly. "All I know is that she's crazy, and she's a witch, and I bet she could kill you just by looking at you, if she wanted to. And we better go home or we're going to get in trouble."

"But I thought you were going to show me Dad's boat," Cassie said, carefully controlling the smile playing around the corners of her mouth. When Miranda had disappeared, she'd noticed, it had been in the direction of the marina. Apparently Jennifer had noticed too.

"I'll show it to you next time," Jennifer promised.

The bells of the Congregational Church began to peal as they started back toward Alder Street, and as the two girls drew near it, the doors opened and the crowd of morning worshipers began flowing out onto the sidewalk. Jennifer began waving to her friends, and suddenly Cassie found herself surrounded by a covey of small children, all of whom listened excitedly as Jennifer told them about having seen Miranda a few minutes before.

"And Cassie looked right at her," Jennifer reported, her voice betraying none of the fear of a few minutes earlier. Some of the children stared up at Cassie in obvious awe. Cassie was about to say something when she felt eyes watching her. Looking up, she saw a blond girl about her own age standing just outside the church door, staring at her. Cassie raised her hand in a tentative wave, but the girl turned pointedly away from her and began talking to someone else.

Although she couldn't hear what was being said, Cassie was almost certain the girl was talking about her. Feeling herself flush with embarrassment, she took Jennifer's hand and drew her away from the small crowd of children. Only when they were around the corner, out of sight of the group gathered in front of the church, did she speak.

"Who was that?" she asked. "The girl who was staring at me?"

Jennifer looked up at her curiously. "I didn't see anyone. Why would anyone stare at you?"

Cassie shrugged helplessly. "I don't know," she said. "But it was a blond girl—" Before she could finish, the same eerie sense that someone was staring at her came over her again. She quickly turned around.

At the corner the same girl was talking to two other girls. Both the other girls were staring at Cassie, but seeing her looking at them, they turned away.

"There," Cassie said to Jennifer. "Who is she?"

But it was too late. Jennifer, spying her father pushing the power mower over the front lawn, had dashed ahead. Cassie hesitated, half tempted to go back to the corner and introduce herself to the three girls. But in the end, her face once again burning with the humiliation of being stared at, she hurried across the lawn and into the house.

"Cassie, is something bothering you?" Rosemary asked after dinner that evening. All of them were in the den, Jennifer sprawled on the floor, her chin propped in her hands as she watched the early movie on television. Keith was leafing through a marine catalog, while Rosemary worked on the sweater she was knitting. Cassie was curled on one end of the sofa, a book open in her lap, but Rosemary noticed that she hadn't turned a page for the last fifteen minutes.

Startled, Cassie glanced up at her stepmother, then shook her head and went back to her book, but Jennifer rolled over on the floor and faced her mother.

"We saw Miranda in the square today," she said. "And Cassie looked right at her."

Rosemary glanced at Keith, who had stopped turning the pages of the catalog. When she spoke, she was careful to keep her voice neutral. "You know perfectly well that there's no harm in looking at Miranda. As long as you weren't staring."

Jennifer gasped. "I wouldn't stare at her. I won't even look at her if I can help it. Wendy Maynard says—"

"I know perfectly well what Wendy Maynard says," Rosemary interrupted her, "and you know as well as I do that it's all so much nonsense. Miranda Sikes is perfectly harmless."

"That's not what all the kids say," Jennifer protested. "And when Cassie looked at her, she looked right back at Cassie too!" She shuddered, letting her imagination run away with her. "It was weird. There she was, in that awful black dress, walking along talking to herself. I made Cassie cross the street, and told her not to look, but she did it anyway."

"I wasn't staring," Cassie said, closing the book. "I just looked at her, that's all."

"That's all it takes," Jennifer pronounced. "I bet she put a spell on you!"

"Oh, for heaven's sakes!" Rosemary said, her voice edged with exasperation. She leaned forward and looked directly at her daughter. "Jennifer, we've been through this a hundred times. Miranda Sikes is a bit eccentric, but she's perfectly harmless."

"Then how come they locked her up?" Jennifer demanded. "How come they put her in the insane asylum?"

"But she's not still there, is she?" Rosemary countered. "If she were still sick, they wouldn't have let her out. She's trying to get well, and the way you and your friends treat her doesn't help her at all!"

Jennifer's face crumpled at the severity of her mother's scolding, but Rosemary couldn't stop herself. "How would you feel if every time your friends saw you, they ran away from you? Don't you think you might start talking to yourself and acting funny too?"

Tears welled up in Jennifer's eyes, and she scrambled to her feet. "I didn't do anything," she wailed. "All I did was cross the street because I'm scared of her. I didn't point at her or look at her or anything!" Bursting into tears, she fled from the room. A moment later her door slammed shut.

The living room was silent until Cassie spoke, her voice soft. "She didn't stare at her, Rosemary. She didn't do anything at all. She was just scared, because Miranda looks so strange." She stood up, leaving her book on the couch. "I'll go up and talk to her—"

"No!" Rosemary broke in, her voice strident. "I'll do it. I was the one who snapped at her, not you." She got to her feet and hurried up the stairs, but before she left the room, she saw the look on Keith's face. Though he said nothing, she could feel his reproach at the way she'd spoken. And, of course, he was right—Cassie had only been trying to help.

After apologizing to Jennifer, she would have to apologize to Cassie too.

She found Jennifer in her room, lying facedown on the bed, her body shaking as she cried into her pillow. "Jen?" Rosemary asked quietly. "May I come in?"

When Jennifer said nothing, Rosemary entered the bedroom and closed the door behind her. Sitting on the edge of the bed, she gathered her daughter into her arms. "I'm sorry I snapped at you, honey," she said.

Jennifer wriggled around and looked up at her. "I didn't do anything—" she began, but Rosemary put her fingers over the child's lips.

"I know," she soothed. "But I just want you to understand that when you act like you're afraid of Miranda, it hurts her."

"But I *am* afraid of her," Jennifer protested, rubbing her eyes with her fists. "All the kids are."

"But what I'm telling you is that you don't have to be. She's just a strange woman, and a little bit different from everyone else, that's all. But she's not wicked, and she's not a witch. There's no such things as witches, at least not the kind that can cast spells on people, or work magic. So there's nothing to be afraid of. All right?"

Jennifer nodded, but Rosemary could see she wasn't convinced. And why should she be? she thought to herself, remembering when she'd been Jennifer's age and all her friends had been as positive as she that the woman who lived in the old house on the corner was a witch. Of course, by the time she was in her teens she'd discovered that the woman wasn't a witch at all—she was simply an alcoholic, and perhaps agoraphobic as well. Someone to be pitied, not feared. But the old stories had certainly served to keep the neighborhood children away, which was probably what the woman had wanted all along. Maybe, after all, Miranda Sikes didn't mind the tales that were circulated about her among the children of False Harbor.

Rosemary decided she'd said enough. "Do you want to go back downstairs and finish watching the movie?"

Jennifer shook her head. "It wasn't any good. It was for kids."

Her mother chuckled affectionately. "Well, preserve us from that, right?"

Jennifer nodded solemnly, then met her eyes. "Cassie said someone was staring at her in front of the church today."

Rosemary's smile faded. "Staring at her? Who?"

"I don't know. I didn't see anybody. But why would anyone stare at Cassie?"

Rosemary shook her head and stood up. "Maybe no one

was," she replied. She bent over and kissed Jennifer on the forehead. "It's eight-thirty, and I want you in bed by nine. All right?"

Jennifer automatically started to argue, but Rosemary held up an admonishing hand. "Not tonight. Nine o'clock, and not a minute later. Okay?"

Jennifer hesitated, then looked up hopefully. "Can Cassie come up and tuck me in?"

Rosemary hesitated as an emotion very much like jealousy stabbed at her. Resolutely, she put the feeling aside. "Of course," she said. "I'll send her up in a little while." Then, kissing her daughter once more, she went back downstairs.

Keith had returned to his catalog, and Cassie was once more involved in her book. Rosemary went back to her knitting, but every few moments she found herself glancing at Cassie. Though Cassie was now turning the pages of the book every couple of minutes, Rosemary was still certain her stepdaughter wasn't reading a word.

Several times Rosemary was tempted to speak to the girl, but each time she changed her mind. Later, she decided. After she's gone upstairs, I'll go up and talk to her.

It was almost ten when Rosemary tapped softly on Cassie's door then let herself into the room, even before Cassie had replied. Cassie lay on the bed, her book propped up on her knees, but once again Rosemary was certain she hadn't been reading.

"I . . . I thought maybe we could talk for a few minutes," Rosemary began uncertainly. She came to perch on the edge of the bed, and reached out as if to take Cassie's hand, but when Cassie made no response to the gesture, she pulled her own hand back. "I just thought you might like to talk," she began again. Then, almost against her will, her eyes flicked to the empty picture frame on the dresser.

"Is that what you want to talk about?" Cassie asked immediately. "My mother's picture?"

Rosemary felt her face burn. "N-no . . ." she stammered. "I mean—"

"I tore it up," Cassie said.

Rosemary took a deep breath, then nodded. "I know,"

she admitted. "I . . . well, I came in earlier, and I couldn't help but notice the empty frame." She reached out again, and this time she took Cassie's hand in her own. "Why did you tear it up, Cassie?"

Cassie hesitated, then shook her head. "I . . . I don't know. This morning when I woke up, I just couldn't stand to look at it anymore."

Rosemary thought she understood. "I know," she said. "It must be terrible for you. But why didn't you just put the picture away? After a while, when you get used to the idea of . . ." She faltered, then chose her words carefully. "When you get used to her being gone, you'll want a picture of her."

Cassie's eyes darkened. She shook her head. "No, I won't," she replied, her voice low. "I don't care if I never see a picture of her again."

"Cassie—"

"Well, I don't!" Cassie exclaimed. "And why should I? She never cared about me. If she had, she wouldn't have—" She cut her own words off, her eyes brimming with tears.

"Wouldn't have died?" Rosemary asked gently. Cassie said nothing, and Rosemary leaned forward and brushed a strand of hair away from the girl's forehead with her free hand. "Cassie, she didn't die on purpose. It was an accident. She loved you very much—"

"She didn't!" Cassie flared. "Nobody's ever loved me. Daddy sent us away when I was just a baby, and all Mom ever did was go out! She didn't care about me! All she ever did was tell me I wasn't doing anything right, and she always made me feel like I was in her way! And the only reason I'm here is because Daddy had to take me!"

"No," Rosemary protested. "That's not true! You're here because your father loves you, and I love you—"

Cassie sat bolt upright and jerked her hand out of Rosemary's. Her eyes were blazing. "No you don't. You don't even know me! Nobody loves me. Nobody at all! And don't tell me you know what I'm feeling! Nobody knows what I'm feeling. Nobody's *ever* known what I feel!"

Once again Rosemary reached out to hold Cassie's hand, but Cassie pulled away, her voice rising. "Leave me alone!" she yelled. "Why can't you just leave me alone?"

Suddenly the door opened and Keith, his face pale,

stood framed against the light from the hall. "Cassie?" he asked. "Cassie, what's wrong?"

Cassie swung around to face her father. "Make her leave me alone," she sobbed. "She's not my mother and she doesn't know me and she doesn't have any right to come in my room! Just make her leave me alone."

Keith stood silently for a moment, then spoke to Rosemary. "What happened?" he asked. "What did you say to her?"

"Nothing," Rosemary said helplessly. "I just came in to talk to her and—" She turned and reached out toward Cassie once again. "Cassie, I'm so sorry. I didn't mean to upset you. I just thought—"

"Leave me alone!" Cassie screamed. "Why can't you just leave me alone?"

"I—" Rosemary began, but this time it was Keith who cut her off.

"I'll take care of her," he said. He came into the room and gestured Rosemary away, then sat on the bed, taking his daughter into his arms. "Just leave us alone a minute, okay, honey?" he asked.

Rosemary hesitated, then nodded quickly and hurried out of the room, closing the door behind her.

"What is it, Punkin?" Keith asked when he was alone with Cassie. "Can you tell me about it?"

Cassie shook her head and turned away. "I'll be all right," she said. "I just . . . I just need to be left alone. Please? Can't you just leave me alone?"

Keith hesitated, certain there was something he should say, something he should do. But finally, feeling helpless to console her, he shrugged and patted Cassie's leg. "All right, Punkin," he said gently. "Whatever you want. But if you want to talk, just remember that I'm here, all right?" He waited for a response from Cassie. When there was none, he got up and quietly left the room. Maybe that was all she needed, he told himself as he went back downstairs. Maybe all she needed right now was to be left alone.

Rosemary was waiting for him downstairs, her face ashen. "Is she all right?" she asked as he came into the den.

Keith gestured helplessly with his hands. "All right?

How can she be all right, given what she's been through? What happened up there?"

As best she could, Rosemary recounted what had happened in Cassie's room. "She wouldn't even talk to me," she finished. "She says no one loves her and no one understands her. I was only trying to help."

"I know," Keith replied. "But maybe the best way we can help her right now is simply to leave her alone so she can work things out for herself."

Rosemary's eyes widened. "Keith, she's only a child—"

"She's almost sixteen," Keith pointed out. "She's not a child, and we can't treat her like one."

"But if she thinks no one loves her—"

"She doesn't," Keith interrupted. "For heaven's sake, Rosemary, I'm her father. She knows I love her. She's just upset right now, and she has a right to be. But she'll get over it."

But what if she doesn't? Rosemary thought. What if she truly believes no one loves her? What will happen to her? But she said nothing, for Keith's jaw had taken on the stubborn set that told her that for tonight, at least, the discussion was over.

Cassie lay on her bed, trying to sort things out. She hadn't meant to yell at Rosemary, not really. But how could she explain to this woman the real reason why she'd torn up the picture of her mother? How could she tell her that when she'd gotten up that morning and seen the picture, a wave of cold anger had washed over her and she'd ripped the picture to shreds before she'd even thought about it.

It wasn't that her mother had died—that wasn't it at all. It was all the things that happened while she was still alive.

It was her mother's voice, constantly correcting her.

It was her eyes, constantly accusing her.

It was all the other things—the things she would never tell Rosemary about, never even tell her father about. And so she'd torn the picture out of its frame and ripped it to pieces.

She couldn't explain it to Rosemary—she never would have understood.

Then she remembered Miranda, remembered the look that had passed between them in the square that morning.

Miranda would have understood. Miranda would have listened to her and nodded. Hadn't Miranda smiled gently at her this morning? Cassie was certain now that the woman had.

Miranda. Cassandra.

The names almost rhymed, almost sounded like music.

The more she thought about it, the more certain she was that Miranda was, indeed, the woman she'd seen in her dreams, the woman who had stood among the flames and wreckage and beckoned to her.

But who was she, really?

Cassie felt a sensation sweep over her, a feeling of yearning—of need—that was so intense it made her shiver. She pulled the quilt on the bed up tight around her neck. She had to see Miranda again, had to know who the woman in black was. She closed her eyes, seeing again the woman in the street, the woman of the dream. Once again, as she drifted toward sleep, she heard Miranda call her name.

She was almost asleep when the first faint scratching sounds intruded on her. She curled deeper into the mattress and pulled the covers closer.

The sounds came again, an odd rasping, as if something were brushing up against the window screen.

She tried to ignore it. She switched on the radio and focused her mind on the soft music. But the sound persisted. Finally she sat up and looked at the window.

At first she saw nothing. Then, in the darkness outside, a shadow moved.

Cassie's heart began to pound and she felt the first stirrings of panic as the darkness in the room began to close around her. Instinctively she reached out, fumbling to find the lamp that stood on the nightstand.

At the window a pair of feral eyes suddenly glowed yellow in the blackness outside.

Cassie gasped as an icy finger of fear played along her spine. The eyes, unblinking, stared in at her.

Slowly she reached out to turn off the radio, and the click seemed to echo loudly in the room. Then the only sound Cassie could hear was the pounding of her own heart.

At last, from the window, another sound came.

The same rasping scratch as before, but this time the yellow eyes blinked, and there was a soft mewing sound.

A cat. It had been nothing more than a cat scratching at the window.

Suddenly feeling foolish, Cassie got out of bed and went to the window. The cat, clinging to a branch of an elm tree, meowed again as she approached, then reached out with one of its forepaws and scratched once more at the screen.

"Hello, cat," Cassie said softly, half expecting the creature to bolt at the sound of her voice. "Do you want to come inside?"

As if it understood her words, the cat reached out and raked the screen yet again.

Cassie groped in the darkness for the hooks that held the screen in place, released them and pushed the screen outward. As soon as the crack was wide enough, the cat leaped from the branch to the windowsill and slithered through. Dropping to the floor, it rubbed up against Cassie's ankles, its long tail twining around her left leg. Then, as Cassie refastened the screen, it bounded across the room and up onto the bed.

Returning to bed, Cassie switched on the lamp again and in the dim light looked more closely at the cat.

It seemed nothing more than an alley cat, its grayish fur marked across the shoulders and down its back with two stripes which were almost black. It sat on the bed, the tip of its tail twitching nervously, staring back at Cassie with eyes so bright that they looked almost golden in the soft light of the lamp.

"Who are you?" Cassie asked. "Do you live here?"

The cat mewed softly, then crept close and began purring as it licked at Cassie's hand.

As Cassie slid back under the quilt, the cat did, too, and as she reached out to switch the light off, she felt it curling up around her feet.

A few minutes later, with the cat purring quietly at the foot of her bed, Cassie finally fell asleep.

That night she saw Miranda in her dreams once more. Miranda smiled at her, then reached into one of her shopping bags and brought forth a wriggling creature, which she handed silently to Cassie.

"This is for you," Miranda said as she placed the animal in Cassie's arms.

Cassie looked down into the cat's eyes. "What's its name?" she asked.

For a long time Miranda said nothing. Then, still smiling, she reached out and stroked the cat. "He has no name," she said. "He is a gift, and it is for you to decide what to name him, and how to use him."

The image of Miranda merged into the blackness, disappearing. For a moment Cassie was startled back into wakefulness.

At her feet the cat stirred restlessly.

And deep in Cassie's subconscious a long-forgotten memory also stirred.

Chapter 5

Monday morning dawned bright and clear, but with a snap to the air that reminded Cassie immediately that she was no longer in southern California. At home on a day like today the temperature would reach eighty degrees before noon, and by lunchtime she and her friends would be talking about cutting the rest of their classes and going to the beach. But here the morning was still far too chilly even to think about the beach. Cassie got out of bed, pulled on the same pair of red jeans she'd been wearing all weekend, and found a clean white shirt to wear under her black sweater. The cat, emerging from under the quilt, sat at the foot of the bed watching her dress, then bounded over to the windowsill. A moment later it looked expectantly back at Cassie.

"You want to go out?" Cassie asked. Crossing to the window, she unhooked the screen and pushed it open. The cat leaped into the tree, jumped from branch to branch, then dropped to the ground and slipped through the fence into the graveyard. Cassie watched it until it disappeared, then frowned thoughtfully. Finally she went to her closet, found a wire coat hanger, and worked it into a brace to hold the window screen open a few inches. Then, leaving the window open, too, she went downstairs.

Her father and Jennifer were already at the table in the corner of the kitchen, eating scrambled eggs and pancakes. From the stove Rosemary smiled at her uncertainly. "Are you all right, Cassie?" she asked. "Maybe . . . maybe you'd rather wait a few days before you start school. I mean . . ."

It took a moment before Cassie understood, but then her eyes met Rosemary's. "You mean because of last night," she said calmly.

Rosemary hesitated for a fraction of a second, then nodded.

"It's okay," Cassie told her. "I'm sorry I yelled at you. I just . . . well, I guess things just sort of got to me, that's all."

Rosemary smiled in relief. She'd lain awake for hours last night, turning the scene with Cassie over in her mind again and again and dreading the coming of morning, certain that when Cassie appeared at the breakfast table—*if* she appeared—she would be sullenly silent. But Cassie seemed to have put the incident behind her. Yet Rosemary still felt uneasy. "Are you sure you want to go to school today? It just seems like it might be too much for you. I mean, you don't really have anything to wear—"

"What's wrong with what I have on?" Cassie asked, frowning. "At home everyone wears jeans to school."

"That's what they do here too," Keith put in. "I think Rosemary's just wondering how clean they are."

Cassie's face clouded. "They're clean enough. Besides, the only other thing I packed was a dress. And nobody wears dresses to school!"

Jennifer snickered, then fixed her eyes gleefully on her mother. "See? I told you so. How come no one ever believes what I say?"

"Because you're eight years old, and everybody knows that eight-year-olds named Jennifer lie their heads off all the time," Keith replied, then ducked away from Jennifer's pummeling fists. "Anyway, even if she wanted to change her clothes, there isn't time. You want some eggs, Cassie?"

Cassie shook her head. "All I ever have in the morning is orange juice and coffee." As her father and stepmother exchanged a glance, she shrugged. "That's all Mo—" She stopped abruptly, then went on. "That's all Diana and I ever had. Neither of us ever ate breakfast."

At Cassie's use of her mother's name, Keith glanced up, but Rosemary shot him a warning glance. "Suit yourself," she said quickly. "But if you get hungry before lunch, don't blame us." As she poured Cassie a cup of coffee there was a soft rap at the back door. Rosemary put the coffeepot down and went to the service porch. A moment later she came back with Eric Cavanaugh behind her. Keith stared at the boy in surprise.

"Eric! What brings you over so early?"

Eric flushed slightly. "I . . . I just thought maybe Cassie might want to walk to school with me. I mean, since it's her first day and everything."

"I was going to drive her—" Rosemary began, but Cassie was already on her feet.

"It's okay. I'd really rather walk. I mean—" Her voice faltered, and she flushed even redder than Eric had a few seconds earlier.

Rosemary's brows arced knowingly. "You mean you're not sure that being driven to school by your stepmother is quite the thing to do?" she asked.

Cassie's flush deepened. "I—I didn't really mean that—"

"It's okay. Really," Rosemary assured her. "In fact it was kind of stupid of me not to have figured it out for myelf. I guess I'm not very good at being a mother to a teenager yet."

"But you're not—" Cassie began, then stopped. For a moment there was an awkward silence, broken finally by Jennifer, who looked up at Eric, her eyes wide.

"Cassie's mother died," she announced. "And that makes my mom her stepmother, and me her halfsister. Isn't that neat?"

Keith stiffened. "Jennifer! I'm sure Eric already knows what happened to Cassie's mother, and I'm sure we don't need to talk about it right now! And from now on your mother is going to be Cassie's mother too. Understood? We don't need any of that 'step' or 'half' nonsense around here."

At the anger in her father's voice, Jennifer's expression froze and her eyes filled with tears. Wordlessly, she looked to Cassie for help.

"It's all right," Cassie said. "Jennifer didn't mean anything, did you, Jen? She was just telling Eric the truth."

Keith hesitated, then nodded. But his expression remained serious. "Okay. But I won't have either of you getting the idea that Rosemary cares more for Jennifer than she does for you."

Cassie stared at her father for a moment, and Rosemary

braced herself for another outburst. But instead of saying anything, Cassie merely bobbed her head and followed Eric out the back door. Only when Jennifer had disappeared up to her room in search of her school bag did Rosemary speak.

"I wish you hadn't said that," she said quietly. "Cassie didn't believe you, and there's no reason why she should have."

"I just don't want her to feel like she's a second-class member of this family," Keith insisted.

"She's not," Rosemary agreed. She smiled wryly. "I guess I'm going to tell you what you told me. Leave her alone, Keith. Let her fit herself in. You can't force her."

Keith reddened slightly. "I'm not—" he began. But he knew that his wife was right. "I'm sorry," he said. "I guess I just want her to feel that she's at home here."

"She will," Rosemary promised. "In time she will." But even as she spoke the words, she wondered if they were true. Remembering Cassie's words from the previous night, she wondered if Cassie had really ever felt at home anywhere, wondered if that was the reason for the pain that seemed constantly to linger in the depths of her eyes.

"I—I'm sorry about your mom," Eric said when they were a block away from the Winslows' house.

Cassie said nothing for a few seconds, then smiled shyly at Eric. "Would you think I was weird if I said I'm not really sorry she's dead?"

Eric frowned, and cocked his head. "But she was your mom, wasn't she? I mean, you have to be sorry your mom died, don't you?"

Cassie bit her lip. "I don't know. I guess I am, in a way. But I . . . well, I just don't really miss her. It's kind of strange. I don't think she ever really wanted me in the first place." She hesitated, then went on. "I always had this neat fantasy that I had another mother—that maybe I was adopted."

Eric was silent for a few seconds. When he spoke again, his voice was very low, as if he were afraid someone would overhear what he was saying. "I wish . . . sometimes I wish I'd been adopted too. At least if you're adopted, you know someone wanted you."

Cassie stopped walking and turned to face Eric. "That's a funny thing to say. Don't your folks want you?"

Eric shrugged. "I don't know," he said at last. "I guess maybe my mom does, and my dad says he does, but I don't believe him. He's always putting me down, telling me I'm no good."

"And he beats up on you, too, doesn't he?" Cassie asked.

Eric stared at her for a long moment. "H-how did you know that?" he asked finally.

Cassie was silent for a long time. There was something she'd never told anyone before, something she'd been determined to keep secret forever. But there was something about Eric—she'd felt it that first moment she'd met him—that was different.

Finally she turned to face him, looking deep into his eyes.

He looked back at her steadily, his blue eyes clear and open, ready to accept whatever she might say.

She made up her mind.

"I knew because it happened to me too," she whispered. "Only it wasn't my father. It was my mother. Every time something went wrong, she used to beat me up . . ." Her voice quavered slightly, but she was determined to finish. "It didn't matter if I hadn't done anything. She did it anyway. She just . . . sometimes she'd just start hitting me! I hated her for it. I really hated her!"

During the rest of the walk to school, neither Cassie nor Eric said anything else.

The first thing Cassie noticed was how small Memorial High was.

At home the high school had spread out over several city blocks, with separate gym buildings for the boys and girls, and so many students that on the days when she decided to skip her afternoon classes, the odds were good that she'd never even be missed. Here there were only two buildings: a large frame structure, three stories tall, capped by a steeply pitched roof with a bell tower on top; and next to it a low building that she knew must be the gymnasium, since it faced a playing field that covered the rest of the block on which the school sat.

There couldn't be more than a couple hundred students in the whole school, she thought, and turned to Eric nervously. "How many kids are there in our grade?"

"Fifty-three," Eric replied. "Fifty-four, including you."

Cassie frowned. "And everyone knows everyone else, don't they?" she asked, her voice reflecting her sudden nervousness.

"Sure they do. We all grew up together."

"What . . . what if they don't like me?"

Eric looked at Cassie curiously. "Why wouldn't they like you? There's nothing wrong with you, is there?"

Cassie hesitated, then shook her head. "But I'm new. And at home whenever someone new came in, everyone . . . well, everyone just sort of ignored them at first. You know what I mean?"

Eric shrugged. "I guess. But nobody's going to ignore you. I know everyone, and I'll introduce you around. Who's your homeroom teacher?"

"I don't know. I guess I'll have to go to the principal's office to find out."

"Right. It's on the main floor, on the left. There's only two classes in our grade, so if you're not in my homeroom, I'll see you at lunch. Okay?"

Cassie nodded, and started up the steps toward the front doors of the school, threading her way through the groups of students chattering among themselves before their first classes began. As she passed among them, they all fell silent around her, as if her very presence had silenced them. Then she stopped, her back tingling once again with the eerie sensation of eyes watching her. The memory of the crowd in front of the church the day before was still fresh in her mind, and when Cassie turned, she wasn't surprised to see the same blond girl staring once again, her angry eyes fixed coldly on her. She was a little smaller than Cassie. When Cassie met her gaze, the other girl quickly looked away, then moved over to Eric Cavanaugh, and slipped her arm through his.

Suddenly Cassie thought she understood. The other girl must be Eric's girlfriend, and she must have thought Cassie was trying to cut in on her. But before she could go over and say anything, the first bell rang and the students on the steps began pushing through the front doors. Eric, with the blond girl still clinging to his arm, disappeared into the building.

When Cassie entered the principal's office a few minutes later, a friendly looking woman of about forty peered up at her over the tops of horned-rimmed half glasses and smiled cheerfully.

"Good morning. I'm Patsy Malone, and you must be Cassandra Winslow."

Cassie's head bobbed. "H-how did you know?"

"You're the only new face I've seen in seven months," the woman replied. "Besides, your stepmother called us last week. You can go right on in—Mrs. Ambler is waiting for you."

For the first time, Cassie noticed the door to an adjoining office; CHARLOTTE AMBLER was neatly stenciled onto the opaque glass set into its upper half. She hesitated, then twisted the knob without knocking. As she slipped inside, though, she could feel Patsy Malone still watching her.

Charlotte Ambler looked up from the papers on her desk, then removed her reading glasses and let them drop. They were fastened to her neck with a heavy gold chain, which was the only jewelry she ever wore. The glasses came to rest on her ample bosom; she had grown so used to having them there that she rarely noticed them anymore, sometimes searching her desk for several minutes before she remembered where to find them. Once, to her chagrin, her secretary had caught her unconsciously putting the glasses on in an effort to make the search for them easier. Though the secretary had said nothing, Mrs. Ambler noted that she was unable to keep from grinning. The next day she'd brought an extra pair of glasses to her office. "So I'll have something to find when I start hunting," she'd explained. As Charlotte hoped, by the end of the day the story had spread through the school, and her carefully nurtured reputation for being just a little vague had grown a little larger.

Charlotte Ambler, though, was anything but vague, and as she rose from her desk to greet her newest student, she used the two seconds to size up the girl who stood nervously next to the door.

"Troubled" was the first word that came to Mrs. Ambler's mind, but she quickly dismissed it. Given Cassie Winslow's circumstances, it would be remarkable if she looked anything but troubled. "Is it Cass, or Cassie?" she asked.

"Cassie."

"Good," Charlotte replied, smiling warmly. "Cassandra's a lovely name, but a bit formal. And Cass is too short. Why don't you sit down?"

Cassie moved across the small office and lowered herself into the wooden captain's chair next to Charlotte Ambler's desk. "Well, what do you think of things so far? False Harbor isn't much like California, is it? And I guarantee you that our school is different from the one you went to at home."

Cassie's eyes widened in surprise. "How do you know about Harrison?"

"I don't, really," Mrs. Ambler admitted. "But according to your records, you were ranked fifty-fifth in a class of over four hundred. That makes your class alone twice as large as our entire school. It's got to be different." As she spoke, she opened a thick folder on her desk and put her glasses back on.

"What's that?" Cassie blurted out, and Mrs. Ambler glanced up once more.

"Your records. Harrison's computer transferred them to ours on Friday afternoon. Amazing, isn't it? It used to be that you couldn't count on records arriving at all. Now they send you more than you could ever want. Sometimes I wonder if computers are really a blessing at all."

As Charlotte Ambler went back to the file on her desk, Cassie sat perfectly still. She stiffened as the principal's brows rose slightly at something she'd read in the file, but the woman said nothing, merely flipped through a few more pages then leaned back and smiled at her. "Well, it doesn't look as though you and I are going to be spending too much time together," she said. "According to these, you managed to get through almost three years at Harrison with no problems at all. Mind telling me what your secret was?"

Cassie felt her face flushing. "I—I guess I just never had time to get in trouble," she said. "I just went to school, and then went home and studied."

Charlotte Ambler cocked her head. "Then you were something special," she remarked. "The way I hear it, most of the big schools are having all kinds of problems now. It seems some of the students only come to school about half the time," she added pointedly.

Cassie said nothing, but her heart sank. Apparently some-one *had* noticed all those afternoons she'd cut.

Though she'd been careful to keep her tone light, the principal had watched Cassie's face carefully as she spoke, and she was certain her words had struck home.

Cassie said nothing. After a few seconds of silence that seemed to her to go on forever, Mrs. Ambler finally spoke again.

"I'm putting you into Mrs. Leeds's class for your home-room, and as it happens, we were able to work in most of the same classes you were taking at Harrison, except for Ad-vanced Art. I'm afraid we're just not big enough to offer anything past Art Two, and that's only for seniors. We can either give you a drama class or a study hall."

"Study hall," Cassie said immediately. This time there was no mistaking Mrs. Ambler's frown.

"Drama might be a better way to get acquainted with people," she suggested, but Cassie only shook her head. Charlotte Ambler hesitated, then decided not to push the issue. She made a note on an enrollment card, then handed it to Cassie. "Just give this to Mrs. Malone and go on along to room 207, upstairs at the other end of the hall. Mrs. Leeds already knows you're coming." She stood and started around her desk to walk Cassie to the door, but Cassie was already on her feet. Clutching the registration cards in her hand, she hurried out of the office.

Charlotte Ambler waited a few seconds, then sat down at her desk again and reopened Cassie Winslow's file. Slowly, wanting to miss nothing, she read it through for the third time.

All she could see were the records of a very bright girl whose only problem was that she had never truly applied herself to her schoolwork.

"Highly imaginative," "very creative mind," and "poten-tial beyond her performance" were the phrases her teachers had most often used to evaluate Cassie. Indeed, if it hadn't been for her lackadaisical attendance record, Charlotte as-sumed that Cassie would have been at the very top of her class.

Then why was it that the moment Cassie had come into

her office, all the instincts Charlotte had developed over the years immediately set her antenna to quivering?

"Troubled" was the word that had come instantly to the principal's mind. And now, as she sat alone in her office, reflecting on Cassie Winslow's arrival in False Harbor, the idea still hung in the atmosphere. For some reason Charlotte Ambler couldn't quite put her finger on, she was certain that Cassie Winslow was going to cause trouble.

Cassie paused in front of room 207, then pulled the door open and stepped inside.

The room was small, and looked old-fashioned. Instead of the green chalkboards she was used to at Harrison, the walls at Memorial High were covered with old-fashioned slate blackboards. Dark-stained wainscotting rose four feet up from the floor; above, the walls were painted a stark white. The wood-framed windows, double hung from the wainscotting to the ceiling and running the full length of the eastern wall, were covered with ancient venetian blinds, and the old student desks were solid wood, their surfaces deeply carved by the knives and ballpoint pens of generations of students.

Mrs. Leeds sat at a large wooden desk at the front of the room, severe-looking in a dark blue suit and high heels. At home Cassie's teachers had dressed almost as casually as the students themselves, but there was nothing casual about Mrs. Leeds.

As the door closed behind her, the rustling of papers in the room suddenly stopped as one by one the students swung around to gaze curiously at the new student. Cassie did her best to smile under the scrutiny of her classmates, but almost immediately she spotted the girl who had been staring at her that morning. She was sure that the blonde, whoever she was, had already been talking about her to the rest of the kids.

After what seemed an eternity to Cassie, Mrs. Leeds finally spoke. "There's a seat next to Eric Cavanaugh. Why don't you sit there?" Cassie saw Eric nodding to her, but beyond him she could also see the blond girl, her eyes flashing wrathfully. Cassie quickly scanned the room for another vacant seat, but there were none, so she reluctantly moved up the aisle and slid into the seat. As she did, she saw the blonde lean over and whisper something to Eric.

"I'm afraid you've arrived in the middle of a test," Mrs. Leeds went on. "Of course, I won't expect you to take it—"

"What's it on?" Cassie asked without really thinking.

The teacher hesitated a moment. "History," she said finally. "The Vietnam war."

Once again Cassie found herself speaking without intending to. "I don't mind taking the test," she said, and in the silence that followed, she felt the class scrutinizing her again.

"All right," Mrs. Leeds agreed. "But if you don't do well, I won't count it." Her eyes left Cassie and swept the rest of the class. "That doesn't go for the rest of you, so you'd better get back to work." She approached Cassie's desk and handed her four sheets of paper stapled together in the upper-left-hand corner. "Don't worry about finishing. There's only twenty minutes left. Do you have your registration card?"

Cassie nodded silently, handed the card to the teacher, then focused her attention on the exam. It was a combination of true and false and multiple choice questions, and covered the same material Cassie had studied in California only a month earlier. Fishing in her bag for a pen, she started working.

There were still five minutes left in the hour when Cassie finished. She looked around, surprised to see that most of the class was still concentrating on the quiz. Finally she looked at Mrs. Leeds, who smiled sympathetically and beckoned her to the front of the room.

"I guess I shouldn't have let you take it after all," the teacher said quietly when Cassie was next to her.

"It's all right," Cassie replied. "I'm finished."

Frowning, Sarah Leeds took the quiz from Cassie and quickly compared it to the answer key on her desk. Her brows rose appreciatively as she marked an A in the corner of the paper. "Three minutes," she announced to the class, and with a wink at Cassie, added, "and I might as well tell you that you have some new competition. Cassie Winslow has finished the test in twenty minutes, with only one wrong answer."

The silence that fell over the class this time was resentful rather than curious, and Cassie quickly realized her mistake. She shouldn't have finished the test—shouldn't have taken it at all. But now it was too late. Though she couldn't bring herself to look at the rest of the kids, she could feel them all staring at her with the same hostility that earlier had come only from the girl next to Eric.

She could practically hear what they were thinking: *Her first day, and she's already trying to look better than us*.

Then—mercifully—the bell rang, and suddenly the class was on its feet, milling around Cassie as the students dropped their test papers onto Mrs. Leeds's desk before churning out into the hall on their way to their next classes. Only when the room was empty did Cassie start toward the door.

"Do you know where you're going?" she heard Mrs. Leeds ask, and stopped short, realizing that she didn't. She turned back to see the teacher writing quickly on a piece of paper.

"Here's your schedule, with all the room numbers and names of your teachers." Mrs. Leeds handed her a scribbled list. "And don't worry about the test. I shouldn't have said anything, but I spoke before I thought. I'm sorry."

"It's all right," Cassie replied after a slight pause. "I just . . . well, tests have always been easy for me. I just remember things."

"Like Eric Cavanaugh," Mrs. Leeds observed. "I'll bet he finished in twenty minutes, too, and I suspect he got a perfect score. But I'll bet I'm the only one who knows how quick he is. He always spends the whole hour going over and over his answers, pretending he's having trouble." She winked at Cassie. "You might try that trick."

Cassie nodded, then hurried out of the room as the warning bell for the next period sounded in the crowded halls. She glanced at the paper in her hand and began working her way toward the staircase at the end of the hall. Suddenly she was bumped from behind and felt herself losing her balance. She reached out, grabbed the banister of the stairwell, and turned to face the person who had bumped into her.

"Can't you watch where you're going?" a voice demanded.

"I'm sorry," Cassie blurted, then recognized the blonde with the angry eyes. Once again the girl was glaring at her.

"You should be sorry," the girl replied. "And you shouldn't be trying to show us all up just because you're from California either!"

"I didn't mean to do anything—" Cassie began, but the girl cut her off.

"And if you think Eric's going to look out for you just because he lives next door to you, you're wrong! He doesn't even like you. Now, would you mind getting out of my way?"

The girl pushed past Cassie, running down the stairs to catch up with two other girls, who were waiting for her on the landing below. As Cassie started down the flight, the other girls disappeared from her view and she heard a burst of laughter.

They were talking about her. It was only her first day, but they were already talking about her.

She told herself it didn't matter, tried to convince herself that she wouldn't even see the girls again.

Except that when she found her second-period classroom, there was only one seat left, and in the next seat the blond girl sat whispering with someone on the other side of the aisle.

"I didn't mean to show anyone up," Cassie said as she slid into the seat. "My name's Cassie. Cassie Winslow."

The girl glared at her. "I know your name," she replied, her voice mocking. "We all do. We just don't care!" Then, twisting in her seat so her back was to Cassie, she went on with her conversation.

For the next hour Cassie sat stiffly at her desk, staring straight ahead.

She would give it until lunchtime. But if things weren't any better by then—if something good didn't happen—she wouldn't be back in her classes when lunch was over.

Rosemary glanced at the clock above the kitchen sink. She still had half an hour before the shop had to be open. Just enough time to change the beds and get the laundry started. She hurried up the stairs, then paused outside the closed door to Cassie's room.

Memories of the previous night came flooding back to her.

Maybe she should ignore Cassie's room, and leave a note for Cassie to change her bed when she got home from school.

But that was ridiculous. All she was going to do was make the bed. Surely Cassie couldn't resent anything as simple as that, could she?

Making up her mind, she turned the knob and opened the door. The first thing she noticed was the chill in the room, and her eyes immediately found the open window. She walked the length of the room quickly and was about to close the window when she noticed the bent coat hanger holding the screen open. She paused, frowning at the mangled piece of wire, trying to imagine what it might be for. Finally, deciding that perhaps the screen had been rattling during the night and that Cassie had propped it open rather than wiring it shut, she took the coat hanger out, rehooked the screen, and shut the window.

Then Rosemary went to the bed and began to pull the quilt back, intending to straighten the bottom sheet.

An angry screech filled the room as the quilt came away from the bed, and a grayish form rose off the mattress and hurled itself at her. Instinctively she raised her right arm to shield her face, and a split second later felt the burning heat of claws sinking into the flesh of her wrist.

Barely able to stifle a scream of pain and shock, she jerked her arm away from the cat's claws and leaped backward. The cat dropped to the floor then shot across the room toward the window, leaping up to the sill as if it expected to be able to slip outside. Thwarted, it turned back, arching its back and hissing.

Rosemary gasped, suddenly understanding why the screen had been propped open.

But where had the cat come from? She'd never seen it before, couldn't remember even seeing one that looked like it.

She started toward it, stopping when the creature's fur stood up and its hissing turned into a dangerous snarl. Rosemary glanced around the room but saw no weapon, nothing with which to fend the cat off. She picked up a pillow and threw it at the angry animal. The cat ducked away from the pillow, leaped from the windowsill, and disappeared under the bed. Instantly Rosemary ran to the window, jerked it open, and fumbled with the hooks. As soon as they were free and the screen was once more loose, she felt the cat brush past her. As she watched in astonishment, it leaped into the tree, dropped to the ground, then disappeared into the cemetery next to the church.

Her heart beating rapidly, Rosemary waited by the window for a moment, trying to catch another glimpse of the cat, but then the burning pain in her arm penetrated her consciousness. Looking down, she saw four deep scratches in her wrist, a line of blood oozing from each of them. Slamming the window shut, she abandoned Cassie's bedroom and hurried into the bathroom to wash her injured wrist.

A cat, she thought. Where on earth had it come from, and what was it doing in Cassie's room? But, of course, she already knew—it had come around begging, and Cassie had let it in. Well, there would be no more of that—if there was one thing Rosemary Winslow had never been able to stand, it was cats.

Chapter 6

"There she is!" Lisa Chambers whispered loudly, leaning forward across the cafeteria table to make sure Teri Bennett and Allayne Garvey could hear her. "Isn't it spooky? I mean, just look at her!" She straightened up, brushing a stray lock of her blond hair back in place, then fell silent as her two best friends shifted their attention to the cafeteria door, where Cassie Winslow stood scanning the room as if she were looking for someone. After a few seconds she moved to the end of the food line and picked up a tray.

"I don't think she looks so weird," Allayne commented, then wished she hadn't said it when Lisa's eyes raked her scornfully.

"Are you nuts?" Lisa demanded, her voice no longer a whisper. "Look at the way she's dressed. She looks like some kind of leftover hippie or something!"

"What's wrong with that?" Teri protested. "And she's dressed just like everyone else, except her jeans are red. If I could find a pair that color, I'd buy them too."

Allayne, feeling more secure now that she knew Teri hadn't seen anything particularly strange about Cassie either, nodded. "And her hair's gorgeous," she added. "It's almost the same color as Eric's, except his is curly and hers is straight." At the mention of Eric's name she saw Lisa's color deepen, and suddenly understood what Lisa really had against Cassie. She grinned mischievously, and her voice took on a needling quality. "In fact I'll bet she and Eric would look neat together, wouldn't they, Teri?"

"They would not," Lisa snapped, instantly rising to Allayne's bait. "Besides, Eric can't stand her."

"Then why did he walk her to school this morning?" Teri asked with a deliberately innocent tone. She was enjoying Lisa's obvious discomfort. Usually it was everyone else who felt uncomfortable while Lisa said whatever was on her mind. As Lisa struggled to find an answer to her question, Teri spoke again, keeping her voice blandly innocent. "Here come Eric and Jeff Maynard. Let's ask Eric."

"Don't you dare," Lisa gasped, her face suddenly paling. "If you ask him, Teri, I swear I'll never speak to you again!" As Eric dropped into the seat next to her, and Jeff into the one next to that, she fell silent.

"What's going on?" Eric asked as the two girls across the table stifled a giggle.

"Nothing," Allayne finally said. "We were just talking about Cassie. Lisa doesn't like her very much." Lisa's eyes flashed her a warning, but Allayne decided to ignore it. "What's she like?"

Eric shrugged. "I don't know. I only talked to her on the way to school this morning."

"Well, what did you talk about?" Teri pressed.

Before Eric could answer, Cassie appeared next to the empty seat beside Teri Bennett.

"Is anybody sitting here?" she asked, her voice betraying nervousness.

Eric was about to shake his head when he felt Lisa's elbow nudge him sharply.

"It's saved," Lisa said. "Teri's boyfriend always sits there, and he'll be here any minute. Sorry."

Cassie hesitated, then moved off toward a small empty table next to the far wall. Teri stared at Lisa.

"My *boy*friend?" she echoed. "Would you mind telling me who that's supposed to be?"

"Well, why should she sit with us?" Lisa protested. "Can't she make her own friends? Just because she lives next door to Eric doesn't make her part of our group. She's just a nobody, and I don't think any of us should have anything to do with her."

A silence fell over the table as the other four teenagers looked at each other, each of them waiting for someone else to speak first. Finally Eric Cavanaugh broke the silence.

"How's she supposed to make friends if nobody will even talk to her?" he asked. Without another word he rewrapped his sandwich and put it back in the bag. Then, with his lunch in one hand and an open carton of milk in the other, he got up and walked over to the table where Cassie sat alone. As his friends watched in silence, he said something to Cassie. She nodded, and then he sat down.

Finally Allayne Garvey leaned across the table. "I thought you said he couldn't stand her."

Lisa's eyes narrowed and her lips tightened with anger, but she said nothing.

When the bell rang twenty minutes later, Eric began stuffing the remains of his lunch into the paper bag. Across from him Cassie didn't seem to have heard the bell at all. "What's your next class?" he asked.

She started slightly, then shook her head. "I—I don't know. Math, I think."

"Mr. Simms," Eric grunted. "He's a real creep. You want me to walk you up there?"

But instead of answering his question, Cassie asked one of her own. "What's Lisa's next class?"

Eric frowned. "Math. So what?"

Cassie took a deep breath then stood up, hooking her right arm through the straps of her bag so she'd have both hands free to pick up her tray. "So, I guess I won't go to class," she said.

"Not go?" Eric asked blankly. What was she talking about? You didn't just decide not to go to classes. "What do you mean?"

"Just that," Cassie replied, her voice calm. "I decided during second period that if things didn't get any better by lunchtime, I was going to leave."

"But you can't leave," Eric protested, scrambling to his feet to follow Cassie as she headed toward the bins of dirty dishes at one end of the long food counter. "Besides, what's been so bad?"

Cassie added her tray to the stack on the counter, then quickly sorted her dishes into the various bins. When she was done, Eric shoved his empty lunch bag into a trash barrel and fell in beside her as they started toward the cafeteria doors.

"I just feel like everybody hates me," Cassie replied. "They're all talking about me, and Lisa's the worst. So if she's in the math class, I'm just not going to go."

"But what'll you do?" Eric asked.

Cassie shrugged. "I don't know. Wander around, I guess. Maybe I'll go to the beach." She glanced at Eric. "Want to come with me? You could show me the beach."

Eric stared at her. He'd thought about cutting school, even talked about it with Jeff Maynard a few times. But he'd never actually done it, because he'd known what would happen if his father ever found out. And yet now, as Cassie challenged him with her eyes, he felt himself wavering. When she spoke again, it was as if she'd read his mind.

"If your father catches you, I'll tell him it was my fault. We'll say I was feeling really sick and you were walking me home, but then I felt better and wanted to go to the beach. And you couldn't just leave me by myself. I mean, what if I got sick again?"

Eric knew his father wouldn't buy a story like that, even if it were true. But as he opened his mouth to tell Cassie it wouldn't work, he found himself agreeing to it.

"Okay," he said. "But if we get caught, I'm gonna be in big trouble."

"We won't get caught," Cassie replied. "Come on."

They walked down Maple Street to Cape Drive, crossed to the beach side, then started walking west, toward the mouth of the harbor. Cassie carried her tote bag in one hand and said little, concentrating instead on the weathered shingled houses that bordered the beach. They were spaced wide apart, and between them were expanses of grassy sand, broken here and there by low picket fences whose paint had long since been worn away by the storms of winter. The houses, their shutters closed, had a lonely look to them. Finally, as they passed the fifth one, Cassie turned to Eric.

"Doesn't anyone live in them?"

"Not this time of year. They won't be opened up until school lets out."

"You mean they're empty all the time except during summer?"

Eric shrugged. "They're just summer houses. Who wants to go to the beach during the winter?"

"I do," Cassie replied. "At home that was one of my favorite times to go to the beach. There'd hardly be anybody there except me, and sometimes I'd go out on the bus all by myself and just walk for miles. The summer's okay at the beach, but it gets too crowded. I mean, at the good beaches there's so many people in the summer, you can hardly move. It gets really gross."

Eric grinned. "It's never that crowded here, even when all the summer people are around. Unless you go out to Provincetown. Out there it gets really jammed."

They came to a path and turned right, then began climbing a series of low grass-covered dunes that separated the road from the beach itself. As they crested the last of the dunes, the soft roar of the surf grew louder. Suddenly the Atlantic lay spread before them. Cassie stopped abruptly, staring at the ocean.

"It looks different," she said, cocking her head thoughtfully. Then she understood. "It's the sun. The sun's coming from a different direction." She dropped down onto the sand, stretched out on her back and stared straight up into the sky. Gulls wheeled overhead, and she could hear them screeching to each other as they dove down every few seconds to snatch something out of the water or off the sandy expanse of beach. Finally she rolled over, jumped to her feet, and ran down the beach toward the water line. A flock of sandpipers skittered away from her, then spread their wings and fluttered into the air. Flying straight out to sea, they suddenly banked around to the right, then glided in to land again, fifty yards farther along. Cassie watched them, entranced, then kicked off her shoes, stuffed them into her tote bag, rolled her jeans up to her knees, and waded into the water. Immediately a shriek burst from her throat. "It's cold!" she shouted to Eric, who had followed her down onto the hard-packed sand of the beach, but not into the water.

"What did you expect?" Eric shouted back. "It's only April!"

"At home everybody's swimming already," Cassie gasped, splashing out of the water. She dashed back up the beach to her tote bag and put her shoes back on. Then something at the far end of the beach caught her eye. "What's that?" she asked.

Eric squinted into the afternoon sun. "It's the marker at Cranberry Point. It shows where the channel starts, so the boats don't wind up in the marsh."

Cassie gazed thoughtfully at the channel marker for a few moments, then turned to face Eric. "Is that where Miranda Sikes lives?" she asked abruptly. "Down that way?"

Eric blinked in surprise. "Why do you want to know that?" he asked.

Cassie regarded Eric carefully. Should she tell him about the dreams she'd had, and that she was almost sure Miranda was the woman she'd seen in the dream? But it would sound crazy to him, wouldn't it? Besides, she didn't even know if it was true or not. Except that she had this feeling, deep inside . . .

"I don't know," she said finally. "I just saw her yesterday, and she . . . well, she looked kind of interesting."

"She's just a bag lady," Eric replied, too quickly. "She's nuts."

Cassie felt a surge of anger. "How do you know?" she demanded. "Have you ever talked to her?"

Eric said nothing.

"Then you shouldn't talk about her," Cassie plunged on. "You don't know what she's like any more than anyone knows what I'm like!" The memory of Lisa's cutting words in the classroom came back to her. "Doesn't anybody around here even want to get to know me? Or do you just not count unless you grew up here?"

"Hey, that's not fair—" Eric began. But then he remembered Lisa gossiping in the cafeteria, and realized that what Cassie had said wasn't very far from the truth. "I want to get to know you," he said quietly.

But Cassie didn't seem to hear him as she kicked moodily at the sand. "Maybe I never should have come here," she said almost to herself.

Eric frowned. "But you had to, didn't you? What were you going to do, stay in California all by yourself?"

Once more Cassie's eyes met his. "Lots of kids my age live on their own. I could do it too."

"Sure," Eric agreed. "And you could wind up hooking in the Combat Zone in Boston, and doing drugs too. Or you could even end up like Miranda."

Cassie's eyes glistened with tears. "Well, maybe it would be better than this," she said. "And what's so awful about Miranda, anyway?"

Eric opened his mouth to say something, then abruptly closed it again and looked out to sea. Cassie said nothing, waiting for Eric to make up his mind. Finally, still not looking at her, he shrugged his shoulders. "I don't know," he said. Then he grinned crookedly, and managed to meet her eyes. "I guess you're right. Nobody knows anything about her, really. She never talks to anybody, and nobody even looks at her anymore."

"Well, where does she live?" Cassie asked. "Does she work?"

Again Eric looked nervous. He shook his head. "She must be on welfare or something. She lives down there," he went on, nodding toward the point. "Down in the marsh. I—I can show you where it is, I guess."

"Then let's go see," Cassie said immediately. She got to her feet again and slung the bag over her shoulder. Without waiting for Eric to reply, she started toward the tall red channel marker barely visible in the distance. When Eric caught up with her a few moments later, her mood seemed to have changed. She glanced over at him, grinning happily. "Now, isn't this better than school?" she asked. "Out here I can almost forget about everything and pretend everything's perfect!"

"It's fun," Eric admitted. "But what if we get caught?"

"If you always worry about what will happen, how can you do anything?" Cassie asked. "Besides, what's so great about school?"

"If you want to go to college, it helps if you go to high school," Eric pointed out.

"I go," Cassie replied. "Anyway, I go enough so I don't get behind. Besides, all you're supposed to do is learn the stuff they teach, so if I learn fast, why should I waste my time sitting in classes all day? Especially with people like Lisa."

Eric kicked self-consciously at the sand. "Lisa's okay."

Cassie looked at Eric out of the corner of her eye. "Is she your girlfriend?"

Eric felt himself flushing. "I—I don't know. I guess she is. Anyway, she thinks she is, and my dad likes her."

Cassie stopped short. "Your *dad* likes her? What's that got to do with anything?"

Eric shrugged uncomfortably. "It—well, it just makes things easier if I go out with people my dad likes." He could feel Cassie's eyes on him then, and he tried not to look at her. At last he couldn't help himself, and his eyes met hers. "That's kind of stupid, isn't it?" he asked.

Cassie said nothing, but nodded her head.

They continued walking along a few feet apart, and though neither of them said anything for a long time, there was nothing uncomfortable about the silence. When Cassie finally spoke again, Eric knew immediately what she was talking about.

"I bet she's rich, isn't she?"

"Uh-huh. Mr. Chambers married Kevin Smythe's aunt, and the Smythes used to own most of False Harbor."

"I bet your dad wishes *he'd* married Kevin Smythe's aunt."

Almost in spite of himself Eric snickered. "She wouldn't have married him. She can't stand my dad."

Cassie's eyes rolled. "So your dad likes Lisa because of who her parents are, and her parents don't like your dad but let Lisa go out with you?"

Eric nodded.

"What a bunch of crap. Doesn't it make you want to puke sometimes?"

Eric frowned. "I'm not sure what you're talking about," he said, even though he thought he knew exactly what she meant.

"Just parents," Cassie said. She tipped her face up into the breeze, enjoying the feel of the crisp air on her face. "They always do things for dumb reasons. Like my mom hated my dad and was always telling me how rotten he was." Her voice took on a hard edge, but her eyes were glistening with tears. "She only kept me around so he couldn't have me. Then she went out and got killed on the freeway, and how was that supposed to make me feel? I mean, Mom wanted me to hate Dad as much as she did, and now I have to live with him 'cause she's dead. . . ." She hesitated, fighting the conflicting emotions that roiled inside her. "Well, it's no big deal that she died—just because she was my mom didn't give her the right to beat me up! And you know what? She was wrong about my dad. He's not a bad guy. But what does he need me for? He's got a whole other family." She sniffled, then determinedly wiped her tears away and managed to smile weakly at Eric. "It makes you wonder why they bother to have kids in the first place."

Eric looked at the sand at his feet, embarrassed by Cassie's outburst. And yet almost everything she'd said were things he himself had thought about. "But what can you do about it?" he asked softly. "You can't choose who your parents are."

Cassie stopped walking and turned to face him. "Maybe I can," she said quietly. "I mean, Dad and Rosemary don't really want me. I'm just in their way. So . . ." She hesitated, wanting to tell Eric about the fantasy but not wanting him to laugh at her. If he laughed at her— But she had to take the risk. "Maybe . . . maybe I can find a mother who really wants me." She hesitated, but Eric didn't laugh. Instead he only looked at her intently.

She decided to tell Eric a little bit of what was in her mind. Not much. Just enough to see what his reaction would be. "I had a dream," she said, a nervous laugh rippling around her words. "I—I dreamed that Miranda Sikes was really my mother. Isn't that weird?"

Eric looked away from her, and when he replied, his voice was low. "I don't know," he said. "Lots of funny things happen in dreams. And—and sometimes they mean something, don't they?"

Feeling suddenly encouraged by Eric's response, Cassie bobbed her head eagerly. "In the dream, she called my name, and she was reaching out to me. I think she wanted me to come to her."

Eric looked at her strangely. "What makes you say that?" he asked.

A stab of fear ran through Cassie. Did he think she was crazy? "I didn't say she did," she added quickly. "It was just a dream."

Eric said nothing for a while. When he finally spoke, his voice was barely audible. "But if she were calling you," he said, "that would mean you'd have to go out there."

Cassie frowned. "Why shouldn't I?"

Eric hesitated for a long time. "No reason," he said at last. "I'll show you where it is. And maybe I'll even show you what happens if you get too close."

Rosemary Winslow heard the tinkling of the bell above the shop door and glanced up from the chair she was working on to see Charlotte Ambler pausing just inside, examining a copy of a Tiffany lamp. It couldn't be after three already, could it? Frowning, Rosemary glanced at her watch.

It wasn't. In fact it was barely two o'clock. Then what was the high school principal doing here? Suddenly alarmed, she rose to her feet and threaded her way through the maze of furniture that cluttered the small store.

"Charlotte?" she asked. "Has something happened to Cassie?"

Charlotte Ambler shook her head. "I doubt it, but I don't know, really," she said. "In fact I was hoping you might know. Is she here, by any chance?"

"Here?" Rosemary repeated. "But . . . well, school isn't even out yet, is it?"

The principal sighed. "No, it isn't. But I'm afraid that Cassie didn't go to any of her classes after lunch. I thought— well, I thought perhaps I might find her down here."

Rosemary shook her head in confusion. "I'm not sure what you mean. Was she ill?"

"Not according to Lisa Chambers," Charlotte said. "It seems that Lisa saw Cassie and Eric Cavanaugh leaving school after lunch. Neither of them have been seen since."

Rosemary's brows arched in surprise. "You're telling me that Eric Cavanaugh cut school?" she asked. *"Eric Cavanaugh?"*

"Well, it's hardly as earth-shattering as the second coming," Charlotte observed dryly, "but yes, that's what I'm telling you. More to the point, I'm also telling you that Cassie cut along with him. I'd hoped she'd at least last out the first day."

Rosemary frowned. What was the woman talking about? "I'm afraid I don't understand."

Charlotte nodded. "That's why I came," she said. "Do you have a minute? I have some things here I think you ought to see."

Her apprehension deepening, Rosemary led Charlotte to the back of the shop, where she had a tiny office. As Charlotte settled herself into a chair, she drew a file folder from her briefcase. "These are Cassie's records from her former school. I thought perhaps you should look at them."

Frowning, Rosemary took the file from the principal with her unbandaged hand and flipped through it. But it was the first page, obviously, that Charlotte Ambler was concerned with.

"I see," she said. "Apparently this isn't the first time she's cut some classes."

"Apparently she's in the *habit* of cutting," Mrs. Ambler corrected her. "I thought perhaps we ought to discuss it face-to-face. Given all the circumstances," she added pointedly.

The principal's tone made Rosemary look up at her. "The circumstances?" she repeated. "What circumstances? Couldn't you have just called me? After all, it's her first day of school in a strange town where she has no friends. Perhaps she shouldn't even have started today."

"I hope you're right," the principal replied, "but I'm afraid there might be more to it than just the simple fact of her being new here." She fell silent, but her eyes remained expectantly on Rosemary.

"I'm sorry," Rosemary said after a moment's silence. "I'm afraid I don't know what you're talking about."

The blank look on Rosemary's face made Charlotte Ambler wonder if coming here had been a mistake. But it was too late now. "I'm not sure how to approach this. . . ." she began.

Rosemary felt a pang of alarm. What on earth was bothering Charlotte? "Directly, I should imagine," she replied.

Charlotte took a deep breath, as if preparing herself for a

plunge into icy water. "I've been a teacher and a principal for a long time, Rosemary," she began. "And I like to think I've developed a sixth sense about children."

Rosemary felt a chill pass through her, and instinctively knew what was coming next.

"And there's something about Cassie," Charlotte went on. "I can't quite put my finger on it. It's just something . . ." She fell silent, as if searching for the right words.

"Something in her eyes?" Rosemary said quietly.

Charlotte Ambler looked at her quickly, startled. Then she nodded. "That's it," she said. "That's it exactly. When she came in this morning, the first thing I noticed was her eyes. They're so deep, and yet I kept having the feeling that I wasn't really seeing into them. I had the feeling there was something else there—something, well, 'hidden' is the word that keeps coming to my mind. And usually when children are hiding something, it's anger. I know this must all sound a little strange, but—"

"But it doesn't, Charlotte," Rosemary broke in. "It's the same thing I've seen. I keep telling myself it doesn't mean anything, that she's been through a lot, and of course she's doing her best to hide her pain, but—well, I guess I keep thinking there's something more."

Charlotte frowned thoughtfully. "Have you talked to Keith about it?"

"I've tried, but you know Keith. He sees what he wants to see, and he never wants to admit that anything's seriously wrong. And he's usually right." She gestured helplessly. "I'm hoping he's right about Cassie too."

Charlotte's head cocked thoughtfully. "I wonder—do you know how Cassie's relationship with her mother was?"

"Not good," Rosemary blurted before she thought it through. Then she paused. "I mean . . . well, apparently she feels some resentment toward her mother, but that's common with children when their parents die, isn't it? They feel abandoned, and then turn their hurt into anger, don't they?"

Charlotte nodded. "It's almost stereotypical," she agreed. "And maybe that's what's happening with Cassie."

But when the principal left a few minutes later, neither she nor Rosemary were satisfied with their conversation.

They both felt that something had been left unsaid, though neither of them had been willing to say it.

What neither of them had talked about was the strange sense of fear that Cassie Winslow induced in both of them.

Rosemary closed the shop early, but instead of going home, she went down to the marina, and as she'd hoped, found Keith aboard the *Morning Star III*, polishing her brass fittings. He grinned as she stepped aboard, and held up a rag.

"Want to help?"

Rosemary shook her head and held up her injured hand. "Good for sanding, but not for Brasso," she said. "Would you believe I found a cat in Cassie's room this morning?"

"A cat?" Keith echoed. "How on earth could it have gotten in?"

Rosemary shrugged. "For some reason she'd propped the screen open this morning. Anyway, it was sleeping in her bed, and it didn't take kindly to me disturbing it. But that isn't why I'm here. I wanted to talk to you before you got home, in case Cassie gets there before we do."

Keith's grin faded. "Cassie? What's wrong?"

"She cut school. She and Eric both."

Keith only shrugged. "What's the big deal? I mean, every kid cuts school now and then, and—"

Before he could finish his sentence, an angry voice erupted from the boat in the next slip. Both he and Rosemary turned to see Ed Cavanaugh, his eyes bleary but blazing with anger, emerging from the hatchway of the *Big Ed*. "I'll tell you what the big deal is," he snarled, wiping grease from his hands with a filthy rag. "The big deal is that *my* boy doesn't cut school. And maybe you don't give a damn about what your girl does, but I do! I'm gonna find Eric, and you better hope that tramp of yours isn't with him. Got that, Winslow?"

Keith's mouth opened, but before he could speak, Rosemary put a restraining hand on his arm, and neither of them said anything until Ed Cavanaugh had shambled off the dock.

"He may be able to talk to Laura like that," Keith finally said, his voice quaking with anger. "But he can't talk to me that way, and he can't talk about Cassie that way."

"He's drunk," Rosemary said. "He doesn't even know what he's saying. And even if he finds them, he won't touch Cassie. Ed's a lout, and he's lazy, but he's not that stupid."

Keith was silent for a long moment, then Rosemary saw the tension drain out of his body. "Hang on for five minutes and you can give me a ride home. On the way we can decide what to do about Cassie."

When they got home ten minutes later, Cassie was not there.

Chapter 7

Cassie stood at the very end of Cranberry Point. The noise of the surf was much quieter here, for a sandbar lay off the mouth of False Harbor, and only beyond the bar was the bottom steep enough to allow the ocean swells to build into breakers. Between the bar and the beach the water was no more than four feet deep, except for the narrow channel visible only by a darkening of the water where its depth had been dredged out. Standing like a beacon in the middle of the harbor's mouth, a red marker rose high out of the water, a light at its top flashing four times every five seconds. Inland of the marker a series of red-painted pilings marched in a gently curving line toward the shelter of the inner harbor.

"Why are they painted red?" Cassie asked, frowning thoughtfully. "If they're marking the channel, shouldn't they be green?"

Eric shook his head. "Red right returning. If you're coming in on a boat, you always keep red markers to your right. So if the pilings were green, everyone would come in on the wrong side of them and run aground in the marsh."

Cassie's gaze shifted then, taking in the weed-choked marsh which was separated from the sea only by the low strand of beach that formed the point. The strangest part about it, she decided, was that you couldn't really tell where it started and where it stopped.

Then, on a rise far out in the middle of the marsh, she saw a thin stand of windblown pines. In their midst, nearly hidden from view, she could just make out the shape of a small cabin.

"What's that?" she asked Eric, but the sudden racing of her heartbeat told her the answer before Eric even spoke.

"That's Miranda's house," Eric said. "It's on the only solid ground in the whole marsh."

"Can we go out there?" Cassie asked.

"You're not supposed to," Eric replied carefully. "It isn't really safe unless you know your way around. I've been doing it all my life, and I know almost all the trails. But you still have to be careful because some of the trails change from year to year. When we have really big storms, with real high tides, the marsh floods completely. Sometimes the paths wash away. Then you have to find new ones."

Cassie frowned. "But what does she do when the marsh floods?"

Eric shrugged. "Just stays there, I guess."

Cassie stared out over the marsh in fascination, trying to imagine what it must be like for Miranda Sikes, living alone in the marsh with only a few ragged trees to protect her from the winter winds. Then, as she gazed at the little cabin, the ancient, unfocused memory from the night before stirred within her once again. There was something about the house that seemed to beckon to her, almost as if it were trying to draw her to itself. She tried to ignore the strange feeling, but couldn't. "Take me out there," she said softly. "I want to see it up close."

Eric's gaze followed Cassie's and fixed on the little house as if he were searching for something. Then, finally, he nodded. "Maybe she's not home. If she isn't . . ." His voice trailed off, and he led Cassie back along the point, finally veering off into the marsh on a path that was barely visible to Cassie's eyes. The ground felt spongy under her.

With each step, she felt the soil compress beneath her weight, leaving footprints that flooded briefly then faded into the swampy ground. "What is it?" she called to Eric, who was a few yards ahead of her. He looked back.

"What's what?"

"What we're standing on. It doesn't look like sand."

"The sand's underneath, except in a few spots where there's

quicksand on the surface. But this is all peat, and it's about thirty feet deep. Come on."

They moved slowly through the thick grass that covered the surface of the marsh. Every few steps birds, disturbed in their feeding, burst into the air, their wings flapping wildly as they screamed their alarm. Twice Cassie heard vague rustling noises that sounded like snakes slithering invisibly around her. She shivered with a sudden chill, then quickened her step to catch up with Eric.

Suddenly Eric stopped short. Cassie nearly bumped into him before she realized he was standing perfectly still, staring off into the grass to the left. "What is it?" she whispered, her eyes following his but seeing nothing.

"A goose. First one I've seen this year. See? Over there, sitting real still. He's watching us."

Still Cassie could see nothing, but then a movement caught her eye and the bird was suddenly perfectly clear. It was waddling placidly now, dipping its head under the surface of the water to feed off the bottom. They watched it for a few moments before Eric started along the path once more. As soon as he began moving, the goose honked loudly and launched itself into the air.

Eric stopped when they were still fifty yards from the base of the little hill on which Miranda's house perched. A network of paths seemed to go off in every direction, but only one path led to the hill and the tiny cabin in the stand of stunted pines. A post had been planted in the marsh here, a weatherbeaten sign warning trespassers away.

"Can't we go any farther?" Cassie asked, instinctively dropping her voice to a whisper.

Eric shook his head and pointed toward the house. "See that?" he asked. "On the roof?" It was sloped on all four sides, and rose steeply to a sharp point in the precise center of the square structure. Cassie searched carefully and finally spotted a white shape perched on the very point of the cabin. "It's hers," Eric went on. "It's an albino hawk, and it's always up there, just sitting and watching. She trained it. Come on."

He veered off to the right, and slowly they began circling the little rise. The house was visible now through the scraggly trees. As they moved slowly around it, Cassie had the feeling they were being watched.

The cabin was perfectly symmetrical, built of peeled logs that had long since weathered to a silvery gray. There was a single window on either side of the front door, and a low porch, only one step above the sandy soil on which the house stood, ran the width of the structure. The door was closed, but the heavy oak shutters that hung at each window were held open by large wrought-iron hooks.

Cassie stared at it for several seconds, trying to imagine how anyone could live here, in so small and cramped and desolate a place. Even the trees around it looked as if they were trying to draw away from the building. A tangle of weeds struggled for survival in the nearly barren soil surrounding it.

As Cassie and Eric began making their way slowly around the cabin, the bird on the roof stirred, its feathers ruffling angrily as it screeched an alarm.

Still perched on the point of the roof, the eerie white hawk began shifting nervously from one foot to the other. It shook itself every few seconds, and its head—dominated by an evil-looking hooked beak—was constantly in motion as the creature's sharp eyes endlessly surveyed its territory. From deep in its throat an ominous clucking sound emerged.

Only when the two teenagers stopped moving did the hawk once more subside into silence.

Each side of the house bore two shuttered windows, and the back, like the front, had a door in its exact center. But instead of twin windows, the back of the house had a single window to the left of the door and a stone chimney to the right. Nor was there a porch along the back wall—only a small step from the threshold to the ground. From a few yards away Cassie could also make out a well, its mouth circled by a low ring of stones. Above the well twin posts supported a wooden roof, with a metal rod and a crank at one end. A rope was wound around the rod, and a bucket stood on the lip of the well.

"Does she still use that well?" Cassie asked, her voice little more than a whisper.

Eric nodded. "There isn't any electricity or anything. All she has is a wood stove, and there's an outhouse over there. See it?"

He pointed off to the left. At the bottom of the hill,

covered with a tangle of vines, Cassie saw a sagging privy, its weathered planking cracked and splintered.

"How can she live here?" she asked. "Why do they even let her?"

Eric tipped his head noncommittally. "She's always lived here, except when she was in the hospital." He faced Cassie, his blue eyes serious. "This is how come everyone thinks she's crazy," he went on. "I mean, you would think you'd have to have something wrong with you to live like this, wouldn't you?"

Cassie bit her lip, her eyes suddenly filling with tears again. "But how come nobody does anything for her?" she asked.

Eric paused, then shrugged his shoulders again. "Mom says people tried a few times, but Miranda wouldn't even let them into the house. She . . ." He hesitated, then went on. "Well, I guess she just likes it out here."

At last—with the hawk eyeing them warily every step of the way—they worked their way back to where they'd begun and Cassie stopped to look at the house once more. As she watched, the front door opened and Miranda, dressed in the same black clothes she had been wearing the day before, stepped out onto the porch.

She stared out over the swamp for a moment, then, as her eyes found them, she slowly raised her arm.

Instantly the white hawk rose from the roof, its wings beating rapidly as it lifted itself into the sky.

As the hawk soared higher and higher and Cassie felt a shudder of sudden fear, a shout floated over the marsh. "Eric? *Eric!*"

"Oh, Jesus," Eric whispered. "It's my father. What are we going to do now?"

Cassie said nothing. She stood motionless, as if hypnotized by the ghostly bird. Then she tore her eyes away and faced Eric. "Nothing," she told him. "We already decided what we'd say if we got caught. So let's go do it. Come on."

With a last quick glance at the strange figure of Miranda standing on her front porch, Cassie turned and began making her way back toward the beach.

The hawk, screaming with fury now, beat its way after them, flying low over the reeds of the marsh. Only when they reached the beach did it finally turn back, screeching once more, to return to the peak of the cabin's roof. Panting, Eric and Cassie watched it for a few seconds then headed for the parking lot that edged the easternmost border of the marsh.

Ed Cavanaugh was leaning against the fender of his truck, his eyes flashing with unconcealed rage.

"What the hell are you doing out here, boy?" he demanded. "You got any idea what time it is?"

"I—I don't know," Eric stammered. "Two-thirty? Three?"

"Don't sass me, Eric. You know what happens when you sass me." The muscles in Ed's jaws twitched dangerously, and his right hand clenched into a fist.

"I'm not sassing you, Dad," Eric said, his voice desperate. "I don't know what time it is, that's all."

"It's four," Ed rasped. "Four o'clock! And if it were two-thirty or three, it wouldn't make a goddamned bit of difference. What the hell are you doing out here?"

"It's my fault, Mr. Cavanaugh," Cassie tried to interrupt, but Cavanaugh raked her scornfully with his eyes.

"I ain't talking to you, you little slut," he snarled. "Get your ass in the truck, Eric! You and I are going to have a little talk when we get home!"

Eric's face paled but he said nothing, only glanced quickly at Cassie before climbing into the passenger seat of the battered white truck.

A second later Ed Cavanaugh's eyes met Cassie's, and she felt a chill of pure terror. *He hates me,* she thought. *He's never even met me, and he hates me.*

Then Cavanaugh swung himself into the driver's seat, slammed the door, and gunned the engine. The truck shot forward, spraying Cassie with a stinging hail of sand and gravel. She instinctively raised her arm to shield her eyes. When she touched her face a moment later, her fingers came away bloody.

Biting her lips against both the pain of the cut on her forehead and the sting of tears in her eyes, she started home. But before she'd gone more than a few yards, she found herself stopping to turn back once more and gaze out over the marsh toward the tiny cabin in the pines. She could barely make out the dark form of Miranda Sikes, still standing on her porch. Seconds, marked only by Cassie's heartbeat, passed. At last, almost tentatively, Cassie raised her arm and waved.

For a moment Cassie thought Miranda hadn't seen her. But then, just as she was about to turn away, she thought she saw Miranda smile.

Whatever anger Keith may have been feeling toward Cassie vanished as she came in through the back door. Her right hand was held against her forehead, and her cheek was stained with a dark smear of drying blood. "Cassie? Honey, what's happened?"

"I'm okay," Cassie said. "I just—it was an accident, that's all." She dropped her tote bag on the kitchen table, then went to the sink and bent over it, washing the cut with warm water. She groped for a paper towel, pressed it against the wound, then straightened up and faced her father. "Are there any Band-Aids?" she asked, managing a weak smile.

"Upstairs in the bathroom," Keith told her. "Come on." Herding Cassie up the stairs ahead of him, he guided her into the bathroom and opened the medicine cabinet. "Maybe we better let a doctor have a look at that," he suggested as he fumbled with the little metal box. "When Rosemary gets back from Jen's dance class, I'll take you."

"It's just a cut. It doesn't even need a big one. Are there any of the little round ones?"

"Got it," Keith said, ripping open the paper cover and extracting the small plastic disk inside. He peeled away the backing, then told Cassie to tip her head back. When she took the paper towel away, he saw that she was right—the cut wasn't nearly as bad as it had looked when she came in. He centered the bandage carefully, then pressed it tightly to her skin.

"Okay," he said when they were both back downstairs, "now let's hear the whole story. Starting with why you left school right after lunch."

Cassie's heart sank. How had he found out so soon? But then she knew the answer: False Harbor wasn't like the San Fernando Valley, where nobody ever noticed what anyone was doing. False Harbor was a tiny little town, and everybody knew everybody else. Someone had seen Eric and her, and told on them.

"School was—" she began. She was about to blurt out the truth, but then remembered the story she had made up for Eric. What would happen to him if she told her father the truth and Mr. Cavanaugh found out about it? "I—I got sick," she began again. "I was having lunch with Eric and I got sick to my stomach. I decided to come home and lie down, and Eric said he'd come with me, in case I started throwing up on the way home."

Keith frowned. "But that was three hours ago," he said. "Where have you been since then?"

Cassie's expression turned wary. "I got better," she replied. "By the time we got home, I was all over it."

Keith eyed her suspiciously. "Then why didn't you go back to school?"

"I didn't *want* to," Cassie said without thinking. "School was horrible, and I hate it. It isn't anything like I'm used to, and everyone was talking about me."

"Talking about you?" Keith repeated, his eyes narrowing slightly. "Why would they do that?"

Cassie shrugged. "One of the girls hates me."

"Hates you? That's a little hard to believe, honey. How could anyone hate you on the first day?"

"It's Lisa Chambers," Cassie replied. "She's Eric's girlfriend, and she thinks I'm trying to take him away from her."

Keith relaxed. "And for that you skipped half a day of school?" he asked, the beginnings of a smile playing around the corners of his mouth.

"It's not funny," Cassie began, just as the back door opened once more and Rosemary came into the kitchen.

"Well, she's right," Rosemary sighed after Keith had repeated what Cassie had told him. "It's not funny, really. Lisa Chambers can be pretty nasty when she wants to be." But just as Cassie was starting to let herself relax, her stepmother turned stern eyes on her. "But that still isn't any reason for you to stay away from school. If you were sick, you should have gone to the nurse's office."

"I—I didn't know there was one," Cassie stammered.

Rosemary's brows arched skeptically. "Did you ask?"

Cassie hesitated, then shook her head and turned to her father. "Mr. Cavanaugh found out we cut too. Eric says he's going to be in trouble."

Keith glanced at his wife, who said nothing, apparently waiting for him to take the lead. "Don't you think you might be in a little trouble too?" he asked with more severity than he was really feeling.

Cassie shrugged. "I don't care. But Eric's father—I think Mr. Cavanaugh's going to beat Eric up."

"Beat him up?" Rosemary echoed, her voice clearly betraying her doubt. "Just for cutting school? What gave you that idea?"

"Eric told me. He says his father hits him when he gets mad. He hit him Saturday night."

Simultaneously both Keith and Rosemary remembered the shouting they'd heard coming from the Cavanaughs' two nights before. Surely it had been no more than an argument, hadn't it? But, of course, they both knew better, for each of them had at one time or another seen the bruises on Laura's and Eric's faces and arms. Eric's injuries had always been explained away as nothing more than accidents on the playing field, but neither Keith nor Rosemary had ever put much faith in Laura's implausible accounts of her own clumsiness.

Suddenly Keith understood the truth of his daughter's tale. "You didn't get sick, did you?" he asked, his voice gentle. "You made that story up for Eric, so his father wouldn't beat him up."

After a moment Cassie nodded unhappily. "You won't tell, will you? It was all my idea. Eric didn't want to go with me, but I talked him into it. Please?"

Keith hesitated, uncertain. When he glanced at his wife, he could see she was still determined to leave the situation up to him. "I don't see what harm it can do," he said at last. "If claiming you got sick will keep Ed Cavanaugh's hands off Eric, I think it's worth it. But I want you to promise me you won't cut school again. Or if you do, at least don't try to talk anyone else into going along. Understood?"

Rosemary saw Cassie glance at her, but said nothing, and after a long silence Cassie finally nodded. "Yes, Daddy," she said quietly.

"Then that's settled," Keith said.

"Not quite," Rosemary interjected. "Don't you think we have to do something about this?"

Now Cassie's eyes met her stepmother's directly, and Rosemary was sure she recognized a challenge in them.

"Why?" Cassie asked. "My mom never did anything when I cut school at home."

"Did she know what you were doing?" Rosemary countered.

"Sure," Cassie replied, her tone just short of belligerence. "I used to do it all the time. What's the big deal? I get good grades, and the classes are so dumb I don't see the point of going."

Rosemary decided to ignore the jibe. "What did you do when you cut school?"

"Nothing much," Cassie replied vaguely. "Sometimes I'd go to the beach, like Eric and I did today. But usually I just went home and read."

"And your mother didn't care?"

Cassie's jaw tightened, but when she spoke, her voice was almost emotionless. "Most of the time she probably didn't even know. She was always at work, and then after Tommy left, she usually went out all the time. Sometimes I didn't even see her except on the weekends."

"I see," Rosemary breathed, suddenly softening. Apparently Keith was right—Diana hadn't really cared about Cassie at all. "Well, under the circumstances I guess we can let it go this time," she said. "But I want you to understand that here we *do* care if you go to school or not. Even though I have my store, I won't be working all the time, and I certainly won't be going out every night. If you have problems at school, we want you to talk about them, not just stop going to classes. Okay?"

Cassie's eyes narrowed slightly, but she bobbed her head. "Can I go up to my room now?"

Rosemary hesitated, feeling certain there was more to be said, but not quite sure what it was. As had already happened a couple of times before, she felt vaguely manipulated. "All right," she sighed. "I'll call you when I need you to come down and help Jennifer set the table." Cassie started toward the stairs when Rosemary suddenly remembered the cuts on her wrist. "Cassie?" she called.

The girl stopped, and turned back questioningly.

"There was a cat in your room this morning," Rosemary said. "It was in your bed, and when I went in to make it, it scratched me." She held up her bandaged hand. "Do you have any idea where it came from?"

Cassie said nothing for a moment, the dream from last night suddenly coming back to her. Then she shook her head. "I don't know. It was in the tree last night, so I let it in. Then I let it out this morning, but it must have come back." She hesitated a second, then: "Can—can I keep him?"

Immediately Rosemary shook her head. "You shouldn't even have let him in. I'm sure he belongs to someone, and I let him out again."

Now it was Cassie who shook her head. "He'll come back," she said. "I know he will. When he does, can I keep him? Please?"

Rosemary glanced at Keith. Wasn't he going to say anything? He certainly knew how she felt about cats—she'd made it perfectly clear last year when Jennifer wanted a kitten. "I—I don't know," she finally temporized. "He probably won't come back, but if he does, we'll talk about it then."

Cassie opened her mouth to say something, but then seemed to change her mind.

A moment later Keith and Rosemary were alone in the kitchen. Rosemary went to the refrigerator and pulled out the bottle of white wine they had opened the night before but hadn't finished. "I know it's a bit early," she said, offering Keith a glass of wine and a rueful smile. "I guess I'm just feeling a little overwhelmed."

Keith raised his glass and tipped it toward her. "Well, if you ask me, you handled that situation like a champ."

"Did I?" Rosemary mused. "I wonder. I have this nagging feeling that maybe we should have insisted on some kind of punishment."

"But you heard her," Keith replied. "It was almost as if she didn't even know that what she did was wrong. And it's obvious she didn't think we'd care."

Rosemary shook her head. "I don't know. She certainly knew there was the possibility of getting in trouble. I mean, she went so far as to make up that story to protect Eric. And I'm also having a problem dealing with the idea that Diana really didn't know what was going on, or didn't care."

"Well, it doesn't surprise me," Keith replied bitterly. "In fact I'm not sure Diana ever really cared about anyone but herself. Even when we were married and she claimed she loved me so much she couldn't stand to have me out of her sight, she wasn't telling the truth. The truth was that she couldn't stand being away from me because she could only convince herself I loved her if I was there every second. And I've never been sure she didn't take Cassie just to keep me from having her."

"My God," Rosemary said, her eyes drifting up to the ceiling toward Cassie's room. "What must it have been like for her?"

Then they both fell silent as they heard Ed Cavanaugh's voice shouting from next door.

"*Lying, stinking, rotten kid!* I'll teach you to talk back to me!"

Laura's voice came next, softer. "Ed—"

"SHUT UP!"

Keith rose to his feet, but Rosemary stopped him. "Don't," she said. "We can call the police, or we can ignore it. But I don't want you to get involved."

"But we are involved, damn it," Keith replied. "We have to listen to it, don't we? And what about Eric and Laura? Do we just let him beat them up?"

Rosemary met his eyes. "Then call the police," she insisted. "If you want to do something, call the police. But let them handle it."

Keith reached for the phone, then, as he always did when he was tempted to report the fights at the Cavanaughs', hung up again before he dialed. If he called the police, Ed Cavanaugh would know immediately who had reported the fight at his house. And there were too many nights when Keith had to be at sea, and Rosemary and the girls would be alone in the house. He couldn't risk Ed taking out his drunken anger on them when Keith himself was hundreds of miles away.

"Shit," he said softly, pouring himself a second glass of

wine. Then he smiled sadly at Rosemary. "I guess Cassie's story didn't work for Eric. But at least she tried, didn't she?"

For a moment Rosemary said nothing. Was that really all the lie had been? An attempt to help Eric? Or had it been meant for them too? She wished she could be sure.

She dismissed the uncharitable thoughts from her mind and made herself smile. "Yes, I guess she did." She reached over and squeezed her husband's hand. "We'll make things work out. She's got some problems, but nothing we can't handle."

"And it's hard to get mad at someone whose always looking out for someone else, isn't it?" Keith added. "She did it for Jennifer the other night, and she did it for Eric today. Whatever mistakes Diana may have made, I think she raised a good kid."

But Rosemary made no reply, for once again her mind was occupied with the strange feeling she had about Cassie, the feeling that the things Cassie was doing, no matter how well-intentioned they seemed on the surface, were cloaking something else. Cassie, she was beginning to believe, was a lot more complicated than she seemed on the surface. Something was going on behind those large brown eyes of hers, and it wasn't something that Rosemary understood.

More and more, she was growing certain that it was something she should fear.

But that's silly, she told herself once again. She's only a child. What can there be in a child to be afraid of? But as the afternoon turned into evening, and the evening turned to night, Rosemary found herself watching Cassie, looking for something.

What it was, she didn't know. . . .

Late that night, as Miranda Sikes carefully banked the fire in the ancient wood-burning stove that sat next to her makeshift kitchen sink, the nondescript grayish cat with the black markings on its back wove around her feet, rubbing itself against her ankles. She finished with the stove, closing the vent to let in only enough air to keep the fire going, then turned the oil lantern on her table down low.

She began stripping off her clothes, hanging them carefully in the armoire against the east wall, and finally slipped into a worn flannel nightgown. As she turned the bed down, the cat leaped up and slithered under the covers, but Miranda shook her head.

"No, no, no, Sumi," she crooned.

Reaching into the depths of the bed, she scooped the cat up and cradled it in her arms. Stroking its belly, she looked down into its glowing yellow eyes. "Didn't we have a long talk yesterday, and didn't I explain to you that you can't come back here anymore?"

The cat mewed softly, and one of its forepaws stroked Miranda's wrist.

"Yes," Miranda crooned. "I know what you want, but you can't always have what you want, can you? And you just can't live here anymore, no matter how much you want to. You have to stay with Cassandra. You have to stay with her and do what she wants you to do. She needs you now, doesn't she?"

Opening the front door, she stooped down and slid the cat out into the night.

The cat hesitated, looking up almost questioningly into Miranda's eyes. But once again Miranda shook her head.

"No, you can't come back in. You know where you live now, and you know what you're to do." Quietly but firmly she shut the door.

The cat stared at the closed door for a moment, then bounded off the porch and down the slope into the darkness of the marsh. It moved quickly, slipping through the reeds and grasses like a dark shadow, its eyes glittering brightly in the starlight.

As the clock in the church tower struck midnight, the cat slipped once more through Cassie's window. A few minutes later it was asleep at its new master's feet.

Chapter 8

By the end of the week Rosemary Winslow was finding that she no longer looked forward to each new day. So on Saturday morning, instead of getting up at her usual time, she allowed herself to sleep in, lingering in bed, not quite asleep, but somehow unwilling to dress and begin the day.

"Are you sure you're all right?" Keith asked when he came up to look for her just after seven.

The look of concern on his face and the slight tremor in his voice almost made Rosemary laugh out loud, but when she had reassured him and he'd gone downstairs again, she lay awake, a strange feeling of ennui overcoming her. Slowly she'd come to realize that she wasn't nearly as all right as she'd told Keith she was, though she still couldn't put her finger on precisely what was wrong.

Part of it was simply the fact of Cassie's being there. She understood that and accepted it. Time would take care of that. It was simply a matter of waiting for new routines to establish themselves. What, after all, had she expected? Had she really thought that a teenaged girl could come into their lives without having anything change? Of course not.

Yet deep down inside she suspected that she had hoped for precisely that. A part of her knew that she'd hoped nothing would change, that somehow Cassie would simply meld into their family, sliding naturally into her role as Jennifer's older sister and her own eldest daughter. Which, of course, was a stupid idea, even if it had been an unconscious one. And if she was completely honest with herself, she also knew that so far everything had gone much better than she could realistically have hoped for.

And yet . . .

She cast her mind back over the week, remembering all the little things that had happened, the little things that really shouldn't have bothered her but somehow did.

The biggest of those things was the cat.

Tuesday morning when Cassie had come down to breakfast, the cat had been with her. Rosemary's first instinct had been to tell her to put it out and not let it come back in again, but when Jennifer had seen it, she'd squealed with excitement and immediately demanded to be allowed to hold it. Rosemary had opened her mouth to protest, but before she could say anything, Cassie had set the cat in Jennifer's lap. It immediately closed its eyes and began purring.

"His name's Sumi," Cassie said.

"Sumi?" Keith repeated. "How did you come up with that?"

"I dreamed it," Cassie replied. She turned to Rosemary, smiling softly. "When you dream something, you should pay attention to it, don't you think?"

Before she could even think, Rosemary had nodded. She wanted to protest again and insist that the cat must go, but Cassie had artfully changed the subject. By the time she was able to turn the conversation back to the cat, it all seemed to be over.

"But I always wanted a cat," Jennifer wailed. "And it's not a kitten, like the other one was. This one's all grown up, and I bet it won't even scratch the furniture or anything."

"You have to admit it's kind of pretty," Keith argued. "It almost looks like a gray Siamese, except I've never heard of such a thing."

"But it's just an alley cat," Rosemary protested. "And it looks far too well-fed to be a stray. It has to belong to someone."

It wasn't until the girls had left for school and Keith had gone down to the marina to work on the *Morning Star*, that Rosemary realized that throughout the discussion Cassie had said nothing. She had merely brought the cat downstairs and let her father and half sister talk Rosemary into letting it stay.

As she'd loaded the breakfast dishes into the washer, the cat had sat quietly on a chair, watching her.

Watching her, Rosemary had thought, as if it knew exactly what had happened, and knew that it—and Cassie—had gotten the best of her.

That's stupid, Rosemary told herself now. It's only a cat, and cats don't think. Even so, all week long, whenever she found herself alone in the house with the cat, she'd kept getting the feeling that the cat was watching her, assessing her somehow. As each day passed, she grew more wary of the animal. More wary, and also more suspicious.

Where had it come from?

What did it want?

Unreasonable as she knew the thought was, she had a growing certainty that the cat did, indeed, want something.

But it wasn't just the cat.

One night—Wednesday night, she remembered—she had asked Cassie how things were going at school.

Cassie had shrugged. "Okay."

"What about the kids?" Rosemary asked as casually as she could. "Do you like them?"

Though Cassie's face had tightened, she had shrugged once more. "They're okay, I guess," she said, though her eyes never left her plate.

Rosemary opened her mouth to speak again, then changed her mind, remembering the conversation she'd had with Cassie on Monday. So far Cassie had not cut school again, nor had she complained of any problems with her classmates.

She hadn't spoken of school at all, in fact. Each day she'd come home and disappear into her room, presumably to do her homework. Once, when Rosemary had been passing through the upstairs hall, she'd paused outside the closed door to Cassie's room and listened.

Within, the soft tones of music from the radio had been barely audible, and above that she'd heard the sound of Cassie's voice, murmuring softly.

Immediately, unbidden, an image of Miranda Sikes had come to Rosemary's mind—Miranda, pushing her grocery cart slowly along the sidewalk, muttering to herself in barely audible tones.

No! Rosemary told herself, forcing the image from her

mind. *She's just talking to Sumi, that's all. Everyone talks to pets, and there's nothing strange about it.*

Then why had she become increasingly uneasy about it as the week had passed? Why had she begun to feel that though Cassie was being perfectly cooperative, appearing whenever she was called and doing whatever was asked of her, she was separating herself from the rest of the family, turning increasingly inward?

Then, late on Thursday afternoon, something else had happened.

She had been in Jennifer's room, finally unable to stand any longer the mess that never seemed to bother Jennifer at all. She was packing Jennifer's toys away in the chest below the window when she'd glanced outside.

In the cemetery on the other side of the fence, kneeling in front of one of the graves, she'd seen Cassie. For several minutes she'd watched in silence.

Cassie seemed to be reading one of the headstones. Then she reached out and touched it. Her hand rested on the granite for a few moments before she moved on to the next one, where she repeated the process.

Finally, after about ten minutes, Rosemary left Jennifer's room, went downstairs and out the back door, then crossed to the low fence that separated the yard from the graveyard.

"Cassie?" she asked, keeping her voice low.

Cassie froze, her left hand, about to touch another of the grave markers, hovering in midair. Slowly, almost furtively, she'd turned around and looked at Rosemary.

"What are you doing?" Rosemary asked.

Cassie's eyes flicked almost guiltily away from Rosemary. "I was just reading the gravestones," she replied. She met Rosemary's gaze, and once more Rosemary saw that look of challenge in her eyes. "They're—they're interesting."

Rosemary's brows creased into a frown. "But you can hardly see them."

Cassie hesitated, then nodded and got to her feet. "It's all right," she said. "I was just about done anyway." She came to the fence and scrambled over it, then looked at Rosemary uncertainly. "Did I do something wrong?" she asked. "I mean, aren't I allowed to go into the graveyard?"

Suddenly flustered, Rosemary shook her head. "No, of

course not," she said. "It's just . . . well, it seemed like an odd thing for you to be doing, I suppose."

Cassie's eyes immediately darkened. "Well, maybe I'm just an odd person," she said, her voice quavering. "But I don't think there's anything wrong with that either!" Covering her face with her hands, she fled toward the house.

Rosemary took a single step after her then stopped. It was too late—once again she'd said the wrong thing, and once again Cassie was upset. She took a deep breath, wondering once more why it was that she seemed to have such a talent for saying the wrong thing to the girl. She was about to go back into the house herself when she changed her mind and carefully climbed the low picket fence into the graveyard. It was nearly dark now, and the huge ancient trees that dotted the little cemetery seemed to be closing their branches overhead, as if trying to shut out what little light remained.

The air in the graveyard seemed to carry a chill Rosemary had not felt a few moments before.

Slowly, almost apprehensively, she moved toward the grave Cassie had been kneeling over when she'd come outside a few minutes ago. It was the grave of Rebecca Sikes, who had been Miranda Sikes's mother.

Next to that was the grave of Charity Sikes, Rebecca's mother.

Rosemary moved slowly down the row of graves, examining the stones that marked the memory of the generations of Sikes women.

It wasn't the first time she'd looked at these graves—indeed, over the years she'd read most of the headstones in the village cemetery. And long ago she'd noted the oddity about the Sikes women.

None of them had ever married, and each of them had borne a single child—a daughter.

Except for Miranda.

Miranda was the last of the line. When she was gone, for the first time since the seventeenth century there would be no Sikeses in False Harbor.

But what was it that Cassie had been looking for? Why had she been touching the stones?

Suddenly Rosemary remembered standing outside Cassie's door, listening to Cassie talking softly in the privacy of her room. She remembered how she'd been reminded of Miranda.

Shivering against the chill and the darkness, Rosemary hurried out of the cemetery.

That night she'd tried to talk to Keith about it. Though he'd listened patiently as she attempted to voice her concerns about Cassie, he became coldly furious when she'd mentioned Miranda.

"What are you trying to say?" he asked. "That Cassie is going to turn into another Miranda, walking around in rags and talking to herself? For Christ's sake, Rosemary, look at things from her point of view. She's an outsider here, and she's having a hard time making friends. So she's lonely. Haven't you ever talked to yourself? And as for the graves, why shouldn't she be interested in them? Miranda's the town character, isn't she? Cassie's probably been asking questions about her, and somebody told her about the graves."

"But she hasn't been talking to anyone," Rosemary protested. "That's the problem—she spends all her time in her room, with that cat."

Keith only shrugged. "Just because you can't stand cats doesn't mean everybody has to hate them," he said. If he noticed how his words stung Rosemary, he gave no sign. "Sumi's a nice cat. Besides, Cassie has a lot to work out for herself, and she hardly knows us. You can't expect her to open up to us right away. Give her a chance, honey. Just give her a chance." He snapped his paper and turned the page, and Rosemary knew the conversation was over.

Feeling dismissed, she retreated into silence.

And then, yesterday, Miranda Sikes had come into her shop.

Many times before, Rosemary had seen her pause in front of the shop to stare inside. She had often wondered if Miranda was really seeing what she was looking at, or if her eyes merely drifted from object to object while she herself watched whatever strange visions might be going on in her head. Over the years Rosemary had been tempted to open the door and speak to her, but when she tried, Miranda had quickly moved on. After a while, understanding that the woman didn't want to be spoken to, Rosemary had given up. Indeed, for the last year or so she'd barely been conscious of the strange figure in black who drifted through the town almost like some sort of ghost.

But on Friday morning Miranda had paused outside the shop again, staring in through the window, and Rosemary had suddenly become aware of the fact that her lips were not moving in their customary whispered monologue. As Rosemary watched, afraid to move lest Miranda dart away, the woman pushed her shopping cart close to the window, carefully tucked the large black shawl she always wore on her head over the tops of the bags, and opened the door.

She stopped cold as the bell tinkled above her, then slowly tipped her head up to stare at the tiny brass object. At last, nodding, she came inside and closed the door behind her.

She looks like a fawn, Rosemary thought. She looks exactly like a frightened fawn. Rosemary stayed where she was, certain now that if she moved, Miranda would bolt out the door.

For a moment Miranda seemed totally disoriented, as if she didn't know quite what to do. She glanced around, then took a tentative step forward and reached out to brush her fingers lightly over the marble top of a Victorian sideboard. As if reassured by the fact that the piece of furniture didn't crumble under her touch, she moved farther into the shop, pausing every few steps to lean down over one of the display cases. Finally she was only a few feet from Rosemary, but still Rosemary didn't speak.

At last Miranda turned and looked directly at her.

As their eyes met, the room seemed to reel, and for a split second Rosemary was afraid she might faint.

Suddenly she knew why she'd been so certain she had seen Cassie's eyes before. She was looking into them now.

Yet Miranda looked nothing like Cassie at all. As Rosemary studied the ruin that was Miranda's face, she could see no resemblance to Cassie's clean, clear features. Whatever beauty Miranda might once have had was long since buried under the sea of wrinkles that had ravaged her flesh. Her gray-streaked black hair was pulled back into a thick braid that had always before been hidden in the folds of the black shawl.

And where Cassie's eyes were dark brown, Miranda's

were the startling blue of sapphires. Always, Rosemary had had the impression that Miranda Sikes's eyes held the strange vacant stare of the mentally disturbed. But now, as the woman faced her, she saw that they held the same strange intimation of darkly hidden secrets that Cassie's eyes contained. In their depths Rosemary was sure she saw an underlying residue of anguish, and something more.

"If you don't want me here, just say so," Miranda said in a voice that was little more than a whisper.

Slowly, deliberately, Rosemary tried to clear away the fog that seemed to have gathered around her mind. Part of her—a part she immediately understood to be irrational— wanted to turn away from Miranda, to banish this grotesque figure from her shop and her mind. But the pain she'd seen in Miranda's eyes was so clearly reflected in the woman's voice that a tear welled up and overflowed onto her cheek. Vainly she searched for her voice. Miranda waited for her to reply, then finally nodded slightly and turned away. Only then did Rosemary manage to get to her feet. "No—no, please don't go," she said.

Miranda turned back.

"I'm sorry," Rosemary floundered. "You—I didn't know what to say. I thought—oh, Lord, I don't know what I thought. . . ."

Miranda smiled then, but instead of replying, she turned away from Rosemary again and looked curiously around the shop. "I've always wanted to come in here, you know," she said at last. "It's my favorite place in the whole village. I always look forward to the days when you change the windows."

Rosemary swallowed. I have to speak, she thought. I have to say something. Anything. "Y-you should have come in then," she heard herself say.

But Miranda shook her head. "I don't go in any of the shops. They don't want me, and I don't want to impose myself."

"But you came in today," Rosemary breathed. And yesterday Cassie was looking at your ancestors' graves, she thought. And the day before that I thought of you while I listened to Cassie. She could feel her heart begin to pound.

A shadow fell over Miranda's eyes. Rosemary noticed for

the first time that she was clasping her hands nervously together.

They were the hands of an old woman, the skin as translucent as parchment, covered with a network of fine wrinkles. Dark brown spots were scattered over their backs, and the fingers seemed permanently bent. She's an old woman, Rosemary thought. So old. But it was impossible. Surely Miranda Sikes couldn't be much past forty.

As if she felt Rosemary's eyes on them, Miranda's hands suddenly disappeared into the folds of her long black skirt. "I wanted to talk to you about Cassandra," she said. "I wanted to tell you that she's going to come to see me."

Rosemary's jaw sagged dumbly. "She's spoken to you?" she asked, her voice hollow. "I didn't know—"

"She hasn't spoken to me," Miranda interrupted, as if she'd read Rosemary's mind. "But she wants to talk to me. She wants to know who I am."

Rosemary shook her head uncomprehendingly. "I—I'm afraid I don't understand. . . ."

"She's going to come tomorrow," Miranda went on. Her eyes took on a faraway look, and she nodded slightly. "Yes, tomorrow. I hope you will let her."

Rosemary's confusion only deepened. Tomorrow? How could Miranda know what was going to happen tomorrow, unless she'd already talked to Cassie? What did Miranda want of her stepdaughter? Rosemary felt a shiver of foreboding pass through her. "What is it?" she pressed. "What is it about Cassie? Why do you want to see her?"

Miranda's eyes met Rosemary's, but she did not answer. She turned away then, and started slowly out of the shop.

Rosemary stood frozen where she was for a moment, trying to absorb the strange words the woman had uttered. And then, without thinking, she spoke. "Miranda!"

Miranda stopped and turned back.

"Miranda," Rosemary asked, "is something wrong with Cassie?"

For a moment Miranda said nothing, then she shook her head. "No," she said in a voice that was oddly empty. "Nothing's wrong with her. But she belongs to me." She fell silent for a moment, then smiled again. "Yes," she repeated. "She belongs to me." Then she turned away again, and left the shop. Outside she removed the black shawl from the shopping cart and carefully wrapped it around her head. Without looking back, she started down the sidewalk, pushing the shopping cart in front of her.

The memory of that strange visit had hung over Rosemary all the rest of that day, and last night she'd found herself watching Cassie.

Perhaps it had been meaningless. Perhaps Miranda was—as everyone thought she was—only harmlessly daft.

But what had she meant? Cassie belonged to her? It was crazy!

She had said nothing the night before, unwilling to try to talk to Keith about it and knowing that to Cassie none of it could possibly make any sense. But still, before Cassie had gone up to her room for the night, Rosemary had asked her what her plans were for the weekend.

Cassie looked at her disinterestedly. "I don't know," she'd said at last. "I don't have any, really. I guess I'll just study."

Then she hasn't talked to Miranda, Rosemary had thought. So it probably doesn't mean a thing. Still, she'd been unable to sleep last night.

It was nearly nine when Rosemary finally went downstairs. She found Keith sitting at the kitchen table, working on a crossword puzzle. There was no sign of either Cassie or Jennifer.

"Where are the girls?" she asked as she poured herself a cup of coffee and settled into the chair opposite her husband.

He glanced up from his paper, shrugging. "The beach," he said. "Cassie was going by herself, but Jennifer made such a nuisance of herself—"

"The beach?" Rosemary echoed hollowly. "Did—did she say why?"

Keith grinned at her. "Why do kids ever go to the beach?" he countered.

But Rosemary knew Cassie hadn't gone to the beach at all.

It was the marsh.

The marsh where Miranda lived.

The fear that had been flitting around the edges of her

consciousness ever since Cassie had come to False Harbor suddenly coalesced into a tight knot in her stomach. Her hands shaking, Rosemary tried to pour herself a cup of coffee. It spilled over the rim, scalding her hands.

Chapter 9

There was a sharp bite to the morning air, but the sky was a deep cloudless blue and the morning sun made the sea sparkle as if it had been scattered with millions of tiny diamonds. A strong wind was blowing in from the east, and a heavy surf was building, the swells close together, so the beach resounded with a steady din of crashing water. There were birds everywhere—gulls and sandpipers covered the beach. A flock of ducks churned over the marsh, rising as one into the air, circling, then dropping back down into the reeds to continue feeding. As Cassie and Jennifer walked along the hard-packed sand, staying just above the highest reach of the surf, the sandpipers skittered out of their way, opening a path before them then closing it again after they'd passed. Jennifer stopped short, clutching at Cassie's hand. "Look!"

From the south, barely visible above the horizon, Cassie could make out a faint line. "What is it?"

"Geese," Jennifer explained. "Sometimes they stop in the marsh."

The birds flew steadily toward them, and Cassie watched, fascinated by the perfect formation. As they drew nearer she could make out the individual birds, their necks stretched out straight, their feet tucked up under their bodies, their wings beating steadily in an almost hypnotic rhythm. By the time the formation reached the coast, everything else in Cassie's consciousness had faded away and she found herself imagining that she was with them, riding on the wind, looking down on the sparkling expanse of water and the thin strip of beach along its edge.

The big Canada geese were flying low, and as they came across the surf line, Cassie could hear the rush of air across their wings and almost feel it on her brow. Her whole body began to tingle with excitement. Then, as if giving a signal, the bird at the center of the V-formation honked loudly and veered off to the left. In perfect synchronization the rest of the flock banked to follow, then the formation suddenly broke as the geese lost altitude, braked in midair, and plummeted into the marsh in a cacophony of flapping wings and excited honkings. Even after they had disappeared from her sight completely, Cassie gazed out over the marsh, the image of the magnificent birds still vivid in her mind. Then, in the distance, she saw something else.

Far out on the rise in the middle of the marsh, Miranda was standing on the porch of her cabin. Though the distance was far too great for Cassie to see clearly, she knew that Miranda, too, had been watching the geese.

Now Miranda was watching her.

Watching her, and silently calling to her.

Already Cassie could feel the first stirrings of the strange force within her, drawing her toward the marsh.

"Isn't it neat?" Jennifer said excitedly, totally unaware of the strange feeling that had come over Cassie. "By next week there'll be so many of them you can hardly believe it. They just keep coming in, and then one day they all take off. They're going up to Canada, and after they're gone there won't be any more until fall." Her eyes widened in wonder as she gazed at the marsh. "How can they do it? How can they fly that far?"

Vaguely, Cassie heard Jennifer speaking, but her eyes never left the figure on the porch of the little cabin, and she made no reply.

Finally Jennifer looked anxiously up at Cassie. "Cassie? Is something wrong?"

"Look," Cassie said quietly. "Look out there."

Puzzled, Jennifer followed the older girl's gaze, and then gasped with sudden alarm. "It's Miranda," she breathed. "Don't look at her, Cassie."

But Cassie seemed not to hear her. She took a step forward.

Sumi, who had followed them from the house and was now sitting quietly at her feet, suddenly leaped to his feet and darted ahead, his tail twitching.

Jennifer's heart began to beat faster as she realized what Cassie had in mind.

"Cassie?" she called. "Cassie, what are you doing?"

Jennifer's voice sounded to Cassie as if it was coming from far away. In her mind, Cassie could hear another voice— Miranda's voice—calling to her.

She had to answer that call—she had to!

She took a step forward, then felt something tugging at her. Almost in a trance now, she looked down to see Jennifer clutching at her arm, trying to hold her back.

"I have to go out there," she said softly. "She wants me."

"No!" Jennifer protested. "You can't go out there. It's dangerous, and Miranda's crazy, and—" She fell silent as she saw the strange faraway look that had come into Cassie's eyes.

"She isn't crazy," Cassie breathed. "And you can't keep me from going out there. Nobody can."

With a short gasp, Jennifer dropped Cassie's arm and backed away. "B-but you'll get lost," she whispered in a final attempt to change her halfsister's mind.

Cassie only shook her head. "Sumi knows the way. He'll show me. Look." A few yards away the cat had stopped and turned around, his eyes fixing on Cassie. His tail twitched impatiently and he uttered a loud meow.

Jennifer backed farther away, her heart thumping now. Cassie took a step toward the frightened child, but when Jennifer shrank back from her, she turned away and began following Sumi along the beach. Jennifer stayed where she was, too afraid to follow, until Cassie was fifty yards away from her. Then her curiosity overcame her fear, and she timidly started after her halfsister.

Sumi angled across the beach, loping easily up the gentle rise of the low dune. He disappeared over the crest, but a moment later Cassie spotted him ranging back and forth at the very edge of the marsh, his tail once again twitching as if to signal her. She moved faster then. When she was within a few feet of Sumi, the cat turned and bounded down one of the narrow paths that led into the tangle of tall grasses and reeds. Cassie hesitated only a second, then followed.

Jennifer stopped short at the edge of the marsh. She stared fearfully at the oozing black water. Visions of slithering snakes and huge spiders made her skin crawl.

"Cassie?" she called out, her voice sounding small and lost against the cries of the birds and the muffled roar of the surf. "Cassie, don't . . ."

But Cassie was gone, already lost from Jennifer's view. She paused for a moment, trying to decide what to do. Should she go home and tell her parents what Cassie was doing? But that was tattling, wasn't it?

Then she had an idea. She wouldn't go into the marsh, but at least she knew a place where she could watch. Her fear easing slightly, she turned and started running down the beach.

Lisa Chambers and Allayne Garvey walked along Oak Street, which skirted the marsh from Bay Street all the way to Cape Drive. It was one of the prettiest streets in False Harbor, for before the village had been laid out, Oak Street had been a cow path that wound along the edge of the wetlands. When the town fathers had laid out a more formal structure of streets, Oak Street's route was allowed to follow the natural contours of the land, as the path had always done, instead of being forced into the puritan uniformity of the rigid grid upon which the rest of the village streets had been surveyed. On both sides of the gently curving road, rows of giant oaks had spread their branches wide. Near the end of the street a strip of the marsh had been reclaimed in the early part of the century to form a grassy park, dotted now with picnic tables, swings, and teeter-totters.

All the beauty of the street was lost on Lisa, however, for her mind was totally occupied with her fury toward Cassie Winslow.

"I don't see why Eric wants to walk her to school every day," she complained, kicking sullenly at an empty Coke can that lay next to one of the trash barrels. "Doesn't he even care what people think?"

"What's he supposed to do?" Allayne argued. "Cross the street every time he sees her?"

"Well, why shouldn't he? She's not part of our group, and she never will be." She stopped in mid-step and turned to face Allayne. "Mom doesn't think she has any class at all, and nobody even knows where her mother came from."

Allayne's eyes rolled, and she started tuning Lisa's voice out. There wasn't much she hadn't already heard about Lisa's own family, and how old it was, and how important. But Allayne knew perfectly well that outside of False Harbor nobody had ever heard of the Chamberses or the Smythes or the Maynards. Nor, for that matter, had they heard of the Garveys, either, and Allayne's family had been around at least as long as any of the others. It was just that in her family, the kind of haughty pride the Chamberses displayed was known as arrogance. "Most of the founding fathers were a pretty sleazy bunch anyway," her father always said. "Stealing the land from the Indians, then snooping on their neighbors all the time. And we all think that just because we haven't had the gumption to get out of here, we're something special. The only special person we have around here is Miranda Sikes, and nobody will even talk to her."

"Including you," Allayne had pointed out, but her father had only dismissed her words with a wave of his hand.

When Allayne had asked him what was special about Miranda Sikes, he'd shaken his head and replied, "If you want to find that out, maybe you ought to go out there and see." Ever since, Allayne had thought about his words and wondered if he was really serious. She also wondered if she'd ever work up the courage to take up his challenge.

Now, as Lisa Chambers's voice droned on, Allayne sighed and glanced at the park in the hopes of finding something that might divert Lisa from her monologue of complaints about Cassie Winslow. Almost immediately she found something. Standing on one of the picnic tables, staring into the marsh, she saw Jennifer Winslow. Allayne watched the little girl for a few seconds, and when she didn't move, gently nudged Lisa. "Look," she said quietly.

Lisa, annoyed at being interrupted, looked irritably toward Jennifer. "So what?" she asked.

"What's she doing? There must be something in the marsh."

"Birds," Lisa said. "That's all that's ever in the marsh. Why don't we go down to the drugstore and get a Coke?"

But Allayne ignored Lisa's words. "I think she's watching something," she said. "Come on, let's find out what it is." She veered off the sidewalk into the park, and after a moment Lisa followed her. "Jennifer?" Allayne called.

Startled, Jennifer jumped, then turned to face them. She looked almost frightened, but as she recognized Allayne, who had been her favorite baby-sitter before Cassie arrived, her expression eased.

"Jen?" Allayne asked. "Is something wrong?"

"It's Cassie," Jennifer breathed. "Look."

She pointed out into the marsh, and a second later Allayne and Lisa saw what the child had been watching.

Far out in the marsh, maybe two hundred and fifty yards away, they could see a figure moving quickly through the weeds.

"But what's she doing out there?" Allayne asked. "Doesn't she know it's dangerous?"

"I told her," Jennifer said solemnly. "But she wouldn't listen to me."

"She's crazy," Lisa Chambers pronounced. "She doesn't know anything about the marsh."

"She isn't either crazy," Jennifer shot back.

"Isn't she?" Lisa taunted. "Well, if she isn't, what's she doing out there?"

"She's going to see Miranda!" Jennifer exclaimed without thinking, then clamped both hands over her mouth as if she could take back her words.

Lisa and Allayne stared at the little girl for a moment, and then suddenly understood. They looked out over the marsh once more, but this time they ignored Cassie, searching instead the low rise on which Miranda Sikes's cabin stood starkly silhouetted in its scraggly grove of trees.

On the porch of the tiny house, standing so still she might have been carved from stone, was Miranda.

A slow, cruel smile spread over Lisa Chambers's face, and her eyes gleamed with malice. "I knew it," she said quietly. "I told you so, didn't I? She's just as crazy as Miranda is!"

But Allayne, fascinated, said nothing, for in the wetlands

beyond the park even the birds had suddenly fallen silent as Cassie slowly approached the strange cabin in the marsh.

Cassie was barely inside the grove of spindly pines when the hawk on the roof of Miranda's cabin suddenly came to life, raising its head from beneath its wing to peer out into the surrounding swamplands. Then, as its eyes found Cassie, it rose up onto its feet, its wings flapping noisily.

With a high-pitched scream of fury, the hawk rose up off the roof, its wings beating hard as it circled up into the cloudless blue of the sky.

Cassie watched as the bird flew higher and began to circle. She turned slowly, both fascinated and frightened by its graceful flight. Then, as she followed the bird's path across the marsh, she saw the three figures in the park. For a split second she thought they were watching the hawk too. Suddenly, with a flash of anger, she realized that they weren't staring at the hawk, but at her.

They were staring at her, and talking about her. She could almost hear the sneering words coming out of Lisa Chambers's mouth. Her surge of anger grew, and for a moment she wished the hawk would see them, too, and know what they were saying, and stop them.

From high above her head another angry screech erupted from the hawk's beak. Instantly, a flock of ducks burst from the reeds. Cassie froze, her heart suddenly beating faster as she remembered the terror she'd felt when she had first seen the bird rise from the roof in a frenzy of beating wings. But then she felt Miranda's eyes upon her once more, and her fear began to abate.

Cassie braced herself, certain that the bird was about to plunge down to attack her.

Instead the white hawk shot away to the east, passing over Cassie's head, blotting out the sun. As Cassie watched it, unable to move, it circled above the park. Then it dove downward.

Allayne looked up just as the hawk, screaming once again, burst through the budding branches of the oaks and chestnuts that circled the picnic table. Her eyes widened in shock as she realized what was happening, and she snatched

Jennifer off the table. "Run!" she shouted as she lowered the child to the ground. "Put your arms over your head and run!" Jennifer, a shriek of fright escaping her lips, obeyed instantly, but Lisa Chambers, too surprised by what had happened to move, was frozen to the spot, staring mutely at the attacking bird.

Only at the last instant did she manage to throw up an arm to fend off the hawk's extended claws. A searing flash of pain shot through her forearm as its talons sliced through her skin and tore at her flesh, then she finally came to life as Allayne grabbed her other arm. Screaming with fear and agony, she stumbled after Allayne.

The attack was over as quickly as it began. The hawk rose once more into the air, caught the wind, and soared skyward without so much as a beat of its wings.

Cassie watched it all. She saw the bird dive, saw Allayne send Jennifer running from the park, saw the hawk slash viciously at Lisa's arm then burst back out of the trees. But as Lisa and Allayne stumbled away, the hawk screamed once more. Cassie looked up into the sky.

This time the hawk was coming toward her.

Cassie felt herself begin to tremble, and her skin turned clammy with a cold sweat as the bird flew over the marsh, gained altitude, then hovered over the pines for a moment.

Then it closed its wings and dived.

Cassie couldn't move. She remained where she was, paralyzed with fear. She closed her eyes and waited for the bird to strike.

At the last moment she heard a fluttering of feathers, then felt a weight on her shoulder. A moment later, something brushed her cheek, and when she finally managed to open her eyes again, the hawk was perched on her shoulder.

Sumi sat at her feet, his tail wrapped around her leg.

From the front porch of the cabin Miranda beckoned. "They are your friends," she said softly. "They'll always be your friends."

Then, reaching her hand out to Cassie, the woman in black drew her inside the cabin.

Chapter 10

"Why the hell would Cassie want to go out and see Miranda?" Keith asked. Though his tone was light, Rosemary knew by the expression on his face that he was really wondering why she'd wasted a whole night worrying about the words of an old woman the whole town knew was half crazy.

"I don't know," Rosemary repeated for the third time. Her lack of sleep was catching up with her, and she felt herself growing angry with Keith. Why was he insisting that she should have simply dismissed whatever Miranda had said to her? Wasn't he even interested? "All I'm telling you is what happened yesterday, and that I think you ought to go out to the marsh and see if she's there. Probably you're right—she's down at the beach with Jen and there's nothing at all the matter. But I just wish you'd take a look. Is that so horrible of me, that I'm worried about your daughter?"

Keith's eyes narrowed. "My daughter," he repeated. "Is that what this is all about? She's my daughter, and you don't really have anything to do with her?"

Rosemary's eyes brimmed with tears. "You know that's not true," she said, her voice quavering. "And I'd go myself, but it seems as though every time I try to talk to her, I say something wrong. If I go, she'll think I'm . . . well, she'll think I'm spying on her."

"Which is what you want me to do, isn't it?" Keith asked. "I have a lot to do today," he went on, "and I'll be damned if I'll waste my time poking around in the marsh just because Miranda was babbling to you yesterday. And if I were you—"

Before he could finish, the back door slammed open and Jennifer plunged into the kitchen, her frightened face stained with tears. Behind her, sobbing uncontrollably, was Lisa Chambers, her right arm bound up with a bloody scarf. At her side was Allayne Garvey. Keith froze in mid-sentence as Jennifer threw herself into his arms. While Lisa continued to sob hysterically, Allayne tried to explain what had happened in the park. Rosemary—her anger at Keith momentarily banished from her mind—carefully unwound the scarf from Lisa's arm and gently rinsed the wound at the kitchen sink.

There were deep slashes in the girl's forearm, each of them almost an inch long, so clean that they might have been made by a razor blade. The skin had shrunk back from them, exposing the torn muscle beneath. Wincing with sympathetic pain as she soaped the cuts, Rosemary tried to follow what Allayne was saying while still keeping half an ear on Keith's hurried call to Paul Samuels, the village's only doctor.

"We'd better take her in," he said after he'd hung up. "Paul says if the cuts are as deep as I told him, she'll need stitches. I'll call Fred Chambers and tell him to meet us at the clinic." Leaving Rosemary to take care of Jennifer, he half carried Lisa out to the car, then, with Allayne tending to Lisa, he drove toward the twelve-bed emergency hospital a few blocks away.

"Lisa said Cassie did it," Jennifer told her mother when she was finally calmed down enough to make sense. Her eyes were wide and her jaw set stubbornly. "All the way home she kept yelling that Cassie did it." Her fear was quickly giving way to anger now. "But that's dumb, isn't it? Cassie wouldn't do something like that! Only a mean person would, and Cassie's not mean! I don't care what Lisa Chambers says. She's a big liar, anyway."

"Slow down, darling," Rosemary protested. "Slow down, and just try to tell me what happened. Everything, from the moment you left the house with Cassie this morning."

Jennifer's face screwed up into an expression of intense concentration as she began telling the story, her eyes fixed anxiously on her mother. "I tried to stop her," she finished. "I told her she shouldn't go in the marsh by herself, but she wouldn't listen to me."

"But where is she now?" Rosemary asked when Jennifer was finally done. Even before Jennifer spoke, she was already certain she knew the answer to her question.

"She went into Miranda's house," Jennifer breathed, her voice trembling with awe. "Allayne saw it. She said the bird just came down and perched on Cassie's shoulder for a minute, and then Cassie followed Miranda into her house."

Twenty minutes later Keith was back, his face flushed with anger. "You want to hear something really wonderful?" he asked tightly. "Fred Chambers says if there's so much as a single mark on Lisa's arm, he's going to sue us. Can you believe that?"

"Sue us?" Rosemary echoed. "What on earth for?"

Keith's voice hardened. "He seems to think he's got lots of grounds. For starters, there's Lisa's cockamamie story about Cassie making the hawk attack her. But it gets worse. There's also the fact you took the scarf off Lisa's arm and tried to clean up the cuts. That, he claims, could be construed as practicing medicine without a license."

Rosemary's eyes flashed indignantly. "That's ridiculous!"

"Of course it is," Keith agreed. "But ridiculous has never stopped Fred Chambers before. Even if he loses, he can make life miserable for us." Shaking his head with barely contained anger, he began shrugging into his pea coat. "I'd better go out there and find Cassie. Maybe she knows what really happened."

But as he left the house, Rosemary noticed that he'd said nothing about the fact that apparently she had been right all along. For whatever reasons, Cassie had, indeed, gone out to see Miranda Sikes.

Just as Miranda had said she would.

Eric Cavanaugh was walking aimlessly over the dunes. The chill wind whipped around him, slowly cooling the anger that still burned inside him. He'd been walking for more than an hour, not really aware of where he was going, and not caring. But now, looking up, he realized he was halfway out Cranberry Point. He paused, breathing deeply of the salt air and enjoying the cool sting of spindrift against his skin. As far as he could see, whitecaps glistened brightly in the sun and the thundering surf had scrubbed the beach clean of every trace of seaweed. The last of his fury seemed to drain into the roiling sea, and when he at last turned away to gaze out over the wetlands on the leeward side of the point, he felt the beginnings of the peacefulness he always found here begin to wash gently over him.

In strange contrast to the churning ocean, there was a placidity about the marsh now. The wind, rushing freely over the open expanse of the Atlantic, had been unable to vent its full strength on the protected marsh, and the reeds were merely swaying in the breeze. Here and there open expanses of black and brackish water rippled gently, reflecting the crystal blue of the sky in a rainbow of hues. A redwing blackbird, its beak filled with a tuft of grass, was industriously pulling reeds together in the first stages of its nest building. Far in the distance Eric could make out the familiar shape of Miranda Sikes's cabin, the ubiquitous white hawk perched on the peak of the roof.

Then, as he watched, someone emerged from the cabin. At first, as the figure hesitated on the porch, he was certain it was Miranda, but a second later he knew it was someone else, for the person bolted off the porch and began running down the slope of the hill.

Cassie. It had to be Cassie.

As she disappeared into the tall grasses, a shout drifted over the marsh, then another. A movement off to the right, near the park, caught Eric's eye, and then he recognized Keith Winslow running along the strip of grass that edged the marsh. As Eric watched, Keith shouted once more, then veered off into the marsh itself.

A moment later the hawk on the roof of Miranda Sikes's cabin came to life, rising off its perch with a single beat of its powerful wings. A second later Eric lost sight of it as its ghostly image disappeared into the brightness of the morning sunlight.

Cassie reappeared for a moment, then was gone again, lost somewhere in the reeds. But even in the split second she'd been visible, Eric knew she was running toward him rather than her father. He hesitated, wondering what could have happened. Had she really gone to Miranda's house alone? But how had she done it? How had she threaded her way through the maze of trails and paths, most of which led nowhere but simply petered out into boggy morasses of peat and treacherous expanses of quicksand?

And what had made her father come looking for her?

And then, over the pounding surf and Keith Winslow's shouts, Eric heard a high-pitched scream. The hawk, no more than a tiny speck high above the marsh, was preparing to dive.

Cassie had no idea of where she was—on both sides of her the reeds seemed to be closing in, reaching out, grasping at her. The pounding of her heart thundered in her ears, but above the throbbing she could hear the cries of the birds in a howling cacophony.

And then her foot slipped and she plunged headlong off the path and into the marsh itself. Screaming, she flailed in the muck and tried to grab at a clump of reeds. The reeds came loose in her hand and she only rolled over, the foul waters of the marsh oozing through her clothes. Struggling to her hands and knees, she looked wildly around, but the path seemed to have disappeared.

"Help!" she yelled. "Somebody help me!"

Staggering to her feet, she took a single step, then tripped again, plunging face first into the mire. The screams of the marsh birds were even louder now, and she imagined she could hear the beat of the hawk's wings as well. She looked up, and at first saw nothing. Then, high above her, she found the pale shape of the hawk, floating on the wind. As she watched, it seemed to discover her, and folding its wings against its body, dropped into a plunging dive.

It couldn't be coming after her—it couldn't! It was her friend, and it wouldn't turn against her. And yet with every second it was swooping closer.

Keith dodged to the right, then to the left. Almost there— just a few more yards. He shouted to Cassie again, but she didn't seem to hear him. She just kept plunging onward, stumbling through the mud.

Why didn't she stop? Why couldn't she hear him?

Her screams were muffled now, but the white hawk was

clearly visible, streaking out of the sky. From its open beak a high-pitched scream of attack rent the air, and its feet were extended, the talons glittering in the sun like deadly jewels. Still running, Keith ripped his pea coat off, preparing to throw it over Cassie.

Only at the last minute did he realize that the hawk was not attacking Cassie at all.

He himself was the target.

He froze, caught in a nightmare as the hawk loomed larger and larger above him. He could see its eyes now—bloodred spots bored into the white mask of its face. Suddenly its wings spread out as it braked in midair, and the creature's talons seemed to spread wide.

At the last instant Keith's arm jerked reflexively upward. The bird's talons closed, but instead of sinking into his own flesh, they tore only into the thick wool of the jacket.

Instantly the hawk's mighty wings spread wide as it tried to launch itself back into the sky with its prize clutched in its claws, but Keith jerked hard on the jacket, and the bird plunged into the reeds, thrashing wildly. Screaming in furious confusion, it rolled over, then found its balance and hurled itself into the air for a second attack.

Keith plunged through the reeds and found Cassie, half mired in the mud, struggling to free herself from the entangling reeds. Grasping her arm, he pulled her to her feet, then shielded his head with his free arm as he prepared for the hawk's next attack.

"Hang on," he shouted. "Just hang on, Cassie!"

Half carrying and half dragging her, his feet sinking into the peat with every step, Keith slogged through the marsh until he found a path. Then, still clutching Cassie's hand, he ran toward the beach.

The hawk, beating against the wind, kept pace with them. As they neared the edge of the wetlands, it spiraled high until it was once again only a shimmering speck against the blue backdrop of the sky. As they reached the dunes and the beach beyond, Keith braced himself for another attack.

But it never came. As he watched, the hawk turned away, then sailed back out over the marsh in a graceful loop, settling once more on the peak of Miranda Sikes's cabin. Only then did Keith finally turn to face his daughter.

Her clothes were black with the reeking waters of the marsh, and her face was smeared with mud. Slimy grasses had tangled themselves in her hair, and her hands were covered with a network of tiny cuts where the sharp edges of swamp plants had slashed her skin. Beneath the mud her face was pale, and her entire body was trembling.

Releasing her father's hand, she sank down onto the beach and choked back a sob.

"What is it, baby?" Keith breathed, dropping to his knees beside her. "What happened out there?"

Cassie looked at him with haunted eyes and shook her head mutely, still overcome by the churning of her emotions and the thoughts reeling through her mind. It was real. It was true. Miranda Sikes was the woman of the dream, the woman in black. And Cassie knew now that she was Miranda's. She belonged to Miranda, and it was to her that Miranda would reveal her incredible powers. But at the same time as she knew this, Cassie also had a terrifying foreboding that something was about to happen. Something terrible. To Miranda. And to her.

Keith stared helplessly at his anguished daughter for a few seconds. She was sobbing uncontrollably now. "She's going to die," Cassie gasped. "I know it."

"Who is, baby? Who's going to die?" Keith whispered, but he got no response. Cassie's hysteria was abating now as she struggled to regain control of herself. At last, Keith drew her to her feet, his arm around her, supporting her. "Come on, baby," he said soothingly. "It's all right. I'm taking you home. I'm taking you home now." Slowly, with Cassie still sobbing against his chest, he led her away.

Only when Cassie and her father were gone from the beach did Eric Cavanaugh stand up in the patch of dune grass where he'd lain hidden. He looked out into the marsh. It was quiet now—its placid calm restored as if the chaotic scene of a few minutes before had never happened.

He stood still for a few minutes, Cassie's words echoing in his mind. Then, moving slowly and deliberately, he started out into the marsh, following the familiar twists and turns that would lead him out to the low hill on which Miranda's cabin stood.

He hadn't really believed Cassie would go out there. No one went out there, no one at all, except . . .

He made up his mind.

It was time for him to go see Miranda.

By the time Keith got Cassie home, her crying had stopped, but she had fallen into a silence that neither Keith nor Rosemary could penetrate. She offered no explanations about why she'd gone out to Miranda's house, no explanations for her strange words. Instead she simply retreated to her room, where she spent the rest of the day alone, with the door closed.

Around noon there was a scratching at the back door, and Rosemary let Sumi in. The cat, ignoring its bowl of food, streaked up the stairs, and a moment later Cassie let it into her room.

As the day wore on, there was still only silence from the second floor. Rosemary went upstairs several times and tapped softly at Cassie's door, but when there was no response, she turned away and went back downstairs, shaking her head at Keith's inquiring glance.

"We should try to *make* her talk about it," Rosemary finally said when dinner was over and Cassie had still not been seen. "Whatever happened out there obviously terrified her."

Once again Keith shook his head. "She'll talk about it when she's ready to," he said, though remembering the stricken look on his daughter's face and her hysterical sobs, he was more worried than he cared to admit.

Rather than precipitate another fight, Rosemary reluctantly agreed to let it go—at least until morning.

Cassie jerked awake, her skin clammy and her heart pounding. In the dream she'd been in the marsh, but the grass had been higher than it really was. It had towered over her head almost like a bamboo forest, and the stems of the cattails and reeds had seemed almost like the trunks of trees.

Ahead of her, Miranda was walking, and though Cassie couldn't quite see her, she knew she was there.

There was someone else there too. Cassie could feel a presence in the darkness, but she didn't know who it was.

The night sounds of the marsh were loud in her ears, and she could distinguish every separate noise, from the soft thruppings of the tree frogs and chirpings of the crickets, to the restless rustling of sleeping birds as they ruffled their feathers. The marsh was filled with odors, too, odors that brought vague images to her mind and made her want to leave the trail and investigate.

But she never did. Instead she stayed on the path, quietly following Miranda.

She had no sense of time, but after a while she began to feel a sensation of foreboding.

Something had gone wrong. Miranda was no longer moving ahead of her.

She moved faster, and as she came around a bend in the path, everything suddenly changed.

The reeds were broken and the grasses crushed down.

Then, a little way off the trail, she saw it.

Miranda was on the ground and there was a shape above her, staring down at her. Miranda was staring back at the looming figure, but neither of them was saying anything. Then the peaceful sounds of the night were interrupted by a stream of angry curses, followed by a loud, broken laugh.

It was the laugh that awakened Cassie.

She sat bolt upright in bed, shivering against the clammy chill of cold sweat that covered her body.

Sumi was sitting in the darkness beside her, his eyes fixed on her as if he knew she'd just awakened from a nightmare. Then he ran to the window, leaping up onto the sill. But instead of disappearing out into the limbs of the tree beyond, he looked back at her, mewling anxiously.

At first she didn't understand. Then, slowly, the realization of what the cat wanted became clear. He wanted her to follow him.

Instantly she knew that this dream was like the other one—the one in which she had seen her mother die and first met Miranda.

It wasn't just a dream. It was a vision. It was real.

Miranda needed her.

But where was she? It didn't matter—wherever Miranda was, Sumi would lead her there.

Slipping out of bed, she pulled on her clothes and went

to the window. A moment later she was gone, climbing down through the tree to the ground, following Sumi into the night. . . .

Rosemary's eyes blinked open and she stared for a moment at the glowing numerals of the clock on the bedside table.

Midnight.

She wasn't sure what had awakened her; she wasn't even sure how long she'd been awake. All she knew was that something in the house felt wrong.

She told herself it was nothing, and turned over. Keith stirred next to her, then rolled over on his back and began gently snoring.

She closed her eyes and tried to ignore the strange feeling of something amiss. But the feeling only grew stronger. At last she sighed, slid out from under the covers, and shoved her arms into the robe that hung over the chair in front of her vanity. Slipping out of the master bedroom, she moved quickly down the hall and opened the door to Jennifer's room. By the bright glow of the moon she could see Jennifer sleeping peacefully, one arm cuddling her favorite doll, a large Raggedy Ann. Her chest rose and fell in the deep steady rhythm of sleep. With a soft click Rosemary pulled the door closed.

She paused outside Cassie's door, listening for any sounds from within.

There were none.

She rapped softly, then hesitantly twisted the knob and pushed the door open.

She caught her breath, then stepped inside. The bed, its covers piled at the foot, was cold. At the far end the window stood open. The screen had been removed from its hinges and stood next to the window, leaning against the wall. Her heart beating faster, Rosemary hurried back to her own room and shook Keith. He mumbled, rolling over, then sleepily opened his eyes.

"She's not here," Rosemary whispered urgently. "Keith, Cassie's gone."

Keith blinked, then sat up and switched on the lamp next to the bed. "Gone?" he repeated. "What do you mean, she's gone?"

Quickly she explained. "We'd better call Gene Templeton," she finished.

Ten minutes later the False Harbor police chief appeared at the front door, his eyes red with sleep, his uniform rumpled. He listened to Rosemary's story silently, then shrugged. "Lots of kids take off like that," he told her. "She's probably just poking around town, having herself an adventure."

But Rosemary shook her head. "She's gone out to the marsh," she said. "I don't know why she's gone out there, but I'm sure that's where she is. I can feel it."

Templeton sighed, and wondered why it was that women always "felt" things. Never men. Men had "hunches." But it was the same thing, and Templeton had long ago learned to act upon his hunches. So now he would act on Rosemary Winslow's feeling. "Okay, I'll go out and take a look around."

"I'll go with you," Keith said, but the police chief shook his head.

"No you won't. You'll stay right here with your wife. The last thing I need is having the father along while I look."

Keith started to protest, but the look of determination in Templeton's eyes stopped him. And, of course, the chief was right. His job was to find Cassie, not deal with Keith.

As Templeton left the house, Jennifer, rubbing her sleepy eyes, came downstairs. "Something woke me up," she said, reaching up to her father. "Is something wrong?"

"It's okay," Keith assured her, lifting her into his arms and kissing her on the cheek. "Cassie just went for a walk, and Mr. Templeton's gone to find her."

Jennifer screwed her face into a worried expression. "Did she go back to Miranda's house?" she asked.

"Now why would she want to do that?" Keith asked.

"Because Miranda's a witch," the little girl said solemnly. "And I bet she cast a spell on Cassie."

Templeton swung the police car into the parking lot at the end of Oak Street, then maneuvered it in a wide curve so the headlights swept out over the marsh like twin searchlights. A few birds, disturbed by the sudden brilliance, burst into the air then settled down again. Seeing nothing, Templeton turned off the ignition and the headlights, then sat for a moment, letting his eyes adjust to the pale glow of the full moon above. At least the night was clear and the moon high, he reflected as he released the flashlight from its clip beneath the dash. He left the car and started toward the marsh. If Cassie Winslow was out there, she wouldn't be too hard to spot.

Unless she didn't want to be spotted.

If that was the case, his job would be the next thing to impossible, for all she would have to do was stay low and there would be no way for him to see her among the reeds. Unless, by sheer chance, he happened to stumble across her.

He chose the widest path he could find and started into the boggy morass, moving carefully but swiftly, his easy grace belying the bulkiness of his six-foot-four-inch frame. He searched for anything that might be construed as fresh foot-prints, but in the saturated soil even his own tracks disappeared almost as soon as his feet left the ground. After a few minutes he stopped looking at the trail ahead, letting his eyes constantly flick out over the marsh itself, looking for a move-ment or a silhouette that might be Cassie. Almost without making a conscious decision, he found himself moving in the general direction of Miranda Sikes's cabin. The paths began to grow narrower, branching off in a haphazard fashion dic-tated more by the contours of the marsh than any particular destination. Around him Templeton could hear the night sounds of frogs and insects, and twice he saw snakes slither across the path to disappear into the tangled safety of the reeds.

He was halfway to the rise on which Miranda's house stood, when he suddenly froze.

Off to the left there had been the barest flicker of move-ment, then nothing. He stood perfectly still, his eyes flicking back and forth as he searched for the source of the movement.

It came again, and then from out of the gloom a shape emerged. Twenty or so yards away, almost lost in the reeds, a figure was making its way carefully along one of the paths.

Cassie, or someone else? Miranda?

Templeton couldn't be sure. But whoever it was, the figure moved very slowly, head tipped down slightly, as if watching something on the trail. Templeton watched for a few moments, then silently began working his way closer. He circled around, always keeping the dark shadow of the figure within his range of vision, until he was ahead of her.

The trail she was following intersected his own a few steps ahead. He crouched down, waiting.

Suddenly a shadow darted across the trail ahead, but it was gone before Templeton could identify it. Then the figure of the person stepped into the intersection of the two trails, and Templeton, every muscle in his body tensed, rose to his feet and switched the flashlight on.

"Hold it!" he said, his words snapping in the quiet like the flick of a whip.

The figure froze, then turned slowly toward him. In the brilliance of the flashlight's halogen bulb, he recognized Cassie Winslow, her skin pale and her eyes frightened. He relaxed and took a step forward.

"It's all right, Cassie," he said gently. "It's Chief Templeton." He turned the flashlight off, and in the shimmering moonlight saw Cassie blink as her eyes tried to adjust to the sudden darkness. He reached out a hand and took her arm to steady her. "What are you doing out here?" he asked.

For a moment Templeton wasn't sure she'd heard him, but then she spoke. Her voice was barely audible, and tears were streaming down her face. "Miranda," she whispered. "She needed me."

Templeton frowned in the darkness. "Miranda needed you? Why?" Cassie made no reply, but her eyes flicked away from Templeton, scanning first the path ahead, then the sky above. "Where is she?" Templeton asked. "Isn't she in her house?"

Cassie slowly shook her head. "There," she said, and her right arm slowly came up, pointing into the sky. "She's over there."

Templeton studied the sky in the direction she was pointing, and at first saw nothing. But then, in the blackness, he saw a sudden flicker of light, then another. Slowly a ghostly shape took form in the darkness, and after a few moments Templeton realized what it was.

The white hawk, sailing silently on the air currents, was slowly circling a spot a hundred yards away. "Come on," Templeton said quietly. "Let's take a look."

Guiding Cassie with his free hand, Templeton started along the trail, lighting their way with the flashlight. Every few seconds he looked up at the hawk, half expecting it to have disappeared. But it was always there, and as they drew closer, its circle seemed to tighten. Ahead Templeton heard a soft mewling.

"Sumi," Cassie breathed. "He's already there."

There was a bend in the trail a few paces farther on, and as they came around it, the flashlight's beam trapped the cat in a circle of brilliance. It was sitting in the middle of the path, its twitching tail curled around its feet, its eyes glowing with an almost unnatural brightness. It suddenly squawled loudly and bounded away. Above them the hawk screamed once then folded its wings and dropped down out of the night sky.

Templeton's eyes followed the hawk, watched it plunge downward into a small area to the right which was free of anything except a thin sheen of shining water. At the last moment it spread its wings to break its fall and landed on something that protruded out of the marsh. Clucking softly, the bird settled its feathers then fell still and silent.

Templeton played the light out over the open area. The bird, red eyes glowing like embers, blinked, but made no attempt to fly away. And then Templeton realized what it had perched on.

From the depths of the quicksand a human hand protruded upward into the night. On its crooked fingers—frozen in death—the hawk had found its roost.

"She needed me," Cassie said once again, her voice cracking. "She needed me, and I had to come. I had to . . ."

Chapter 11

At three o'clock on Tuesday afternoon Cassie, wearing a navy-blue skirt with a white blouse and dark blue sweater that her stepmother had bought for her the day before, walked up the steps in front of the Congregational Church. Keith and Rosemary were on either side of her, and Jennifer, clutching her mother's hand tightly, did her best to keep up with Rosemary's quick stride.

The four of them walked down the aisle and slipped into the front pew. In front of the altar a plain white coffin containing Miranda Sikes's body sat on a small catafalque. Its lid was closed, and on top of it lay the spray of flowers that Rosemary had ordered that morning.

Other than that single spray, the church was barren of any decoration whatsoever.

The organist sat at the console, staring straight ahead, her thin lips forming a disapproving line across her face. As soon as the Winslows had seated themselves, she began playing. The music echoed oddly in the silent church. A moment later the little door behind the empty choir box opened and the dour-faced Congregational minister stepped out, a bible held tightly in his hand. As he closed the door behind him and stepped to the pulpit, Rosemary glanced over her shoulder.

Except for the Winslows, the church was totally empty.

His reedy voice sounding hollow in the nearly deserted

church, the minister began the short service in memory of Miranda Sikes.

There was no choir, no eulogy, only a short prayer and brief recounting of the life of a woman to whom the minister had never spoken in all his years in False Harbor. Twenty minutes later it was over, and the doors of the church were opened. Six pallbearers hired for the occasion by the undertaker in Barnstable marched quickly down the aisle, picked up the coffin, then began their slow retreat from the church.

The Winslows rose to their feet.

Cassie, with her family behind her, followed the coffin and the minister out into the spring afternoon. The bearers carried the coffin around the church to the graveyard, where an open grave awaited, the newest—and last—in the even row that contained the earthly remains of all the generations of Sikes women. As the Winslows gathered around the grave, the minister began intoning the prayers for the dead.

It was during the prayers that Cassie first felt eyes watching her. The skin on the back of her neck began to prickle. Finally, when she could stand it no longer, she turned around.

Just beyond the fence separating the graveyard from the sidewalk, she recognized Wendy Maynard, pulling at her mother's arm. But Lavinia Maynard was ignoring her daughter. Instead she was staring at Cassie as if examining a bug on the end of a pin. As soon as their eyes met, though, Mrs. Maynard turned away, then she hurried down the sidewalk with her daughter, the two quickly disappearing around the corner. Cassie turned back to face the minister again, but in a few moments felt her skin begin to crawl once more. When she looked back this time, she saw Lisa Chambers standing across the street in the square with some of her friends. They were whispering to each other while watching Cassie.

She felt a tear well in her eye, but didn't brush it away until she'd turned her back on Lisa.

At last the minister finished his prayer and reached down to pick up a clod of earth. He crushed the lump between his fingers and the dirt dropped onto the casket the pallbearers were lowering slowly into the grave.

As the casket disappeared from view, Sumi slipped out from behind one of the gravestones and darted over to peer into the open grave. The fur on his neck rose, and a soft mewing emerged from his throat. Then he backed away, his eyes fixed on the yawning chasm in the earth, until he came in contact with Cassie's leg. She bent over slightly, and he leaped up into her arms and licked gently at her cheek.

As the casket touched the bottom of the grave, Cassie had a sudden urge to look up into the sky.

So high up it was barely visible, the white hawk was floating above the graveyard, its wings fixed as it effortlessly rode the wind coming in off the sea. As Cassie watched, it turned and soared away.

Finally it was over, and with Sumi still cradled in her arms, Cassie was led out of the cemetery and back around the church to the house on Alder Street.

Before she went inside, she glanced out toward the marsh. It wasn't fair, she thought. She'd barely met Miranda, and already she was gone.

Except that deep within her Cassie had a feeling that Miranda wasn't gone at all.

This funeral—Miranda's funeral—hadn't been at all like her mother's. All through the ceremony she'd found herself reliving once again those few moments she'd spent with Miranda, feeling once again the power of the connection between them, hearing once again the words Miranda had spoken to her.

"You are mine. You've come home again, and now you belong to me. Forevermore you belong to me."

And Cassie knew that she had heard those words before. The memory was becoming clearer, though it was still not complete.

But Cassie knew that though Miranda was dead, she wasn't gone. Not the way Cassie's mother was gone.

Miranda's spirit, the spirit to which Cassie had felt herself drawn from the moment she'd first seen the strange woman who lived in the marsh, was still alive.

Alive within Cassie herself.

Gene Templeton tipped back in the large chair behind his desk and propped his feet up on the open drawer which had been designed to hold an array of files but had long since been converted into a convenient storage bin for the endless snacks with which he filled his stomach. Someday, he supposed, he would pay for his constant grazing, and his stomach would begin bulging out over the wide black belt of his uniform. But it hadn't happened yet, despite the dire warnings of his wife Ellie. His weight hadn't changed an ounce from the two hundred ten pounds he'd carried when he graduated from college thirty-odd years ago. Though Ellie liked to tease him that forty of those pounds had converted themselves over the years from muscle to fat, Gene knew it wasn't true: his body was as hard as it had ever been. Metabolism, he always told her. That was the key to it: a good, healthy metabolism.

Except that the whole thing with Miranda Sikes was making him overeat, and if he wasn't careful, he would throw that precious metabolism off balance. Then watch out. He could picture himself ballooning up fifty pounds overnight, and having to forego most of the meals Ellie liked fixing for him.

Which wasn't, he knew, really the point. He was thinking about food to avoid thinking about what had happened to Miranda and what the implications of his investigation might mean. Besides, things like finding Miranda Sikes's body in the marsh weren't supposed to happen, not in quiet little towns like False Harbor.

In Boston, where he'd worked for more than twenty years, you expected bodies to turn up unexpectedly dead, and more often than not you wound up never finding out exactly what had happened, or why.

But Miranda Sikes had lived in the marsh all her life and knew every inch of it as well as Templeton knew the inside of his snack drawer. Could she really have simply wandered off one of the paths in the middle of the night and gotten caught in quicksand? Of course, it was possible that she had committed suicide. But suicide didn't really make much sense either; if she were going to kill herself, surely she would have found a less macabre way to go than to hurl herself into quicksand.

And there was also the question of Cassie Winslow.

It wasn't simply the fact that Cassie had not only been in the marsh when Miranda had died, and even been able to lead him to her body. That could have been coincidence, and it was, in truth, the hawk that had led both of them to the body.

But there were also the words she had spoken to her father on Saturday afternoon.

"She's going to die. . . ." Had Cassie had some uncanny premonition? Had she somehow known what was going to happen? Or had she been somehow involved? Templeton leaned forward in the chair and heard the springs screech in protest at the sudden shift of his weight. The words, written in his own hand, seemed to leap off the page at him. But what, exactly, did they mean?

If Cassie had known Miranda was going to kill herself why hadn't she told anyone? You didn't listen to someone announce she was going to commit suicide, and then just not tell anyone, did you?

On the other hand, he remembered watching her at the moment they had discovered Miranda's corpse. The expression on her face had been one of pure horror. Nothing about her had suggested that she knew what they were going to find, nor did anything she said. "She needed me, and I had to come." Those had been her words, and Templeton was certain that she had hoped to find the old woman alive.

He sighed heavily. He had to make up his mind what to do. Should he talk to Cassie again? But what good would it do? What could she tell him that she hadn't told him already?

He also had to consider the harm it might do. Nothing had been easy for Cassie since the day she'd arrived in False Harbor, and it wasn't about to get any easier. And if he kept after her, the rumors that had already begun—the rumors that she must have had something to do with Miranda's death—were only going to spread.

Spread, and grow.

And in the end what would be accomplished? Nothing. For in the end there was no evidence. No weapon had been involved, and no injuries had been apparent on Miranda's body. Nor was there a motive.

In his gut Templeton didn't truly believe that Cassie Winslow had killed Miranda.

He made up his mind, and filled in the one remaining blank on the report of Miranda Sikes's death. *Cause of Death: Accidental Drowning*.

Then he closed the file on Miranda Sikes.

*   *   *

Cassie knew she had to be alone for a while, had to deal with everything that had happened. As soon as she'd changed her clothes, she slipped out of the house and started toward the marsh. But when she got to the park, she found herself unable to cross it and move into the marsh itself.

The memory of Saturday night was still too raw, too painful.

Instead she turned toward the beach, walking slowly, reliving the night Miranda had died.

She came to the beach finally and walked out into the dunes, settling in a patch of grass from which she could see both the ocean and the marsh.

She sat gazing out at the cabin, thinking again about the vision she'd had Saturday night, the vision that at first she'd thought was a dream.

She had said nothing to the police chief about the vision—had said nothing to anyone. Who would believe her?

No one.

But ever since, she'd been going over the vision again and again, trying to see clearly the figure that had been looming over Miranda while she died.

It had done no good. Even in the vision it had been too dark and she'd been too far away.

Since that night a knot of grief had held her in its grip, and the cold shroud of loneliness that had wrapped her in its folds so long ago closed even tighter around her.

Sometimes—times like now, when she sat alone in the dunes, staring out at the sea—she wished that it was she herself who had died in the marsh.

And yet there were the words Miranda had spoken to her in those hours they had spent together. They were, indeed, the last words Miranda had spoken.

"It's all right. I will die soon, but I will never leave you. Remember the things I've taught you, and I will live on within you. I will live on, and you will never be alone again."

But what did the words mean?

Cassie didn't know, but as she sat watching the heaving sea, a certain knowledge began to grow within her that soon she would find out.

Even from the grave Miranda would find a way to tell her.

* * *

Eric Cavanaugh had avoided the village square after school that day, knowing that his friends had made plans to go down and watch the burial of Miranda Sikes from outside the cemetery fence.

What they really planned to do, he knew, was watch Cassie Winslow.

He'd been listening to them talking about her all that day and the day before, speculating on whether or not she would come back to school on Wednesday.

Or, possibly, not at all.

"I hope she never comes back," Lisa Chambers had said angrily at lunch hour. Her injured arm, freed of the unnecessary sling she wore around her neck, was displayed on the table as if it were an indictment. "If you ask me, she's just as crazy as Miranda was, and even if she didn't kill her, she doesn't belong here. And if she comes back, I don't think any of us ought to speak to her at all!"

Eric had said nothing, and when Lisa—and most of his other friends as well—had trooped down to the square after school, he'd gone to the beach instead, and spent an hour walking slowly along the dunes, watching the birds and enjoying the feeling of the wind on his face.

And enjoying the solitude.

When he'd seen a figure in the distance, he almost turned away and started walking west again. But then he'd realized it was Cassie Winslow and quickened his step. She was sitting on the grass in the dunes, looking out over the marsh. As he approached, she'd looked up at him, her eyes large and rimmed red with tears.

"Hi," he said, shifting his weight from one foot to the other, uncertain about what to say. Finally, deciding it didn't really matter, he dropped down onto the sand beside her. "Is it all over with?"

Cassie nodded, and bit her lip. "Some of the kids were in the square while they were burying her," she said softly, her eyes still fixed on the marsh.

"I know," Eric replied. "They wanted me to go with them, but I wouldn't."

Cassie turned to see him then. "Why not?" she asked, her voice bitter. "You could have laughed at me too."

Eric flinched, and the pain she saw in his eyes made her wish she could take back the words. "I'm sorry," she whispered. "I just . . . well, I wish you'd come to the funeral."

"I—I couldn't," Eric stammered. "I had to go to school." He looked away quickly, afraid his face would betray his thoughts. Cassie only nodded silently, then, after what seemed an eternity to Eric, spoke again. "Nobody else came either."

Eric's eyes widened. "Nobody?" he echoed.

"My dad, and Rosemary, and Jennifer. But they had to go, I guess. And then afterward, in the cemetery, everyone was staring at me from across the street." Her voice broke, and Eric saw a tear welling up in her eye. She blinked it back, then looked at him shyly. "Are you going to start staring at me too?" she asked, her voice barely audible. "Is that why you came out here?"

Eric frowned. "Why would I do that?"

"Because that's what everyone else is doing. They all think I'm crazy, don't they?" She saw Eric start to shake his head then think better of it. "Well, I'm not," she went on, her voice rising slightly, "and Miranda wasn't either! And I didn't do anything to her. I don't care what anybody thinks, I didn't do anything to her!"

"Hey," Eric protested. "How come you're mad at me? I didn't say anything, and if I was going to start staring at you, I would have been with everybody else, wouldn't I?"

Cassie hesitated, her eyes flickering with uncertainty. "Does that mean you're going to be my friend?" she asked, and once more her voice had turned shy.

Eric looked at her out of the corner of his eye. "I thought we were already friends," he said carefully. "If I wasn't your friend, I wouldn't be here right now, would I?"

Now Cassie turned to face him squarely, and as their eyes met, he had a peculiar feeling that she was looking beyond his eyes—was looking straight into the depths of his soul. It was a strange sensation, almost frightening, and for a moment he wanted to look away again. But then she nodded, and smiled at him.

"You *are* my friend," she said quietly, and stood up. "Would you like to see my house?"

Eric frowned. "Your house?"

Cassie nodded, and pointed out into the marsh.

"Miranda's house," she said softly. "It's mine now."

Hers? Eric thought. What was she talking about? Miranda wouldn't have given her the cabin. She *couldn't* have.

"I think that . . ." Cassie went on uncertainly, "Well, I just have a feeling she wants me to have it. So I've decided it's mine." She smiled crookedly. "You won't tell anyone, will you? I mean—well, I guess it sounds sort of crazy, doesn't it?"

Eric hesitated only a moment. "I don't think so," he said. "If that's the way you feel, that's the way you feel." Pausing, he added, "I guess she wasn't going to give it to anyone else." His eyes went to the cabin, and he saw the white hawk on the rooftop suddenly lift up and spread its wings. A shrill whistling sound drifted across the wetlands.

"It's all right," Cassie said, certain she knew what he was thinking. "He won't hurt you. He won't hurt anyone who's my friend."

Eric shook his head. "I can't stay," he told her. "My dad—I promised my dad I'd be home early."

Cassie smiled sadly. "All right," she said. "Tomorrow. I'll show it to you tomorrow."

As Eric hurried away, she started walking slowly out into the marsh. The white hawk rose up off the rooftop, his wings beating rapidly as he flew toward her.

Chapter 12

Eric sat silently at the breakfast table the next morning, his eyes carefully avoiding his father's, for he had known the moment he came into the kitchen that his father's anger was still seething just below the surface. Finally, though, Ed spoke to him.

"You not going to say good morning to your old man?" he asked, his voice rising and falling in the sarcastic singsong that was always a sure signal he was looking for a fight.

"Morning, Dad," Eric mumbled, glancing up to see his father's eyes—little more than narrow red-rimmed slits this morning—fixed balefully on him.

"I been thinking," Ed went on. "And I decided something. I don't want you hanging around with Cassie Winslow. You only got enough time for Lisa Chambers."

"What's wrong with Cassie?" Eric protested. "And I'm not hanging around with her. All I did was—"

"Don't you argue with me!" Ed commanded, rising slightly out of his chair. "You were messin' around with her again yesterday afternoon!"

Now Eric felt his own anger beginning to rise inside him. "We didn't do anything," he replied. "All we were doing was talking. What's the big deal?"

"Don't you sass me, boy," Ed snarled. He was on his feet now, looming over Eric, his right hand reflexively clenching into a fist.

"No!" Laura Cavanaugh suddenly exclaimed. Though her

eyes were wide and frightened, the strength in her voice deflected Ed's wrath from his son to his wife. He swung around to face her.

"What did you say?" he rasped, his voice dangerously low.

"Don't hit him," Laura pleaded. "Do you want him to have to go to school with a black eye? What will people say?"

"They wouldn't say a damned thing," Ed growled. "What's the big deal if a kid takes a swat from his old man now and then? I got my share from my pa, and I didn't turn out so bad, did I?" He glared at his wife and son, as if daring them to challenge him. Then he was gone, slamming out the back door. A moment later they heard a grinding sound as the engine of the old pickup reluctantly turned over, then caught and roared into life. The screeching of spinning tires followed, the truck shooting backward down the driveway and out into the street.

A strained silence hung over the kitchen. Laura gazed at Eric beseechingly but saw that his eyes had gone dark and his jaw had tightened in unconscious imitation of his father.

Laura, her voice little more than a sob, finally spoke. "Why?" she breathed. "Why does he hate us so much?"

"I wish he wouldn't come back. I wish he'd just go away and disappear."

"I know," Laura said tiredly, getting to her feet to begin clearing the breakfast dishes away. "Sometimes I wish the same thing. But it won't happen." She smiled with wan encouragement. "But in another year you'll be away at college."

"Yeah," Eric agreed, making no attempt to keep the bitterness out of his voice. "That'll be really great, won't it? I'll be gone, and you'll be stuck here with him all by yourself. How come you don't just kick him out, Mom?"

"I can't," Laura said. "What would I do? How would you and I live?"

As she spoke Eric's pity for his mother's defenselessness turned to rage.

"How do we live now, Ma?" he demanded. "We're scared witless all the time, and half the time he beats us up. And all we ever do is pretend nothing's happening! You call that living? I sure as hell don't!" Before Laura could reply, he grabbed his book bag and stormed out the back door.

Just like his father, Laura found herself thinking. He walked out the same way his father does. She started washing the dishes, but her mind kept drifting away from her work as she saw over and over again the image of her son—as filled with rage as his father—stamping out of the house. What if it was too late? she wondered. What if she'd stayed with Ed Cavanaugh too long, and the fury and hatred that had already consumed Ed was working now in Eric as well?

Cassie caught up with Eric just as he was leaving the Common to start down Wharf Street. "How come you didn't stop this morning?" she asked shyly, falling into step beside him.

Eric said nothing for a moment, then managed to give her a weak smile. "It wasn't you," he explained. "It was my dad. He says he doesn't want me to spend any time with you anymore."

Cassie said nothing as she continued to walk silently beside him. By the time they'd turned the corner on Hartford Street, with Memorial High four more blocks away, she could contain herself no longer. "He thinks I'm crazy, doesn't he?"

Eric hesitated, then nodded once. "I guess."

"They're all going to act like that, aren't they?" Cassie went on. "It's not just going to be your father. It's going to be your friends too."

"So what?" Eric asked carefully.

"So I was just wondering what's going to happen, that's all," Cassie replied. "I mean, what are you going to do if everyone starts treating you the way they've been treating me? Are you still going to be my friend?"

Eric nodded, his jaw setting stubbornly. "It doesn't matter what my friends think, and I don't give a damn what my dad says either," he insisted.

A hopeful smile touched Cassie's lips, but her eyes seemed to plead with him. "Then meet me after school this afternoon," she said. "I—I really want to show you my house. I mean Miranda's house," she corrected herself quickly.

Eric hesitated, then shook his head. "I—I don't think I better," he said, and the pleading in Cassie's eyes dissolved into unconcealed pain. "I mean, I have baseball practice today. I skipped it yesterday, and if I do it again, Simms'll kill me."

"I'll wait for you," Cassie decided. "In fact I'll come out and watch you practice. I've never done anything like that before."

Eric cocked his head quizzically, relieved that the subject of the conversation had shifted. "How come? Lots of the guys' girlfriends come out and watch them practice. Didn't they do that in California?"

He hadn't told her not to come, Cassie thought. Maybe he really was still going to be her friend. "That's what I'm talking about," she said. "It was always the airheads that went out to watch the boys. And none of my friends had boyfriends. I mean, we all had friends that were boys, but they weren't boyfriends." Suddenly her eyes turned wary again. "If I come out and watch you, is everyone going to think I'm your girlfriend? What's Lisa going to think?"

Eric grinned. "Do you care?"

Cassie hesitated. "I just . . . well, I just don't want her to think I'm after you, that's all."

Eric's grin widened. "Don't worry about Lisa," he said, with more confidence than he felt.

They started up the steps of the school, and for the first time since Miranda had died, Cassie was genuinely smiling. But suddenly Lisa Chambers detached herself from a group of her friends, her eyes flashing with anger when she saw Cassie with Eric.

"What's so funny?" she demanded of Cassie, slipping her arm possessively through Eric's. Cassie's smile faded away, and she hurried up the steps and disappeared into the building.

"We were just talking, that's all," Eric explained. He faltered, seeing the jealousy in Lisa's eyes. "It didn't mean anything. I mean—"

"I know what you meant, Eric," Lisa said, dropping his arm as her voice turned chillingly cold. Silence fell over the group on the steps as they all listened. "And if you want to spend your time with someone like her, I'm sure I don't care." She turned back to the group she'd left seconds before, leaving Eric standing helplessly alone as all the rest of the kids stared at him.

This is how Cassie felt last week, Eric thought. *Just like some kind of freak.*

When the last bell of the day finally rang, Cassie still hadn't made up her mind what she was going to do. Today had been even worse than last week. She'd made it through the morning only by telling herself repeatedly that she'd see Eric at noon and at least she wouldn't have to eat at a table by herself, with everyone staring at her. But when she got to the cafeteria, Eric was nowhere to be seen. She'd waited at the door for ten minutes, hoping he'd show up, but when they finally began closing down the steam table, she took a tray, chose some food without really looking at it, and started toward the same table she'd occupied the week before.

As she moved through the cafeteria she felt the rest of the students staring at her, and heard them whispering to each other after she passed their tables. Though she couldn't hear all that they said, she heard enough.

"Everybody *knows* she did something," Lisa Chambers said as Cassie passed the table where Lisa sat with Allayne Garvey and Teri Bennett. Lisa hadn't even bothered to lower her voice. "I mean, my mother actually *saw* Mr. Templeton's car in front of their house yesterday!"

"But what's going to happen?" Teri demanded. "If she killed Miranda, why don't they arrest her?"

"Maybe she didn't do anything at all," Allayne Garvey suggested, but by the time she spoke, Cassie was out of earshot. "Maybe you're just mad, Lisa, because Eric came to school with her again."

"I don't care about Eric," Lisa insisted. She raised her voice to make sure it would carry across the room to the table where Cassie sat by herself. "If he wants to spend all his time with someone who's crazy, why should I care? But he better watch out—she might do the same thing to him that she did to Miranda Sikes!"

A wave of rage washed over Cassie and she wanted to scream at Lisa. But she didn't. Instead she made herself remember the words Miranda had spoken to her the day she'd died.

'It doesn't matter what they say about me, and it doesn't matter what they say about you. Some people are set apart from everyone else, Cassie. But whatever they say about you, they can never truly hurt you.' She'd smiled then, a small, cryptic smile that Cassie hadn't understood. 'I made certain of that. So don't worry about what they say. Just don't let them hurt you. Be true to yourself, and always remember that you must never let them hurt you.'

So instead of saying anything, Cassie simply sat alone at her table, concentrating on forcing the tasteless food into her mouth and trying not to gag as she swallowed it. The lunch hour seemed endless, and when the bell finally rang, she began the afternoon ordeal, moving somnolently from class to class, the stares and whispers of her classmates stinging her soul.

At last it was three o'clock, and she had to make up her mind.

Should she go out to the baseball diamond to wait for Eric, or should she just leave and spend the afternoon by herself? She thought about the beach and the little house in the marsh, and the prospect of being alone with nothing but the seabirds and the crashing of the surf for company. At least out there no one could stare at her, and if people were whispering, she couldn't hear them.

Then she remembered Eric, and his absence from the cafeteria at lunchtime. Making up her mind, she shoved her books into her bag and left the building by the back door. A small set of bleachers stood behind the backstop. Already a group of girls was clustered at the far end of the lowest three tiers. They turned away from Cassie as she approached, and began giggling among themselves. Every few seconds, one of them would surreptitiously glance at Cassie. Head held high, Cassie pretended she didn't notice.

There was no one on the baseball diamond yet, so Cassie fished her math book out of the bag and began working on the homework assignments from the last two days, which Mr. Simms had insisted be completed even though Cassie had missed the classes. "After all," he'd pointed out in front of the whole class, his voice edged with sarcasm, "it isn't as if you were sick, is it? No one else went to Miranda Sikes's funeral, did they? It's beginning to look as if you don't think school is worth bothering with."

Cassie's face had burned as a ripple of snickering had passed over the class. "But she was my friend," she'd breathed.

Simms's thin lips had only curled into a scornful sneer. "Even if that were true, Cassie, you hardly knew her. And if you had, you'd know she was nothing more than a mental case who should never have been let out of the hospital. In my opinion you simply used Miranda Sikes's unfortunate demise as another opportunity to cut classes. Your parents may approve, but I don't. Please have the assignments completed by tomorrow."

Cassie had forced herself to stifle an urge to run from the room. It didn't matter, she told herself once again. He can't hurt you. None of them can. So instead of running away, she'd controlled her tears, and her anger, and her pain. And now, as she looked at the assignment, she was glad she had. The problems in algebra were so simple she could work most of them in her head. Shutting everything else out of her mind, she quickly began writing down the equations and their solutions.

Twenty minutes later, just as she finished the last problem, the baseball team trotted onto the field to warm up. Eric hesitated for a split second, and Cassie felt a quick pang of fear that he was going to ignore her, but then he waved before he and Jeff Maynard began tossing a ball back and forth along the first-base line. At last the coach came out of the gym, but it wasn't until he'd actually arrived at the diamond that Cassie recognized him.

It was Mr. Simms.

His mouth was twisted into the same ugly smile he'd worn while humiliating Cassie earlier that day, and she knew instantly that something else was about to happen. But this time she couldn't be the target—he hadn't even seen her.

He blew his whistle, and the team immediately gathered around him. He said nothing for a few seconds, and the boys fell silent, squirming uncomfortably as they cast sidelong glances toward Eric. In the bleachers Cassie suddenly understood who Simms's new victim was.

"Decide to join us today, Cavanaugh?" Simms finally asked, his small, close-set eyes fixing on Eric.

Eric nodded. "I—I'm sorry about yesterday," he said. "I shouldn't have skipped practice, and I won't do it again."

"What you do or don't do isn't really of interest to me, Cavanaugh." Simms's eyes glittered with pleasure at Eric's discomfort. "If you can do without us, we can certainly do without you. As of now you're off the team. Smythe, you'll be taking over as pitcher."

Eric's eyes widened as the coach's words sunk in. "Off the team?" he repeated. "But—but you can't do that."

"Can't I?" Simms replied with an exaggerated drawl. "And what makes you say that?"

"It's not fair," Eric pleaded. "I'm the best pitcher in the school, and I have to play baseball."

"Really?" the coach pressed, now openly relishing Eric's misery. "And why is that?"

Eric's voice fell to a whisper. "If I'm going to college, I have to have a scholarship," he managed. "And if I can get one in baseball, I can go to—"

"Too bad you didn't think of that yesterday," the coach interrupted. "But it's too late now, isn't it?" He turned his back on Eric and faced the rest of the team. "All right, let's get it going, guys," he called. "Let's have a lot of chatter out there, okay?"

The boys glanced at each other, uncertain what to do. Kevin Smythe, his eyes smoldering angrily, was about to say something, when Cassie, whose own fury had been growing as she'd listened to Simms talk to Eric, scrambled off the bleachers and hurried out onto the field.

"Mr. Simms?" she called.

The coach swung around and looked at her. "Well, look who's here," he said, glancing at the boys then facing Cassie again. "I would have thought you'd be long gone." Two of the boys snickered quietly but fell silent when the others didn't join in. "What is it?" Simms asked. "If it's a question about your assignments, save it for class."

"It isn't," Cassie said. "I just wanted to turn the work in now."

Simms hesitated, and his sarcastic smile gave way to an uncertain frown. "You're done?"

Cassie shrugged. "I'm going to talk to Mrs. Ambler about changing classes," she said, her voice perfectly level.

Simms's smile returned. "If the work's too hard—"

"It's not," Cassie replied. "It's too easy. But I guess if the school needs a baseball coach that badly, they have to give you something else to do, don't they?" She let her voice drift off, and shrugged again. Then, as the baseball team stared at her in stunned silence, she turned and walked away from the baseball diamond. She could feel Simms's fury bore into her as she left, and knew she'd gone too far. What if there was no other class for her to transfer into? What if she had to stay in Simms's class for the rest of the year? It didn't matter, she decided: what he'd done to Eric wasn't fair, and she'd had to do something. She'd *had* to.

She was three blocks from the school when Eric, panting, caught up with her. "I thought you were going to wait for me."

"I—I wasn't sure you'd want me to," Cassie stammered. "I mean, after what happened."

Eric rolled his eyes. "What happened is nothing next to what's going to happen. You should have seen Simms after you left. All the guys started laughing at him, and I thought he was going to go crazy. Now he's going to be out to get you."

Cassie nodded. "I know. But I was so mad, I didn't even think about it." She hesitated, then met Eric's eyes. "Is it true? That you have to get a baseball scholarship if you want to go to college?"

Eric nodded, his jaw setting angrily, and he fell into step beside Cassie. "I don't see how I can make it any other way. God knows, my dad doesn't make enough money to help me out. And he probably wouldn't, even if he could." He shook his head bitterly. "Now I'm going to have to talk to Mrs. Ambler tomorrow and try to get her to fix it with Simms. He thinks he's a big deal, but he's scared to death of her. At least she still likes me." He shifted his book bag to his other hand and glanced at Cassie. "So what are you going to do? He's the only math teacher, and you've gotta take math."

Cassie shook her head. "What *can* I do? I'll just make sure I do all the work and pass all the tests. And next year I'll get someone else."

Eric shook his head. "I told you, there isn't anyone else. Simms has senior math, too. The only way you're going to get away from him is if he quits, and he'll never do that." He grinned. "Unless we could figure out some way to make him quit."

Cassie stopped walking and turned to face Eric. "You're kidding, aren't you?"

Eric's jaw clenched. "Maybe I am. I mean, he didn't have to kick me off the team just because I skipped practice, did he? It isn't fair. Besides, there isn't any harm in thinking about it, is there? I mean, as long as we don't actually do anything to him."

Cassie thought about it for a few seconds, and once more Miranda's words echoed in her mind.

"Don't let them hurt you. Never let them hurt you."

But what if they *did* hurt you?

"Why not?" she thought out loud. "You can't hurt someone just by thinking about it, can you?"

Eric glanced at her out of the corner of his eye, but said nothing.

They were still a hundred yards from the house in the marsh when the pale form of the white hawk rose up into the afternoon sky, screeching loudly. Eric froze, his eyes tracking the bird until it suddenly disappeared into the sun and the brilliant glare made him turn away.

"It's all right," Cassie told him. "His name's Kiska and he's my friend. As long as you're with me, he won't do anything at all." She started forward, but Eric didn't move. He was staring up into the sky once more, watching the hawk circling above them. "Watch," Cassie said quietly.

She gazed up into the sky and her eyes locked onto the soaring bird. Then, slowly, she raised her right arm, with her index finger pointed directly at the cabin.

As if she'd issued a command, the bird instantly banked and began beating its wings against the breeze. A moment later it settled onto the peak of the house and began preening its feathers.

Eric's heart pounded. He turned to face Cassie. "How did you do that?" he asked. "Did—did Miranda teach you that?"

Cassie smiled at him, nodding happily. "I told you he's my friend. He was Miranda's friend, but now he's mine." Her smile widened into a grin. "He'll do anything I want him to."

Eric looked at her sharply. "What do you mean?"

But instead of answering him, Cassie merely smiled.

With Eric following behind her and keeping a watchful eye on the restless hawk on the roof, she led him toward the little cabin on the hill.

On the porch, his tail curled around his feet, they found Sumi waiting. He jumped into Cassie's arms, and she cuddled him for a moment. Then they stepped through the cabin's door.

Though on the outside the cabin seemed dilapidated and about to collapse, the walls inside were paneled with pine, all of it waxed to a soft golden sheen which appeared to glow from within. There was a large walnut armoire against one wall, and against another, tucked into one of the corners, was a small bed. A table sat in the very center of the cabin's single room, and the back wall was half occupied by a stone fireplace, to which a cast-iron wood-burning cooking stove had been added at some time in the distant past. Along the other half of the wall was a wooden counter with a sink mounted in it, and above the counter, on either side of the window, pine cabinets.

Aside from the two chairs at the center table, there was an old wooden rocker next to a small table by one of the front windows. There was no other furniture.

Though everything in the cabin was very old, and obviously made by hand, each object had been perfectly cared for. There was not even so much as a speck of dust in the room, nor was there any sign of the clutter with which everyone in False Harbor had always assumed Miranda surrounded herself.

Eric grinned to himself. It was nothing like anyone thought it was. And that, he decided, was the strangest thing about the cabin. You couldn't tell from the outside what was happening on the inside. In some ways, the cabin was just like himself.

He looked up.

The four triangular panels of the peaked ceiling were each painted a different color, and all of them were covered with strange designs that time had faded until they were nearly invisible.

"What is it?" he asked. "Did she ever tell you what they mean?"

"It's astrology," Cassie explained. "She told me this house

is special because it's in tune with everything around it." She hesitated a moment, but when Eric said nothing, she went on. "She told me it's a magical place."

Eric's eyes avoided hers, but when he spoke, she heard no trace of mockery in his voice. "Did you believe her?" he asked.

"I—I don't know," Cassie replied. "I'm not even sure what she meant. But I know she believed it."

"But didn't she tell you?" Eric asked, his tone more insistent now. "She must have said something else."

"She did," Cassie said, sinking down onto one of the chairs at the table. Eric was looking at her, and she searched his eyes but was sure she saw nothing in them except curiosity. He wasn't looking at her the way the rest of the kids had.

She decided she could trust him.

"She said I was special," she told him. "She said she was giving me a gift and that I could . . . well, that I could do things. And she said I shouldn't let people hurt me."

Eric's heart beat faster. "You mean, like Mr. Simms hurt us," he said.

Cassie thought a moment. "I—I guess so," she said finally.

Eric dropped onto the chair opposite her and picked up Sumi, who was anxiously pacing the floor beneath the table. "But what can you do?" he asked.

"I don't know," Cassie breathed. "But I'm going to try to find out." She closed her eyes and her lips began to move, though no sound emerged from her throat.

Eric watched her as the seconds slowly stretched into minutes. Silently, fixing his gaze on her in fascination, he watched until he saw Sumi slide out from under his caressing fingers and off his lap.

A moment later the cat slipped out the door.

Harold Simms lounged against the wall of the locker room until the last of the boys had dressed and left, then went into the little office he shared with the other coaches and closed the door.

Still seething with anger at what Cassie Winslow had said to him earlier that afternoon, he finally picked up the sheaf of paper on which she'd neatly laid out the two days of homework that should have taken her at least two hours to complete.

All of it was done perfectly.

Obviously, he decided, she must have cheated. Even if she'd spent the hour of her study hall working on it, she shouldn't have been able to finish the assignments so quickly. He concluded that she'd just done today's assignment, and Eric Cavanaugh had given her the answers to yesterday's. Smiling to himself, he marked both papers with an F, and added an admonition that cheating would not be tolerated in his class. And just let her try to argue, he thought to himself. She's in big enough trouble already, and if she starts backtalking, I'll have her suspended. In fact he hoped she *would* talk back to him, and give him an acceptable excuse to punish her for the humiliation she'd caused him. He could still hear the laughter from the baseball team, still see them looking at him with mocking eyes.

It wasn't that they cared about Cassie Winslow—they were just mad at him for what he'd done to Eric Cavanaugh. But he'd been right in throwing Eric off the team—the kid had always been everybody's favorite, and he'd been waiting a long time to knock him off his pedestal. Simms's only regret was that he wouldn't be there to see what happened to Eric when Ed Cavanaugh found out his son had been dropped from the baseball team. Eric would be lucky to come out of that one with all his teeth intact.

Simms snapped out of his reverie. He had an uncanny feeling that he was no longer alone in the building. He glanced around, half expecting to see someone else at the other desk, but there was no one. Frowning, he left his chair and went to the door. Opening it, he gazed out into the empty locker room and the showers at the far end.

"Hello?" he called. "Anybody in here?"

His voice echoed hollowly off the concrete walls of the gym. Frowning, he reclosed the door and returned to the desk, intending to pack his briefcase before leaving for the day.

His back was still to the door when he heard it slowly creak open.

He froze, his heart pounding, then turned.

Crouched in the doorway, its tail twitching spasmodically, was a gray cat.

Simms frowned. He hated cats—had hated them as long as he could remember. Tentatively he took a step forward.

But instead of backing away, the cat rose to its feet, its back arching as its fur stood up. It bared its teeth, and a hiss emerged from its throat.

"What the hell?" Simms muttered. He took another step forward, and drew his right foot back to kick the cat. But before he could swing his leg forward, the cat leaped at him, all four of its legs outstretched, its claws extended.

Simms screamed as the animal hit his chest and its claws slashed through his T-shirt and into his skin. He lurched backward, grabbing at the cat, but it seemed to slip through his grip. A moment later he felt a burning pain as its claws slashed across his face. He raised his right arm to try to knock the animal away, but before the blow struck, he lost his balance, falling backward over his desk and rolling off onto the floor on the other side.

Sprawled on his back, he looked up to see the cat poised over him, hissing furiously. Before it could launch its next attack, Simms struggled to his feet and hurled himself away, crashing into the bare concrete wall of the office. Swearing, he turned to see the cat leaping toward him.

The door.

He had to get to the door, had to get out.

He whirled, but the door slammed shut as the cat struck his back. Simms screamed with pain as he smashed into the door then sank to his knees. He felt the cat's teeth sink into the flesh on the back of his neck, felt blood begin to ooze out of the open wound.

Terrified now, he threw himself to the floor and rolled, trying to crush the animal beneath his own weight. But no matter where he turned, the cat seemed to be there, its fury growing constantly. Its claws slashed at his face, and its teeth tore pieces of flesh from his arms and torso.

His screams grew louder, and he staggered to his feet once more, but there was no escaping the torture. Everywhere he turned the beast was there first, and over and over he felt its claws and fangs slashing into his flesh. Finally, whimpering, he wedged himself into the kneehole under his desk and wrapped his arms around his bleeding head. And then, at last, the attack ended and a silence fell over the room.

It was broken by the sound of soft laughter, and as Harold Simms sank slowly into unconsciousness, he thought he recognized the laughing voice.

It sounded like Cassie Winslow's voice, mocking him.

Half an hour later the door opened once more, and Jake Palmer, who had been the janitor at False Harbor's high school for forty years, stepped inside. He set his mop and bucket down, then glanced around the room.

"Holy Jesus," he whispered softly to himself. "What the hell they been doing in here today?" Everywhere he looked, the walls were stained with red smears, and the floor looked as if a wild animal, mortally wounded, had spent its last moments thrashing around in a violent search for some unseen enemy. As Jake's mind tried to accept what his eyes were seeing, he heard a low moaning sound from a few feet away. Slowly, carefully, he made his way around to the other side of the room, then bent over to look under the desk.

Staring back at him, Jack saw the pale visage of Harold Simms, his skin torn away, his flesh oozing blood.

"It was her," he heard Simms moan. "It was that crazy girl. She . . . she tried to kill me." Then Simms's eyes closed as he slid into unconsciousness for a second time.

In the cabin Cassie's eyes blinked open and she saw Eric watching her intently. "What—what happened?" she asked.

Eric shook his head. "Nothing. You were just sitting there, and your lips were moving, and then—well, then you started laughing."

Cassie cocked her head thoughtfully. She'd been thinking about Mr. Simms, and then she had drifted off, as if in a dream. But what had happened in the dream?

She couldn't remember.

Frowning, she looked around.

Something was different. Then she realized what it was. The cat was gone.

Her eyes flicked back to Eric. "What happened to Sumi?" she asked.

Eric was silent for a moment, then shrugged. "Who

knows?" he said. "He was on my lap, and then he just sort of took off."

Then he grinned. "Maybe he went after Simms," he suggested. "Maybe you sicked him on him."

Chapter 13

Gene Templeton left Memorial High by the side door, fishing in his pocket for his car keys. Only the day after the funeral, and already it had started. Templeton was pretty sure he was on a wild-goose chase, for the story he'd heard at the school made no sense at all. But still, he had to check it out, he thought, as the squad car cruised slowly through the village toward the Winslows' house.

He got out of the car and approached the house, sighing as he pressed the doorbell. A moment later the door opened. Rosemary Winslow stared at him apprehensively.

"What is it?" she asked. "It's not something else about Miranda, is it? I thought we were all through with that."

Templeton held up his hands in a reassuring gesture. "Nothing to do with Miranda at all, Rosemary. It's . . . well, uh, it's something else. I wonder if I might come inside?"

Relief apparent in her eyes, Rosemary stepped back and held the door open. As Templeton stepped into the foyer, Jennifer Winslow came crashing down the stairs.

"Hi, Mr. Templeton!" she said, grinning up at him with her hand held out expectantly. Grinning back at her, Templeton fished in his jacket pocket and pulled out one of the jawbreakers he habitually carried there, insisting to anyone who asked that they were only for bribing children, that he never ate them himself. It was a lie, but everyone knew it, so it didn't matter.

"Hi, yourself," Templeton replied, holding the jawbreaker

just out of Jennifer's reach. "You being a good girl? Haven't tried to rob the bank this week?"

"No," Jennifer shrieked. "Can I have it? Please?"

Templeton glanced at Rosemary, who nodded, then gave the candy to Jennifer, who immediately stuffed it into her mouth, her right cheek bulging grotesquely. "Now run along," he said. "I have to talk to your mom about something."

"Can't I listen?" Jen begged, her words garbled by the mass in her mouth.

"No, you can't," Rosemary told her.

Faced with the unanimous decision of two adults, Jennifer retreated back up the stairs. When she was gone, Rosemary led Templeton toward the kitchen.

"I have a little pie, but I'm afraid that's all," she apologized. She poured them each a cup of coffee and pulled the last slice of last night's apple pie out of the refrigerator before sitting down to face Templeton, her eyes still worried. "Now, what's going on?"

Templeton's expression turned serious, and he shook his head. "I'm not really sure. But I'm hoping maybe I can nip this one in the bud real quick. Do you happen to know where Cassie's been this afternoon?"

The worry cleared from Rosemary's face. "That's easy," she said. "She's with Eric. They're right here, upstairs in Cassie's room."

Templeton's brows rose a fraction of an inch. "Cassie's room?" he repeated, and Rosemary chuckled.

"Times have changed, Gene. All the kids have their friends in their rooms now, boys and girls both. It's not like when you were young. Or me, either, for that matter."

"Thanks for that, at least," Templeton grumped. "So, how long have they been there?"

Rosemary shrugged. "All afternoon, as far as I know."

The relief Templeton had been momentarily feeling vanished. "As far as you know?"

"Well, I've only been home half an hour. I did a little shopping after I closed the store, but they were here when I got home. Now, would you mind telling me what this is all about?"

Sparing her as many of the details as he could, Templeton described the scene he'd found in the high school gym office an hour before. "And what's happened," he finished, "is that just before Simms passed out, he told Jake Palmer that 'the crazy girl did it.' "

Rosemary gasped, and her face paled. "He . . . what?"

"It's not quite as bad as it sounds," Templeton added. "And Jake said he didn't actually name Cassie. But, well . . ." He floundered for a moment, then fell into an embarrassed silence.

"There's only one girl in town that they're calling crazy," Rosemary finished for him, her voice cold. "Is that it, Gene?"

Templeton nodded. "Rosemary, I'm sorry. I know how all this sounds, but I still have to do my job. And anyway, it might not be so bad—he didn't actually name her, and nobody saw Cassie around the school at all. In fact a couple of the kids saw her leave, and saw Eric catching up with her. After that, no one saw either one of them at the school again. So if I can place Cassie somewhere else, we can put an end to this right now."

"Then let's do it," Rosemary said. "The last thing we need right now are more rumors flying around." She went out into the hall and called up the stairs. A minute later Eric and Cassie appeared at the kitchen door. Recognizing Templeton, both their expressions turned worried.

"What's wrong?" Cassie asked.

Rosemary started to speak, but Gene Templeton held up a hand to stop her. "You kids mind telling me where you've been all afternoon?" he asked.

Eric and Cassie glanced at each other, then Eric shrugged helplessly. "We've been here for about an hour, I guess," he said.

"An hour," Templeton repeated. Whatever had happened to Simms, it had happened more than an hour ago. "What about before that?" Eric's eyes suddenly took on a wary cast, and he said nothing. Instead he glanced at Cassie, and Templeton's stomach knotted as he realized that maybe, after all, there was some truth to Simms's disjointed words. When Cassie finally spoke, the nervousness in her voice only tightened the knot.

"We—we were out in the marsh," she said. "I was showing Eric Miranda's house."

Templeton glanced at Rosemary, who seemed to be as

surprised at the words as he was. "All right," he said carefully. "Do you mind telling me why you went out there?"

Cassie's eyes darkened. "I already told you," she said. "I was showing Miranda's house to Eric. Why shouldn't I? Miranda was my friend. I can go there if I want to."

"Whoa," Templeton protested, holding up his hands in an exaggerated gesture of defense. "Slow down. I didn't say you had no right to go there. I just wondered if there was any special reason why you went."

Cassie was silent for a moment, then nodded. "We were mad," she said. "Mr. Simms kicked Eric off the baseball team this afternoon."

Rosemary gasped, but Templeton managed not to react to the words at all. Suddenly everything made even less sense than it had before, for Cassie had just blandly confessed to a motive. "Mind telling me about that?" he asked Eric, watching the boy carefully. But as Eric told him the story, Templeton could see nothing in his manner that seemed anything other than completely spontaneous.

"Simms is weird sometimes," Eric finished. "But I'll go talk to Mrs. Ambler tomorrow, and she'll straighten it out. But what's happening, anyway?"

His eyes still fixed on the two teenagers, Templeton told them what had happened at the school that afternoon. "Simms is in the hospital. And I'm here because he said something that might have meant he thought Cassie attacked him. From what I saw, it looked like whoever did it must have used a knife." He saw Cassie and Eric glance at each other, and there was something in that exchange of looks that bothered him. It was more than surprise—there was something else there, something he couldn't quite put his finger on. But what? "And you two say you were down in the marsh and then here all afternoon, right?"

Cassie nodded. "We were."

"By yourselves," Templeton pointed out.

Cassie hesitated, then shook her head. "Jennifer saw us in the marsh," she said. "Ask her."

Rosemary hesitated, then went to the bottom of the stairs and called Jennifer. A moment later the little girl came running down the stairs and followed her mother into the kitchen.

"But how do you know they were in Miranda's house all the time?" Gene Templeton asked five minutes later, after Jennifer had confirmed what Cassie and Eric had told him.

Jennifer blushed, and stared shamefaced at the floor. "I was watching," she finally admitted, her voice tiny. "All the time they were in there, I was playing on the swing in the park, and I kept watching to see if anything was going to happen. But nothing did. They just went in, and after a while they came out." Her eyes went fearfully to Cassie. "I'm sorry," she said. "But I wasn't really spying on you. I just wanted to see what you were doing."

"It's okay, Jen," Cassie told her, a little smile playing around her lips. "And it's okay for you to tell them what we were doing too."

Jennifer's eyes shifted to appeal to her mother. "They weren't doing anything," she said. "They just came over here and went up to Cassie's room and started listening to the radio."

The tension drained out of Rosemary, and she turned to the police chief. "Well, at least we know that whatever happened to Harold Simms, Cassie and Eric weren't involved."

Gene Templeton nodded absently, but his eyes were still watching Cassie and Eric. He was certain there was something they were holding back. "Miranda's house," he said finally. "What were you doing in there?"

Once again that strange look passed between the two teenagers, and for a moment Templeton thought Eric was going to speak. But before he could utter the first word, Cassie rushed in.

"We were talking about Mr. Simms," she said, her eyes meeting Templeton's. And though her eyes were clear—as if she had nothing to hide—there was a challenge in them. "We were talking about what a creep he is, and wishing something would happen to him. That's weird, isn't it? I mean, that while we were wishing it, something really did happen to him?"

"Cassie!" Rosemary exclaimed.

"Well, why should I lie about it?" Cassie asked. "It's not like we did anything to him. And I'm not sorry about what happened to Mr. Simms either. He was awful to me, and what he did to Eric wasn't fair at all. If someone beat him up, I'm not going to claim I'm sorry!"

Before anyone could say anything else, she turned and fled from the kitchen. Rosemary glanced at Templeton and started to go after her, when the policeman shook his head. "Let her go," he said gently. "She must be sick of me asking her questions all the time, and I think it's pretty obvious she didn't have anything to do with Simms." He unfolded himself from the chair and closed his notebook. "You have anything else to say, Eric?" he asked.

Eric shook his head.

"Okay." He let himself out the back door and was just about to start down the driveway when a sudden movement caught his eye. Turning, he saw a gray cat slip through the fence between the Winslows' yard and the cemetery next to the church. It dashed across the lawn and slithered up into a large oak tree. When it reached the lowest branch, it paused, then turned to glare balefully at Templeton. Its mouth yawned open and a menacing hiss boiled out of its throat. Then, in a flash, it leaped up through the branches of the tree and disappeared through an open window on the second floor.

"Sumi?" he heard Cassie's voice asking anxiously. "Did you really do it? Did you do what I wanted you to?"

His brow creased in thought, Templeton continued down the driveway.

"Upstairs," Ed Cavanaugh growled. He'd watched Eric come out of the Winslows' house a few minutes after the police chief had left, and by the time the boy had crossed the common driveway and come through the back door, Ed had worked himself into a fury. It hadn't taken him long to get the whole story out of his son. As he listened, his rage had grown. Now his eyes fixed malevolently on Eric. "Move!" he snapped when Eric failed to react to his command.

"Ed, don't," Laura protested. Ed said nothing, but his hand flashed out, striking Laura's face with enough force to knock her back into her chair. "*Now!*" he bellowed, then reached out and grabbed Eric by his shirt collar, dragging him out of the kitchen. As Laura sat trembling in the chair, she heard her husband manhandling their son up the stairs.

Why? she thought bitterly. *Why did he ever think he wanted a son in the first place?*

Eric started to go into his own room, but Ed grabbed his wrist, twisted his arm up behind his back, and shoved him into the little room that would have been a guest room had anyone ever come to visit the Cavanaughs.

Eric's heart sank, for when his father took him in here, it meant things were really going to be bad. "Strip!" his father commanded, already pulling his belt out of the loops in his pants.

Eric's eyes widened. "No," he whimpered. "Come on, Dad—I didn't do anything—"

"You disobeyed me, and you got yourself kicked off the team," Ed rasped. "I don't call that nothing." He reached out with his free hand, grasped Eric's shirt, and ripped it off. Eric cringed, but knowing there was no escape, quickly removed his pants and underwear, then stretched out on the bed.

The belt whistled in the air before it lashed across Eric's naked buttocks, but Eric knew better than to scream out with pain. When his father was like this, the sounds of his agony only seemed to make it worse. He clenched his teeth, his hands gripping the posts at the head of the bed.

Again the leather strap whistled in the air and struck.

With each lash, Eric's rage increased.

"Well, it fits with what I've found," Dr. Paul Samuels commented, after listening to everything Gene Templeton had to say. "As far as I can tell, he wasn't attacked by any kind of weapon at all."

Charlotte Ambler looked at the doctor in surprise. She'd followed the ambulance over from the school, then waited impatiently while Simms was being examined, anxious to know exactly what had transpired in the gymnasium. "No weapon?" she repeated, her voice taking on the acerbic quality she usually reserved for her students, forgetting that it had been twelve years since Paul Samuels had been one of them. "For heaven's sake, Paul, I saw Harold myself!"

"And something happened to him," Samuels agreed. "But it doesn't look to me like he was attacked by anybody, at least not with a knife."

"You want to expand on that?" Gene asked, glancing at

the clock. It was now thirty minutes past dinner time. He sighed silently and turned his attention back to the doctor.

"A knife makes a clean cut," Samuels explained. "If you slash someone with a knife, you're going to stab them deep, or lay them open, but the edges of the cuts are going to be clean. And there won't be any pattern. But that's not the way it is with Harold Simms. It looks to me as though he was attacked by some kind of animal. At least at first."

The memory of the hissing animal in the tree outside Cassie's room came into Templeton's mind. "Could it have been a cat?" he asked.

Samuels thought a moment, then nodded. "Could be. I certainly wouldn't rule it out."

"But Harold was very certain that he heard someone laughing," Charlotte Ambler reminded them.

"Who simply doesn't seem to have been there," Templeton observed wearily. "I'm sorry, Charlotte, but whatever happened, I can't see how Cassie could have had anything to do with it. And Simms could have been wrong."

Charlotte turned impatiently to the doctor. "Is that true?"

Samuels shrugged noncommittally. "It's possible. It's even possible that he did most of the damage to himself."

"Did it to himself?" Charlotte repeated indignantly. "What on earth are you saying?"

"Just that," Samuels replied. "I think it's pretty clear what happened, particularly after what the chief's told us. Simms had just thrown Eric off the team, and then Cassie managed to humiliate him in front of the kids. And you yourself have already told me that Simms was—what? Highstrung? Weren't those the words you used?"

Charlotte's eyes narrowed. "He had some problems, yes—"

"Well, if you ask me, he just snapped," Samuels went on. "There's no way of saying exactly what happened, and some of the marks were certainly inflicted by some kind of animal. But I don't think there was anyone in that office with him. I think that something set him off and he just came apart in there. He literally started bouncing off the walls. I don't doubt that he thought he was being attacked by Cassie. In fact I wouldn't be surprised if he claimed he actually saw her. But I'd be just as willing to bet that it was an hallucination."

"But the wounds . . ." Charlotte pressed.

"Except for the deepest scratches and bite marks, the wounds are all consistent with someone striking hard against concrete block walls. The bruises, the abrasions, everything. There isn't much that couldn't have been self-inflicted."

Templeton regarded the doctor thoughtfully, his fingers absently rubbing at the stubble on his chin. "What you're saying is that he just went nuts?"

Samuels's brows arched. " 'Just went nuts' isn't precisely the terminology I would use, no. I'd be more inclined to label it a psychotic episode."

"Is there a difference?" Templeton drawled, and Samuels, despite the circumstances, couldn't quite suppress a chuckle.

"In some cases, not really," he admitted. "But with Simms, it's too early to tell. 'Just went nuts,' as you put it, always seems to me to imply a permanent condition. A psychotic episode can be quite a temporary thing."

"How temporary?" Templeton asked.

"A few minutes. An hour. A day. Who knows?" Now he turned once more to Charlotte Ambler. "What can you tell me about Simms's condition the last few days?"

Charlotte hesitated, then sighed. "Well, actually, I've been worried about Harold. He's seemed to be wound up about a lot of things lately, and I know he's been taking it out on some of his classes. It hasn't been too serious, and so far no one has complained. But it *has* been there. I'd hoped he'd make it through the year and then get a good rest. But I've also had some reservations about renewing his contract. Frankly, I'm not sure he's cut out to teach. He . . . well, I've always had the feeling that deep down, he just doesn't like the students."

"And if he came apart, he'd be likely to blame it on one of the kids?" Samuels suggested.

Charlotte's lips tightened. "I'm afraid I find that a little hard to believe." She paused and met the doctor's eyes. "May I talk to him again? Is he conscious?"

Samuels nodded. All three of them stood up and left the doctor's office, walking down the hall to the last of the six rooms which were all the False Harbor hospital required. Inside the room, strapped to a bed, they found Harold Simms.

Charlotte moved to the bedside and looked down at the math teacher's face. The blood had been washed away, and now she could see that the lacerations were not as serious as they'd first appeared. His cheeks were scratched, and on Simms's forehead a large round black and blue spot marked the point at which something had struck his forehead.

But what? The wall? Or even, perhaps, the underside of the desk beneath which the teacher had been found?

Simms's eyes blinked open and for a moment he seemed to stare unseeingly at the ceiling. Then his gaze flickered around the room, finally focusing on Charlotte Ambler's face. Then he began struggling against the restraints that held his arms, legs, and torso immobile, meanwhile mumbling broken fragments of words. Templeton listened closely, but nothing the man said made any sense. It was nothing more than a disconnected stream of syllables.

Simms's voice rose to a scream and the words became garbled beyond recognition. He was thrashing on the bed now, straining against the heavy leather straps, his hands clenching into fists so tight that his knuckles turned white and the palms began to bleed where his fingernails pierced his own skin.

"Jesus Christ, Doc," Gene Templeton whispered. "Can't you do something?"

His words were unnecessary. Samuels had already picked up a syringe from a table that lay near the door, filled it, and was in the process of plunging it into Simms's arm. After a few seconds the drug began to take hold, and slowly Simms began to relax.

"What are you going to do?" Charlotte Ambler finally asked, her voice bleak.

"We're moving him tomorrow," Samuels replied. "He'll be taken up to the state hospital near Eastbury."

Templetoon shook his head sadly and turned away. "Hope they bring a straitjacket," he muttered softly as he started out the door. "Looks to me like that guy's going to need one."

And yet, as he left the hospital he still couldn't get Cassie's words out of his mind.

"Sumi? Did you really do it? Did you do what I wanted you to?"

Chapter 14

"I don't be*lieve* it!" Teri Bennett squealed excitedly. "You really *saw* it?"

Kevin Smythe nodded, glancing at his watch out of the corner of his eye to make sure there was time to tell the story once more. So far he'd had to repeat it twice, but each time new arrivals appeared on the front steps of the school, and they wanted to hear it too. Feigning boredom with the repetition, he began again. "I was just coming around the corner from Pine Street, and there was an ambulance right there in front of the entrance on Hartford. I almost just went on by, 'cause at first I didn't think anything was happening. But then the doors opened and they brought him out. Man, it was weird—they had him all strapped down, and there was one of those bottles with a rubber hose on it, and everything! Then they stuck him in the back of the ambulance and the lights started flashing and they took off!"

"But where are they taking him?" Allayne Garvey demanded. "I mean, are they really going to lock him up?"

Kevin shrugged with exaggerated casualness. "Search me," he said, and then his voice dropped to a level that implied he was about to divulge a secret. "But my dad said he went absolutely spacey after it happened—"

"After what happened?" Jeff Maynard asked, trotting up the stairs to join the group on the top step. "What's going on?"

Kevin and the two girls stared at Jeff in disbelief. "You

179

mean you didn't hear?" Kevin asked. "Cassie Winslow hung around after school yesterday and tried to kill Mr. Simms."

Jeff's mouth dropped open. "Are you nuts?" he demanded. "She left right after Simms kicked Eric off the team. And—" He suddenly fell silent, staring at the street. The eyes of the others followed his gaze, and they, too, stopped talking.

Walking along the sidewalk, their heads close together, as if they were whispering to each other, were Eric Cavanaugh and Cassie Winslow. By the time they got to the foot of the steps, not a sound was to be heard from any of the thirty or so students gathered in front of the school, all of whom were now staring at the latest arrivals.

Cassie glanced up and knew immediately what had happened. But for Eric it seemed to take a moment.

"Hey!" he called to Jeff Maynard. "What's going on?"

Jeff looked back at him uncertainly, then his eyes shifted to Kevin Smythe. It was Kevin who finally spoke.

"What are you doing with *her*?" he asked, the belligerence in his voice tempered by nervousness. To him Cassie Winslow suddenly looked dangerous.

Eric frowned. "What are you talking about? Why shouldn't I be with Cassie?" His gaze shifted to Teri and Allayne, but both of them were now looking somewhere else. And then he, too, understood. "Hey," he said, "she didn't do anything to Simms. I was with her, and we were out at the marsh at—" He stopped himself as he saw his friends exchange doubtful looks.

Lisa Chambers—who had been silent until now, trying to sort out the truth from all the strange things she'd heard last night and this morning—suddenly made up her mind. She glared down at Eric. "You were in Miranda's house, weren't you?" she accused. "What were you doing there? Helping Cassie figure out how to do it? Or did you help her do it yourself?"

Eric's jaw tightened. "Do it?" he demanded. "Do what? You guys don't think she did anything to Simms, do you? And even if she did, so what? Every one of you hated his guts! We all did!" No one said anything as Eric slowly searched the faces of the people who only yesterday had been his friends. Only Jeff Maynard seemed to be uncertain. "Jeff? You don't think Cassie and I did anything, do you?"

Jeff felt like a trapped animal, caught between his best friend and practically everyone else he knew. "I—I don't know," he stammered. "I just got here. Teri says—"

"What does she know?" Cassie demanded, her eyes flashing with anger. "Were you there? Did you see what happened to Mr. Simms? Maybe *she* did it!"

Teri's face turned scarlet with indignation. "Don't you try to blame me, Cassie Winslow!" she shouted. "All I know is what my mother told me, and she says you did it and they ought to lock you up! So don't try to blame it on me!" Bursting into tears, she wheeled around and rushed into the building, Allayne and Lisa hurrying after her.

Eric, now as angry as Cassie, started up the steps, his hands clenching into fists. But then he abruptly changed his mind, and took Cassie's hand in his own. "Let's just go," he said, his voice so quiet no one but she could hear him. "It doesn't matter what they thought about Simms. They just want to blame you."

They were already a block away when the school P.A. system came to life and an announcement that the first class of the day would be replaced by an assembly was broadcast through the halls and out over the grounds.

Neither Eric nor Cassie heard it.

Charlotte Ambler stood behind the podium atop the choir platform hastily assembled fifteen minutes earlier, and looked out at the assembled students of Memorial High. Ordinarily they tumbled happily into the auditorium, laughing and chattering among themselves, looking forward to an assembly—any assembly—as a release from an hour of classes. But today it was different. They were still chattering, but their voices were subdued, and as they huddled together in small groups, they seemed to glance furtively around them, as if sensing that they were talking about something none of them had any information about and that they shouldn't be talking about at all. Charlotte Ambler was about to give them the information they wanted, but she had a sinking feeling that it might already be too late, for nowhere in the sea of faces could she spot either Eric Cavanaugh or Cassie Winslow.

Rapping sharply on the podium with a gavel, she waited for the hubbub to die down, then cleared her throat.

"I'm sure most of you are aware of the unfortunate incident of yesterday afternoon," she began, determined to choose her words as carefully as possible. If she couldn't defuse the situation now—and quell the rumors that had already begun—there was a distinct possibility that the rest of the term would be a complete loss. If, indeed, it wasn't too late already. "One of our teachers," she went on, "Mr. Simms, has suffered a form of illness that is not at all uncommon in our day and age. Mr. Simms has been under a great deal of pressure—"

"And maybe a few knives?" someone yelled from the back of the room.

There was a gasp, followed by dead silence, and Charlotte Ambler slowly removed her glasses, letting them drop down to her breast. Abandoning the short speech she'd written a few minutes before, she stepped around the podium and moved forward to the edge of the platform. When she spoke again, her voice needed no amplification from the microphone.

"I shall not ask who said that," she said, her words echoing coldly through the room, "because if I found out, that person would no longer be a part of this high school." She paused for a split second, then went on. "What has happened is this: Mr. Simms suffered a sort of mental breakdown in the gymnasium yesterday afternoon, and it caused him to inflict a certain amount of harm upon himself. He is being taken to a hospital in Eastbury, where he will be treated for an indefinite period. For the remainder of this term his coaching duties will be handled by Mr. Johnson, and his classes by myself." She paused, as if waiting for any of the students to dare make comment on her selection of substitutes for the absent teacher. When there was no response, she continued. "There may be certain scheduling changes, and you will be notified of those in due course. As for the rumors that have been circulating this morning, there is no evidence that Mr. Simms was attacked by anyone, or that there were any weapons involved. That is all. You may return to your homerooms."

She stepped off the platform and immediately disappeared out the side door of the auditorium, unwilling to allow even a moment for any of the students to ask a question she might not be prepared to answer.

There was a moment of silence before the realization that the assembly was over sank in. Then, slowly, the students got to their feet and began drifting toward the doors. But everywhere there was a soft buzz of whispered conversation as the teenagers tried to decipher the truth of what had happened in the gymnasium the day before.

By the time the auditorium had emptied, a consensus had been reached, and though Charlotte Ambler wasn't there to hear it, it would not have surprised her.

Lisa Chambers summed it up as she left the auditorium, the center of a group that only a few days before had always pivoted around Eric.

"I don't care what anybody says," Lisa announced. "I could tell Cassie Winslow was weird the first time I saw her. If Mr. Simms said she tried to kill him, I believe it. And if you ask me, Eric better stay away from her before she does something to him too."

"We can't just ignore it, Keith," Rosemary insisted. "If you keep trying to bury your head in the sand, things are just going to get worse and worse!"

"Bury my head?" Keith demanded. He glanced at the clock above the kitchen sink. It was nearly nine. He should have been down at the marina an hour ago, but Rosemary seemed determined to keep arguing with him until he admitted that there was something wrong with Cassie. "I'm not burying my head in any sand, and I'm getting a little tired of you saying I am. If Gene thought there were anything to Harold Simms's story, don't you think he'd have been back here by now?" His strong jaw set in an expression of grim determination. "What the hell do you want? Cassie and Eric say they were out at Miranda's house, and Jennifer backs them up. Even if Eric and Cassie were lying—which I don't believe—why would Jen lie?"

Rosemary shook her head doggedly, determined that this time she wouldn't be swayed by Keith's stubbornness. "You weren't here," she insisted. "If you'd heard her, you'd be worried too! I know you would!"

Keith took a final swallow of his coffee, then drained the

rest into the sink. "All right, so she said she wished something would happen to Simms. Why the hell wouldn't she? He's always been a mean little wimp, and I don't blame her for wishing him the worst." He set the cup on the drainboard, placing it with the overly careful precision that was a certain clue to his growing impatience. "If he'd treated me the way he did the kids, I'd want to kill him too." He turned to face Rosemary once more, and his voice took on a patronizing tone that made her simmer with anger. "But wanting to do something and actually doing it are two different things. If Templeton accepted her story, I don't see why you can't." The patronizing tone gave way to a sarcastic edge. "Don't you think I've noticed how you're always watching her, as if you're just waiting to catch her in a lie, or make a mistake? My God, Rosemary, even when she does something nice you've acted like she's trying to get something for herself!"

"That's not true!" Rosemary breathed, her heart pounding with indignation. And yet, deep inside, she knew that there was some truth to Keith's words.

All those strange feelings she'd had about Cassie, which she'd tried to keep to herself. Apparently she hadn't been successful.

"All right," she admitted, sagging into one of the kitchen chairs. "I have been suspicious. There's just something about her, Keith. I keep getting the feeling that she's hiding something from us."

"That's ridiculous," Keith snapped. "She's a perfectly normal fifteen-year-old, and when she came here we were perfect strangers to her. Even me, when you get down to it. What did you expect? That she'd open up to us the first minute she was here?"

Rosemary studied Keith beseechingly, trying to find the love that she'd always seen in his eyes. Right now there was none. Only a coldness that made her want to shiver. "But after all that's happened . . ." she began again, struggling to keep her voice steady.

"Nothing's happened, Rosemary," Keith broke in. He was wiping the cup with a dish towel, then abruptly slammed it down on the counter with such force that it shattered. Keith ignored the fragments of broken china. "All you're doing is giving in to a whole lot of unfounded gossip."

It was too much, and Rosemary's temper suddenly snapped. "I don't believe it!" she said, angrily snatching up the pieces of the smashed cup, punctuating her words by hurling them into the trash basket in the corner. "Is Miranda being dead nothing but unfounded gossip? What about Harold Simms? Is what happened to him nothing but unfounded gossip too? Isn't he really in the hospital at all, Keith?"

"You know that's not what I meant," Keith replied, his voice icy. "Of course those things happened. What I'm telling you—and what seems quite obvious to me—is that Cassie didn't have anything to do with them!"

"Then why was she out there?" Rosemary flared. "Why is it that when Miranda died, and when Harold Simms was attacked, Cassie was out there in the marsh, doing . . . God only knows what?"

A heavy silence fell over the kitchen as Keith and Rosemary faced each other. Finally Keith shook his head. His anger seemed to dissipate visibly, to be replaced by a melancholy sadness. "Listen to us," he whispered. "Will you just listen to us? What are you trying to say? That Cassie's some kind of witch?"

"Oh, for God's sake," Rosemary wailed. "Of course not!"

But it was too late. Snatching his coat from the hook by the door, Keith slammed out the back door. A second later Rosemary heard the sound of his car starting, and then he was gone. But when she was alone, it wasn't Keith's words that stuck in her mind, it was her own.

What *had* Cassie been doing in the marsh? But it wasn't the marsh. It was the cabin in the marsh, the run-down shack that had stood out there, housing generation after generation of Sikes women, apparently each of them as strange as the one who had come before.

Coming to a quick decision, Rosemary abandoned the remains of the morning's breakfast and put on her own jacket. Locking the back door behind her, she hurried down the driveway then cut across the lawn toward Cambridge Street, at the foot of which lay the park, and beyond it, the marsh surrounding Miranda Sikes's cabin. It was time she herself had a look at the place that seemed to have such a fascination for her stepdaughter.

Just as she turned the corner onto Cambridge Street, a

gray shadow slipped out the open window of Cassie's room and dropped nimbly through the tree to the ground.

Crouching low, Sumi began stalking after Rosemary.

Laura Cavanaugh glanced at the clock over the kitchen sink and wondered if she should go upstairs and waken Ed. She didn't want to, yet at the same time she was almost afraid not to. But it didn't matter, really—whatever she did would be wrong. If she woke him, he'd be mad at her for not letting him sleep, and if she didn't wake him, he'd be furious at her for letting him oversleep. She decided to compromise—ten more minutes wouldn't matter anyway, and it was nice to have the house quiet, at least for a little while. Except that at times like this morning, even the quiet had a tension to it, like the eye of a hurricane; a moment of calm, but with storm clouds pressing in from every direction.

She filled Ed's thermos with coffee, then clamped it into the top of his lunch pail. There were already three sandwiches and an apple in the pail. After hesitating a moment, she added a can of beer—Ed would take beer on the boat with him anyway, and if she left it out of his pail, he would only accuse her of implying that he drank too much. She was just closing the lunch bucket when she heard him lumbering down the stairs. Then he was in the kitchen, smiling at her.

I don't believe it, she thought. Last night he whipped Eric and slapped me around the bedroom, and this morning he acts as though nothing happened.

"What's for breakfast, doll face?" he asked, sliding into the breakfast nook and pulling the sports page out of the pile of newspapers Eric had left on the table.

Laura looked at him uncertainly. "I—I thought you'd just take a Danish and eat it on the boat," she said. "It's already after nine, and if you're not out by nine-thirty, the tide will be too low, won't it?"

The smile faded from Ed's face and his eyes flashed dangerously. "What the hell does the tide matter?"

Laura searched her memory for anything he might have said last night about not working today, but there was nothing. "I thought . . . I thought—"

"*I thought!*" Ed mimicked. "Jesus, Laura, can't you let me do the thinking around here? I told you last night I wasn't going out today. Can't you remember the simplest goddamned thing?" Tossing the paper aside, he went to the refrigerator, jerked it open, and fished around on the bottom shelf for a beer. Twisting the cap off, he tossed it into the sink then tipped the bottle and drained half of it in one long swig. Wiping his lips with his forearm, he shook his head. "I'm goin' down to the high school to talk to that snotty principal about Eric. I'm gonna see to it she puts him back on the baseball team."

Laura shuddered, remembering the last time Ed had gone to talk to Mrs. Ambler. He'd stopped off at the Whaler's Inn on the way, and by the time he'd gotten to the school, he'd been so drunk he'd barely been able to stand up. Mrs. Ambler had listened to him for only two minutes before calling up Gene Templeton and having Ed escorted out of the building. Gene had taken Ed down to the police station and put him in the town's single jail cell for the rest of the morning, then sent him home. "Maybe it would be better if—"

Ed's jaw tightened and his eyes narrowed. "Better if what?" he demanded, his voice dropping to the snarl that was always a warning of impending violence. But it didn't matter. This time Laura was determined to try to stop her husband.

"Better if you just let everything alone for once," she said. "Don't you think you've done enough? Don't you think I know what you did to Eric in the guest room last night? You're sick, Ed. You don't need to go talk to Mrs. Ambler about Eric—you need to go talk to a doctor about yourself!"

Ed's eyes glowed with a manic rage, and Laura knew she'd gone too far. She started to back away, but Ed came after her, his fingers already working spasmodically. He reached out and grabbed her hair with his left hand, jerking her head back as he slapped her across the cheek with his free hand. "I'm sick?" he demanded. "Me? Who the hell are you to be talking? Who the hell do you think keeps this family together? You think I like sacrificing my life for the likes of you? I shoulda gotten rid of you a long time ago!" He slapped her again, then hurled her across the room. Her hip smashed into the counter and she yelped with pain, then sank to the floor, sobbing. "It's all your fault," Ed told her, moving across the room. He drew his foot back and kicked her viciously in the ribs.

"No!" Laura screamed. "Ed, I didn't do anything—I'm sorry! I'm sorry!"

"Sorry?" Ed mocked. "You're sorry?"

"But it isn't my fault!" Laura wailed. "I've never done anything to you! I've never done—"

"*Shut up!*" Ed roared. "*Goddamn it, woman, will you just shut up?*"

His foot swung back once more, but this time Laura rolled away, scrambling to her feet and managing to bolt out the back door. Ed started after her, but by the time he got outside, she was already up the driveway and limping across the street. He watched her go, then shook his head in disgust.

He'd have one more beer, then head for the school. Let Laura go hide out with the people across the street—he'd deal with her tonight.

Chapter 15

Charlotte Ambler wondered if she should signal Patsy Malone to call Gene Templeton, or try to handle the situation herself. But, of course, it was too late now. If she was going to call the police chief, she should have done it thirty minutes ago, when she'd first seen Ed Cavanaugh sitting in his truck, drinking from a bottle of whiskey he hadn't even tried to hide in a brown paper bag, and glowering darkly in the direction of her office. When she'd first noticed him, she'd stood at her window staring back, putting him on notice that he'd been seen. Usually that was enough, and after sulking in his truck for a few minutes, he would drive away, presumably to the Whaler's Inn, where, Charlotte knew, he would sit at the bar and brag to whoever would listen about how he'd "set that uppity Ambler woman straight on a few things." All of which was fine with her. If he wanted to puff himself up that way, it wasn't any skin off her nose. The one time she had actually called the police, Ed had bided his time through the day, then taken his rage out on his wife and son that evening. When Eric had shown up with bruises on his face the next day, Charlotte had tried to convince him that he should report what had happened to the police, but Eric had refused, insisting that nothing had happened—he'd simply tripped and fallen down the stairs that morning.

Strange, she reflected cynically to herself as she watched Ed climb out of his truck and shamble up the steps of the school, how the drunken fools like Ed Cavanaugh never trip and break their necks. She heard him lumber into the outer office, and went back to her desk. When he pushed her own door open a moment later, she was staring at him calmly and coldly. "I don't believe we have an appointment, Mr. Cavanaugh," she began, but he only sneered at her.

"I don't need an appointment where my boy is concerned," he said, advancing across the room to lean over Charlotte's desk. The reek of his breath made the principal lean back, but her eyes never left his.

"Eric's situation will be dealt with in a—"

"Don't give me that pious bullshit, lady." His eyes had narrowed to slits, and his jaw was clenched tight. "None of what's happened is his fault anyway. It's all that trashy Winslow girl. If it wasn't for her, none of this would have happened!"

Charlotte decided there was no point in arguing—Ed was far too drunk for that. "I'm sure you're right—" she began, but once more Ed cut her off, this time with his fist pounding on her desk.

"And don't you patronize me!" Ed roared. "I already took care of Eric for cutting school and getting himself dumped from the baseball team. All I want from you is your word that you'll see to it he gets back on the team! And I want you to keep him away from that girl too!"

Suddenly Charlotte Ambler had had enough. The strain of the last fifteen hours suddenly telescoped, and her temper snapped. She rose to her feet. Though her height was no match for Ed's, the fury in her eyes seemed to cut through his alcoholic haze. "Is it!" she spat. "Is that what you want? Well, let me tell you what I want! I want you to get out of my office and off my campus. I want you to stop drinking, and stop beating your wife and son! I want you to start being a decent husband and father! And then, when I get what I want, perhaps I'll be willing to listen to what you want! But until that happens, keep in mind where you are, and who you are, and who I am! Now get out of this office, and if you have anything further to say, put it in writing and send it to the school board. If you *can* write!"

Ed's face turned ashen and his fist rose up threateningly.

"Do it," Charlotte challenged him, her voice dropping, but taking on a cutting edge. "Just do it. But don't expect me to keep my mouth shut about it. You might be able to bully your family, but you can't bully me. I'll have you in front of a judge before the blood even dries. Now either get out of my office or swing that fist."

Ed stood still for a moment, his entire body trembling with rage, and for a moment Charlotte thought she'd pushed him too far. But then she realized that she didn't care. Indeed, she found herself half hoping he *would* try to slap her around. Let him think about it in jail for a while. As she watched him warily, he seemed to regain control of himself.

"You can't talk to me that way," he rasped, but the menace was gone from his voice. "I know what you think of me—I know what everybody thinks of me in this crummy town. But I can take care of myself, and I can take care of my family. And ain't you or anybody else gonna stop me. So you think about that, Mrs. High-and-Mighty, 'cause if that girl gets my boy in any more trouble, I can tell you there's gonna be hell to pay!" He turned around and shambled out of the office, leaving the door open behind him. Only when the outer door had slammed shut did Patsy Malone appear nervously in her office, her face pale.

"Are you all right?" the secretary asked. "I was just about to call Gene Templeton."

"I trust," Charlotte observed dryly, "that if he'd actually hit me, you would have followed through on that impulse."

"I . . . well, I don't . . . well, of course I would," Patsy floundered, and for the first time since Harold Simms had been found in the gym the day before, Charlotte Ambler found herself chuckling.

"Well, that's nice to know." She eyed Patsy mischievously. "And can I also trust that you won't say anything about that little scene?"

"Why . . . why, of course not!"

"Good," Charlotte replied, knowing as well as Patsy did that by the end of lunch hour there wouldn't be a person at the school who hadn't heard every detail of what had just transpired. If nothing else, the story should put an end to any further discipline problems for the year. The way Patsy would tell it, it would sound as if Charlotte had actually given Ed Cavanaugh a thrashing. "Now perhaps we can get on with the day, all right?"

The secretary's head bobbed, and she quietly pulled the door closed, leaving Charlotte alone in her office. Charlotte went over to the window and saw Ed Cavanaugh's truck still sitting in front of the school, and Ed himself still glaring at her. But when she nodded to him, he started the engine, slammed the truck into gear, and careened down the street, his wheels shrieking in protest as they skidded over the pavement. Only when the truck had disappeared around the corner did Charlotte return to her desk and lower herself tiredly into her chair. She leaned back, removed her glasses, and closed her eyes, rubbing at them for a moment. In her mind Ed Cavanaugh's last words kept re-echoing.

Hell to pay.

Didn't he realize that since Cassie Winslow had come to False Harbor there had already been hell to pay?

And unless Charlotte missed her guess, it was all just beginning. Despite her words to the students that morning, and despite what Paul Samuels had told her, Charlotte Ambler was still not convinced that Cassie had nothing to do with what had happened to Harold Simms.

She recalled all too clearly that first meeting with Cassie, when she'd instinctively sensed trouble. And her first instincts, as always, were proving to be correct.

Cassie Winslow was, indeed, proving to be trouble.

"You can't just never go to school again."

"Why not?"

Eric and Cassie had been sitting on the beach, staring out over the water, saying nothing. After leaving the high school an hour ago, they'd cut over Maple Street to Cape Drive, but instead of walking along Cape until they came to the public path, Cassie had insisted they go through someone's yard. Eric thought about arguing, then realized that Cassie was right—the more quickly they put the beach and dunes between themselves and the village, the less chance there was of someone spotting them and reporting them to his father. And so they'd slipped through one of the beach-house gates, ducked around the corner of the house itself, then scrambled down a low bank to the beach. From there they'd walked along the deserted expanse of sand, finally flopping down to watch the sea and the birds.

"Because you just can't do that," Eric argued now. He regarded Cassie carefully out of the corner of his eye. "Besides, if you don't go back to school, everyone's going to think you're afraid to."

Cassie was silent for a moment, and when she finally spoke, there was a tremor in her voice. "Maybe I *am* afraid to go back."

"Why?" Eric asked, his voice almost teasing. "You didn't do anything, did you?"

"Maybe—maybe I did," Cassie whispered. "Maybe we both did."

Eric hesitated, then shook his head. "That's stupid."

"But what about yesterday?" Cassie asked. "What I thought about really happened."

Eric reached down and scooped up a handful of sand, then let it run slowly through his fingers. "Nobody even knows what happened to old Simms. Not really. And it doesn't matter what he said—you didn't beat him up."

Cassie turned to face Eric. "But we wanted something to happen to him, and it did!"

Eric shrugged. "So what? You didn't really do anything, and it isn't your fault if old Simms cracked up."

"But what if it is?" Cassie blurted out. "Miranda said I had a gift, and what if that's what she meant? That I can make things happen just by thinking about them?"

Eric was silent, but his fist closed on the rest of the sand, squeezing it hard for a moment. Then he threw it down, stood up and started walking away.

"Eric?" Cassie called after him, scrambling to her feet. "Are you mad at me, too, now?"

Eric stopped and turned around. He stared hard at her, then said, "I don't know. I don't know what you're talking about. But, you know, Cassie, it sounds kind of crazy."

Cassie gasped, but Eric didn't seem to hear her. "And maybe you feel like you can never go back to school again, but I can. So I'm going for a walk and think things over. Okay?"

Cassie helplessly watched him walk quickly away, disappearing into the distance, his head down. She wanted to follow him, wanted to try to talk to him some more, try to explain the confusion she was feeling. But she couldn't bring herself to do it—the look in his eyes as he'd stared at her a moment before, a look that resembled pure hatred—stopped her. He didn't hate her, did he? Eric was her only friend. If he started treating her the way everyone else did—

She shuddered, and tried to close the thought out of her mind. If Eric turned against her now, she wouldn't have anyone left at all. But there was nothing she could do. Nothing at all. Turning in the opposite direction from where Eric had gone, she headed toward Cranberry Point and the marsh.

For the first time in years Rosemary found herself really looking at the marsh. How long, she wondered, had it been since she'd last gone for a walk in it?

She remembered the first time she'd seen it, soon after she'd met Keith and come to False Harbor. It had been spring, and the day had been much like this one—clear, with just a touch of crispness still lingering from the winter. The wetlands had been full of geese that day, and the air vibrant with their honkings and the quacking of ducks. It had been a beautiful sight, bursting with life, and she'd made Keith walk in it with her for hours.

But that had been ten years ago, and as time had passed, the marsh became just another familiar fixture of False Harbor, until finally she'd grown so used to it that she barely noticed it at all.

Until now.

But as she looked at it today, it seemed to have changed. A feeling of foreboding appeared to have settled over it, and where once she had sensed new life stirring within it, now she was most conscious of the stifling odor of decay, as if deep within it, somewhere below its shimmering waters, there was a rotten core threatening to bubble to the surface.

But, of course, she was wrong—nothing in the marsh had changed at all. It was her feelings toward it, for as she stood at the edge of the park, gazing out over the green expanse of grasses and quivering reeds, she realized that in the last few days she'd come to associate the marsh with the uneasy tensions that had begun to wrap themselves around her like the coils of a serpent.

And in the center of the marsh, rising like a boil on an otherwise smooth skin, was the barren hummock that supported Miranda Sikes's cabin, with its half-starved trees reaching upward like the hands of a corpse trying to claw its way out of the grave.

Stop it, Rosemary commanded herself. *Just stop it. It's only a marsh, and an empty shack. There's nothing to be frightened of at all.*

Determinedly she pushed her way through the barrier of tall weeds that separated the park from the wetlands, and found one of the soggy trails that led out into the bog itself.

She made her way slowly, for the path she had chosen was narrow and nearly overgrown with rushes and cattails. Every few yards, it seemed, the trail split off and she had to make a decision about which direction to take.

More than half the decisions appeared to be wrong, the trail petering out entirely, the grasses closing in around her, the earth giving way beneath her feet.

Twice she felt the deceptive firmness of quicksand that seemed solid when she put her weight on it, only to give way a second later, sucking at her shoe like something alive. Both times she jerked loose, her heart beating fast as panic welled up inside her. But both times she forced the panic back into its cage and backed away to find solid ground.

Several times, when she realized she'd made a mistake and turned around to retrace her steps, she saw a flash of movement out of the corner of her eye, as if something had been following her on the trail and darted off as she turned, to disappear into the reeds.

The third time it happened, she stood perfectly still, only her eyes flicking over the marsh, searching for a telltale movement that would expose the animal. But the seconds crept by, and she saw nothing. Her skin began to crawl. Though she could not see them, she knew that there were eyes on her, watching her from some hidden ambush, waiting for her.

Once again she had to force herself to go on, had to fight back the urge to retreat to the park, with its secure footing and protective groves of trees.

But the cabin was closer now, and she could see it clearly.

And she could see the hawk, perched at the very peak of the roof, stretching its wings restlessly, its head bobbing back and forth as its red eyes fixed on her.

And then, when she was only a hundred yards from the cabin, the bird rose into the air, its great white wings lifting it onto the wind then locking into position as it effortlessly soared toward her.

Rosemary stared at it, mesmerized, and in her mind's eye she saw once again the deep slashes the bird's talons had left in Lisa Chambers's arm.

The hawk passed between Cassie and the sun, and its shadow flashing over her face jerked Cassie out of her silent reverie. She glanced up to find that she had walked nearly the whole length of the beach. Only a few yards ahead the concrete cylinder of the Cranberry Point light rose up from the end of the peninsula, and for a moment Cassie thought that was what she'd seen. But then she spotted the pale white form of the hawk circling high above the marsh.

As she watched, she thought he was searching for something, but then she realized that he wasn't searching at all. Whatever he was looking for, he'd already found it.

Frowning, she scanned the area of the marsh the bird was hovering above. She saw nothing. Then, almost invisible against the green expanse of the wetlands, she found the hawk's target.

There was someone out there, staring fixedly up into the sky, and Cassie realized that the reason she hadn't seen the figure right away was because it was clad in a jacket that was nearly the same color as the marsh itself.

But who was it? She strained her eyes, but the distance was too great.

Then Cassie understood what was about to happen. Whoever was out there was on his way to the cabin—her cabin—and the hawk was preparing to attack. Cassie watched in fascination. What should she do? Should she try to shout a warning?

But why should she? Whoever it was had no right to go into her cabin.

If something happened to a trespasser, it was his own fault, wasn't it?

But what if she was wrong? What if the person was just wandering around and didn't realize he'd gone too close?

She vacillated, part of her wanting to cry out to the person or try to distract the hawk.

But another part of her wanted to watch, to see what would happen. Her eyes fixed on the great bird, Cassie almost unconsciously moved closer to the marsh.

The hawk circled higher and its spirals grew ever tighter. In another moment, Cassie knew, it would draw its wings in and plunge into the streaking dive of its attack.

Rosemary knew what was going to happen, and knew she had to do something, but panic was coursing through her now, setting her heart pounding and draining the strength from her limbs. She tried to tear her eyes away from the bird, certain that if she could break the creature's hypnotic spell, she could bring herself back to life. But it was as if she'd lost control of her own will. Even as the bird suddenly folded its wings tight against its body and began dropping out of the sky toward her, she could do nothing but stare at it in horrified fascination.

It grew larger and larger as it picked up speed, and as the bird lunged toward her, time seemed to stand still, each second becoming an eternity.

She could see its gaping mouth now, the pointed hook of its beak hurtling toward her like the curved blade of a miniature scythe, ready to tear into her flesh. Her own mouth opened then, but her throat felt numb and no scream came out.

And then it was on her, its legs outstretched, its talons poised to slash into her. Still Rosemary couldn't move. Her heartbeat was pounding in her head and icy tentacles of fear held her firmly in their grip. She could smell the bird, the rank odor of its raw-meat diet emanating off its skin and filling her nostrils with the putrid scent of rotting flesh. At the last possible instant her arm came up and she felt the bird's talons close down on it, tearing through the thin material of her jacket to slash deep into her flesh.

She ducked her head away, but even that movement came too late, and she felt a searing flash of pain as the razor-sharp beak sliced into her right cheek.

Instantly she felt a hot gush of blood pour out of the wound, and a moment later her mouth filled with the salty taste of fresh blood.

The pain of the attack brought Rosemary back to life, and a surge of adrenaline shot through her. With her uninjured arm she swung wildly at the bird, and suddenly its talons released her arm. It jerked spasmodically as it tumbled to the ground, an angry screech of frustration erupting from its throat. Then it regained control of itself, its wings beating wildly as it took to the air once more.

She felt its tail feathers brush against her face, then heard the peculiar whumping sound of its wings as it pulled away. A moment later it was gone, streaking away low over the grasses, its wing tips barely clearing the cattails and reeds.

Blood oozing from the cut on her face, her right hand clutching at her damaged left arm, Rosemary turned and fled through the marsh, ripping and tearing at the weeds and vines that threatened to entangle her. At last, her breath rasping in her lungs, she hurled herself onto the firm ground of the park and sank sobbing onto the lawn. For a long time she didn't move, fighting the waves of pain that wracked her body. Then, slowly, her pounding heartbeat began to ease and her breathing returned to normal. At last—she didn't know how much later—she sat up and wiped the tears and blood away from her eyes. Her vision slowly cleared, and she looked around.

A few yards away, sitting with his tail curled around his legs, was Sumi.

Rosemary's eyes met the cat's, and burning yellow eyes held hers for a moment. Then the cat ducked his head, his tail twitched, and he darted away into the marsh. Instinctively Rosemary knew where he was going.

Had it been Sumi she'd seen in the marsh, following her? But why?

And why had the hawk, after striking her down suddenly abandoned its attack?

She struggled to her feet, every fiber of her body aching with exhaustion. She had to get home, had to lie down. But as she started out of the park, something pulled at her, made her pause and turn back.

She saw Cassie standing on the porch of the cabin. As Rosemary watched, she saw the gray cat dash out of the marsh and up the gentle slope of the hummock.

As the hawk perched calmly on the rooftop, the cat leaped into Cassie's arms.

Chapter 16

Rosemary winced as the needle pierced her skin, and her knuckles turned white as she gripped the arms of the chair in Paul Samuels's office.

"Almost done," Samuels told her, his voice soothing. "Just one more."

She felt the needle jab again, followed by the eerie rasping sensation of the suture being drawn through her skin. Her left eye followed the movement of Samuels's deft fingers as he tied a knot then covered the stitches with a bandage. "That's it," he said, winking at her. "Want a lollipop?"

Rosemary managed a weak smile, and shook her head. "What about a scar? Will there be one?"

Samuels raised his hands in a gesture of incredulous dismay. "A *scar*? Would these fingers leave a *scar*?"

"I don't know," Rosemary replied, managing only the faintest hint of a smile, then instantly wincing with pain. "That's why I'm asking."

The doctor shook his head. "Shouldn't. The cut wasn't as bad as it looked, and in a couple of weeks—maybe a month—you shouldn't even know it was there. Actually, your arm was in worse shape than your cheek, but at least you kept that damned bird away from your eyes." His expression darkened slightly. "Have you told Gene Templeton about this?"

"That's where I'm going next," Rosemary replied. She got out of the chair, took off the smock that had covered her clothes, and began searching in her purse for a comb. "Somehow it seemed more important to get this mess cleaned up first." Her eyes met the doctor's in the mirror above his office sink. "But let me tell you, I can understand now why Lisa Chambers was so upset last week. I don't think I've ever been so frightened in my life. And the worst of it was, I couldn't do anything! I just stood there, Paul. I just stood there and let it happen."

"Panic," the doctor told her. "It does that sometimes. But it's something else too. There's an instinct to freeze when you sense danger. But then at the last second, when you know you can't hide, instinct takes over. That's what saved your eyes," he added pointedly. He moved to his desk and began making some notations in Rosemary's file. "I want you to go talk to Gene. If something isn't done about that bird, it's going to do real damage someday."

"Don't worry," Rosemary replied, her voice grim. "If he won't do anything about it, I'll have Keith go out and shoot it himself." She put her comb back in her purse, then picked up the shredded remains of her poplin jacket. "Anything else? Do I need any antibiotics or anything?"

"I've got the prescription all ready." Samuels handed her a slip of paper, then walked with her out to the hospital's small waiting room. Just as Rosemary was about to leave, he stopped her. "What about Cassie?" he asked. "You said you saw her out there. And there was a cat, too, wasn't there?"

Rosemary looked at the doctor blankly, then the meaning of his words began to sink in. "Paul, are you saying what I think you are?"

"I'm not saying anything," Samuels replied neutrally. "I'm just asking a question."

"And I'll answer it," Rosemary told him. "Yes, Cassie was out there, and yes, her cat was out there. But the cat didn't attack me, and I'm absolutely positive that Cassie *was* there. I didn't imagine seeing her. So if you're wondering if I had the same kind of hysterical attack that Harold Simms had, the answer is no. The hawk attacked me, Paul. That's all that happened."

But as she left Samuels's office to walk the two blocks to the town hall, she replayed the entire incident in her mind. And she remembered Lisa Chambers's insistence that Cassie had made the hawk attack her. But it wasn't possible, was it?

Of course not.

* * *

Templeton listened to Rosemary's story silently, taking a few notes in between munches on his mid-morning doughnut. When she was finished, he sighed heavily. "Well, it looks like it's time for me to go hunting again, doesn't it?"

"Then you'll do it?"

"I'll try," he agreed. "But I'm not going to promise you anything. I've gone after that bird before, but it's never done me any good. It's almost like it knows I'm coming and just takes off. And in the meantime I'll post the marsh. At least maybe we can keep people out of there for a while."

When Rosemary was gone, he left the police station and drove home. Thirty minutes after that, carrying his favorite hunting rifle—equipped with a telescopic sight—he headed for the marsh.

It was almost noon, and the sun was high in the sky. The last of the morning chill had left the air, but Templeton kept his uniform jacket on. If the hawk attacked him, at least he would have the protection of the heavy gabardine covering his arms and chest. He locked the squad car, and cradling the gun in his left arm, started out toward Cranberry Point. Before he started shooting, he'd damned well better make sure the marsh was deserted.

There was no one on the beach, and only the constant fluttering of the feeding birds disturbed the tranquillity of the wetlands. Tightening his grip on the gun, Templeton began making his way toward the cabin.

Cassie sat in the rocking chair by the window, with Sumi curled up in her lap, purring contentedly. But Cassie herself was not content.

She was worried. Worried and frightened.

She had watched from the beach as Kiska attacked the person in the marsh, and then, after the green-clad figure had struggled to its feet and hobbled back to the park, she had hurried out into the marsh herself.

She wasn't afraid of it anymore, wasn't worried about getting lost in the tangled maze of paths, or stumbling into one of the patches of quicksand that dotted the bog where the peat had never built up. It was almost as if there were some kind of invisible map in her head, guiding her. Today, in fact, she'd almost felt as if she were one of the birds soaring above the reeds, and that she could look down and pick the quickest, safest route from the beach to the cabin. Finally she'd gotten to the cabin and was just about to open the door and step inside, when she sensed something coming toward her. She turned, and out of the marsh, darting up the hill toward her, came Sumi. The cat had hit the porch then bounded into her arms, nuzzling against her cheek.

As the cat nuzzled her, her eyes were suddenly drawn to the person in the park—the person wearing the torn green jacket—and she suddenly knew who it was.

Rosemary.

But how had she known? She watched the figure carefully, squinting against the sun, but the distance was too far. Even though she knew who it was—*knew it*—she couldn't distinguish her stepmother's features. Finally, when Rosemary had limped out of the park, clutching her injured arm with one hand and holding the other to her bleeding face, Cassie had turned away and gone into the cabin.

Immediately a sense of peace had come over her. She settled herself into the chair by the window, rocking gently, cuddling Sumi in her lap.

The cat had looked up at her, and their eyes met. Then, as her fingers rubbed at the cat's fur, she felt a tingling sensation on her skin and vague images began to form in her mind.

She had a sense of being surrounded by something like seaweed, and all around her there was nothing but a swirling green cloud. She concentrated, and slowly the flickering images began to come into focus.

Not seaweed. Grass.

The grasses of the marsh, but larger, towering over her head, as they seemed to the night of her vision of Miranda's death. She had the sensation of being in the marsh herself, but not on any of the paths. Instead she was close to the ground, threading her way through the tangle, moving quickly and smoothly, almost as if her feet weren't touching the soggy earth at all.

The tingling in her fingers grew stronger, and the vision in her mind suddenly changed. She was out of the marsh now, gliding over a thick carpet of coarse grass, and around her immense trees, much larger than she'd ever seen before, towered overhead. A little bit ahead of her she saw a form lying on the ground and heard the rasping sounds of labored breathing. But there was something strange about the breathing, and as she concentrated even harder, she realized that it sounded amplified.

Indeed, everything was being amplified.

She could actually hear the sounds of the blades of grass as they rubbed against each other beneath her, and a few yards away she heard a soft rustling sound which she instantly knew was a mouse searching in a thicket for food.

Then the form lying on the grass moved and looked up.

It was Rosemary, her face bleeding from a deep gash on her right cheek. Her left hand was still clamped over the cuts on her right arm and tears were flowing from her eyes.

Now Cassie understood what was happening.

I'm seeing it. I'm seeing it all through Sumi's eyes, just as he saw it a few minutes ago. . . .

Slowly the vision dissolved and her mind cleared. Once again she was looking into Sumi's glowing golden eyes, and as the tingling faded from her fingers, she felt once more the soft warmth of his fur.

"You told me, didn't you?" she said softly. "When you jumped up into my arms, that's the first thing you did."

As if he understood her words, the cat began purring agreeably, and nestled deeper into her lap. Then his eyes closed, his ears flicked a couple of times, and he went to sleep.

Ever since, Cassie had been sitting by the window, trying to decide what it meant.

Maybe it wasn't Rosemary at all. Maybe she had only imagined the whole thing. But she knew she hadn't, knew that what she'd felt emanating from the memory of the cat into her fingers and then up into her own mind had been the truth.

So that was what Miranda had been talking about, that was the gift she'd given her. She could communicate with Sumi. She could see what the cat saw, and hear what it heard.

Instantly she knew that the dream she'd had the night Miranda died was no dream at all. Sumi had actually seen Miranda die, and then come back home and shown it to her. So there *had* been someone out there that night.

Someone who had killed Miranda.

But who? And why?

And then, unbidden, another memory came back to her.

Eric staring at her on the beach.

In her mind she melded his image with the one she'd seen in Sumi's memory, then rejected it.

It couldn't be right. It simply couldn't!

She squeezed her eyes shut and tried once again to visualize the figure as it bent over Miranda, but she could not make it out. Though she tried with every ounce of concentration she could bring to bear, the face eluded her as though her inner vision had been blocked.

Tears flooding her eyes, she looked down at Sumi once more. Could he do the same thing? Could he see what she saw, and feel what she felt? Could he really understand her?

Deep in her soul she felt that he could. There was some kind of bond between them, and yesterday, when she had imagined Sumi attacking Mr. Simms, the cat had understood and carried out her wishes.

But she hadn't really meant to hurt Mr. Simms, had she?

She searched in the deep recesses of her mind, and after a while found a cold black place that was filled with anger— and she knew that there, where all her darkest demons dwelt, was a part of her that could easily have killed Mr. Simms yesterday if it had been given a chance.

But everyone had a place like that. It was where you hid your worst hatreds away, concealing them from yourself as well as everyone else, and you didn't do anything about them. You put them away there, and kept them under control, and after a while you forgot about them.

That was the part of herself she'd been exploring yesterday when Sumi had attacked the teacher. But somehow the cat had understood her anger and acted upon it.

Was that what Sumi was? Some kind of weapon her very mind could use to strike back?

As if in answer to her unspoken question, the cat stirred

in her lap and its pink tongue came out to lick gently at her fingers.

Then what was Kiska, the ghostly white hawk that perched constantly on the rooftop?

But she already knew the answer to that.

He was her guardian, there to protect her, to drive off anyone or anything that threatened her.

But why had he attacked Rosemary? What had Rosemary wanted? Perhaps she hadn't wanted anything, and the bird would attack anyone unless Cassie herself told him not to.

And she could have.

She'd sensed it while she was on the beach, known that if she pointed up at the bird and told it to go back to the rooftop, it would have obeyed her instantly.

But she hadn't.

Instead she'd let it attack.

But she hadn't known who it was, she told herself. She hadn't known who it was or what the person wanted. And besides, Kiska wasn't really her bird. He just lived there, didn't he? It wasn't her fault he'd attacked. And what if she hadn't been there? Then there wouldn't have been anybody to stop him.

But she *was* there, and she *hadn't* stopped him.

She shivered slightly. From now on, she knew, she would have to be very careful. She couldn't allow herself ever again to get as angry as she had been at Mr. Simms, couldn't allow herself to imagine hurting anyone else.

Slowly she began to understand Miranda's words. 'Don't let them hurt you. You must never let them hurt you.' She couldn't let anyone hurt her anymore, because if she did, she might be tempted to release the demons in that dark place in her mind, and along with the demons, the animals that understood her darkest fantasies. . . .

Something glinted in the sun beyond the window, and the flash of light in her eye brought Cassie out of her reverie. Turning, she looked out at the marsh and recognized Gene Templeton making his way toward the cabin through the reeds. With each step the sun flashed off the reflective lenses of his sunglasses, and Cassie blinked against the sudden glare. Cradling Sumi in her right arm, she got out of the chair and went closer to the window. She could see that the police chief was carrying something, but for a second she didn't realize what it was. Then she recognized the object.

A rifle.

She gasped as she realized what it must mean, and hurried to the front door. As she opened it she heard a quick rustling of wings, and realized that Kiska had already taken off from his perch. She stepped out onto the front porch and looked up, shading her eyes against the sun.

The bird was spiraling upward in what Cassie knew was a first preparation for an attack.

Gene Templeton stopped short when the white hawk suddenly lifted off the rooftop and raised the rifle to his shoulder. He put his eye to the telescopic sight and a moment later found his target. But the bird was circling rapidly, and he knew that until it reached altitude and started toward him, he wouldn't be able to hold the gun on target long enough to get a shot. Only when the bird chose a direction and he could gauge its speed closely enough to determine how far to lead it, could he risk taking a shot, for he knew that if he missed on the first one, he wouldn't get a second chance. His attention riveted on the bird, he didn't see the cabin door open and Cassie step out onto the low porch.

Cassie herself wasn't sure what to do. Should she summon the bird back to the roof, or just let him go? But what if he went after the policeman? Her mind in turmoil, she watched anxiously as the hawk reached the apex of its climb and leveled off. And then she realized that he was going to be all right.

Kiska knew what was going to happen and was flying the other way. She let out a sigh of relief.

The target steady in the sight, Templeton carefully lined up the cross hairs. In the magnification of the lens the bird loomed large, its wings beating steadily, the muscles of its back working rhythmically. It was flying almost directly away from him, and Templeton realized he needn't lead it at all.

Simply line it up and squeeze the trigger.

Slowly, carefully, he steadied the gun and gently began to apply pressure to the trigger.

A sharp report exploded from the barrel and the stock of the gun recoiled into his shoulder. In the sky the bird jerked and a few feathers seemed to pop away from it. Templeton quickly put his eye to the sight again and found the target.

It was tumbling through the air now, a red stain spreading through its feathers.

Then, as he watched the bird fall toward the ground, a piercing scream rent the quiet that had followed the gunshot.

Cassie, still standing on the porch, heard the gun's report and saw Kiska suddenly tumble in the sky. But the scream that erupted from her throat was not one of fury, but of pain, for at the moment the bullet had struck the white hawk, a searing pain had shot through her back and into her chest. As Sumi yowled in sudden alarm and leaped out of her arms, Cassie's knees buckled and she sank down onto the porch, then rolled off the single step and onto the ground itself. The pain burned within her, and her hands clutched at her breast as if attempting to close a wound.

Templeton, startled by the scream, let the rifle drop away from his shoulder and looked at the cabin just as Cassie collapsed to the ground.

"What the hell . . . ?" Templeton whispered under his breath, already breaking into a lumbering run. What had happened? He couldn't have shot her—he'd only fired a single shell, and he'd seen the bullet hit the bird. And even if he'd fired twice, he couldn't have shot that wildly. He couldn't have!

He burst out of the marsh and pounded up the low hill, then dropped onto the ground next to the writhing girl. Her face was twisted into a mask of pain and low moans bubbled out of her lips.

"It's all right, Cassie," Templeton told her. "It's all right. I'm here!"

Setting the rifle aside, he grasped her wrists to pull her hands away from the wound she was clutching. She fought against him, twisting away, trying to escape his grip, but he was much too strong for her. At last she let her arms relax slightly, and her hands came away from her chest.

Nothing.

No blood, no hole where a bullet might have passed through the man's white shirt she was wearing, nothing at all.

Still whimpering, she rolled over and Templeton was able to examine her back as well.

It, too, showed no signs of any kind of wound.

And yet there was no question the girl was in terrible pain, for her eyes had glazed over with shock and she was still moaning softly.

He ran his hands over her limbs, looking for broken bones, but found none. Finally, leaving the rifle where it lay, he picked her up and started back through the marsh, toward the squad car.

Cassie lay in the hospital bed, staring out the window at the setting sun. The pain still throbbed in her chest, and she knew that no matter what the doctor said, she wasn't imagining it.

"But something *must* have happened to her," she heard her father insisting through the open door to the hall. "You heard what Gene said. She was in shock, for Christ's sake!"

"I know what Gene said," Samuels replied patiently, "but I also know that I've examined her and I can't find anything wrong. Nothing at all. No marks, no cuts, nothing. I've looked at the X rays at least five times, and there's no internal damage either. If you want to, we can go over them again. The only thing I can tell you is that she's not hurt."

"Then what happened?" Keith asked. "Gene claims he shot the bird—though what the hell he was doing out there with a gun when Cassie was out there, too, is something that's beyond me—but he can't find the bird. He says he saw it drop, and knows where it came down. But it's not there. So how do we know he shot it at all?"

Samuels shrugged, but when he spoke, his voice clearly revealed that he was running out of patience. "Fine. He didn't shoot it. Frankly, I don't really give a damn about the hawk, but his not finding it doesn't prove a thing either. By the time he got back, a raccoon could have gotten it. But he didn't shoot Cassie. You don't shoot someone and not leave a wound. It's a physical impossibility."

Keith's eyes narrowed angrily. "So you're telling me Cassie's faking, is that it?"

The doctor licked his lips and shook his head. "I'm not

telling you that at all. In fact I'm sure her pain is quite real. But that doesn't mean a bullet caused it."

"Then what did?" Keith asked, his voice icy.

"A hysterical response. She saw the bird get shot, and she felt the pain herself."

"That's your answer to everything this week, isn't it?" Keith asked, making no attempt to keep the sarcasm from his voice. "Isn't that pretty much what you had to say about Harold Simms?"

Samuels's eyes glinted darkly but he kept his anger under control. "All I can do is tell you my diagnosis," he said evenly. "If you want a second opinion, I'll be more than happy to refer you to someone. But frankly, I think any other doctor will agree with me. There just aren't any wounds." Noticing the open door to Cassie's room, he reached out and closed it, then lowered his voice. "If you want my opinion, Keith, I think you might want to have her talk to a psychiatrist. After everything she's been through in the last couple of weeks, she's got to be in a lot of emotional pain. What we're seeing today could be symptomatic of that."

Keith's brows arched. "So we send her off to Eastbury along with Simms, and don't deal with it, right? Sorry, Paul, I don't work that way, not with my own daughter." Before the doctor could say anything else, Keith turned away and let himself into Cassie's room, closing the door behind him.

"Hi, Punkin," he said gently, forcing a smile. "How're you feeling?"

Cassie looked at him suspiciously. Why had they closed the door a minute ago? What were they saying that they didn't want her to hear? But she already knew.

They were talking about whether she was crazy or not. But she knew she wasn't.

But if they decided she was . . .

"I'm okay," she said softly, struggling not to let the pain in her chest show on her face. "I just—I don't know what happened, Daddy. But I'm all right now. Really I am. Can—can I go home?"

Keith frowned. "Are you sure you feel well enough?"

Cassie nodded. "It's almost gone," she said, though the pain still felt like a hot poker had been stabbed into her.

Then her eyes met her father's. "How's Rosemary?" she asked. "Is she all right?"

Keith nodded. "Dr. Samuels says it's not bad at all."

"I'm sorry," Cassie said. "If I'd known it was her, I wouldn't have let Kiska do it."

"Let him do it? What do you mean?"

"I didn't know who it was," Cassie explained. "If I'd known, I would have told him to leave her alone. Really I would."

Keith grinned crookedly. "Honey, you can't tell a hawk what to do. Not unless you've been training him for years. And even then you can't always stop them from attacking. It wasn't your fault. Anyway, none of it matters anymore. The hawk's dead."

Cassie shook her head. "Mr. Templeton shot him, but he's not dead."

The grin faded from Keith's face and his eyes darkened. "He isn't?" he asked. "How do you know that?"

Cassie hesitated, then shrugged. "I just know, that's all."

She wasn't about to tell her father that during the hours she had spent in the hospital, she'd figured out what was happening to her. It sounded too crazy.

But she knew that the pain in her chest wasn't her pain at all.

It was Kiska's pain, and it was being transmitted to her.

But it was all right, and she could bear it, for she knew what the pain meant.

It meant that Kiska was alive somewhere. He was injured, but he was alive.

If he was dead, she wouldn't still be feeling the pain, for it would have died with him.

Now she had to conceal the pain until he got well and came back to her.

Chapter 17

For five days Cassie stayed in her room, lying on her bed—fighting against the deep burning pain in her chest. But each time Rosemary suggested that she should see the doctor again, Cassie had shaken her head.

"It's getting better," she'd insisted. "And there isn't anything he can do. I just have to get over it."

On Monday Rosemary went to Samuels herself, and while he changed the bandages on her cheek and forehead, she talked worriedly about her stepdaughter. But to her surprise, the doctor agreed with Cassie. "She's having an emotional reaction," he told her. "The best thing you can do is simply give her some time. If it weren't getting better, I'd agree with you. In fact I'd insist she see a psychiatrist. But if she says she's feeling better, just leave her alone. Keep an eye on her, but don't push her."

Samuels's advice seemed to work, and for the next four days Cassie came downstairs each morning, picking at her breakfast then insisting on doing the dishes and cleaning up the kitchen before returning to her room.

Then, on Friday morning, Cassie came down from her room dressed for school, her face pale but set in determination. "I'm going back to school," she announced.

Keith's eyes clouded with doubt. "Are you sure that's a good idea? Maybe you ought to wait until Monday. Missing one more day isn't—"

"But I want to go back," Cassie insisted. "I'm fine now,

and if I go today, at least I can get all the work I missed and do it over the weekend."

She left the house right after breakfast and walked slowly through the town, surprised by how quickly spring had taken over. The morning was warm, and there was a softness to the air. The trees, their leaves only budding ten days ago, were bursting with a vibrant green, and tulips were blooming everywhere, dotting the village with bright patches of color. There was a freshness and promise of new beginnings to everything which imbued Cassie with a sense of well-being she had never felt before.

The last vague twinges of pain in her chest left her, and as she approached the school, even it seemed to have changed. The chestnut trees surrounding the old frame building were in full leaf, softening the lines of the structure, and the lawn of the playing field had taken on a brighter green than it had displayed ten days ago.

But as she mounted the front steps, Cassie's good feelings began to fade away. She passed through the knots of chattering teenagers and conversations suddenly stopped, voices dropping to whispers.

Her skin tingled with the now familiar sensation of eyes watching her.

It doesn't matter, she told herself. None of it matters, and this time I'm not going to run away. Eric was right—I can't not ever go to school again. So I'll ignore them, and after a while they'll forget all about me.

Taking a deep breath, she quickly climbed the stairs to the second floor, and long before the first bell rang, she was already in her seat. Today, at least, she wouldn't feel everyone staring at her as she came in late.

The morning dragged by, and each time she had to change classrooms, Cassie moved through the halls with the strange detached air of a zombie. It was as if there were some sort of force field around her, and wherever she went, the crowds in the corridors seemed to part for her, as if the other students were now afraid even of brushing up against her. She did her best to pretend she didn't notice, looking straight ahead, her face an expressionless mask.

By the end of the third period the urge to run away was upon her, but she refused to give in to it.

Don't let them hurt you, she reminded herself over and over again. Slowly the rhythm of the words became a silent chant, and eventually she imagined that Miranda herself was with her, whispering the words in her ear, giving her strength.

Maybe Miranda really is with me, Cassie thought as the last bell of the morning rang and she started slowly toward the cafeteria, willing her feet to move even though every fiber of her being wanted to turn and flee. After all, this is how Miranda had felt.

Every day of her life Miranda felt like this, Cassie thought—no one speaking to her, no one even smiling at her.

But staring at her.

Always staring at her.

The noise in the cafeteria seemed to dry up the moment Cassie opened the door and stepped inside, but she did her best to ignore it once more, moving slowly down the line, pushing the plastic tray in front of her, selecting food automatically, without even realizing what she was putting on her tray.

And all the time she could feel the eyes of the gathered students boring into her back, watching her slow progress toward the cashier.

Wordlessly she fished in her book bag for her wallet and paid the cashier, who glanced up at her for a moment, then looked again.

"Are you all right?" the woman asked tentatively.

Cassie nodded mutely, though she could feel a clammy sheen of sweat on her forehead and her legs were trembling. But the cashier wasn't satisfied.

"Maybe you ought to go to the office and lie down for a few minutes," she said. "My goodness, you're so pale you look like you've seen a ghost!"

Instantly the cafeteria erupted with laughter. Cassie's eyes brimmed with tears as she tried to pick up the tray, but her hands were shaking too badly, and the glass overturned, splashing water into the bowl of macaroni and cheese.

Then she heard a voice behind her.

Eric's voice.

"I'll take it," he said. "There's a table over there by the window. Come on."

Relief flooding through her, Cassie let Eric take the tray, then followed him as he walked quickly through the tables filled with snickering teenagers. One of them stuck a foot in Eric's way, but he deftly stepped over it, throwing the boy a dirty look as he passed. By the time they reached the table, the last of the giggles had died away, but when Cassie glanced around, she could see the kids whispering among themselves.

Eric seemed to read her mind.

"If you let them get to you, they'll never quit," he said, setting Cassie's tray on the table. He fished his sack lunch out of the depths of his book bag, looked at the contents of the brown paper bag sourly, then grinned crookedly at Cassie. "Trade you a soggy sandwich for the macaroni and cheese."

"It's soggy too," Cassie replied, her voice quavering as she struggled to keep her emotions in check.

"That's okay," Eric told her. "I'm just so sick of tomato sandwiches, I could puke." He held up the unappetizing mess of white bread, limp lettuce, and thin slices of tomato, but Cassie shook her head.

"Take the macaroni and cheese anyway," she said. "I hate it, and I'm not very hungry."

"Then why'd you buy it?"

Cassie shrugged. "I had to buy something, didn't I? Anyway, I wasn't really looking at the food." She fell silent, but her eyes darted around the room, and Eric nodded.

"Want to know what they've been saying?"

Cassie swallowed hard, trying to clear the lump that had risen in her throat, but she nodded.

"Well, everybody has a slightly different version, but the main idea is that you're crazy."

Cassie flinched but said nothing, and Eric managed another grin. "But it's not so bad, really."

"Not so bad?" Cassie breathed. "You don't know—they've been staring at me all morning, and nobody will talk to me. It's—it's the same way everybody treated Miranda."

Eric met her eyes. "I know," he said. "They're treating me the same way."

Cassie stared back at him. "You? But—but—"

"It's because of Simms. Everyone's sure you did some-

thing to him, and since I was with you, they think I must
have helped you."

"But we didn't do anything to him," Cassie protested.

"No one cares what we say," Eric said, his voice bitter.
He leaned closer. "But it isn't just that," he whispered. "I've
been spending a lot of time out in the marsh."

"The marsh?"

Eric nodded. "Everybody heard about what happened
out there. So I went out and looked for Kiska." He glanced
around quickly, and his voice dropped even further. "Cassie,
I found him."

Cassie gasped, then covered her mouth with her hand.
"Where is he?" she asked. "Is he all right?"

Eric nodded quickly. "He was almost dead when I found
him. He was about a quarter of a mile from the cabin. There's
a big bush out there with vines all over it, and he was inside
the bush. When I found him he couldn't even walk, and for a
minute I thought he was dead. There was blood all over him.
Anyway, I took a cage out there and sort of bandaged him up,
and I've been going out there every day, taking him food."

"And he's really okay?" Cassie asked anxiously.

"He's almost well again. He can stand up, and he takes
the food right out of my hand—"

"Monday," Cassie said softly, her eyes suddenly boring
into Eric. "He started standing up again on Monday, didn't
he?"

Eric looked at her quizzically. "How'd you know that?"

"Because that's the day I got up," Cassie replied, her
voice taking on an edge of excitement. "I knew I was feeling
what Kiska was feeling, and that proves it, doesn't it? I was
getting better, but I couldn't really get up until Monday. And
now I'm all right again." Suddenly her eyes were sparkling.
"And I bet that means Kiska can fly now. Let's go out there.
Right after school, let's go let him out of the cage."

But Eric shook his head. "I can't. Not right after school.
I got back on the baseball team, and I can't miss practice.
And if anybody sees you go out there . . ." His voice trailed
off, but Cassie knew what he meant.

She glanced quickly around and saw Lisa Chambers
glaring at them. "Is that why they've started staring at you
too?" she asked. "Because someone saw you going out there?"

Eric's gaze wavered for a split second, then he nodded. "I—I always act like I'm going to the cabin, but then I go down the hill on the other side of it." Suddenly his eyes flashed with anger. "Anyway, it doesn't matter. If they all want to think I'm crazy, let them. They're all just like my dad—it doesn't matter what you do, it's always the wrong thing."

"But why didn't you tell them?" Cassie asked. "All you were doing was taking care of Kiska—"

"Are you serious?" Eric demanded. "They would have told, and then Templeton would have gone out and killed him. Why do you think I left him there in the first place?"

"But it's not fair," Cassie protested.

Eric's eyes darkened. "So who ever said anything was supposed to be fair? Nobody was ever fair to Miranda, either, and look what happened to her. But it's not going to happen to us," he added, his voice taking on a bitter edge. "I won't let it happen to us."

Cassie looked at him, her eyes frightened almost as much by his tone as his words. "But—but what can we do?" she asked.

"There's some things," he said, and smiled. "For starters we can let them all know they're not getting to us. From now on we act like nothing's the matter at all. If they want to stare, let them stare. If they want to talk, let them talk. And tomorrow we'll go let Kiska out of his cage. Okay?"

Cassie smiled gratefully. "Okay," she agreed.

"Come on," Eric said. He shoved the remnants of his lunch back in the bag and dropped the crumpled bag on Cassie's tray. Then, with his book bag in one hand and the tray in the other, he weaved his way between the tables, Cassie right behind him. They were halfway to the doors when Lisa Chambers's voice stopped them.

"What are you doing, Eric?" she asked, her tone saccharine sweet. "Playing nursemaid to the poor little crazy girl?"

Cassie felt her face burn with humiliation, but as she tried to hurry past the table, Eric dropped his book bag and grasped her arm, stopping her. "If that's what you want to think, Lisa, fine," he said. "But if you really want to know, it isn't that at all."

Lisa blinked uncertainly. She'd expected Eric to blush as

deeply as Cassie, and ignore her. Instead he was looking right at her, his eyes mocking her.

"Actually I was inviting her to the dance tomorrow night. See you there." He dropped Cassie's arm, reached down and picked up the book bag, then started once more toward the door, Cassie hurrying after him.

Lisa sat still, a wave of cold anger washing over her.

What was Eric doing?

Until today—without Cassie Winslow coming to school—everything had been just as it always had been. Every day Eric sat with her at lunch, and she waited for him until baseball practice was over, then he walked her home. He'd never even mentioned Cassie Winslow.

And the day before yesterday he'd asked *her* to the dance.

Now she could feel her friends staring at her, and hear Allayne Garvey snickering. She glared at Allayne, daring her to say anything.

Allayne's snickering only grew into a laugh. "Didn't you say he was all done with her?" she asked, throwing Teri Bennett a knowing look. "I thought he was taking *you* to the dance."

"He was," Lisa said stiffly, doing her best to conceal both her anger and her disappointment. "But I changed my mind. I broke the date yesterday."

Allayne rolled her eyes. "Sure you did," she said. "That must have been while I was flying to the moon, wasn't it? Come off it, Lisa—he dumped you again. All she had to do was show up, and he went right back to her." She winked at Teri. "And you can't really blame him, can you? I mean, she *is* pretty."

Lisa's lips tightened and her eyes narrowed to angry slits, but she said nothing. A cold knot of hatred toward Cassie Winslow formed in her belly like a lead weight. Somehow, she would get even with Cassie.

She didn't know how, but she would find a way.

"What were you talking about?" Cassie asked. There were still a few minutes before the lunch hour would end, and they were sitting outside, their faces tipped up to the sun. "You didn't ask me to a dance. What dance?"

Eric glanced over at her, then closed his eyes again. "The one tomorrow night. Don't you want to go?"

Cassie started to shake her head. It was bad enough having everyone stare at her at school all day long. But to have to spend an entire evening—

She couldn't stand it. Just the idea of it terrified her. Then she remembered what Eric had told her at lunch time, and Miranda's words. "All right," she said quietly. "I'll go."

Eric smiled at her. "I knew you would."

Chapter 18

When Rosemary came downstairs Saturday morning she found Keith already sitting at the breakfast table, his marine charts and tide tables spread out before him. That, together with the phone call he'd gotten earlier, could mean only one thing.

"You have a charter?" she asked.

Keith nodded, not looking up. "Some guys from Boston. They'll be here at noon."

"It—it's awfully short notice, isn't it?" she asked.

Keith glanced up at her, the quaver in her voice catching his attention. He shrugged. "That's the way this business is. You take the jobs as they come, and if you turn them down, they don't call again."

"But . . ." She fell silent. It wasn't the first time this had happened, and it wouldn't be the last.

Under normal circumstances, it wouldn't have bothered her. But the circumstances weren't normal. Hadn't been normal since the day Cassie had come to live with them. Now, for the first time, he was going to leave her alone with this strange girl she hardly knew, and of whom she was beginning to be desperately afraid.

Cassie herself, her food untouched, was staring out the window, a faraway look in her eyes as she gently stroked Sumi's gray fur.

Jennifer, her eyes wary—as if she knew something had

gone wrong in the house but wasn't sure what—was poking nervously at her eggs.

"Hurry up and finish them," Rosemary said automatically. "As soon as they're gone, you can go outside and play."

Jennifer frowned. "I don't want to go outside. There isn't anyone to play with."

Rosemary shot a glance at Keith, who had finally pushed his charts aside and was looking at Jennifer now. "Why don't you go to the park?" she heard him ask. "There's always someone over there, isn't there?"

Jennifer nodded uncertainly. "But Wendy Maynard always goes there, and she doesn't like me anymore."

"She doesn't?" Keith asked. Rosemary saw his eyes flick toward her then return to his youngest daughter. "Why not?"

Jennifer opened her mouth to say something, glanced at Cassie, and seemed to change her mind. "I don't know," she said, but her eyes evaded her father's. She slid off her chair. "May I be excused, please?"

Keith hesitated, then nodded.

Now Cassie emerged from her reverie and smiled at Jennifer. "What if I go with you?" she asked. "Would that be fun?"

The little girl looked uncertain. "I—I don't know."

"Come on," Cassie urged. "We can play on the swings and do the teeter-totter, and anything else you want." Jennifer still seemed unconvinced, and Cassie turned anxiously to her father. "It's all right, isn't it?"

Keith shrugged. "If you're sure you're up to it."

"I'm fine," Cassie said. And indeed, this morning she was feeling even better than yesterday. There was only a trace of the pain left in her chest, and on her back, where she'd first felt the blinding stab of agony when Kiska had been shot, there was only a faint itching, like a scab that was about to fall off.

"Great," Keith said. He swung Jennifer off her feet as she tried to dart past him, and planted a kiss on her cheek. "Aren't you going to say good-bye to your old dad?"

" 'Bye," Jennifer replied, kissing him back.

He put her back down and she dashed out into the morning sunshine. Grinning happily, Keith turned to Cassie once more. "Take good care of your sister while I'm gone, okay?"

Cassie nodded, then she, too, disappeared out the back door. When she was gone, the smile on Keith's face faded and he turned to Rosemary. "Now, what is all this?" he asked. "It's obvious you don't want me to take this charter. And I presume it has to do with Cassie. Right?"

Rosemary took a deep breath. "I just . . . well, I just don't feel comfortable with her, that's all."

Keith's eyes rolled impatiently. "For God's sake, haven't we been through this before? She's fine now."

"She's not fine!" Rosemary snapped. "She wouldn't leave the house for over a week, and when she came home yesterday, she didn't say a word about school. All she did was go over to the cemetery and sit by Miranda's grave. She sat there for more than an hour, Keith. I watched her and it was— Well, it was just weird. She had that awful cat on her lap, and she was sitting on the grass next to the grave, petting the cat and talking to herself. Maybe you call that normal, but I don't!"

"Oh, for God's sake," Keith rasped. "She's having a rough time, and except for Eric, Miranda was the only person in town who was nice to her. So is it a crime that she went to visit her grave?"

"But it isn't just that," Rosemary pleaded.

"Then what is it?" Keith demanded.

Rosemary cast around in her mind for something concrete, something Keith couldn't simply dismiss. "All right. Before we came downstairs I told her she had to clean her room this morning. Instead she's off playing in the park with Jen."

"So? Maybe she forgot."

Now Rosemary's eyes flashed. "Or maybe she was just playing us off against each other!"

"Make up your mind," Keith said, his voice taking on a cutting edge of sarcasm. "Is she crazy, or is she manipulative, or is she both?" The sarcasm gave way to cold anger. "Or are you just imagining things?" Turning his back on her, Keith returned to his marine charts.

When he started out of the house twenty minutes later, the anger between them still hung heavy in the atmosphere.

Rosemary knew he wouldn't be back before he took the boat out. "Keith?" she blurted. He turned back, but his hand stayed on the half-open screen door. As their eyes met, she could see that he was in as much pain as she.

"I'm sorry," she whispered. She went to him and slipped her arms around him, burying her face against his chest. "We can't just leave it like this. Please?"

She felt him stiffen for a moment, but his arms went around her and he held her close. "It's going to be all right, baby," he whispered. "I'm sorry too. But I just can't believe there's anything really wrong with her."

Rosemary hesitated, then nodded, her head pressed close to his chest. "When will you be back?"

"Tuesday, maybe Wednesday. They weren't sure." He held her away from him then. "And you can always get me on the radio. You know that. Okay?"

She hesitated, wanting to beg him not to go, to back out of the charter just this once. But in the end she nodded again. "I love you."

"I love you too."

And then he was gone, and Rosemary was alone.

Cassie was pushing Jennifer on one of the swings when she first saw Lisa Chambers and Teri Bennett walking along Oak Street. At first she thought they were going to pass by without noticing her. But then Lisa glanced in her direction and came to an abrupt stop, putting out a hand to stop Teri as well. At Cassie's feet Sumi opened his eyes and stood, a soft mewing emerging from him as he pressed himself against her legs and twined his tail around her calf.

"Would you look at that?" Cassie heard Lisa say loudly to Teri, intending to be overheard. "Do you believe Mrs. Winslow's letting her take care of Jennifer? She must be as crazy as Cassie is!"

Swallowing the sudden surge of anger that rose in her, Cassie forgot the swing.

"Push me," Jennifer called out. "How come you stopped?" Then, as the swing gradually came to a stop, Jennifer saw the two girls standing at the edge of the park, watching them. "Just pretend they're not there," she told Cassie. "Maybe they'll go away."

Instead, Lisa left the sidewalk and started across the lawn toward them. When she was a few yards away she stopped again, her lips twisted into a cruel smile. "Didn't anyone tell you about Cassie?" she asked, her eyes fixed on Jennifer.

Jennifer got up from the swing and moved next to Cassie. "Tell me what?" she asked, her eyes narrowing suspiciously.

Lisa's eyes glinted maliciously. "That she's a witch, just like Miranda was."

Jennifer gasped. "Th-that's not true," she stammered. But in her head she heard an echo of Wendy Maynard's singsong chant after school yesterday. "Cassie is a wi-itch. Cassie is a wi-itch."

"How do you know?" Lisa taunted. "She has a cat, doesn't she? Don't all witches have cats?"

Cassie, her temples throbbing with anger, stepped forward. "Stop it, Lisa," she said. "Why do you want to scare her? She's only a little girl."

"Why should I stop it?" Lisa sneered. "Maybe it's true! Besides, what can you do about it? You don't have Miranda's hawk anymore, do you? Mr. Templeton shot it! So what are you going to do?"

Cassie's eyes narrowed and she reached down to pick Sumi up. His body was tense, and the fur on his hackles was standing up stiffly. His soft mewling had turned into a hiss, and she could feel his claws flexing.

"Do you want me to let Sumi go?" she asked. "Is that what you want me to do?"

Lisa's twisted grin faded slightly. "You think I'm afraid of a crummy cat?" she asked. "Or are you going to put a hex on me?" Bolstered by her own words, she grinned again and turned her attention back to Jennifer. "That's what she did to Mr. Simms, Jennifer. She put a hex on him and made him go crazy. Is that what you want her to do to you too? Make you as crazy as Mr. Simms?"

Jennifer was trembling now. Suddenly all the stories she'd heard about Miranda came back to her. Instinctively she took a step away from Cassie, and Lisa saw the movement.

"That's right. You'd better get away from her. If I were you, I wouldn't even want to sleep in the same house with her. You don't know what she might do to you in the middle of the night, do you?"

With that, Cassie's anger erupted. "Stop it!" she shouted. "Stop it right now!"

"Why?" Lisa taunted. "What are you going to do about it?"

Cassie froze, and Miranda's words echoed once more in her mind. *Don't let them hurt you.*

But it was too late, and she ignored Miranda's words, letting her anger run free.

"I'll kill you," she shouted, her eyes burning with tears. "If you don't leave me alone, I'll kill you!"

For a moment Lisa said nothing, but then her mouth opened and an ugly peal of laughter burst from her throat. "You can go to hell, Cassie Winslow," she shouted. "In fact, why don't you? Nobody wants you around here!" Still laughing, she turned back to Teri Bennett. "Come on," she said. "Let's get out of here before she cracks up completely."

Cassie stared after Lisa, fury churning inside her. She could feel it coursing through her, making her whole body shake.

Her limbs trembled with it, and after a moment she felt Sumi begin trembling too. Suddenly the cat leaped from her arms and streaked across the park after Lisa.

No! Cassie thought. *Stop!*

Instantly the cat stopped running and turned back to look at Cassie. Both the girl and the animal stood frozen for a split second. Then the cat—as if obeying some unspoken order—trotted back and rubbed itself against Cassie's leg.

The tight knot of anger in Eric Cavanaugh's belly hadn't relaxed in the slightest, despite the three hours of hard work he'd put himself through since the fight with his father that morning.

He still wasn't exactly sure what had triggered Ed's explosion, unless it had been the mere sight of Cassie Winslow coming out of the house next door.

"What you starin' at, boy?" his father had growled.

Eric looked up from his plate of greasy hominy cakes— the breakfast his father insisted on every Saturday morning, and which Eric and Laura did their best to pretend they liked, though the very sight of them made both of them slightly nauseated. He shook his head. "I'm not staring at anything—"

"Don't you lie to me, Mr. Smartmouth," Ed had cut in, his eyes glittering dangerously. "Don't you think I know what goes on in that head of yours?"

Frowning in puzzlement, Eric had glanced out the window just in time to see Cassie and Jennifer disappearing around the corner onto Cambridge Avenue. "I wasn't staring at anything, Dad," he insisted, though he knew that arguing with his father was useless. Once Ed had made up his mind about something, there was no changing it.

"You were starin' at *her*!" his father snapped, pushing his chair back and rising to his feet so abruptly that the chair tipped over and crashed to the floor. Eric flinched involuntarily, and his father's mouth twisted into a vicious smile of victory. "Thought you could fool me, didn't you?"

"Leave him alone, Ed," Laura pleaded, standing next to the sink. "Can't you just let him finish his breakfast? He wasn't looking at anyone!"

Ed's hangover-induced fury quickly shifted focus, and he sneered at Laura. "How's anybody 'sposed to eat this slop?" he demanded.

"I thought you liked it—" Laura blurted, then stopped herself. But it was too late.

Ed's hand snaked out to strike her across the face with enough force to knock her off balance. She stumbled, then fell to the floor, her head banging against the door of the cupboard below the sink. "Don't you argue with me, you worthless bitch," he stormed.

"Stop it, Dad!" Eric yelled. "She didn't do anything to you, and neither did I. Why don't you just go get drunk and leave us alone!"

Trembling, Ed faced his son, but this time Eric, who was on his feet now, showed no fear. "Try it, Dad," he said quietly. "Just go ahead and try it. I'm done letting you beat up on me for things I never did."

Ed's eyes flickered uncertainly. "You ain't big enough to take your old man," he snarled, certain that the words alone would be enough to cow Eric.

But Eric's jaw only tightened. "Try it, Dad," he challenged. "Just go ahead and try it. I'll kick the shit out of you so fast you won't even remember what happened."

For a moment Ed wavered, and Eric had been certain his father was going to swing at him. If he did, Eric would have to make up his mind what to do. Would he really strike back at his own father? No, not yet. It wasn't quite time. Not quite.

But instead of taking a swing at him, Ed had shambled toward the door. "Some goddamn son you are," he mumbled. "What kind of kid threatens his old man?" Then he was gone, and both Eric and Laura knew where he was going. He'd start out drinking on his boat, then move to the Whaler's Inn. And when he was drunk enough, he'd come home.

When they were alone, Eric had tried to help his mother, but she'd shaken her head and waved him away. "Just leave me alone," she said, her voice muffled. "I'll be all right."

He'd gone outside then, and begun the weekly routine of yardwork, but even the work hadn't helped. His mind refused to concentrate on the job.

Instead he kept thinking about the rage growing within him.

It wasn't just his father anymore, he knew. The anger was spilling over now, onto his mother too. . . .

Before—when the rage had grown to the point where he thought he might burst—he'd always gone to the marsh and talked to Miranda.

Always—since he was ten years old, and Miranda had come home from the hospital—she'd been there for him. He had been able to go out to her cabin and sit with her—Sumi snuggled comfortably in his lap—and pour out the rage. And no matter how bad it had been—how filled with hatred he'd been—Miranda had always listened to him, comforted him, and accepted him. She'd been his friend, always there.

She had taught him how to control the rage, how to use it, how to bury it so deep that no one else even knew it was there.

She had taught him how to survive.

And then Cassie had come, and Miranda—the only person who had ever been Eric's alone—had taken her in too.

"She's just like you, Eric," Miranda had told him on that last afternoon when he'd gone to visit her. "And I've known her just as long. I found her the same day I found you, when you were both so young. And I won't turn away from her. I won't, and you mustn't either. She needs us, Eric. She needs both of us."

That day his rage had turned for the first time on Miranda. But he'd kept it under control, hidden it so deep that even she—who could see everything—hadn't been able to see it. And then, late that night, he'd gone back to the marsh.

But even after Miranda had died, even after he'd finally given in to the rage within him, it hadn't stopped.

Instead the fury only seemed to feed on itself, growing ever stronger.

And then, the day Simms threw him off the baseball team, Miranda's words came back to him. But Miranda had been wrong. He suddenly understood that it wasn't Cassie who needed him.

It was he who needed Cassie.

Needed her so that when he finally released all the rage that had built up within him over the years, it would be Cassie who took the blame.

And it would begin today, when they released Kiska.

He put the mower back in the garage and hung the edging clippers on their nail in the wall. After he closed the garage door, he crossed the double driveway and knocked at the Winslows' back door. A moment later Rosemary Winslow stepped out into the service porch and held the screen door open for him.

He composed his features into the friendly smile that had long ago become the mask behind which he hid the furies burning within him. "Is Cassie here?"

Rosemary frowned uncertainly. "I—well, yes, she is. But I'm not sure she's feeling too well. When she got back from the park, she went up to her room, and she hasn't come down again."

"Oh," Eric said, feeling a twinge of disappointment. "Well, when she comes back down, would you tell her I was here?"

"Of course," Rosemary replied. She was about to let the door swing shut on its spring when Cassie suddenly called out from the kitchen.

"It's okay. I'm here."

Surprised, Rosemary turned to face Cassie. When she'd come back from the park an hour ago, it was obvious that something had gone wrong, but Cassie had refused to tell her what. Instead she'd disappeared up the stairs, retreating once more into the solitude of her room, shutting Rosemary out. Jennifer, though, told her what had happened, and Rosemary had been tempted to call Harriet Chambers.

Except that you didn't do that when two teenagers had a spat, did you?

Had it been Jennifer and one of her friends, fine—the two mothers could do their best to straighten it out. But when the kids were Cassie's and Lisa's age, shouldn't she stay out of it?

Now she felt foolish for even having thought of calling Harriet, for obviously Cassie's anger had passed. She was smiling at Eric now as if she hadn't a care in the world.

"Hi," Cassie said to Eric. "You ready?"

Eric nodded. "I would have been here earlier, but— well, you know."

Cassie's smile faded. "Your dad?"

Eric shrugged dismissively. "You know what he's like. Come on."

As the two teenagers started out the back door, Rosemary reached out and stopped Cassie. "What about your room? Have you cleaned it?"

"I'll do it later," Cassie replied. She started to move around Rosemary, but Rosemary stepped sideways to block her path. "You got out of it earlier by taking Jennifer to the park. Now, before you do anything else, I want that room cleaned."

Cassie's eyes darkened. "I'll do it later," she said again. "Besides, you're not my mother, and you can't tell me what to do!"

While Rosemary stared after her in shocked silence, Cassie disappeared out the back door, letting the screen slam behind her.

For just a moment Rosemary considered going after her, then abandoned the idea.

She was going to have at least four days alone with Cassie. She didn't want to start them off with a fight.

*   *   *

From the *Big Ed*'s pilothouse Ed Cavanaugh watched the *Morning Star III* move sedately out of the harbor as Keith Winslow carefully maneuvered it past the channel markers.

From the provisions he'd watched Keith stowing aboard, it looked like he was planning to be out quite a while. That meant his wife would be alone in the house with Jennifer.

Jennifer, and Cassie.

His mind darkened as he thought of the girl.

He'd seen her watching him. It had been going on ever since Miranda had died, and gotten worse in the last few days, after she'd locked herself up in that room of hers.

Almost every day he'd seen her standing at her window, looking down at him, accusing him, like maybe she thought *he'd* killed Miranda.

But he hadn't done anything, no matter what the girl thought. Not that he cared that Miranda was dead—in fact he was glad. At least Eric wouldn't be wasting any more time going out to that cabin of hers, listening to whatever crap the crazy bitch had been telling him all those years. And Eric thought he was so smart, thought no one knew where he was going all those times when he sneaked out of the house on weekends, leaving all the work for him to do.

He should have stopped it years ago, Ed thought. Would have, too, if there'd been any way he could have kept his eye on the kid all the time. But there wasn't.

Once he'd even tried to go out to the cabin himself and slap some sense into Miranda. Tell her to leave his kid alone! And after he'd told her—

But he'd never even gotten close to the cabin. The goddamn hawk had seen to that.

So when the old witch had finally gotten what was coming to her, he hadn't shed any tears.

Except that now Cassie was picking up where Miranda Sikes had left off. Now it was Cassie who Eric was always talking to. And he knew what Eric was telling her.

He was telling her the same things he'd told Miranda— telling her what a jerk his old man was!

And she was listening to Eric, too, just like Miranda had. And why wouldn't she? He'd seen what the little tramp was after right from the beginning, staring at the boy with those big brown eyes and getting him into all sorts of trouble, cutting school and being wise with his father. Cassie Winslow and Miranda Sikes were two of a kind. Well, he might not have been able to do anything about Miranda, but he knew what he could do about Cassie Winslow.

He already knew Rosemary Winslow didn't like her. So tonight he'd go pay a little call on Rosemary. With her smart-ass husband gone, she'd pay attention to him. He'd tell her exactly what Cassie was all about, and let her know what would happen if she didn't see to it that Cassie stayed away from Eric. If she wanted to live with a nut in the house, that was fine with him. But she'd damn well keep the kid away from his son.

And after they'd talked . . .

Ed's eyes glistened as he thought about what he might do to Rosemary Winslow.

Hell, he thought, she probably wouldn't even scream. She'd probably like it. She'd sure given him the eye enough times.

He opened the little icebox next to the sinkful of dirty dishes and fished around for a beer. When there wasn't any, he slammed the icebox closed and locked the *Big Ed*.

The Whaler's Inn always had beer, and people to talk to. Good people—people who liked him.

Not sluts like his wife, and Rosemary Winslow, and Cassie.

Well, he'd show them. He'd show them all. And he'd start tonight.

Chapter 19

The hawk cocked his head, his pink eye fixing on Cassie, the feathers on his neck ruffling nervously.

The cage had been completely invisible as they approached; indeed, Cassie hadn't even been sure toward which bush Eric was leading her. To her eye the entire area to the west of the hillock seemed choked with vegetation, and the path Eric had followed had been all but completely grown over with vines and reeds.

But a few moments ago she'd felt a tingling sensation come over her, almost as if there were unseen eyes watching her. She'd paused, looking around, and Eric had looked at her sharply. "You can feel him, can't you?"

Cassie hesitated. "I—I can feel *some*thing," she said. "Are we close?"

Eric nodded. "Over there. The big bush, with the clump of cattails growing out of it."

Cassie had scanned the area ahead, then spotted the bush Eric was pointing at. She'd started toward it, and the tingling sensation grew stronger. Finally, with Eric behind her, she'd knelt down on the damp earth and pushed her way through the dense foliage. The cage was hidden among the branches, near the trunk of the shrub.

Inside the cage, his talons wrapped around a makeshift perch, Kiska had gazed warily at her, soft clicking sounds emerging from his throat.

Eric crept up beside her, then fished in the pocket of his

232

jacket. "Here," he breathed. "Give him this." He put something in her hand.

Cassie glanced down, gasping as she recognized the small shape of a dead mouse sitting in her right palm. Her stomach recoiled and her hand jerked reflexively, the mouse falling to the ground.

The hawk stretched up from the perch, its neck extending as it reached for the small gray form. Cassie looked fearfully at Eric. "What should I do?"

"Pick it up," Eric told her. "Hold it on your hand, but keep your hand flat. Then put your hand in the cage. He'll take it right away."

Cassie swallowed hard, then gingerly picked up the dead mouse and laid it in the palm of her hand.

Kiska clucked eagerly, his head bobbing and weaving as he kept his eyes on the furry shape.

Cassie carefully opened the cage door just wide enough to slip her hand inside. Kiska's head flashed forward, and suddenly the mouse was in his beak.

Cassie quickly pulled her hand out of the cage and shut the door. Then, as they watched, the bird began eating the mouse.

He dropped it to the floor of the cage and pounced on it, his talons puncturing the creature's hide, sinking into its flesh as his curved beak began tearing chunks of skin and meat from the small skeleton. As soon as a piece came loose, the bird jerked his head back, his tongue stuffing the morsel back into his throat. Even before the first piece was swallowed, he was tearing at the corpse once more. In seconds the mouse had disappeared, even its bones torn apart and forced down the bird's gullet.

"Did you ever see anything like it?" Eric breathed, his eyes still on Kiska, who was back on his perch now, methodically preening his feathers with his beak.

Cassie, still fighting a wave of nausea, shook her head. "You've really been doing this every day?" she asked. "Where did you get the mice?"

Eric said nothing for a moment, then shrugged. "The cellar of our house. Dad dumps everything down there, and there's mice all over the place. I just set some traps. A couple of days ago I had three for him."

"But what are we going to do with him?" Cassie asked. "We can't just keep him out here forever."

Eric glanced at her out of the corner of his eye. "And we can't just let him go, can we?"

"But he's okay now," Cassie said. "I know he is."

"But what about Templeton?" Eric asked. "If he sees him, he'll shoot him again."

Cassie fell silent, her eyes fixed on the bird for several long seconds. Inside the cage Kiska stopped preening his feathers, standing perfectly still as he stared back at Cassie.

The soft cluckings in his throat died away.

Finally Cassie reached out once more and opened the door of the cage. Immediately the hawk hopped from the perch to the floor of the cage and extended his head through the opening.

Slowly, warily, Cassie moved her hand down until her wrist was just outside the door.

Kiska bounded onto her wrist, his talons closing around her flesh as they had around the mouse's a few minutes earlier. But the pressure was light, and the needle-sharp points of his claws didn't pierce her skin.

A soft sigh escaped her lips, and she smiled at Eric. "It's all right," she said. "I can feel him, and it's all right."

As if to prove her words, the hawk suddenly leaped from her arm, his wings spreading as he beat his way through the thick foliage and burst into the sky above the marsh. Cassie and Eric pushed out of the tangled branches of the bush and scrambled to their feet. Above them the hawk was circling higher and higher, his wings moving strongly as he searched for the wind. Then he found it and his wings locked into position as he soared on the breeze, his tail spread wide, a screech of excitement bursting from his throat. A moment later he dived, swooping low over the pine trees around the cabin, flushing a flock of ravens from their nests. Cawing loudly, the black birds fluttered into the air, streaking after the hawk. He rose high again, with the ravens chasing after him, then dived straight into the flock. Frustrated and furious, the ravens tumbled through the air then spread out, surrounding the hawk. One by one they darted in at him, but each time he dived away, gradually leading them out over the sea.

"What's happening?" Cassie asked. "What are they doing?"

"He's playing with them," Eric told her. "First he flushed them out to make them mad, and now he's teasing them. Watch!"

The ravens tumbled around the hawk, rolling in the air as they darted toward the bigger bird, then dropping away before he could attack them. Finally he wheeled over the sea, found the wind once more, and sailed serenely back, ignoring the screaming ravens as he dropped to the peak of the cabin roof.

For a few minutes the ravens circled him, attempting to lure him back into the air, but he sat calmly where he was, his beak once more methodically combing through his feathers. Losing interest at last, the ravens drifted back to their nests. Within a few minutes the marsh was quiet again, only the soft murmurings of the feeding ducks occasionally punctuating the rhythmic washing of the surf beyond the dunes.

Feeling the warmth of the sun on their backs, Cassie and Eric started walking slowly back toward the cabin. A deep sense of peace settled over Cassie, and once more she understood why Miranda had been able to live here by herself, why she'd loved the marsh so much. It was a universe sufficient to itself, teeming with life and activity, but somehow set apart from the rest of the world.

Then, a second later, the quiet that hung over the marsh was shattered by a high-pitched screech as Kiska leaped from the roof, climbing into the air.

"What is it?" Cassie gasped. "What's wrong with him?"

Eric said nothing for a moment as he gazed into the sky, one arm shielding his eyes from the sun. The bird spiraled higher, then leveled off, soaring across the marsh toward the park.

A moment later he disappeared from their view.

"Where's he going?" Cassie cried. "If anyone sees him—"

Eric grabbed her hand. "Come on," he yelled. "I think I know where he's gone. I'm sure of it!" Pulling Cassie with him for the first few steps, he began running through the twisted labyrinth of trails. Cassie hurried after him, doing her best to keep up, her feet slipping in the mud every few steps. As Eric reached the edge of the marsh and paused to catch his breath, she caught up.

"What is it?" she asked. "Eric, where are we going?"

"After Kiska," Eric gasped. "Will you stop asking questions and just come on?"

"Look!" Eric shouted. He came to a sudden stop, and Cassie had to throw herself to one side to keep from crashing into him. She stumbled, then she caught herself, regained her balance and followed Eric's gaze.

They had come up Commonwealth Avenue, and the square opened before them. But Eric wasn't looking at the square. He was pointing off toward the Congregational Church.

Cassie searched the sky for a moment, before finding what she'd been looking for.

High up, almost out of sight, Kiska was circling in an ever-tightening downward spiral. Slowly the speck in the sky grew larger, and then Cassie heard once more the faint sounds of his screams as he cried out in preparation for an attack.

"But what is it?" she asked. "It's just the church—"

"Not the church!" Eric yelled. "The graveyard! He's over the graveyard, Cassie!"

Her heart pounding anew, Cassie rushed around the corner then across the street and into the square. The little cemetery next to the church came into view, and she could see clearly what Kiska had somehow known and Eric had guessed.

In the graveyard, crouched in front of Miranda Sikes's grave, was Lisa Chambers.

Around her were half a dozen of her friends. Cassie recognized Jeff Maynard and Kevin Smythe, along with Teri Bennett and Allayne Garvey. The others were faces she'd seen before, but had no names for.

But she knew what they were doing, knew it just as surely as had Kiska and Eric.

"No!" she screamed. "Don't do that!"

Lisa looked up, and when she saw Cassie and Eric, a cold grin spread across her face. "I can do what I want," she taunted. "There's nothing you can do to stop me!"

"Yes there is!" Eric shouted from behind Cassie. "Look!"

He pointed into the sky. Lisa and her friends looked up, then froze where they were.

Kiska was streaking down, his high-pitched scream of attack electrifying the air, his talons reaching out.

Cassie gasped, staring at the strange spectacle, knowing what would happen in just a few more seconds.

And she wanted to let it happen, wanted to let Kiska tear into Lisa the way he had torn into the corpse of the mouse only a little while ago.

But once more Miranda's voice welled out of her memory, speaking softly to her.

She tried not to listen, tried to shut out the words. But she couldn't do it.

Miranda spoke, and she had to listen.

"No!" she screamed out loud. "Kiska, don't!"

The hawk, already into his final dive as he prepared to attack the crowd of terrified teenagers, whirled in the air, flapped wildly for a moment until he caught the wind, then reversed his course and began climbing upward once more. A few seconds later he leveled off and wheeled back toward the marsh.

Eric and Cassie watched until he'd disappeared, then Eric's eyes narrowed. "You should have let him do it," he said, his voice bitter.

Cassie shook her head. "I couldn't. Miranda—" She broke off, but Eric looked at her, his eyes penetrating.

"What?" he pressed. "What about Miranda?"

"She never wanted to hurt anybody," Cassie said quietly. She started across the street to the graveyard, where Lisa and her friends were now backing away. As Cassie stepped through the gate into the cemetery itself, they turned and fled. But it wasn't until they were gone, and she and Eric were alone, that she finished what she'd been saying. She looked down at the defaced headstone that marked Miranda's grave, and the shredded remains of the uprooted flowers she'd planted there so short a time ago. "She never wanted to hurt anyone," Cassie said again. "And she doesn't want me to hurt anyone either."

Eric's jaw tightened. "But she's dead! She doesn't care what you do."

Once more Cassie shook her head. "But I don't feel as though she's dead," she said quietly. "I feel as though she's still alive inside me, and sometimes I can . . . well, I can almost hear her talking to me. And she doesn't want me to hurt anybody."

"Even if they hurt you?" Eric challenged.

Cassie hesitated. "They—they can't hurt me," she faltered. "Not unless I let them."

"But they *are* hurting you," Eric insisted. "When Lisa does something like this, it hurts you just as much as your mother hurt you and my father hurts me." The bitterness in his voice hardened into anger. "Just because they aren't beating up on you doesn't mean they're not hurting you. And they won't stop as long as they know they're succeeding."

She knew he was right, knew that what Lisa and her friends were doing stung just as much as any of the slaps she'd ever received from her mother.

But how could she stop them?

Then, slowly, an idea began to take shape in her mind.

Maybe, after all, there was a way. Maybe Eric was right. If they thought they weren't hurting her at all . . .

Quickly, before she lost her nerve, she made up her mind. And when she told Eric what she was going to do, he nodded his agreement.

"It's perfect," he said. "It's just perfect."

Then they began repairing the damage Lisa had done to Miranda's grave.

It was almost eight-thirty when Cassie and Eric walked around the end of the school building and cut across the playing field to the gymnasium entrance. The double front doors to the gym stood open, light from the foyer spilling out onto the front steps and the yard beyond. A couple of kids were standing at the edge of the lighted area, passing a cigarette back and forth between them.

Cassie paused in the comforting shelter of the darkness, then spoke quietly. "Maybe—maybe we shouldn't go in at all."

"But we already decided," Eric replied. "Besides, I can hardly wait to see their faces."

Cassie felt a knot of fear tighten in her stomach as she

remembered the expression on her stepmother's face when she'd come downstairs half an hour ago.

Rosemary had been sitting in the little den at the front of the house. When Cassie stepped in from the foyer, she'd glanced up from her knitting and gasped, her eyes widening in shock. But before she could speak, Cassie had hurried out the front door and down the street, where Eric was waiting for her on the corner in front of the church.

"Did she say anything?" he asked.

Cassie had shaken her head. "She didn't have a chance." She'd chuckled. "For a second I thought she was going to faint."

But now, as the throbbing rhythms of rock music reverberated from the building and she thought of the crowd of teenagers inside—all of them friends of Lisa Chambers—she was beginning to lose her nerve.

As if sensing what was happening, Eric took her arm. "Come on," he said. "You can't back out now." His grip on her arm tightening, he led her out of the shadows, and they hurried up the steps into the gym.

Charlotte Ambler stood at the door to the gym itself, keeping a watchful eye on the crowd that covered the dance floor. So far everything seemed to be perfectly normal, and she was enjoying a brief respite from the tension that had permeated the school almost from the day Cassie Winslow had arrived. When she'd heard the rumor that Eric Cavanaugh had broken his date with Lisa Chambers for tonight and was planning to bring Cassie Winslow to the dance, she'd had a sinking feeling that something was going to go terribly wrong. So she'd made sure she got to the gym and taken up her station even before the doors had opened, hoping her very presence could avert whatever trouble might be brewing. During the last hour, with no sign of either Eric or Cassie, she'd begun to let herself relax. Apparently they weren't coming at all.

As the band wound up its first set of the night, the last electronic wailings of the synthesizer fading away, she sensed someone behind her and turned, prepared to welcome the latest arrivals.

Turned and froze.

Standing perfectly still, her face an ashen white, her eyes wide, stood Cassie Winslow.

Except that it wasn't Cassie.

It was Miranda Sikes.

The black skirt—the same black skirt Miranda had worn every day of her life—fell from Cassie's waist to the floor.

She wore Miranda's thick black woolen sweater, and wrapped around her head in loose folds that almost concealed her face, was Miranda's black shawl.

She cradled Sumi in her left arm while the fingers of her right hand slowly stroked his fur.

The cat's eyes, large and golden, glowed dangerously in the soft light from the gymnasium.

"C-Cassie—" Charlotte breathed. A wave of dizziness swept over her, and she had to reach out to the wall to steady herself.

"Cassie?" the eerie apparition said, her voice echoing with the oddly detached quality of Miranda Sikes. "I'm not Cassie. Cassie's gone. I'm Miranda. I'm Miranda Sikes."

Moving slowly and deliberately, she walked past Charlotte and paused in the doorway that led to the dance floor.

It was only then that Charlotte saw Eric Cavanaugh standing just inside the building, his face pale, his eyes fixed on Cassie. Her heart thumping erratically, Charlotte hurried over to him. "What's going on, Eric?" she asked, her fear giving way to sudden anger. "Is this some kind of a joke?"

Eric only shook his head, pretending to be puzzled. "I—I don't know," he stammered. "When I picked her up, she was dressed that way, and all the way over here she wouldn't say a word. I—I tried to talk to her, but she wouldn't answer me. I'm not even sure she heard me."

Charlotte closed her eyes for a moment in a vain effort to shut out the strange image of Miranda that Cassie had managed to create, shut out the reality of what must have happened.

A hush fell over the crowd of teenagers inside the gym as one by one they became aware of the dark figure that stood framed in the doorway.

Cassie didn't move. She simply stayed where she was, her fingers stroking Sumi, her eyes—wide and unblinking—flicking over the crowd. And then, across the room, she found what she was looking for.

Lisa Chambers, her back toward Cassie, was standing with Teri Bennett and Allayne Garvey next to the punch bowl.

Her eyes fixed on Lisa, Cassie moved slowly across the now silent room.

The crowd parted before her, watching her slow progress. When she was ten feet from Lisa Chambers, she stopped.

Lisa suddenly realized the room had grown totally silent, and her skin began to crawl as she felt eyes watching her.

She turned around.

The cup of punch in her hand crashed to the floor as she stared at the black-clad figure that stood ten feet away.

It was Cassie.

It *had* to be Cassie.

But somehow it wasn't.

It was Miranda, her empty eyes glaring balefully.

She felt Teri and Allayne move away, and suddenly she was standing alone, facing the accusing eyes. Icy fingers of panic began to close around her, and her legs began to tremble.

The cat hissed dangerously, its fur rising up to stand on end.

Then Cassie's hand came up, her forefinger pointing directly at Lisa. "You," she breathed. "It was you. . . ."

Once again she moved forward, and as she came closer to Lisa, the hand of fear squeezed tighter on the other girl.

The cat's teeth were bared now, and its back had arched as it once more spat out at Lisa. Then it crouched down, its tail twitching as it prepared to spring from Cassie's arm.

As Cassie took one more step, Lisa screamed and twisted away from the approaching figure.

Stumbling, she lurched into the table. Its legs gave way, and the table, with its punch bowl and cups, crashed to the floor, Lisa sprawling on top of it. She tried to scrabble away across the floor, but the tablecloth entangled itself around her and she flailed helplessly, still shrieking with fright.

Then, behind her, she heard a peal of laughter. Whirling around, she stared up at Cassie, who was smiling mockingly at her as she pulled the shawl off her head.

"You said I was crazy, didn't you?" Cassie asked. "Isn't that what you told everyone? Well, I just decided to be what you said I was. How did you like it?"

There was a moment of dead silence as everyone in the room realized what had happened.

Then, from a few feet away, another laugh broke out.

And another.

And another.

Lisa, her dress stained with punch, struggled furiously to her feet. "It's not funny!" she screamed, her voice trembling with fury and her face contorted into a twisted grimace of rage. "Look what she did to me!" She turned to Allayne and Teri, but they, too, were laughing.

"She got you," Allayne told her, unable to suppress her giggling. "She got all of us!"

As the laughter swept through the rest of the room, Eric appeared at Cassie's side, his eyes glittering. "Well?" he asked. "You didn't answer Cassie's question. How did you like it?"

Still trembling with fury, Lisa glared at her laughing classmates. "You did it," she spat at Eric. "She couldn't have thought of anything like this. It was you!" Her hand lashed out and she slapped Eric across the cheek.

Instantly the humor disappeared from Eric's eyes, replaced with a chilling cold. "You shouldn't have done that," he said, his voice tight, anger boiling inside him. "You shouldn't have done that at all."

Lisa only slapped him again, her face scarlet with fury. "I'll do anything I want!" she screeched. "I'll get both of you for what you did! You'll be sorry! You'll both be sorry!" Then, tears of rage and humiliation streaming down her cheeks, she shoved her way through the crowd and stormed out into the night.

A moment later, as her classmates crowded around her, Cassie realized that Sumi was gone. "We've got to find him," she whispered to Eric as soon as she could get close enough for him to hear her. "What if he finds Lisa? What'll he do to her?"

But as they made their way out of the gym, and Eric still felt the sting of Lisa's slaps on his cheek, he knew that he didn't care what the cat did to Lisa.

In fact, if he had his way, Sumi would kill Lisa Chambers.

Chapter 20

Rosemary Winslow glanced at the clock for the fifth time in fifteen minutes. She had promised herself not to do any of what she thought of as "serious" worrying until midnight, but it was becoming harder to keep that promise as each minute dragged by.

What could Cassie have been thinking of? That moment still burned in Rosemary's memory—that eerie moment of certainty that she was actually seeing a ghost—when Cassie had stood in the doorway, her face all but lost in the shadows of Miranda's shawl. If her intention had been to frighten Rosemary, she'd certainly succeeded. But what would happen when she got to the dance?

By the time Rosemary had recovered enough to go after Cassie, the girl was gone, swallowed up into the night. For a moment Rosemary had considered going after her in the car, but then gave up the idea, certain that even if she found Cassie, there would only be a scene as she demanded that Cassie come home and change her clothes and Cassie refused. So she'd spent the evening with Jennifer, half expecting Cassie to come home early in tears, humiliated by the taunting of her classmates.

But Cassie had not come home.

Rosemary put Jennifer to bed at nine, and settled down in the den with her knitting, deciding that everything must have turned out all right after all. Then the clock in the living room had struck eleven and her worries returned. For the last fifteen minutes she'd been pacing restlessly through the house, wondering what to do.

The radio that could put her in instant contact with Keith seemed to beckon to her, but so far she had resisted its seduction. Still, she was standing at the den door for the fourth time in the last hour, chewing at her lower lip as she once more weighed the seriousness of the situation, when the soft tapping at the back door intruded on her consciousness. Had it not been for that, she would have given in and called Keith, begging him to come home. Of course, she would have had to call him back when Cassie finally did come home—as Rosemary was positive she sooner or later would—and tell him that it had all been a false alarm. She was thinking this as she abandoned the den and hurried into the kitchen.

To Rosemary's surprise, Laura Cavanaugh was standing on the back step, her face pale and drawn in the light from the service porch. When she opened the door and saw her neighbor more clearly, Rosemary couldn't stifle a gasp.

Laura's eyes were puffy, each of them circled with a dark ring of bruises. There was a cut on her left cheek extending nearly to her ear, and her right cheek was swollen, its edematous flesh mottled with an ugly purplish color.

The two women stared at each other in silence for a moment as tears welled in Laura's damaged eyes. "I know how I look," she said apologetically. "I suppose I shouldn't have come over—"

Rosemary's hands rose in an instinctive gesture of protest. "Not come over? Why on earth not? Laura, what's happened? Did Ed—" She broke off when she saw Jennifer, rubbing sleepily at her eyes, standing in the kitchen door and staring curiously at Laura.

"I couldn't sleep," the little girl said. "I thought maybe Cassie was home."

"Go back up to your room, sweetheart. Mrs. Cavanaugh and I are just going to have a little talk." Jennifer hesitated, frowning, then decided that this was not the time to argue with her mother. A moment later she was gone, and Rosemary turned her attention back to Laura. "Did Ed do that to you?" she asked, the hardness in her voice indicating that she assumed he had.

Laura started to shake her head, but then, almost against her will, nodded. "It's not too bad, though—really. And it's not why I came. It's Eric—he hasn't come home yet. I—well, I was wondering if he was over here with Cassie." Her eyes went to the ceiling, as if she might be able to pierce the wood and plaster that separated the two floors of the house. "I hate to be a bother, but Ed could come home any minute, and if Eric's over here, well . . ." Her voice faltered, then she fell silent, sinking helplessly onto one of the straight-backed kitchen chairs.

"Have you called Gene Templeton?" Rosemary asked. Without asking Laura if she wanted any, she began preparing a pot of tea.

"Gene?" Laura echoed vaguely. "Why would I call Gene? It's not like something's happened to Eric—"

"I'm not talking about Eric!" Rosemary broke in. "I'm talking about you. For heaven's sakes, Laura, how long are you going to put up with this? You can't just let Ed beat you up every time he gets mad!"

Laura shook her head helplessly. "He doesn't—"

"Yes, he does!" Rosemary insisted. "My God, Laura, it's not as if it was a secret. Everyone in town knows what he does to you. But if you won't stick up for yourself, what can anyone do?"

Laura's hands went to her face, and she rocked back and forth in her chair. Rosemary watched her for a moment, wondering if she should go to Laura, put her arms around her, try to comfort her. She knew, though, that what Laura Cavanaugh truly needed was not pity, but a discovery of the strength that would finally allow her to walk out on Ed. And no amount of comforting would give her that. Sighing heavily, Rosemary poured hot water over three tea bags, let the tea steep for a while, then poured a cup of the steaming brew and set it in front of Laura Cavanaugh. At last Laura seemed to regain control of herself.

"I'm sorry," she said. "I know you're right! But it's Eric I'm worried about right now. He said he was going to the dance with Cassie—"

"And Ed hates Cassie," Rosemary broke in. "I know. But he's not here, and neither is she."

"But where are they?" Laura gasped. "If Ed comes

home—" Once again she fell silent, but this time her eyes went fearfully to the kitchen window. Following Laura's gaze, Rosemary saw Ed Cavanaugh's white pickup truck weave down the driveway, its brakes squealing as he slammed it to a stop. Both women watched in silence as he slid out of the truck and lumbered unsteadily toward the back door of his house.

"Drunk, of course!" Rosemary said disgustedly as he disappeared from their view. Then they heard him roaring his wife's name, and his son's. A few seconds later he reappeared at the back door and Laura and Rosemary could see him staring speculatively at the Winslows' house. The sharp intake of Laura's breath rasped with unnatural loudness as Ed started across the driveway separating the two houses.

She lurched to her feet. "He can't find me here," she whispered. "If he does—"

But it was too late.

Ed Cavanaugh, his bloodshot eyes glowing with malevolence, jerked the back door open without knocking and was suddenly framed in the service-porch door, his fleshy mouth twisted into a scornful sneer.

"Mighta known you'd come sniveling over here." He spat the words at Laura with a viciousness that made her wince, then turned his attention to Rosemary. "Where's Eric?" he demanded. "He with that crazy brat of yours?"

Rosemary rose to her feet, her fear of his drunkenness washed away by indignation. "Eric isn't here, and neither is Cassie," she told him. "They're still at the dance. And if you're still here in two minutes, I'm going to call the police."

Ed regarded her with contemptuous eyes, then waved his hand dismissively at his wife. "Get the fuck outta here, Laur—me and the uppity lady here are gonna have a little talk."

"Ed—" Laura began, but before she could speak another word Ed raised his hand and, in what seemed to Rosemary an almost idle gesture, spun Laura around and shoved her out of the kitchen. Laura hesitated only a fraction of a second before pushing through the back door and hurrying into her own house, her hands once more covering her face as she sobbed in pain and humiliation. Only when the Cavanaughs' back door had closed behind her did Rosemary finally speak, and when she did, it was from the telephone.

"I'm calling Gene Templeton," she said. "I'm going to tell him exactly what happened, and I hope Laura will finally file some charges against you."

But before she could finish dialing, Ed had crossed the room, the bulk of his body pressing Rosemary against the wall as he twisted the receiver out of her hand and dropped it to dangle from its cord a few inches above the floor.

"That what you gonna do, uppity lady?" he asked. "Now why would you want to do a thing like that? I didn't hurt her none. Fact is, she likes it. But now she's gone, and ain't nobody home but you and me, is there? Your snotty husband ain't coming home at all, and his creepy kid's off gettin' my kid into more trouble, ain't she? So what do you say you and I get in a little trouble of our own?"

His face moved closer to hers, and Rosemary suddenly realized what he intended to do. His mouth was only a few inches from her own, and his sour breath made her gorge rise. She tried to push him away, but his weight seemed immovable. Then, from the door to the dining room, she heard Jennifer's voice.

"Mommy? Mommy, is he hurting you?"

Rosemary struggled, but Ed's hamlike hands had closed on her wrist and he held her immobile against the wall. She twisted her head to one side just as his mouth was about to press against hers. "Get out, Jenny!" she yelled. "Run across the street and get help. Tell them to call the police!"

"Goddamn you—" She heard Ed growl as his hands tightened on her wrists like twin vises.

"*Now*, Jen!" she yelled. She heard Jennifer yelp in sudden fear, and out of the corner of her eye saw her daughter dart away. Finally, summoning the last reserves of her strength, she jerked her leg up, plunging her knee into Ed Cavanaugh's groin.

A strangled howl burst from his throat, and his grip was momentarily loosened by the searing pain that rose from his groin to slash upward through his body. Rosemary twisted away from him, shoving hard.

Losing his balance, Ed tumbled backward into the kitchen

table then fell to the floor, his hands gripping his crotch as he glared furiously up at Rosemary.

"Crazy," she heard him say as she dashed past him, toward the back door and the safety outside. "You're as crazy as the girl. All you hadda do was be nice. . . ."

A few minutes later, from the shelter of the neighbors' house across the street, Rosemary saw him stagger out the back door of her house, pause for a moment as if making up his mind what to do next, then get back into his truck. Thirty seconds after Ed was gone, Gene Templeton turned onto the block, the red lights flashing on top of his car.

Ed drove blindly, fighting the nausea that roiled through his body. The pain in his groin seemed untempered by the alcohol in his blood; indeed, the two seemed to combine into a raging fury that grew within him like a separate being, driving him on, banishing the last vestiges of reason from his mind.

He knew where he was going; knew where to look to find the source of his fury.

And he knew what he would do when he got there.

Cassie Winslow was just like Miranda Sikes.

She'd put a spell on the boy, and if Ed didn't do something about it, she'd put a spell on everybody else too.

He decided she'd already put some kind of spell on Rosemary Winslow. She must have, or Rosemary wouldn't have done what she did. After all, Rosemary wanted him as bad as he wanted her, didn't she? Sure she did—he'd seen the way she'd looked at him, seen the lust in her eyes.

But today, when she finally could have had him, she'd kicked him.

She'd actually tried to hurt him.

No woman had ever done that.

So Cassie must have done something to Rosemary.

Maybe he should go back and try to explain it all to her. That was it! That was where he'd gone wrong!

He'd gone over there to talk to Rosemary, but Laura had been there and he hadn't had a chance to explain things to Rosemary.

It was all Laura's fault! She'd spoiled it for him, just like she'd always spoiled everything for him!

And now it was too late. Rosemary Winslow wouldn't listen to him now. None of them would, not as long as Cassie could keep working her witchcraft.

Witchcraft.

The word echoed in Ed's fogged mind, but as he kept driving, his eyes barely seeing into the darkness beyond the windshield, he knew he'd stumbled on to the truth.

She was a witch, just as Miranda Sikes had been, and she'd cast a spell over his son, just as Miranda had!

Well, he'd fix that, as soon as he found them.

He might not know much, he told himself, but he sure as hell knew what to do with women.

Chapter 21

It was Cassie's fault—all of it!

And Lisa was about to make her sorry.

She walked quickly along Oak Street, glancing furtively to each side whenever she stepped into the pools of illumination cast by the streetlamps. She tried to tell herself that it didn't matter if anyone saw her. It wasn't even midnight yet, and she had a perfect right to be out walking.

Except that if anyone saw her, and remembered seeing her . . .

She hadn't known what she was going to do when she'd gotten home from the dance. Still furious, she'd ripped off her ruined dress, changing into jeans and one of her father's old sweaters, then stuffed the dress into the trash barrel behind the garage. At least her parents weren't home, so she didn't have to explain to them what had happened. She'd turned on the television set, but only sat staring unseeingly at it, her fury steadily growing, focusing on Cassie. There had to be a way to get even with her. There had to be!

It was during the eleven o'clock news that the idea came to her. She hadn't really been watching the television until the screen glowed brightly with flickering reds and oranges, catching her attention. With her anger still burning, she listened to the report of a fire in Boston.

A fire that had been set deliberately, with a book of matches and a can of lighter fluid. . . .

Her father kept lighter fluid in his den, along with all the

251

other junk he used to take care of the pipes her mother hated
so much but that he wouldn't give up.

By the time the news ended, she'd made up her mind,
and by eleven thirty-five she'd found what she needed and
slipped out of the house.

So far it had all been easy.

She came to the park and left the sidewalk, pushing her
way into a clump of lilac bushes that edged the lawn. As the
heavy foliage closed around her, she breathed a sigh of relief
and let herself relax. Though clouds were scudding across the
sky now, enough moonlight filtered through the branches so
she could see where she was going, and it occurred to her she
might not need the flashlight in her pocket at all.

Lisa worked her way through the bushes slowly and
carefully, the anxiety she'd felt on the sidewalk quickly trans-
formed into a thrill of excitement.

She came to the edge of the lilacs and paused. Twenty
yards of open lawn separated her from the next thicket.

Should she run, hoping to make it across the open
space before anyone could notice her, or should she simply
step out onto the lawn and not worry if anyone saw her?

But why would she be alone in the park at night? The
sidewalk was one thing—she could be going anywhere. But
the park was something else again. She crouched in the thicket
for a few more seconds, then made up her mind.

Taking a deep breath, she stepped deliberately out of
the bushes and slowly sauntered across the grass, doing her
best to look as if she hadn't a care in the world. Only when
she was within a few yards of her goal did she lose her nerve
and break into a quick trot. And then, once again, she was
safe from any prying eyes. From here on it would be easy.

She moved more confidently now, pausing again only
when she came to the far side of the thicket. Parting the
leaves with her hands, she looked out over the marsh.

The evening breeze had died away, and the only sound
Lisa could hear was the rhythmic pounding of the surf on the
beach. With the strange amplification of sound at night, she
could hear even the soft hiss of each dying wave as it spent its
energy on the sand, followed by a short silence as the next
wave built up for its assault on the shore.

Over the marsh itself there was an eerie stillness that

almost made Lisa change her mind. Her confidence ebbed away, and she shivered involuntarily at the thought of going out into the bog alone. For the first time in years she remembered the stories she'd heard when she was little, about the ghosts that haunted both the marsh and the cabin it surrounded. But they were only stories, and Lisa knew there were no such things as ghosts.

Indeed, the only truly fearful things that had ever been in the marsh were Miranda and her hawk, and now Miranda was dead.

But what about the hawk? Where was it?

She lingered a few more moments, unwilling to take that first step into the bog, and when she finally left the shadowy security of the lilac thicket, she stayed on the narrow path skirting the marsh, leading toward the friendly familiarity of the beach and Cranberry Point.

There was no hurry, she told herself. She had plenty of time.

Her step quickened, and as she neared the beach, her cold anger fed her confidence. It was going to be all right.

Already she could see the cabin—the cabin that Cassie Winslow loved so much—burning brightly against the night sky. By morning, only a heap of smoking ashes would be left.

Inside the cabin a single oil lantern burned on the table beneath the peak of the roof—its wick turned so low that only a soft glow suffused the room, leaving the corners in shadowy darkness. Eric had built a fire in the stove, damping it down so that it was no more than slowly burning embers, the little smoke that escaped up the chimney invisible against the blackness of the night sky. The cabin was warm, and had a cozy feeling to it that his own house had never had. It seemed to welcome them, shielding them from the rest of the world. And even with the lamplight and the fire, Eric knew that from the outside the cabin would still appear to be deserted. He grinned at Cassie. "How long do you suppose we could stay here before anyone found us?"

"Sometimes I wish it could be forever," Cassie replied, scratching at Sumi's ears. He was curled in her lap now, purring contentedly. They'd found him outside the gym, skulking in the darkness, but when Cassie had called to him, instead of running to her and leaping into her arms, he'd dashed the other way, then paused, his tail twitching as he twisted his head around to look at them. For the next thirty minutes he'd darted away, just out of Cassie's reach, then waited, leading them on until they realized where he was going.

"I wonder why he brought us out here?" Eric mused, his eyes drifting from Cassie to the animal in her lap. "It almost seems as if he knows something we don't."

"Sometimes I think he does," Cassie replied. She tried to explain to Eric the strange connection she had with the cat, talking hesitantly at first, afraid he might laugh at her.

But he didn't laugh.

Instead he listened to her intently, and when she was done, asked her a question: "Is that the way it is with Kiska too?"

Cassie nodded. "When Mr. Templeton shot him, I could feel it. It sounds crazy, doesn't it?"

Eric hadn't answered the question directly. Instead his eyes had taken on a faraway look, as if he were thinking about something else entirely. "Lots of things are crazy," he'd said at last. Then, almost reluctantly, he stood up. "I've got to go home," he said.

"Why?" Cassie asked. "Your dad doesn't want you around, and Rosemary doesn't want me around. Why can't we just stay here?"

Eric hesitated only a split second. "I can't. If I do, my dad'll find out and he'll kill me." When Cassie didn't move, he cocked his head uncertainly. "You coming with me?" he asked.

Cassie hesitated. She knew she ought to go home, knew that if she didn't, Rosemary would be furious with her. But Rosemary, she was certain, was furious with her already. And there was a warmth and comfort about the cabin that made her feel closer than ever to Miranda. She shook her head. "I'm staying here." Her eyes met Eric's. "If Rosemary asks you, don't tell her where I am. All right?"

Eric shrugged. "I guess. You sure you'll be okay?"

Cassie smiled at him reassuringly. "Of course I will. This place feels like it's really mine—it's the first place I've ever been where I really feel I belong."

A moment later Eric was gone, and Cassie was alone in the little cabin, with only Sumi for company.

Lisa froze.

Twenty yards away a dark figure had stepped out of the marsh onto the dunes that formed Cranberry Point. But that wasn't possible, was it? She'd been watching the marsh so carefully, looking for any signs of movement, and she could have sworn there were none.

And yet someone was there, standing still, staring out over the moonlit sea. Then the figure moved, and started toward her.

She stepped back, pressing herself into the small clump of shrubs that stood alone at the corner of the parking lot which served both the park and the beach. If she stood perfectly still, maybe the person would pass by without seeing her.

As the figure grew closer, she knew who it was.

Eric.

Her whole body tensed with anger. But what was he doing out here? Was Cassie with him? No—he was alone.

Then she understood.

He'd been out in Miranda's cabin, and Cassie must still be there.

She smiled darkly—that would make it even better.

She shrank deeper into the bushes, holding her breath.

A twig snapped.

She saw Eric stop, saw him turn toward her. But maybe it still wasn't too late. If she held perfectly still—

"Who's there?"

Eric's voice was startlingly loud in the stillness of the night. Despite herself, Lisa jumped slightly. Instantly Eric's body shifted, and she knew he'd seen her. There was only one thing left to do.

"It's me!" she exclaimed loudly, stepping out of the bushes into the moonlight.

Eric stared at her. She'd changed her clothes, and was dressed in jeans and a black sweater now, with a scarf tied around her head. But why was she here? What was she doing, sneaking around in the middle of the night?

The memory of her slaps stung sharply, and his eyes narrowed. "What are you doing out here?"

"J-just taking a walk," Lisa replied, but the hesitation in her voice told Eric there was more to it than that. "You won't tell anyone you saw me, will you?" Lisa asked anxiously.

"Not tell anyone?" Eric demanded. "Why shouldn't I? And what the hell are you doing, hiding in the bushes?"

"I—I didn't know who you were," Lisa stammered. But almost against her will her hand closed on the can of lighter fluid and the book of matches in her pocket. Eric saw the movement.

"What have you got?" he demanded. "You *are* doing something, aren't you?"

"No!" Lisa said, too loudly. "I was just—I just wanted to go for a walk," she said, her voice taking on a belligerent tone. "Isn't that all right with you? You don't own the beach, do you? Or is it only you and Cassie who are allowed to come out here?"

Eric looked at her carefully. She *was* up to something—he was sure of it. But what? And why was she dressed like Cassie? "What's in your pocket, Lisa?" he asked. "What are you going to do?"

"Nothing!" Lisa insisted, her temper once more slipping away from her. She took a step backward but missed her footing and stumbled in the sand.

Eric moved closer, grabbing at her arm. "You tell me what you're doing!" he demanded. Lisa struggled in his grip but couldn't wriggle free.

Then, from the road beyond the parking lot, Eric heard something and looked up.

On Cape Drive he saw the familiar shape of his father's pickup truck. It was weaving slightly, and instantly Eric knew his father was drunk and looking for him.

"Come on," he said to Lisa. "It's my dad." Jerking roughly on her arm, he pulled her out into the dunes and the beach beyond.

The marsh, Ed Cavanaugh thought. That's where he'd found them last time, and that's where he'd find them this time. He pressed his foot down on the accelerator while slamming the transmission into a lower gear. There was a satisfying shriek as the tires spun wildly for a second then caught, shooting the truck forward. Ed's eyes fixed on the pavement ahead as he raced past the summer houses that lined Cape Drive. Just ahead was the expanse of tall grass that marked the beginning of the marsh. Then, out in the dunes that separated the marsh from the beach, he saw two running figures—a boy and a girl—their hands clasped together.

Eric and Cassie, he thought.

Ed's grip tightened on the steering wheel as his fury grew. Ahead, on the left, he saw the parking lot and veered the truck off the road. It wasn't until he was nearly across the lot that he realized he had no intention of stopping.

Tonight there would be no shouting from the cab of his truck.

Through a haze of alcohol he imagined he could see them clearly now—see the grins on their faces. Hell, he could even hear them, and knew what they were laughing at.

They were laughing at him.

But they wouldn't laugh much longer. When he got done with them, they'd never laugh at him again.

Cassie sat quietly, enjoying the solitude of the cabin, feeling the peace that Miranda must have felt here. Though there was no one else around, she didn't feel alone. If she listened carefully, she could hear the sounds of the sleeping birds murmuring in the marsh, and the raccoons and other creatures as they moved through the wetlands, searching for food.

Strangely, she felt less lonely now, with only the birds and animals around her, than she ever had before. And then—his back arching as an angry hiss boiled out of his throat—Sumi leaped out of her lap and darted over to the door. She looked at him curiously, then understood.

Someone was out there.

Someone who meant her harm.

Tears of frustration flooded her eyes. Why couldn't they just leave her alone? Why couldn't they just let her be?

Without thinking, she went to the door and opened it a few inches. "Go see, Sumi," she said softly. "Go find out who it is."

Like a ghost, his padded feet making no sound at all, the cat disappeared into the night.

Eric jerked Lisa to a stop. Turning, his eyes fixed on the truck. It should have stopped in the parking lot. But it hadn't. Instead it was still coming, jumping slightly as its tires struck the low curbing that separated the paved lot from the sand of the beach. Now it was crossing the beach itself, slogging through the soft sand toward the water. When it reached the hard-packed wet sand near the water's edge and turned toward them, he realized what was happening.

Lisa understood at the same moment. "He's coming right at us," she gasped, her anger suddenly forgotten. Now it was she who reached out to grasp Eric's hand.

Eric cursed under his breath. His father really intended to kill him this time! For an instant his body froze, then he summoned all his energy. "Come on!" he yelled. Jerking her hard, he leaped sideways out of the truck's path. It swept past them—its horn blaring, its tires spitting a stinging sleet of sand into their faces. As they watched in growing fright, the truck slowed then spun around to face them again.

"What are we going to do?" Lisa wailed. "What does he want?"

But Eric was too terrified to answer. The truck was gathering speed again, and he had to decide which way to go. Before he could make up his mind, the issue was decided for him. The truck bore down on them, and there was nothing Eric could do but drag Lisa into the protection of the water itself.

"He's drunk!" he yelled as he stumbled into the roiling surf. "He wants to kill us!"

Lisa's eyes widened, and she turned to stare at the truck, which had passed them once more and was even now circling around to try again.

"Get out of the water!" she heard Eric yelling. "When he comes back, he'll try to push us in again and he'll swerve down the slope. But this time we'll go the other way."

The truck was gathering speed now, and Lisa stared at it in detached fascination. It bore down on her like some kind of raging beast, but she couldn't move. Instead she stood still, frozen like a rabbit in the glare of the headlights.

She felt Eric yank on her arm, felt herself being pulled

out of the path of the screaming juggernaut. Eric had been right. At the last second the truck swerved down the sloping beach, its left tires hitting the water. As it passed, Lisa got a clear look into the cab.

Behind the wheel, his face contorted into a twisted grin and his eyes lit with a strangely glowing madness, she saw Ed Cavanaugh. An icy chill of pure terror sliced through her. Once again she knew that Eric was right.

He meant to kill them.

She started screaming as Eric dragged her up the beach toward the edge of the marsh.

Goddamn it, Ed swore to himself. He should have had her that time, should have felt the impact as the front fender crashed into her body, slamming her down into the sand and crushing her under the wheels.

But Eric had outsmarted him. Pulled her the wrong way, so all he'd done was drive the fucking truck into the water. He fought to control the slewing tires, pulling the wheel hard to the right. But it was as if the water itself was fighting him now, trying to pull both the truck and him out to sea. Then, slowly, the ocean seemed to release its grip and the truck surged back onto the hard-packed sand. But the windshield was covered with salt spray now, and he could barely see out. Clutching the wheel with his right hand, he began groping along the dash with his left.

At last the wipers came on and the windshield cleared. He jerked the truck into another U-turn, then he saw them racing across the beach, toward the marsh. If they got in there, he'd never catch them.

He slammed his foot onto the accelerator and the truck lunged forward, hurtling across the wet sand. He leaned on the horn and listened as its blaring rose above the pounding of the surf behind him. The truck slowed as it plowed into the soft sand above the tide line and surged up the gentle slope of the dunes.

But it didn't slow enough to make any difference.

He'd cut them off this time and drive them back down toward the water. He slammed the transmission into a lower gear, and the extra power made the truck leap forward.

As he shot past them he could see the terror in their

eyes. Even the blasting of the horn couldn't drown out the girl's scream.

"He's going to kill us!" Lisa shrieked as the truck shot past, only inches away. Once again she'd seen Ed clearly, his greasy hair matted against his forehead, his drunken eyes glazed over as he stared drunkenly back at her.

And he was laughing.

Even over the awful cacophony of the racing engine and blasting horn, she'd heard an unearthly laughter pour from his throat.

"He's trying to push us back in the water," Eric gasped. "Come on!"

Half dragging Lisa now, he lurched to his feet and started once more toward the marsh. The truck was only a few yards away, floundering in the sand as Ed struggled to turn it toward them once again. Then the lights swept around, blinding Eric for a moment, and he tightened his grip on Lisa's hand.

"Run!" he yelled, but over the mass of sound that seemed to roll over the beach, he could barely hear his own voice.

Then he was over the dunes, and one of the paths into the marsh opened before him. Hauling Lisa behind him, he lurched into the reeds and stopped, gasping for breath.

Behind him Lisa collapsed to the ground, panting. Sobs of fear wracked her body, and when she looked up at Eric, her face was streaked with tears and sand.

"What's he doing?" she wailed. "What's wrong with him?"

"He's gone nuts," Eric replied, kneeling beside her and straining to see out onto the dunes and the beach. The head-lights had destroyed his night vision, and though he couldn't see the truck itself now, he could see its twin beams of light and hear its engine roaring like an infuriated animal that had momentarily lost its prey. "We've got to get out of here. If he finds us—"

"How?" Lisa demanded. "We should have stayed on the beach! We can't get through here—we're trapped!" She stared fearfully into the depths of the marsh, remembering the maze of nearly invisible paths, some of which led somewhere, some of which simply disappeared into the reeds and the quick-sand. Why had she ever come out here in the first place? Why had she ever thought she could get all the way out to

Miranda's house all by herself? "I didn't mean it," she suddenly sobbed. "I shouldn't have come out here at all! I didn't mean it! I swear I didn't mean it!"

Eric turned to face her, his eyes suddenly blazing. "Didn't mean what?" he demanded. "You tell me what you were doing, damn it!"

"The cabin," Lisa wailed. "I was going to burn it down! I was going to get even with Cassie by burning the cabin!"

The anger inside of Eric suddenly boiled to the surface. "You're just like him, aren't you?" he grated through clenched teeth. "You think you can do anything, and everybody's always going to let you get away with it!"

"Stop it," Lisa whimpered. "I didn't mean—"

"You didn't mean what? You didn't mean to do what you just said you were going to do? You didn't mean to slap me? What didn't you mean, Lisa? What!"

But Lisa didn't hear him, for the truck was moving again, its headlights slowly sweeping the marsh, twin eyes searching for them.

"Maybe—maybe he won't be able to see us," Lisa gasped. "Maybe if we just stay still—"

And then the lights were on her, and without thinking Lisa stood up. She stood perfectly still, frozen in the blinding glare.

Like a bug on a fucking pin, Ed Cavanaugh crowed to himself. There she stood, a scarf wrapped around her head, her black sweater almost invisible against the background of the night. But it was her, all right. He could almost see those eyes of hers, those accusing eyes—and he could almost taste the fear in her. But where was Eric? But it no longer mattered, not really. He could take care of Eric anytime.

But he might never get another shot at Cassie as good as this one. He gunned the engine and popped the clutch. The rear end of the truck dropped lower and the wheels once more dug into the sand.

The sudden movement of the truck seemed to free Lisa, and she screamed.

"Run! He's coming again. *Run!*" Without thinking, she

spun around and lurched off the path, into the reeds and grasses that choked the marsh.

Water flooded into her shoes and she stumbled, then caught herself and plunged on, no longer caring whether she was on a path, caring only about hiding herself from Eric's father and the truck. But the lights seemed to stay on her no matter how she twisted and dodged. It was almost as if they were playing with her.

Eric moved quickly down the path, his fury still growing. Suddenly he hoped his father *would* find her. Let her find out what could really happen to her! He didn't care anymore. He didn't care about any of them! And then, a few steps ahead of him, he saw a shape on the path—no more than a small dark mass, crouching low to the ground.

And two yellow eyes, glowing brightly in the darkness.

Sumi.

Eric paused, staring at the cat.

Cassie's cat. Or so they all thought.

There was a reason why he was here, why he had stumbled across him—he was sure of it.

As he looked into Sumi's glowing eyes, he knew what the reason was.

He thought quickly, then knew what he had to do. He crouched down and whispered soothingly to the cat. Sumi's tail twitched, then he crept slowly forward, into Eric's waiting hands.

Slowly, concentrating on the fury pent up inside him—and on the sting of Lisa's slap—he began stroking Sumi's soft fur.

Beneath his fingers he could feel the cat's body tense up. It was working. It was all working.

The gray shape rose in front of Lisa like a shadow out of the night, and her hands instinctively came up to shield her face.

Too late.

With the speed of lightning Sumi's claws sank into the flesh of Lisa's cheeks, and she screamed in sudden pain. Stumbling, she lurched sideways, and suddenly the grasses seemed to wrap themselves around her.

But far worse than the slime and reeds of the marsh was the creature tearing at her now.

Where had it come from?

Why was it attacking her?

She thrashed against it, trying to tear it away, but it only clung closer, its claws sinking deeper and deeper. A searing pain slashed through her as its jaws closed on her cheek and ripped a piece of flesh away.

She rolled violently, trying to escape the animal's fury, and then the ground suddenly gave way beneath her and she felt herself begin to sink through the brackish water, into the sucking mixture of mud and sand below.

She screamed again, flailing at the muck that held her in its grasp, managing to knock the cat aside. Sobbing, she struggled to her hands and knees, but then the cat was on her again. She felt her right leg plunge knee deep in the quicksand as the animal's claws stripped the skin away from her forehead. As she clawed at the cat with her hands, she tried to jerk her leg free, but only felt her left leg begin to sink too.

"No!" she screamed. Then: "Eric! Eric—help me!" For a second nothing happened, but then she heard the roar of the truck's engine once more. Suddenly the lights were on her again, slicing through the tangle of reeds which now seemed to threaten her.

"Please," she sobbed. "Please, help me . . . please. . . ." But the marsh held her firmly in its grip, and the cat's attack went relentlessly on.

The harder she struggled, the deeper into the quicksand she sank. Then, as the shallow layer of water above the quicksand closed over her, the cat suddenly abandoned her.

Swim.

The thought rose out of the depths of her subconscious, and she began trying to fight the panic that had already overwhelmed her. But it was too late, and as she flailed her arms, the reeds and grasses only wrapped themselves more tightly around her . . . until she felt she could struggle no more. All she could do was wait, whimpering and bleeding, to die.

Eric burst out of the marsh and paused to catch his breath. His heart was pounding and he could feel the blood throbbing through his veins with so much pressure it made his head ache and his vision blur. But when he looked back toward the beach, he could still see the lights of the truck.

Only they were still now, reaching out into the marsh.

Had his father found Lisa yet? And if he had, what had he found . . . ?

He turned away and forced himself to run once more. Then he found the house he was looking for, and pounded up onto its front porch to pummel at the door with his fists. After what seemed to be an eternity, the door finally opened and Charlotte Ambler, clutching at the bodice of her robe, stared out at him.

"It—it's Lisa," Eric gasped. "In the marsh. He—he's trying to kill her, Mrs. Ambler."

Charlotte's eyes widened. "Kill her?" she repeated. "Who, Eric? Who's trying to kill Lisa?"

"My father," Eric rasped. "My father!"

Charlotte Ambler stared at Eric. What on earth could he be talking about? After what had happened at the dance—

Her mind reeling, she pulled Eric into her house.

A moment later she was calling the False Harbor police department. It seemed as though it took forever before a bored voice finally answered the phone.

Ed Cavanaugh sat in his truck, watching the girl die. It seemed to take a long time, but it didn't matter. It was good to see it happen, good to enjoy every moment of it.

As she struggled, he began to feel the same strange pleasure he always felt after he'd put Laura in her place, or given Eric a whipping.

He left the truck and picked his way slowly into the marsh, until at last he was standing in the muck only a few feet from her. Now, out of her torn and bleeding face, he could see her eyes watching him in the glow of the headlights. There was terror in them, the kind of terror he had never seen in Laura's eyes, or in Eric's, and he smiled as he watched her writhing in the tangle of reeds and ooze. But even through his drunkenness, he could sense that something wasn't quite right.

It was her eyes. There was something about them that was wrong.

Maybe, he decided, it was just because she was dying.

* * *

Lisa looked up into the twisted face above her.

He wasn't going to help her, wasn't going to release her from the grip of death.

He was smiling at her, smiling at her with an expression she had never seen before.

He was going to watch her, and he was going to enjoy every moment of her agony.

No, she told herself. *No. I won't let him do that. I won't*.

Making up her mind, she tensed her body for the final effort, then lunged—

—downward.

She twisted deeper into the muck, and felt it close over her head and begin to ooze up into her nostrils.

She opened her mouth, but no scream emerged as the thick sludge filled her mouth, then her throat.

Even as her body revolted, retching against the vile invasion, she forced herself yet deeper, until she felt the mud and sand close over her.

It wasn't right. She wasn't supposed to die tonight. If anyone was supposed to die, it should have been Cassie. But she hadn't even come out here to kill Cassie. Not really.

She was only going to burn the cabin.

That was all. Just burn the cabin down.

Then, as the oxygen slowly leeched out of her bloodstream, a strange euphoria began to overtake her.

In the final moments of her life, the fear and terror drained out of Lisa Chambers, and she felt a great calmness seize her spirit. Then the blackness overcame her, and the last thing she saw, its tail twitching as its eyes glowed a bright gold in the yellow beam of a headlight, was the cat—Cassie's cat—watching. Watching, and remembering everything that happened.

It knew, Lisa thought. It knew what I was going to do.

Then it was over.

Chapter 22

Gene Templeton stifled a yawn and tried to ignore the weariness that was slowly infusing his body. Twenty years ago he'd just be getting his second wind along about now. But not anymore. He was just too old. Still, a long night stretched ahead of him. He glanced at the notes he'd taken while Eric Cavanaugh repeated his story of what had happened on the beach an hour before, then shifted his attention to the boy himself. Eric's eyes betrayed his nervousness, but he was much calmer than he'd been when Templeton arrived. He sat stiffly on the edge of the Victorian sofa in Charlotte Ambler's living room, his mother beside him.

The bruises on Laura's face were still clearly visible.

"Ed did that to you, didn't he," he stated, his voice flat.

Laura stiffened, then shook her head. "I—I fell," she murmured.

Fell. Did she really expect him to believe her? She knew he'd just come from talking to Rosemary Winslow. She'd seen him there before he'd picked her up and brought her here. Well, he wasn't going to argue with her right now. Sighing heavily, he turned back to Eric, whose expression clearly indicated that he wasn't sure the police chief believed his story any more than he believed Laura's. "You're sure it was your dad?" Templeton asked once more.

Eric nodded his head obstinately. "I already told you. I saw him, and so did Lisa. It was Dad, all right."

Templeton flipped his notebook closed and tucked it into

the inside pocket of his jacket. "Okay. I'll go out to the beach and have a look around." He turned to Charlotte Ambler, who had been sitting in silence, carefully listening to every word Eric had spoken. But so far she'd said nothing. "Can I use your phone? Before I start combing the beach I'd like to call Fred Chambers. Maybe Lisa's already home."

Charlotte rose to her feet. "In the kitchen," she said, though there was a telephone sitting on the table at Templeton's elbow. "It's more private," she added. She led the police chief into the kitchen and nodded to the wall phone next to the sink. But instead of leaving him alone to make his call, she stayed where she was, obviously thinking about something. But only after Templeton finished talking to Fred Chambers did she speak.

"She's not home, is she?" she asked softly.

He turned to the high school principal and shook his head. "Something's on your mind, Charlotte. If it has anything to do with this, you might as well tell me now."

Charlotte Ambler took a deep breath. "I keep wondering what Cassie was doing all that time. I mean, I could hear Ed's horn blaring. I didn't think much about it—it happens all the time when the kids are out there. But if Cassie was in Miranda's cabin, she must have heard it too. Wouldn't she have come out to find out what was going on?"

"Same thing I've been thinking," Templeton agreed. "And you can bet that that's where I'm going first. If Lisa did go into the marsh, she'd probably have tried to get to the cabin. With any luck at all, that's where she is right now." He shook his head. "I wish to Christ Laura had filed charges against that son of a bitch years ago. Something like this was bound to happen sooner or later."

"Laura should have left him," Charlotte agreed. "She should have thrown him out."

"Well, the fact is she didn't, and it sure looks like he's gone around the bend this time. I'll let you know what I find out at the beach. If I find anything," he added darkly.

A moment later he was gone, and a few minutes after that Laura and Eric left too.

"Are you sure you want to go home?" Charlotte asked them. "If Ed's there—"

"I can take care of him," Eric replied quietly. "I told him

this morning I was through with him pushing me around. That's why he came after me with the truck. But he can't bring the truck in the house. We'll be all right."

After they were gone, Charlotte Ambler sat silently in her living room, waiting.

While they'd been talking, a spring squall had gathered, and now she heard the patter of rain begin on the roof.

It struck her as an omen.

They're coming for me, Cassie thought. *They're going to think I'm crazy, and take me away. . . .*

She knew Lisa was dead, had known it as soon as Sumi came back and leaped into her arms.

She'd felt the familiar tingling sensation, and then the images had begun to form.

And she'd watched Lisa die.

She'd stayed in the cabin for a while, but then, when she saw the flashing light of the police car and watched it speed down Oak Street and pull up in front of one of the houses across from the park, she'd known what was going to happen.

What if they found her here, sitting all by herself in Miranda's house, with Miranda's cat curled up on her lap? What if they made her tell them what Sumi had shown her? They'd think she was crazy. They'd think she'd killed Lisa herself, and then they'd lock her up.

Panic began to build up in her, and she quickly closed the damper on the old cast-iron stove then put out the lamp. At last she left the cabin, pushing her way through the marsh as fast as she could.

If she got home soon enough—if they didn't find her— she could say she'd left the cabin right after Eric did. She wouldn't have to tell them what had happened, or what she'd seen through Sumi's eyes.

It seemed to take forever, but finally she came to the edge of the marsh and slipped into the thicket of bushes on the fringe of the park. Unaware that she was retracing the route Lisa Chambers had used earlier, she forced herself through the lilacs, working her way toward Oak Street. When she got there, she paused for a moment, searching the street for cars. There were none. Taking a deep breath, she bolted out of the bushes, dashed across the street, and ran up

Cambridge to Alder. Only when she was within sight of the house did she pause to catch her breath. Then, as the rain started to fall, she dashed across the street and down the driveway to the back door.

Rosemary was sitting at the kitchen table, her face pale, a cup of tea clutched between her hands. When Cassie came into the kitchen, she gasped slightly, and rose to her feet. She took a step toward the girl, but Cassie shrank back.

In Cassie's arms Sumi hissed softly.

Rosemary hesitated, but then everything that had happened that evening suddenly jelled into anger. "Where have you been?" she demanded. "You walked out of here wearing those—those *rags*—looking like you'd lost your mind or something, and then you're gone most of the night! Do you really think you can just walk in and out of here like it's some kind of hotel?"

Cassie gasped, and her eyes widened fearfully. "Eric and I—something happened at the dance, and we left early. So we went out to Miranda's cabin. . . ."

Rosemary glared at the girl furiously. *Miranda's cabin,* she thought dumbly. *Everything I've been through, and she went for a walk in the marsh. All the things I imagined, all the things I was afraid of, and they were out hiking!* The last vestige of her self-control dissolved. "How dare you? I don't know if Diana put up with this kind of thing, but I can tell you that I won't. I know you've been through a lot, and I know your father thinks I'm too hard on you! But let me tell you something, young lady—your father isn't here now, and as long as you're in my house, you will obey my rules!"

Cassie's eyes glistened with tears. "I didn't do anything—" she began, but Rosemary cut her off.

"Didn't do anything? This afternoon you walked out of here against my wishes, and were rude to me as well. And tonight you promised to be home no later than eleven o'clock. You didn't come back when you said you would, and you didn't even bother to phone. Do you really think you can just walk back in and not expect anything to happen? I was about to call your father!"

Cassie felt a chill of fear. Rosemary was going to call her father just because she'd stayed out too late? But that didn't make any sense. She must already know about Lisa. "You're going to call Dad?" she asked, her voice trembling slightly. "Wh-why?"

Rosemary glared at her, about to lash out again, but then checked her fury. It wasn't Cassie's fault—not all of it. For a moment she was tempted to tell Cassie what had happened with Ed Cavanaugh, then changed her mind. There wasn't any point, and besides, it was all over now. "It doesn't matter," she said. "At least you're home and you're all right."

But Cassie didn't hear her, for the panic she'd felt in the cabin was flooding back over her now. "You've been talking about me, haven't you?" she demanded.

Rosemary gasped in surprise at the accusation. "Cassie—"

"You have, haven't you?" Cassie insisted. Who was it? What had they said? And why wouldn't Rosemary tell her? "Was it that doctor? The one who thinks I'm crazy?"

"Cassie . . ." Rosemary said again. She took a step toward her, and Cassie backed away. Her eyes looked wild now, darting from one corner of the room to another, as if she were searching for something she expected to attack her at any moment.

"You're just like Lisa, aren't you?" she demanded, her voice breaking as she choked back a sob. "She hates me—she hates me, and she wanted to kill me tonight! But it wasn't my fault! I didn't do anything, but everybody hates me!" She spun around and fled from the room, and a moment later Rosemary could hear her feet pounding up the stairs.

Rosemary sat still for a moment, then forced her body to relax. What had happened? What on earth had gone wrong? She hadn't accused Cassie of anything at all. She'd been angry, yes. But not that angry.

And yet—

Cassie's words echoed in her mind.

I didn't do anything, but everybody hates me. . . .

But nobody hated her, not really. And to say that Lisa Chambers wanted to kill her . . . it sounded . . .

She hesitated, then let herself formulate the word in her mind.

It sounded paranoid.

Suddenly her fears—all of them—closed in on Rosemary once again, and once again she felt the urge to call Keith. He couldn't get home tonight, but tomorrow . . .

No! she told herself. You're upset, and you're not thinking clearly, and you're overreacting to everything. Stop it! Just stop it!

Doing her best to shut out everything that had happened that day, she began going through the habitual motions of closing up the house for the night. Not that there was any point to locking up, she thought ruefully.

Deep in her gut she knew that the day was not yet over, and that she would get no sleep tonight.

"We have to get rid of him, Mom," Eric said.

His voice was emotionless, but the cold hatred in his eyes twisted at Laura's heart. *Not him, too,* she prayed silently. *Don't let him turn out like his father. Please!* "We can't," she whispered. "Please, Eric—don't talk like that!"

"Why not!" Eric demanded. "He beat you up this morning, and he hit you again tonight! For God's sake, Mom. What are we supposed to do? Just wait around until he actually kills one of us?"

Laura's eyes widened, and her hand dropped away from the new bruise on her cheek. "Eric! He's your father, and he loves you. You mustn't talk like that."

"Why not? And he doesn't love me, any more than he loves you. For God's sake, Mom, he tried to kill me tonight!"

"He was just angry," Laura tried to explain, but the words sounded hollow even to herself. "You shouldn't have gone off with Cassie like that. You know what he told you, and you deliberately disobeyed him."

"So now it's my fault that he beats us up?" Eric exploded. "You don't expect me to buy that, do you? Now, are you going to tell me what happened or not?"

"He—he found me over at the Winslows'," Laura whispered. "I thought you and Cassie might be there. And he found me there."

"He hit you just because you went over to the neighbors?" Eric's rage drove the last vestiges of fear out of his mind. "I'm gonna call Templeton again. Maybe you won't tell him what happened, but I bet Mrs. Winslow will." He reached for the phone, but Laura put out a hand and stopped him.

"He was here," she whispered, her voice twisted with

the sobs she was struggling to control. "Rosemary called him after . . . after . . ."

"After what?" Eric said tightly. His jaw was working, and his voice was taut with fury. "Did he beat her up too?"

Laura shook her head, and buried her face in her hands. When she spoke, Eric could barely hear her. He had to ask her to repeat her words. Finally she dropped her hands from her face and stared at her son expressionlessly. When she spoke again, her voice was flat, as if the words no longer meant anything to her. "She says your father tried to rape her. And she says she's going to press charges against him."

Eric stared at his mother speechlessly, then sank into a chair. His mind was whirling, trying to sort it out. His father must have gone crazy. Finally, after it had sunk in, he looked at his mother with bleak eyes. "I hope she does," he said softly. "And I hope they lock him up."

"Eric—" Laura tried to protest, but he only shook his head.

"He was trying to kill us, Mom. I don't know why he was pissed at Lisa, but—" He fell silent as he realized the truth. "Oh, Jesus," he whispered, his face turning ashen.

"Eric?" Laura breathed. "What is it?"

"It wasn't Lisa at all. She was dressed like Cassie. That's who he thought it was. He thought Lisa was Cassie. And he wanted to kill her so bad, he would have killed me too."

Laura clamped her hands over her ears, trying to shut out what Eric was saying. "No," she whimpered, rocking back and forth in her chair. "No, it isn't true . . . none of it—"

"It is, Mom," Eric said softly. "And it's only going to get worse." His voice hardened, and his eyes flashed dangerously. "But he won't hurt us anymore, Mom. I won't let him. I'll kill him, Mom. If he tries to hurt me again, I swear to God I'll kill him."

Gene Templeton got out of his car and started out into the blackness over the beach and the marsh. He reached back into the car, switched the headlights on, and twin beams of light cut through the rain, casting an eerie glow over the sand and the surf beyond. As far as he could tell, there was no sign of the white pickup truck. He started to slam the car door, then thought again and switched on the flashing lights on top. If Lisa Chambers was still out there somewhere, there was no use letting her think Ed Cavanaugh had come back again. Finally, flipping on the powerful flashlight he always carried in the car, he started through the rain toward the cabin where Miranda Sikes had lived. With any luck at all he would find Lisa Chambers there.

Twenty minutes later he was back.

The cabin had been empty, but the stove was still warm. So at least part of Eric Cavanaugh's story had been true. But what about the rest of it?

His bones beginning to ache, he began his search of the beach. It was easy to find the tire tracks where the truck had left the parking lot and started across the sand, but the tracks quickly disappeared where the rising tide and the pounding surf had washed the beach clean. He began walking east toward Cranberry Point, playing the light on the sand just above the surf line. About a hundred yards up the beach he found what he was looking for.

More tire tracks, this time leading toward the marsh. He followed them across the beach and over the dunes, then traced them as they led back and forth along the edge of the wetlands. The truck seemed to have turned twice then found what it was looking for. Though the rain, increasing now, was quickly washing them away, there were still the remnants of two short tire tracks perpendicular to the tide line, where it appeared that the truck had been parked for a while.

Cautiously, Gene Templeton approached the marsh, searching with his light for a break in the reeds. Three times he called out Lisa's name, but the rain muffled his voice, and he could hear no answer except for the flappings of a bird.

Finally he found a narrow path with two sets of footprints still faintly visible in the packed mud and sand. He followed them for a few yards and came to a place where it looked as though someone had either knelt or fallen. From there a single pair of footprints continued along the path.

But off to the left some of the reeds had been broken and the marsh grasses were bent.

Here, apparently, was where Lisa Chambers had left the path. Templeton played his light out into the marsh, wondering vaguely whether he was hoping to get a glimpse of her or not. If she was still here and had neither seen him nor responded to his calls—

He abandoned the thought, knowing too well where it led.

The darkness was momentarily washed away by a sweep of headlights, then by another set of beams. Templeton turned and saw two cars turning off Cape Drive into the parking lot. A moment later they were joined by a third, then a fourth.

Great, he reflected sourly. Just what I need. A search party that thinks it can comb a fucking swamp in the middle of the fucking night. I'll wind up with half the town caught in quicksand. He quickly retraced his steps and started down the beach. By the time he got back to the parking lot, Fred Chambers was busy giving orders to three of his friends, all of whom, the police chief noted silently, had kids about the same age as Lisa. As he stepped into the group, Chambers eyed him almost belligerently.

"Did you find her?" Lisa's father demanded.

"I just got here, Fred," Templeton replied. "How come you're not home with Harriet?"

"You think I'm going to sit at home when my little girl's missing? I'm not that kind of man, and you know it!"

"I also know there isn't much any of us can do out here right now," Templeton said. "I was just about to call a couple of my boys to give me a hand, and I could use some of the fire volunteers too." He nodded toward Clyde Bennett, who was the unpaid assistant fire chief of the village. "You want to take care of that for me?" Bennett's eyes flicked toward Fred Chambers, then he nodded and went to Templeton's car. A few seconds later he spoke quickly but quietly into the microphone of the car's radio. "As for the rest of you," Templeton continued, "if you want to poke around, I can't stop you. But I don't want any of you going into the marsh. Not tonight. It's too dangerous, and I can't worry about you guys and Lisa too."

The two men he was speaking to said nothing. Both of them seemed to be waiting for Fred Chambers to contradict the police chief. But when he spoke, Chambers didn't argue.

"What about Cavanaugh?" he asked instead. "Have you picked him up yet?"

Templeton shook his head. "Nope. Right now I'm a lot more interested in finding Lisa than I am in finding Ed."

"But what if he's got her?" Chambers began.

Templeton cut him off. "If he does, then we're too late already. I'm betting he was so drunk he didn't even know what he was doing. And if he was, Lisa probably got away from him, which means she might still be out there somewhere. But I can't find her if I have to stand here with you all night. Go home, Fred. Go home and take care of Harriet, and as soon as I know what's happening, I'll let you know. Okay?"

For a moment Templeton thought the banker was going to argue with him, but then he saw Chambers's shoulders sag in resignation.

"Okay," Fred agreed, all the authority in his voice suddenly gone. "It's just—Christ, Gene, I just feel so helpless. And you know how I am. . . ."

"I know," Templeton agreed. *Got to try to run everything, whether you know what you're doing or not,* he said silently to himself. Then, aloud: "It'll be okay, Fred. We'll find her."

He led Chambers back to his car, still trying to reassure him, and as his deputies and the members of the fire department began to arrive, turned his attention to organizing a search party. "I want you to work in pairs," he told them. "It's dangerous out there. So be careful. But we're going to search the marsh foot by foot. Let's just hope she's out there somewhere." Finally, as the men began moving carefully over the treacherous paths of the marsh, he returned to his own car.

It was time to find Ed Cavanaugh.

The bottle of bourbon on the greasy dinette table was only one-fourth full, and the sink of the galley held half-a-dozen empty beer bottles. But for some reason the alcohol hadn't made Ed feel any better. He reached down and fished in the little refrigerator under his seat for another beer, then cursed softly when he realized there wasn't any more. Tipping the bottle of bourbon to his lips, he poured a long slug into his mouth, then slammed the bottle back onto the table as the fiery liquid burned its way down his throat to his stomach. Vaguely, he heard the topside hatch open, and glanced up to see Gene Templeton standing at the top of the companionway. "Well, look who's here," he drawled, gesturing toward the empty seat opposite him. "Pull up a bunk and have a drink. I'm buyin'."

Templeton's eyes flicked over the cabin, and he found himself almost relieved that there was no sign of Lisa Chambers. "Thought you and I ought to have a little chat, Ed," he said. He moved into the grubby interior of the fishing boat, and wondered how even Ed Cavanaugh could stand the mess. Everything in sight was covered with grease, and the sole of the cabin was strewn with a tangle of ropes, tools, floats, and odd bits of net. Trying to ignore it, he slid into the dinette opposite Cavanaugh and poured himself a shot of whiskey he had no intention of drinking.

"Saw your truck up on the street," he said, doing his best to sound casual. Ed was so drunk, he might just be able to catch him completely off guard. "Just thought I'd drop in and say hello."

Cavanaugh's brows arched skeptically. "Well, ain't you the sociable one," he grunted. "And why shouldn't my truck be up there? It against the law to park on the street now?"

"Just thought you might have let Eric have it tonight," he offered. "It being Saturday night. Know what I mean?" he added, forcing the kind of lewd wink Cavanaugh was so good at.

Ed snickered drunkenly. "Little shit'll be lucky if I even let 'im live, after tonight." He laughed mirthlessly. "An' I bet he's so scared he never even says boo to me again."

"Scared?" Templeton asked. It was working. Cavanaugh was going to admit to the whole thing. "How come he should be scared?"

" 'Cause of what I did," Ed told him, a boozy cackle bubbling out of his throat. "Caught him down on the beach with Cassie Winslow and scared the piss out of both of them."

Now it was Templeton who frowned with puzzlement. "What are you talking about, Ed? What did you do?"

Suddenly Cavanaugh's expression took on a look of cunning. "Oh, no," he said. "I know what you're trying to do. You're trying to pin it on me, ain't you? But I didn't do nothin'. All I did was chase 'em around, till they ran into the marsh. An' I tried to save her. I really did."

"Tried to save her?" Templeton echoed, a tight knot of fear forming in his stomach. "Tried to save who?"

Ed eyed him blearily. "Cassie," he mumbled. "Ain't you listenin', Templeton? Goddamn bitch went off the trail and got caught in the quicksand. Tried to get to her, but jus' couldn't do it. Jus' couldn't do it . . ." His voice faded away. He reached for the bourbon bottle, but before he could grasp it, Gene Templeton's hand closed on his wrist.

"You've had enough, Ed," he said quietly. "In fact you've had a lot more than enough. I'm taking you in."

Ed's eyes opened in drunken surprise. "Me? What for? What did I do?"

Templeton regarded the other man with a mixture of pity and contempt. "You don't know, do you?" he asked quietly. "You really don't know."

Chapter 23

It's not real. None of it is really happening at all. It's all a bad dream, and I'm going to wake up, and everything's going to be fine. Even as the thoughts flitted through her mind, Rosemary knew it wasn't a dream and that she wasn't going to wake up. A numbness had settled over her, and when her eyes wandered to the clock above the sink, she could barely believe it was only a little after two A.M. The weariness that suffused her mind and body insisted that it must be close to dawn.

And at dawn, she was now certain, she would still be numbly awake, still be dressed, still be sitting up somewhere in the house, waiting.

Waiting for what?

For word that Lisa Chambers had been found? But all of them knew, though no one had yet said it, that when Lisa was found she was going to be—

She couldn't say it, couldn't deal with it.

Tiredly, she faced Gene Templeton, knowing that whatever had to be said, had to be said by her. Laura Cavanaugh seemed to have retreated into some secret place inside herself, and Eric and Cassie had sat listening impassively as Templeton repeated what Ed Cavanaugh had told him. Once or twice Eric shook his head as if to deny his father's version of what had happened on the beach. Cassie had revealed no reaction whatsoever, but merely listened in silence, her expression completely impassive. As Rosemary had watched the

278

girl, she had the strange feeling that Cassie already knew what Ed had told the police chief.

"Then what are you going to do?" Rosemary asked. "What is it you want us to do?"

Templeton shrugged, betraying his helplessness. "I can keep Ed locked up for the rest of the night, but tomorrow, I don't know. If Laura won't charge him—"

"But I'll bring charges," Rosemary insisted. "For God's sake, Gene, he tried to rape me!"

"Did he?" Templeton replied, reluctantly assuming the role of devil's advocate. "We went through this earlier, Rosemary. There isn't a mark on you, and there are no witnesses—"

"Jennifer saw—"

"We already know what Jennifer saw," Templeton repeated for the third time. "She saw you on the telephone, and Ed standing next to you. That's all. If you had a bruise, a scratch, anything!—I might have something to go on. As it is, though, if you bring charges against him he'll just countersue. And when I strip-searched him an hour ago, I found the bruise he needs to back himself up, which you've already admitted you gave him." His lips twisted into a rueful grin. "The odds are, though, that he was too drunk to remember exactly what happened. So there we are—he swears he didn't see Lisa on the beach at all, and right now he's absolutely certain that Cassie is dead. He insists he saw her go into the quicksand but couldn't get to her in time to save her. Not that I can put much credence in anything Ed says, given his condition."

"He didn't even try. He hates me, you know." The words had come from Cassie.

Templeton studied Cassie carefully for a moment. She was holding something back, he was almost certain of it. But what? And why would Ed Cavanaugh hate her? But her eyes had taken on a veiled look that told him she'd said all she was going to.

Appalled by the realization of what she had said, Cassie sat silently, hands tightly clasped in front of her. She wanted to tell them she knew exactly what had happened to Lisa, tell them that Mr. Cavanaugh could have saved her, but instead he'd stood there and watched her die. But what could she say that would make them believe her? If she told them the

truth—that she'd seen the whole thing through Sumi's eyes—
they'd only think she was crazy. "He—he wouldn't have
tried," she stammered as her stepmother and the police chief
continued to stare at her. "If he thought Lisa was me, he
wouldn't have done anything. He—he hates me. He didn't
even want Eric to talk to me anymore!"

"All right," Templeton said heavily, standing up and
pulling his raincoat on. "I'd better get out to the marsh and
see what's happened. Ed can sit in a cell the rest of the night,
and in the morning I'll think of something to charge him
with. I can try failure to report evidence of a crime or
something." He turned to face Laura. "Unless you decide to
change your mind."

Laura looked up fearfully. "I can't." Her voice was a
whisper. "I just can't. You have to understand. . . ."

Templeton nodded wearily. He did, indeed, understand,
for the position Laura had taken tonight was no different from
what he'd seen again and again as a policeman in Boston:
women who were absolutely certain that the only way to save
themselves from worse beatings was to keep silent about the
ones they had already suffered. And in a way they were right,
for too many men had come out of courtrooms swearing they
had changed, only to return to their wives with their hatreds
festering deeper than ever.

Some of those women, Templeton knew, had paid with
their lives for assuming the law could protect them. Laura
Cavanaugh had no intention of becoming one of those.

"Okay," he said, his voice gentle. "I'll do what I can to
hold him, but I can't tell you he's not going to do it again,
Laura. You know he is."

Now it was Eric who broke his long silence. "He won't,"
he said, his voice clear. "I told Mom, and I'll tell you too. If
he ever tries to beat either one of us again, I'll kill him."

Templeton gazed silently at the boy. Something in Eric,
he realized, had changed. Always before there had been a
gentleness and kindness in Eric that he'd always marveled at.
By rights the boy should have been silent and brooding,
striking out at others in retribution for the injustices he
suffered at home.

In Templeton's experience, most boys Eric's age and
with Eric's background had long since shown some rebellion.

But Eric never had. Always he'd seemed to rise above his father's hatred, had appeared almost untouched by it. But now there was a hardness in the boy's eyes, a detached coldness. Eric's words had not been uttered in momentary anger.

"That won't be an answer, Eric," he said quietly. "In a few more years you'll be out of it. If you can't stand it now, file charges against him yourself, or take off. But don't even think about killing him. He'd probably kill you first, but even if he didn't, you'd never get away with it. You're a good kid, Eric—you always have been. Don't let him push you into destroying your own life."

Eric's lips tightened, and the expression in his eyes didn't change. Finally, with nothing left to be said, Templeton buttoned up his raincoat and disappeared out into the night. When he was gone, Rosemary looked nervously at Eric, but he didn't seem aware of her gaze. His eyes were fixed on Cassie with an intensity that made Rosemary turn to look at her stepdaughter.

Cassie was returning Eric's steady gaze.

An icy chill passed through Rosemary's body. *They're hiding something*, she thought. *They know something that neither of them wants to talk about.*

The rain finally stopped as dawn began to break, but still the morning light came slowly. Leaden clouds hung low over the sea, and the horizon seemed not to exist at all. It was as if False Harbor, that morning, had been suspended in both space and time.

Charlotte Ambler opened the drapes over the front windows of her house and looked out into the gray morning. A somnolent foreboding hung over the village, and there was none of the usual Sunday morning peacefulness that had always been her favorite part of her week. On any other rainy Sunday morning she would be lighting a fire in her fireplace and curling up in her robe to slowly peruse the thick weekend edition of the Boston paper. But this morning was not like other Sunday mornings.

She gazed out toward the marsh, where the tired figures of the searchers were now clearly silhouetted against the gun-metal sky. A knot of people had already gathered in the parking lot at the end of Oak Street, and as she watched them quietly talking among themselves, she realized that she was seeing a reflection of both the best and the worst of village living.

In another place—a larger city—Lisa Chambers's disappearance would have been noted in the morning paper, and the search would have gone quietly on, almost unnoticed. And for most people, life, too, would have gone quietly on, essentially unchanged for the absence of a single member of their society.

But in False Harbor there was no morning paper; indeed, none was needed, for by now, Charlotte was quite certain, there wasn't a soul in town who was unaware of what had happened last night, at least in its barest essentials. But in the realm of detail there would be as many versions filtering from ear to ear as there were mouths to speak them, and until the truth about what had happened to Lisa was discovered, there would be scant attention paid to any other subject.

She turned away from her front window and went to the kitchen. Soon people would begin noticing that her drapes were open and would start dropping by, some looking for news, some only needing a respite from the vigil by the beach. Her large percolator had just begun to simmer when the doorbell rang for the first time. When she opened the front door, she wasn't surprised to see Gene Templeton standing on the front porch, looking every bit as tired as she herself felt.

"Anything?" she asked.

Templeton shook his head. "Not yet."

"What about Ed Cavanaugh?"

Templeton shrugged. "I found him on his boat, dead drunk. He—well, he claims there's a body out there all right. But he says it's Cassie Winslow's. He says he saw her in some quicksand but couldn't get to her."

"Cassie?" Charlotte echoed. "But Eric said—"

"I know," Templeton interrupted. "And if there *is* a body out there, it isn't Cassie. She's at home with Rosemary. Anyway, a little while ago I got to thinking . . ." He fell silent, reluctant to reveal the thought that had been nibbling at the edge of his mind for the last hour or so.

Charlotte frowned in puzzlement.

"I keep thinking about Simms," Templeton said finally.

"Harold?" Charlotte breathed. "I—I'm afraid I don't understand."

The police chief licked his lips nervously. "Remember what happened that day? He'd been riding Cassie pretty hard, and Eric too." He paused. Then: "Lisa's been giving Cassie a rough time, too, hasn't she?"

Charlotte's frown deepened as she grasped what Templeton was suggesting. Before she could speak again, a shout rose up from the marsh and both she and Templeton turned to see one of the deputies waving frantically. Templeton's stomach knotted as he realized that the man was standing only a few yards inside the marsh, very close to the place where last night he'd seen the fading marks of tire tracks on the beach. It was, he realized now, almost as if they had been pointing at the spot where Harve Lamont now stood.

Swearing softly, Templeton took the front steps of Charlotte Ambler's house two at a time and began loping back toward the marsh. Pausing only to pull her mackintosh from the hook by the front door, Charlotte followed as quickly as she could.

"How'd you find her?" Templeton asked, his voice low enough that only the heavyset deputy would be able to hear him. Harve Lamont said nothing for a moment. His eyes were still fixed on the specter of Lisa Chambers's face, barely visible beneath the thin layer of brackish water that covered the surface of the marsh.

"The reeds," Harve finally managed to say. "I couldn't really see her at all. But the reeds were all broken here, and the grass was kind of squished down. It looked to me as though there'd been some kind of struggle or something. So I came out a little closer, and there was just enough light, so . . . so—" His voice cracked and he was unable to go on.

She was nearly buried in the mud, only her face visible. Her mouth, wide open, seemed still to be forming a silent scream, while her eyes stared sightlessly up through the water. The lacerations that covered her face had been washed clean, and the damage that had been inflicted showed clearly through the water. The skin on her forehead was all but torn away, and a large chunk was missing from one of her cheeks.

And everywhere—in every place in which her flesh was still intact—there were deep parallel rows of cuts that looked to Gene Templeton almost exactly like the wounds that had covered Harold Simms's face.

Lisa's left arm was buried in the mud, but her right, almost completely entangled in a matting of swamp grass, was crossed over her body. From her position Templeton was almost certain she had continued struggling right up until the end, then—in a last terrified grasp at survival—managed to turn herself over. But it had already been too late.

Templeton nodded curtly, then signaled two of the firemen to bring a stretcher. Clyde Bennett and another man appeared with it. Behind them came two other deputies carrying wide planks, which they carefully laid on the surface of the marsh, one on each side of the corpse.

It took the four men several minutes to work Lisa's remains loose from the oozing sands. When at last her stiffened body came free, there was an ugly sucking noise as the marsh gave up its prize. But then, as Templeton watched in a kind of awe, the mud flowed swiftly together. In moments only the broken reeds still testified to the fact that only hours before a girl had died there.

In a strange cortege, Templeton led the four men bearing Lisa Chambers's body slowly back to the path and the beach beyond. Waiting for them at the point where the reeds met the sand was Harriet Chambers, her face ashen, her hands trembling.

She stared at the body for a few seconds, her lips working to stifle the scream building in her throat.

"No," she whispered at last, and then the word was repeated, rising into a keening wail that sliced through the quiet of the morning. *"Noooooo . . ."*

She was about to throw herself on her daughter's corpse when Templeton slid a firm arm around her, holding her back while he signaled to Fred Chambers with his free hand. Instantly Fred was next to his wife, supporting her while he glared at the police chief over her shoulder.

"Well?" he demanded. "Are you satisfied now? Now are you going to lock that drunken son of a bitch up?"

Templeton stared at the man for a moment, then decided it was useless to try to argue with him now. If he wasn't in shock yet, he would be in another few minutes, and though the police chief felt pity for Lisa's distraught parents, he had to attend to pressing matters. To his relief the Chamberses' friends were already beginning to surround them even as he stepped away to begin issuing orders to have Lisa's body taken to the clinic, where it would be examined by Paul Samuels.

Starting back toward the parking lot and his car, Templeton saw Charlotte Ambler, who appeared to have been frozen in her tracks by the sight of Lisa's body. But as he came abreast of her, she put out a hand and grasped his wrist.

"What does it mean?" she asked. "It—it *is* just like Harold Simms. But what does it mean?"

Templeton shook his head grimly. "I don't know yet," he said. "And I'm not going to even venture a guess until the doc's taken a look at her."

He tried to move on, but Mrs. Ambler didn't release her grip. Templeton felt her fingers tighten on his arm.

"What if it is?" she pressed. "What if it really is just like Harold?" Her eyes held Templeton's. "Are you going to say she did it to herself?"

Templeton's eyes flashed toward the group of onlookers who were staring curiously at Charlotte now, straining to hear her words. "I'm not saying anything yet, Charlotte." He spoke quietly but with an urgency he hoped she would understand. But Charlotte seemed not to have heard him at all.

"What if Harold was right?" she went on. "What if he really did see Cassie that day? And what if Ed Cavanaugh really saw her last night?"

Templeton heard the faint gasp that passed over the small crowd, immediately followed by a buzz of whispering.

That does it, he thought. Within an hour the rumors would be all over town.

Ed Cavanaugh woke up quickly: a sharp pain was jabbing through his head, as if someone had shoved a knitting needle into his ear then jerked it viciously up and down. His eyes, still closed in a futile effort to shut out the throbbing ache in his head, felt like they had ground glass in them, and his tongue—a thick slab in his dry mouth—had a sour taste to it. His body felt clammy, and remnants of the nausea that had first awakened him sometime before dawn were still clawing at him, warning him that if he moved too fast, he would find himself on his knees, retching.

A siren sounded somewhere, exacerbating the agony inside his skull, and he tried to raise his hands to clamp them over his ears, but the movement was too much for his polluted body to stand, and his stomach heaved in protest. He dropped his hands back down and concentrated on summoning the energy to bellow to Laura for a cup of coffee.

Or maybe he should just go back to sleep for an hour.

His fingers closed on the sheets, ready to pull the covers up over his head. Dimly, he became aware that something was wrong.

His hands, instead of clutching the sheets and soft blankets of his own bed, had closed on some kind of rough wool. He held still for a moment, trying to think through the pain in his brain. Then he groaned and opened his eyes a crack.

What he saw confirmed the vague memory he had summoned from the depths of his consciousness.

Above the metal cot on which he lay, there was a concrete wall, its gray paint chipped and etched with obscenities. Halfway up the wall there was a small window, covered on the outside with a heavy grillwork of bars. He stared at the barred window for a few seconds, numbly wondering if perhaps he was only dreaming.

But he knew he wasn't.

Carefully twisting his neck, the throbbing in his head building to a crescendo of pain at the movement, he saw a toilet bolted to the opposite wall.

Another memory stirred, and he vaguely recalled having rolled off the cot during the night to lean over the toilet while the contents of his stomach boiled up from his throat. The stench in the air told him that when he'd finally returned to the makeshift bed, he hadn't bothered to flush the toilet. Slowly, almost tentatively, he reached out and pressed the button that protruded from the wall next to the toilet. Instantly the roar of water under pressure filled the cell, then faded away as the mess in the metal toilet bowl disappeared into the sewers. Ed Cavanaugh groaned, turned his head to the wall and clamped his eyes closed again, as if the action itself could change the reality around him. A moment later, though, the clang of a heavy metal door made him roll back and reopen his bloodshot eyes.

Fuzzily, he recognized Gene Templeton staring at him with a face of stone from outside the cell.

"Heard the toilet flush," Templeton said.

Ed managed a nod. "Sick," he muttered. "Puked my guts out during the night."

"Tough," Templeton replied. "Wash up. You're getting out of here."

Taking a deep breath, Ed heaved himself into a sitting position and dropped his feet to the floor. His shirt, smeared with his own vomit, clung to his body like cellophane, and when he cradled his head in his hands, the smell from his shirt assaulted his nostrils with a force that once more threatened the stability of his aching stomach. "What happened?" he asked. "What am I doing here?"

Templeton regarded him silently for a moment. "You don't remember?"

Cavanaugh hesitated, then slowly shook his head. "I was on my boat," he finally managed. "I was on my boat, and then . . . then . . ." His voice trailed off into silence as slowly, a piece at a time, memories of the previous night trickled back to him. "Fuckin' bitch wife didn't have the guts to file any charges, did she?" he finally asked, his lips twisting into an ugly grin.

Now it was Templeton who took a deep breath, his hands unconsciously clenching into fists as he stared with disgust at the man in the cell. "She not only wouldn't charge you, she showed up an hour ago and put up bail for the only charge I could dream up." His lips tightened grimly. "I did my damnedest to talk her out of it, but she's afraid of what you'd do to her if she left you here. But sooner or later you'll go too far, and when you do, it's going to be my pleasure to ship you off to the slammer, Ed. Then we'll all see how tough you are. The only thing those guys hate more than a rapist is a guy who slaps his wife and kid around. Now clean yourself up. You're disgusting."

Templeton turned away, taking a malicious pleasure in slamming the metal door as he left the block of three small cells. Returning to his desk in the corner of the squad room, he dropped into his chair. His stomach growled in protest against the fact that it was now nine o'clock in the morning and he had missed—so far—two complete meals, not to mention several snacks. He picked up the phone to call Ellie, knowing his wife would cheerfully bring an enormous breakfast to his desk, then dropped the phone back on the hook as he realized that he wasn't really hungry, despite the fact he hadn't eaten since noon the day before.

It was Paul Samuels's report on the manner of Lisa Chambers's death that had cost him his appetite. Not the fact of her death—Templeton had long since learned to deal with death itself. But what Samuels told him a few minutes ago had left him feeling completely helpless.

As he'd feared, there was not a mark on Lisa that Samuels could definitely identify as having been made by human hands. She had died by strangulation, but the doctor was certain that it had been mud in her throat and trachea that had killed her, not some external force closing around her neck. Nor were there bruises on her flesh where hands might have clamped on her, forcing her down into the mud.

"But she fought," the doctor had assured him as they went over the report together. "Some kind of animal attacked her, and she struggled to fight it off. I found traces of fur under her fingernails, but it'll have to be analyzed before I can tell you what it's from. The main thing is, she fought hard, and if it was Ed Cavanaugh she was fighting, he'll have some marks to show for it. But frankly, I don't think he did it. As near as I can figure it, she was trying to fight off whatever jumped her, but she stumbled into the quicksand and lost her footing. And that was it."

There were a few cuts on her arms, but the ones that weren't easily identifiable as having been made by an animal's claws had the exact characteristics of the lacerations made by two varieties of marsh grass. In several of the cuts Samuels had discovered minute traces of the grasses themselves.

"If she'd kept her head," Samuels had finished, "she might have been all right. Whatever it was probably abandoned the attack when she fell into the quicksand, and she could have lain there all night. She'd have been cold and miserable, but she would have lived. Still, you can't blame her for panicking, can you?"

Of course he couldn't. In fact, he couldn't blame anyone yet. Despite all the talk and speculation in the village there was no proof of anything. In Templeton's gut, however, he was now certain that in some way he didn't yet understand, Cassie Winslow was involved.

Cassie's words from last night still haunted him. *He didn't even try.* Her face expressionless, her eyes fixed as though she were staring into the distance, she had spoken in a strange monotone—as though she were reliving something she had already seen.

And then there were the eerie similarities between the wounds on Lisa's face and the angry slashes that had marked Harold Simms.

"What about a cat?" he'd asked Samuels just before he left the clinic.

"It's possible," the doctor had replied. "But it did a hell of a lot of damage. If it was a cat, it sure was no ordinary house pet."

It all added up to zero: no evidence to charge Ed Cavanaugh with Lisa Chambers's death, and no satisfactory explanation for what had happened to her.

And with Laura bailing Ed out of the single charge Gene had been able to devise—obstructing justice by not reporting the discovery of Lisa's body—Templeton couldn't even keep the son of a bitch off the streets for a few days.

His thoughts were interrupted by a banging on the steel door to the cell block, and he got up to bring Ed Cavanaugh into the squad room. Fleetingly he wondered if he could get away with punching the smug look off Cavanaugh's bloated face, but knew he couldn't—bullies like Cavanaugh were the loudest screamers when someone finally gave them what they deserved. Instead he contented himself with telling Cavanaugh exactly what he thought of him while he unlocked the safe and retrieved the other man's keys and wallet.

Not that it did much good.

"Aren't you gonna drive me home?" was all that Cavanaugh said when Templeton's warnings were over.

"Walk," Templeton growled. "The fresh air won't kill

you. And if we all get lucky, you might just be hung over enough to get hit by a truck. Now get out of here."

When Cavanaugh was done, Templeton considered going back to his desk, then gave it up. With a nod to the deputy, he headed home. Maybe with a little sleep—and a good meal—he could start to make sense out of what was happening in False Harbor.

Chapter 24

Ed Cavanaugh let himself in through the back door. Laura was standing at the kitchen sink, washing up the dishes from the breakfast neither she nor Eric had been able to eat. He said nothing, but stripped off his soiled shirt, dumped it into the washing machine, then slipped his arms around Laura's waist and gave her a gentle squeeze. When she stiffened in his arms, he felt a surge of anger, but quickly put it down. He nuzzled her neck for a moment, then pressed his mouth close to her ear.

"I'm sorry," he whispered. "I'm sorry about everything. I just—well, I guess I let things get out of control last night."

Laura twisted away from him. Her voice was cold. "Last night?" she repeated. "What happened last night wasn't anything new, and you know it! You don't expect me just to forget it, do you?"

When he replied, Ed's voice had taken on the slight whine that had become familiar to Laura over the years. "But you have to forgive me, honey. You're all I've got. I just—well, sometimes I love you so much that when I think about losing you I go all to pieces. But last night was it. I promise you that if you forgive me this time, it'll never happen again. Never."

"Until you get drunk again," Laura blurted out, then wished she could reclaim the words. But she'd heard it all so often before. He'd drink, then beat her, then—the next

morning—swear it was the last time. And always she wanted
to believe him. Wanted to hope.

As if he were reading her thoughts, Ed pulled her closer
and pressed her head against his chest. Though the sour odor
of vomit still clung faintly to him, Laura could feel his heart
beating, and the gentle throbbing gave her a strange sense of
security. I don't understand, she thought. I don't understand
how he can still make me feel so safe sometimes.

"I had a long time to think about things in jail," Ed said,
stroking her head now. "Maybe that was what I needed—for
Gene to haul me in. And I want you to know I don't hold it
against him. I'm not holding anything against anybody, sweetheart. Not against you, or Eric, or even Rosemary Winslow.
All we have to do is start fresh. I'm going to stop drinking,
and start taking care of you and Eric. But I can only do it if I
know you still love me. You do, don't you?" he added anxiously. "Isn't that why you bailed me out?"

Laura felt herself weakening. He sounds as if he means it
this time, she found herself thinking. But then she reminded
herself that he'd always sounded as if he'd meant it when he
apologized. Not once had it ever made a difference. "I bailed
you out because I didn't want Eric to have to face his friends
knowing his father was in jail." It was only half true, she
knew, but this time she wasn't just going to give in to him.

Once again he seemed to read her thoughts.

"But this time it's really true. I swear it is. I never
landed in jail before, and it scared me, Laura. It scared the
shit out of me. I lay there all night thinking about my life,
and your life, and what I've done to you, and I felt like a
heel. If you left me, I don't know what I'd do. I—I think I
might go crazy."

He was kissing her neck now, his lips working gently
over her skin. Despite herself, Laura felt the first stirrings of
excitement rising in her. Almost involuntarily her arms slid
around his neck and her fingers ran through his hair. A
moment later he picked her up and carried her upstairs.

Eric was sitting at his desk when he heard his bedroom
door open, but he didn't turn around. For half an hour he'd
been trying not to hear the sounds emanating from his parents' room, sounds he hated to hear almost more than he

hated to hear the sounds of his father beating his mother. How could she do it? How could she let him touch her, after the things he'd done? When he first heard his father coming up the stairs, he'd gotten his baseball bat out of the closet and stood in the middle of the room clutching the bat, waiting for Ed to open the door. But instead his father had walked on by. In a few moments Eric had understood what was happening.

He'd had a terrible urge to rush into his parents' room and kill his father right then. Had his mother screamed—just once—he knew he would have done it. But she didn't scream, not at all. Instead he heard only moans of pleasure, and his grip tightened on the bat as his rage grew even wilder. But he didn't lose control. When he became aware that he had actually taken several steps toward the door, and understood what he was about to do, he forced himself to turn around and go to his desk, put the bat on the floor next to his chair, and open one of his textbooks. It was the wrong time; the wrong place. Since then he'd been staring unseeingly at the same page, battling to keep his emotions in check.

Now his father stood in the doorway to his room, and Eric had to turn around and face him. Ed was clad only in a pair of underwear. "I want to apologize," he said, taking a tentative step into the room. When he saw Eric reach down and pick up the baseball bat, he stopped where he was, a look of puzzlement coming over him. "You don't want to do that, Eric," he said softly. "You don't want to hurt the old man. Hell, I told Templeton you didn't have anything to do with what happened last night."

Eric said nothing.

"I didn't kill her," Ed went on, his voice taking on its whining edge once again. And he hadn't, not really. Some of it had come back to him as he'd walked home. He had a vague memory of being on the beach, chasing Eric and Cassie in the truck. He remembered Eric disappearing down one of the paths in the marsh, but Cassie . . .

Cassie had not been able to get away from him. Finally she'd stumbled into the quicksand. He'd watched her die. But he hadn't killed her. If he had, why would Templeton have let him out of jail? "I didn't do it, son." He licked his lips nervously and his mind raced as he saw the cold fury in

Eric's eyes. "I'm sorry she's dead," he lied. "But you can't hold it against me, can you? Hell, you hardly even knew her. And you've still got Lisa. . . ."

Eric's eyes widened. He doesn't know, he thought numbly. He doesn't even know who was out there.

Then, as Eric watched his father with an almost detached curiosity, he saw the blood drain from Cavanaugh's face and a look of terror come into his eyes.

"No," his father snorted. *"No . . ."*

Eric realized that Ed was no longer looking at him. His eyes, wide with shock now, were fastened on the window. Eric's own eyes followed his father's gaze. Then he understood.

Standing in her window, staring at Ed Cavanaugh with an unblinking gaze, was Cassie Winslow.

"No," Ed Cavanaugh breathed once more as he stared at the girl who should have been dead. "It can't be her! She's dead, goddamn it! She's dead!" Wildly he tore his eyes from Cassie and glared furiously at Eric. "I saw it!" he managed to say, his voice strangling now. "I tell you I was there, and I saw her die!"

Eric shook his head, his lips curling into a faint smile. "It wasn't Cassie, Dad," he said quietly. "It was Lisa. You killed Lisa!"

His face purpling with rage, Ed took another step toward Eric, but Eric raised the bat.

"Don't touch me! Don't you come near me, or I swear to God I'll kill you, even though you are my father!"

Ed froze, staring at the bat and at Eric. Now his voice turned venomous. "She's really got you, doesn't she?" he snarled. "Just like Miranda. She's got you the same way Miranda had you!" His eyes sparkled malevolently. "Miranda should have let you die out there, boy! She should have let both of you die! Nobody ever wanted either one of you anyway!" An evil laugh bubbled up from his throat, and he lurched out of the room, his mind suddenly consumed with a single thought.

A drink. He had to have a drink.

Eric didn't know how long he'd been lying on his bed, didn't know whether he'd been sleeping or awake.

His father's words still echoed in his mind.

He knew they were true; had always known. . . .

He pulled himself upright, his body stiff, his mind muddled. An image of his father seemed burned into his memory, and he could still feel the venomous look Ed had given him and recall the words he'd uttered.

He stood silently for a moment, then crossed the room to the window. When he looked out, Cassie was still at her window.

But now she was staring at him.

He left his room and started toward the stairs, pausing at the landing to listen to the house and sense the atmosphere. He heard no sound, but neither did he feel the tension that always hung in the air when his father was at home. Slowly, almost against his own wishes, he started down the stairs.

He found his mother in the parlor, sitting stiffly on one of the wing-back chairs which were only used on special occasions, her eyes fixed on some point beyond the window. When he spoke to her, she didn't seem to hear him, but finally, just as he was about to speak again, she swung around to look at him. Her eyes, usually filled with fear, had taken on a look of tired resignation, as if she had finally faced herself and found herself wanting.

"I'll never get out," she said, and the emptiness in her eyes was matched by her voice. "After everything he's done, I forgave him. How could I have done that, Eric? How could I?"

Eric's eyes glittered with barely contained fury. "What happened?" he demanded, his voice low but with an edge so sharp it made Laura flinch. "He said Miranda should have let us die. He said no one ever wanted us. Tell me what happened, Mother. Tell me what he was talking about!"

Laura gazed blankly at her son for a moment, then seemed to focus. "Miranda," she breathed, nodding slowly. "But it was so long ago. So very long ago. . . ."

It had been a Saturday. One of those hot humid Saturdays when the house was almost unbearable. Ed had been on edge all day, and she'd done her best not to do anything that might annoy him. After lunch, when he suggested he take Eric to the beach, she was relieved. It would give her a chance to catch up with the laundry and the thousand-and-

one other things she somehow never quite found the time to keep on top of. And so she'd packed a change of clothes for Eric and sent them off. But a couple of hours later, when she'd finished the laundry, the heat had finally gotten to her.

She'd decided to join Ed and Eric at the beach.

She knew where they always went—far out to Cranberry Point, where the summer people never went. And it hadn't taken long to find them.

Find Ed, at least.

He was lying on a blanket making love to Diana Winslow, the two of them locked in a passionate embrace. Then Ed must have sensed her presence, for he looked up. As Laura stared at him, speechless with shock and disappointment, she saw his humiliation turn to rage.

And the children—Eric and Cassie—were gone.

She never remembered much about what happened in the next half hour. All she'd known was that she had to find Eric.

And she'd found him.

Found him in Miranda's house.

Miranda had smiled at her as she'd come through the front door—a strange smile that chilled Laura's heart.

"I found them," Miranda told her. "I found them in the quicksand, and they're mine now. They belong to me."

Laura said nothing. Instead she snatched both of the children up into her arms and fled from the cabin in the marsh, rushing almost blindly through the bog until she was back on the beach. And there she had found Ed and Diana, waiting for her. She demanded to know how they could dare behave as they had. Didn't they know the children could have been killed in the marsh?

Neither of them had said a word, and as Laura watched them, she slowly realized why they weren't speaking to her.

They weren't speaking because they had nothing to say.

Consumed by their own desires, neither of them, neither Eric's father nor Cassie's mother, had cared if the children lived or died.

Laura never spoke of the incident afterward, never told anyone what had happened that day on the beach. A month later Diana had left False Harbor, taking Cassie with her.

And Laura—unable to face raising Eric alone—had stayed with Ed.

After that day on the beach the beatings began. In his own mind, Ed had blamed her. Blamed her—and Eric too—for what she witnessed that day. Now, brokenly, painfully tearing away the scars that had hidden her wounds for years, she told Eric the whole story. "That's why he hates us, Eric," she finished, her voice barely audible. "He hates us because of his own shame—shame for betraying me, shame because he knows that you could have died and it would have been his fault. He hates me because I *know*," she finished, her voice cracking. "He must have thought I'd leave him. But I couldn't—I just couldn't!"

Eric froze, staring at his mother, who finally turned back once more to face him with beseeching eyes.

"You have to forgive me, Eric," she pleaded. "You have to."

The room reeled, and a black abyss seemed to yawn at Eric's feet. As his mind spun with his effort to grasp what his mother had said, the memories came flooding back to him.

He saw a face looming over a bed—his bed. Eyes filled with hatred glared down at him from above, and a horrible odor hung in the air. He tried to roll away from it, but every time he tried to squirm under the blankets, rough hands—hands so big they could have crushed him—reached down to snatch the blanket away. And there was a voice, and words he'd never been able to remember before. Now they rang clear in his memory.

"You're nothing," the voice had said. "You should be dead now, you understand me? Nobody wants you, boy. And I'm gonna make you wish you *had* died!"

After a while the voice had stopped, but the beatings had started. And all his life, no matter what he'd done, it had never been right, never been quite good enough, never pleased his father.

And all because of something that had happened when he was only two years old.

"Why?" He uttered the word as an almost formless croak, but he could see that his mother understood.

"It was the shame," Laura said brokenly. "Can't you see, Eric? It was the shame. He never got over the shame. . . ."

"Shame?" Eric repeated, the shattered fragments of his life suddenly coalescing into a rage that surpassed all the anger he had ever felt before. "He wasn't ashamed of what he did! He was ashamed that he got caught! But he's never been ashamed of what he's done to us! And what about you? Didn't you care what he was doing to me? I figured out a long time ago you don't give a damn what he does to you! But what about me? I didn't know what he'd done. I was just a baby! How could you let him do that to me?"

He was shouting now, and Laura cowered on the chair, shrinking away from his words.

"How?" he screamed. "How could you let it happen?"

Laura pushed herself to her feet and took a step toward Eric, but he backed away.

"Don't touch me," he whispered. "Don't you ever touch me again."

"No, Eric," Laura pleaded. "No. I love you, Eric . . . I've always loved you. Please . . . ?"

"Loved me?" Eric wailed. "If you loved me, you wouldn't have let it happen!"

"I couldn't help it, Eric. I tried . . . I tried so hard—"

Eric's hand clenched into a fist and he drew his arm back, ready to strike the pathetic figure before him. Laura froze—like a rabbit trapped in the glare of a headlight—waiting for the blow.

"Do it," she whispered. "You hurt so much, and you're so angry. Do it, Eric."

Slowly, through an agonized exercise of sheer will, Eric unclenched his fist and dropped his arm to his side.

Something in his eyes changed, and Laura felt her blood run cold. In that moment when Eric had refused to strike her, she knew she had lost him forever. "I didn't mean for it to happen," she said quietly. "If I'd known what would happen— "

"But you did know, Mother," Eric said quietly. "You knew right from the beginning. You knew what he did to me. And you didn't do anything about it."

As he turned and walked out of the house, Laura sank back into her chair.

He's gone, she thought. *He's gone and he'll never be back*.

* * *

She's dead, Ed Cavanaugh thought. *I was there and saw her die, and if she hadn't died, I would have killed her!*

But she wasn't dead.

She had been standing there in her bedroom window, staring at him as if she could see right into his brain, and she'd been smiling at him.

She knew. She knew what he'd tried to do, knew what he'd wanted to do. Somehow she had tricked him.

He turned the key in the ignition of the *Big Ed,* then waited for the glow-plug indicator to go out. The engine turned over slowly, started to die, then caught. It coughed loudly, and a plume of black exhaust belched up from the stern, filling the cabin with choking fumes.

Ed stumbled toward a window, pushed it open, and breathed deeply of the fresh air outside. Then, while the engine warmed up, he took a swig from the fresh bottle of bourbon sitting on the chart table next to the helm, and went out to start casting off his mooring lines.

He had to get away, had to think it all out.

The engine smoothed out to a steady rumble, and Ed cast off the last line then stepped to the secondary helm on the after deck of the trawler. He put the transmission in reverse and began backing out of the slip.

The bow of the *Big Ed* swung around, hitting the starboard side of the boat next to it and scraping its entire length before clearing the slip to drift out into the channel. Ignoring the damage he'd done to the other boat, Ed went back inside the cabin and slid onto the helmsman's seat. Throwing the transmission into forward, he pushed the big engine up a notch, then gulped another shot of bourbon out of the bottle. Tending the wheel with one hand, he maneuvered the trawler down the channel toward the open sea. Not until he had passed Cranberry Point did he begin to feel safe.

They couldn't get at him now.

Maybe he'd head toward Hyannis and spend a day or two there. He had a lot of friends in Hyannis, and most of them owed him a drink.

* * *

I have to *do* something, Laura Cavanaugh thought. I can't just keep sitting here, waiting for something to happen. I have to do something.

Outside, the light was beginning to fade as the sun set, and it occurred to Laura that she hadn't moved all day. She'd simply sat, her mind numb, staring sightlessly out the window, waiting. . . .

Waiting for what?

For Eric to come home?

But Eric wasn't coming home. Deep in her heart she was certain that Eric would never come home again.

Ed, then.

Ed would come home. And then what would happen? Would she tell him that Eric was gone and wouldn't be coming back?

He would blame it on her, and then—

She couldn't go on with the thought, knowing too clearly where it would lead.

She had to get out. If she was still there when Ed came home, this time he would kill her.

She tried to move but couldn't, and a terrifying feeling of being trapped swept over her. She wasn't going to be able to get out of the house, wasn't even going to be able to stand up. Her mind seemed to have lost control over her muscles, and when she gave herself the command to rise up from the chair, her legs refused to respond. She waited a moment, forcing herself to be calm, then tried again. At last, aching from the hours of immobility, her legs reluctantly responded, and she shakily got to her feet. She left the living room, moving slowly down the short hall to the kitchen, feeling the emptiness of the house.

Neither of them is coming back.

The thought flashed through her mind, and though she tried to reject it, there was a feeling of abandonment in the house now, which told her with more certainty than any words ever could have that she was never going to see either her husband or her son again.

She moved through the kitchen unseeingly, then went out the back door. Without thinking, she crossed the driveway that separated her own house from the Winslows' and knocked on the back door. After what seemed a long time,

Rosemary Winslow, her eyes red, opened the door and looked out at her. It was the look on Rosemary's face that reminded Laura that she had neither washed nor dressed since Ed had left so many hours ago. As her right hand clutched at her worn housecoat, her left ran spasmodically through her hair in a futile attempt to put it in order.

"I'm sorry . . ." she said. "I shouldn't have—"

But Rosemary pushed the door open wide. "Laura? Laura, what is it? What's happened?"

"They're gone," Laura said hollowly as she allowed herself to be led down the hall to the living room. "They're both gone."

Jennifer, who was sprawled on the floor with a book open in front of her, looked curiously up at Laura. "Who's gone?" she asked.

Laura's eyes fixed vacantly on Rosemary, and when she replied, it was as if Rosemary herself had asked the question. "Eric. And Ed. They both left, Rosemary. They both left, and they aren't coming back. What am I going to do?"

Rosemary glanced at Jennifer, and considered sending her back up to her room, then rejected the idea. "Come on," she said. "I'll fix you a cup of coffee." But when they got back to the kitchen and she fished in the cupboard above the counter for a mug, Laura shook her head.

"A drink," she said quietly. "I haven't had one in years— because of Ed, you know—but I really need one." She sank down on one of the chairs at the table, then immediately stood up again, moving restlessly around the kitchen, finally leaning against the sink as she tried to find the words to explain to Rosemary what had happened.

All the years of lying for Ed, and covering up, and finally I have to tell the truth, she thought. I wonder if I even still know how.

Slowly, tears welling in her eyes, she began telling Rosemary what had happened that morning.

Chapter 25

Cassie moved slowly along the beach, oblivious to the terns and gulls wheeling overhead and the sandpipers skittering ahead of her as they searched the tidelands for morsels of food. The storm had passed, and the sea was calm now. Sumi padded along at Cassie's feet, darting off every few seconds in pursuit of one of the birds, only to be driven back by the gently lapping surf.

She'd had another fight with Rosemary that morning, and she knew she should go back home and apologize to her.

Except that the Winslows' house wasn't home anymore, and she knew that Rosemary didn't want her there. Home was the cabin in the marsh now, the cabin Miranda had lived in and that she knew someday—somehow—she would live in too.

Last night, even after Eric left, it had felt right to her.

Safe.

And then . . .

And then, what? She knew what had happened in the marsh, knew that Sumi had attacked Lisa. But why? She wasn't even angry at Lisa anymore, and when she'd stopped Sumi in the park yesterday morning, the cat had obeyed. But last night Sumi had attacked.

There had to be a reason.

She turned away from the beach and started out into the marsh, carefully avoiding the place where they'd found Lisa early that morning. There were still a lot of people there, talking among themselves. As Cassie passed, they fell silent.

She could·feel them watching her.

Just as they had watched Miranda.

The hostility coming from them was almost palpable. Cassie shuddered, then reached down and picked up Sumi, cuddling the cat close. Why did they hate her so much? She hadn't meant to hurt anyone, not really.

Except that she had. Deep inside, she had let herself get angry with Mr. Simms, and with Lisa Chambers.

She had let them hurt her, and she had struck out at them. She mustn't do it again. Never again.

Except there was still Mr. Cavanaugh.

He wanted to kill her. Last night, in fact, he thought he had killed her. She'd known it when Sumi came back and crept into her arms, and the images had come into her mind. She had seen Eric's father standing above Lisa and felt the hatred coming from him. But it wasn't Lisa he had hated.

It was her.

And then, this morning, when she'd seen him staring at her from Eric's window, she'd felt it again, felt it even more strongly than last night.

She came to the low rise on which the cabin stood, and stepped into the circle of trees surrounding it. Almost immediately a feeling of peace came over her. Then a thought came into her mind, fully formed.

He can't get me here. As long as I stay here, he can't get me.

Silently, cradling Sumi against her chest, she went into the cabin.

Cassie didn't know how long she'd been alone in Miranda's house before Eric arrived. She was sitting in the rocking chair, her eyes closed, listening to the calming sounds of the marsh. It was only when Sumi stirred in her lap that she sensed his presence.

She opened her eyes to find him standing in the doorway, watching her.

"I know what happened," Eric said. "And I know why he hates you so much. You're part of it, you see. You and your mother."

As Cassie listened, Eric began to tell her what had happened that day so many years ago. The day they had both met Miranda for the first time.

"Where are you going?" Rosemary demanded.

"I'm going to find Cassie!" Keith replied, his voice trembling with rage. "I'm her father—what else do you expect me to do?"

Rosemary felt a lump rise in her throat. "I expect you to help me try to figure out what's happening. Isn't that why you came back? To help me?"

"I came back to help Cassie," Keith shot back. He'd only been home for an hour, but after listening to Rosemary's story, he wasn't sure he should have come back at all. Four perfectly good customers, and now they were all furious because he'd insisted on rushing home when Rosemary had called him on the radio that morning. And for what! Some cockamamie story that Cassie had somehow managed to kill Lisa Chambers last night.

"You mean you actually believe it?" he'd asked when Rosemary had told him everything she knew about what happened. "You really believe Cassie could have had anything to do with any of this?"

"I only know what Gene Templeton told me," Rosemary said miserably. "They found cat hairs under Lisa's fingernails, and the cuts on her face matched the ones on Harold Simms. That's when I decided to call you. And if you'd seen her last night when she went out—"

That was when Keith lost his temper. "So now the story is that Cassie sent the cat to attack Harold Simms and kill Lisa Chambers? For Christ's sake, Rosemary! You're an intelligent woman. How can you buy crap like that?"

"It's not *my* crap!" Rosemary shot back. "All I know is what Paul Samuels said. Lisa Chambers is dead, Keith, and it doesn't matter what you think—everyone else in town already believes Cassie had something to do with it!"

"So this whole town's gone nuts in the last two days!"

"Maybe it has," Rosemary agreed, her voice etched with acid. "But Lisa's still dead, and Ed Cavanaugh was trying to kill Eric and Cassie! Not just Eric! Cassie too! Why won't you face the fact that ever since Cassie's been here things have gone wrong, and somehow she's always at the center of it?"

Keith had stood up from the table so abruptly that his chair crashed over onto the floor. He snatched his coat off the hook in the service porch and was halfway out the door, his eyes blazing, when he heard Jennifer's plaintive voice.

"Don't," the little girl said, her chin trembling as she struggled against her own tears. "Please don't yell at each other. Please?"

Keith's and Rosemary's eyes met.

"What are we doing?" Rosemary finally asked. "Dear God, Keith, what are we doing to ourselves?" Then, as Jennifer ran to her mother, Keith put his arms around both of them.

"It's going to be all right," he told them. "We'll be all right, and Cassie will be all right too. We won't let anything happen to any of us." He gave them a hug, then released them and finished pulling his jacket on. When he spoke, his voice was gentle. "I have to go see if I can find her," he said, reaching out to touch Rosemary's cheek. "I guess I'm just starting to understand what the last couple of days have been like for you. But think what they've been like for Cassie, darling. I don't care what anyone else thinks. I don't believe Cassie would willingly hurt anyone. I just don't believe it." And then he was gone.

Keith paused at the foot of the low rise upon which Miranda Sikes's cabin stood. Cassie was there—he could sense it even before he saw the thin wisp of smoke drifting up from the chimney.

And on the roof of the cabin, eyeing him warily, the white hawk was perched, its feathers ruffling as it moved restlessly from one foot to the other.

"Cassie?" Keith called. Then again, "Cassie! It's your father!"

He took a single step forward, then froze as the hawk launched itself from the rooftop, found the wind, and began spiraling upward. From the cabin he heard a single word.

"No!"

Instantly the hawk changed course, dropping out of the air to settle back onto the peak of the roof. Only when it had landed did Keith shift his eyes from the bird to the figure on the porch of the cabin.

It was Cassie, her brows knit into an uncertain frown. She was watching him warily.

"It's me, Punkin," Keith said quietly.

For a moment Cassie was silent, and when she spoke, her voice was heavy with suspicion. "I didn't do anything," she said. "I know what everybody thinks, but I didn't do anything."

Keith felt his heart twist with pain. He wanted to go to her, take her in his arms, hold her. "I know," he said, the words quavering as he struggled to hold his emotions in check. "That's why I came out here. I came to help you, sweetheart." Almost involuntarily his eyes flicked upward toward the watchful hawk. "Can I come up there?"

Time seemed to stand still as Cassie watched her father, and then she nodded.

Feeling the hawk's eyes on him every step of the way, Keith climbed the hill and stepped into the cabin.

"I don't know what to say," Keith told his daughter an hour later. He felt sick as all the pieces of the puzzle finally began to come together. No wonder Diana had been jealous of him: she'd been certain he'd been doing the same things she'd been doing. "I never knew any of it. If I'd known, I never would have let your mother take you away."

"But why did she even want to?" Cassie asked, her voice quavering. "If she didn't care enough about me even to watch me on the beach, why did she want to take me with her?"

Keith shook his head helplessly. "It wasn't you, honey. It was never you. She just didn't want me to have you. She knew how much I loved you. And she knew how much it hurt me when she took you."

"And she never told you what happened?" Cassie asked, her disbelief apparent. "She never told you I almost drowned in the quicksand?"

"She couldn't," Keith replied bitterly. "She knew if she did, I'd have wanted to know how you got lost in the first place. And if I'd found *that* out, she never would have been able to take you away from me." He turned to Eric, who was sitting silently at the table. "I don't know what to say to you either. All those years . . ."

Eric spoke in a nearly toneless voice. "Maybe Miranda shouldn't have saved us. Maybe she should have just let us drown. Nobody cared. Nobody at all."

"That's not true—" Keith started to protest, then changed his mind. It was the children who had lived through all those years, who had received the beatings, and who had lived without love. How *could* they believe that anybody had cared?

"What was she like?" he asked softly. "What was Miranda really like?"

"She was my friend," Cassie replied. Her eyes filled with tears as she remembered those few hours she'd spent with Miranda. "She listened to me. When I talked to her, she knew exactly how I felt. She knew how alone I was, and how different I was, and how much—" Her voice broke, but she forced herself to go on. "She knew how much I hurt." She met her father's eyes. "She wasn't crazy, Daddy. She wasn't crazy at all. She just didn't have any friends, except Sumi and Kiska. That's why she knew how I felt. She always felt the same way. And she never wanted to hurt anybody either. She told me that just because people didn't understand me, it wasn't any reason to hurt them."

In her lap Sumi meowed softly, and Cassie gently scratched his ears. "That's why she gave me Sumi," she went on. "She wanted me to have a friend that really understood me."

Keith felt a chill as he remembered what Rosemary had told him when he came home. "Understands you," he said quietly. "You don't really mean the cat understands what you say, do you?"

Cassie hesitated, then nodded. "He understands what I'm feeling, and he does what I want him to do. So does Kiska. That's why he didn't go after you. I made him stop."

"But, honey, that's crazy," Keith began, then wished he could take back the words when he saw the pain in Cassie's eyes. "I'm sorry," he said quickly. "It's just—well, people can't really do things like that."

Cassie's eyes met his unwaveringly. "Most people can't," she said. "But Miranda could, and I can too. The animals were all she had, and she left them to me." She swallowed hard, then forced herself to go on. "That's what I did to Mr. Simms. I—I sent Sumi after him. I didn't really know I could, but . . ." She fell silent, watching her father fearfully.

Keith said nothing for several long minutes. If it was true, what did it mean? And was it really true? He had to know. "Show me," he said at last.

Cassie blinked uncertainly. "H-how?"

"Make him attack me. If you can make him attack me, I'll believe you. Then we'll figure out what to do."

Cassie glanced at Eric but said nothing. "I don't want to hurt you," Cassie whispered, looking back to her father.

"Make him attack me, then make him stop," Keith pressed. "If I'm going to help you, I have to know what happened."

Cassie stared at him for several seconds without speaking. Then her eyes closed.

She can't do it, Keith thought. She thinks she can but—

In a sudden flash of movement Sumi hissed angrily and tensed in Cassie's lap. As Keith stared in shock, the cat hurled himself toward him. A screech of fury roiled from his throat, and his lips curled back from his fangs. Keith threw up his hands to protect his face, but just before the cat struck him, he heard once more the single word that Cassie had spoken earlier on the porch.

"No!"

The shriek of attack died in Sumi's throat, and he dropped lightly into Keith's lap. His tail twitched once or twice, then he licked Keith's hand and settled down, purring contentedly.

For a long time no one said anything. Then Cassie broke the silence.

"I didn't kill Lisa, Daddy," she said softly. "Really, I didn't."

Keith hesitated, then nodded. "I believe you, Punkin," he said. "I believe you."

Eric said nothing at all.

Rosemary was playing Chinese checkers with Jennifer on the floor of the den when the doorbell rang. She was tempted not to answer it.

All day, as the rumors had spread through the village, she'd seen a steady trickle of people passing by the house—

people who didn't live in the neighborhood and didn't ordinarily go for walks along Alder Street. But today had been different, and finally Jennifer, looking curiously out the window, had asked what they were doing.

"They're just looking, honey," Rosemary had assured her. "I guess they just don't have anything better to do."

"Can I go out?" Jennifer had asked.

Rosemary shook her head, knowing all too well the sort of things Jennifer was likely to overhear on the streets that day. And so after Keith left, she'd settled down with Jennifer in the den, partly to keep the little girl entertained, but also, she knew, to keep her own mind off everything that had happened.

The bell rang again. "Aren't you going to answer it?" Jennifer asked.

Rosemary sighed, and got stiffly to her feet. But when she opened the front door, she wished she'd followed her first impulse to pretend that nobody was home. Fred Chambers, his eyes red and puffy, glared angrily at her.

"It's her fault!" he said, his voice trembling with a mixture of grief and bitter fury. "Everything was fine here until that crazy daughter of Keith's showed up. And now look what's happened! My daughter's dead, Rosemary! Do you understand that? Dead! It wasn't Ed Cavanaugh at all. It was Cassie! And she knew what she was doing too! From the minute she showed up at that dance all dressed up in Miranda's clothes, she knew what she was doing! She's as crazy as Miranda was!"

Rosemary stared at Fred Chambers, her heart pounding. "Stop it, Fred," she said, struggling to keep her voice under control. "I know what's happened, and I can't tell you how sorry I am. But we don't know that Cassie had anything to do with it. We don't know!" she repeated, her voice taking on a note of desperation. "The cat might have been anyone's," she added, though she knew she didn't believe her own words.

"Bullshit!" Fred Chambers exploded. "You think anyone's going to believe that? Teri Bennett saw that cat go after Lisa just yesterday! And it went after Harold Simms, too, didn't it? I don't know what Lisa was doing out there, but we know it was Cassie who killed her. She's doing something to us, and we all know it! She tried to kill Harold Simms, and she *did* kill my daughter. And if Templeton won't do something about it, the rest of us will! She's nuts!" He backed away a couple of steps, then wheeled around and charged off the porch. Halfway to the street he spun around to face Rosemary once more. "She's crazy, Rosemary! She's as crazy as Miranda was! She's some kind of witch, and she ought to be locked up!" A moment later he slammed the door of his car and started the engine, his tires screeching as he pressed his foot down on the accelerator. Rosemary, breathing hard, waited until the car had disappeared around the corner before she finally closed the door and returned to the den.

Jennifer, her face ashen, sat silently on the floor, staring at her.

"I don't like him," the little girl finally said. "I don't like him saying bad things about Cassie." She stood up and came to Rosemary, putting her arms around her mother and burying her face in Rosemary's skirt. "She wouldn't hurt anyone. I know she wouldn't."

Rosemary reached down and stroked her daughter's hair, wishing she could offer some words of comfort. But she couldn't, for she knew that despite everything Keith had said, her questions about Cassie were as great as ever, and that deep in her soul she had no real argument with what Fred Chambers had said.

But maybe—just maybe—when Keith brought Cassie home, she would find out that she'd been wrong, that there was a rational explanation for everything that had happened.

But the day turned into night, and Keith didn't come home.

It wasn't the first time Laura Cavanaugh had spent the night alone in the house, but this time it was different. Always before, she'd spent the evening comfortably, doing exactly as she pleased, enjoying the brief respites from the constant tension of her husband's drinking and violence. Even having Eric gone for a night had never bothered her, for she'd always known exactly where he was and when he'd be back.

But tonight was different. Eric would not be back, and she hadn't the slightest idea of where he was. For a while she'd considered calling Gene Templeton, but in the end hadn't been able to. Though she'd poured the whole story out to Rosemary Winslow, she was not yet ready to face anyone else with it—and certainly not the police chief. So she'd spent the evening drifting nervously around the house, starting one task or another, only to abandon it after a few minutes, unable to concentrate. Finally at nine o'clock she'd retreated to the bedroom—not the bedroom she had shared with Ed, but the guest room, where the memories were fewest.

She'd lain awake for hours, listening to the noises of the house. Until tonight she'd always found the soft creakings and groanings of its timbers reassuring. But tonight they sounded different to her, almost like living things going through some strange torture she could neither comprehend nor alleviate. And then, when finally she did drift into a fitful sleep, nightmares plagued her and she tossed and turned, twisting the sheets around her like a shroud.

Ed came to her dreams, but he had changed into the devil incarnate, determined to punish her for sins she could never hope to understand. And yet in the dreams she accepted her guilt, for why else was she being punished? And so she submitted willingly to the devil's tortures and silently prayed for death to rescue her from her agony.

Finally she thought death was near, and opened her eyes to welcome it, only to find that blackness surrounded her.

She lay still, waiting for the next sting of the whip or burn of the coals the devil had placed against her flesh, but it didn't come.

Slowly Laura realized that she had awakened and the dream was over. But her body, clammy with sweat, still shivered with the terror of the dream, and she tried to gather a blanket around her.

As she reached for the blanket she saw the cat perched on the sill of the open window, a dark silhouette against the pale silver of the moonlit night. Its eyes glowed a golden yellow in the darkness, and Laura had an eerie sensation that it was grinning at her, its lips curled back from teeth that emerged as pointed fangs from bloody gums. She gasped in sudden fear and drew back, clutching the blanket defensively to her breast.

The cat leaped nimbly from the windowsill and disappeared into a dark corner of the room. A moment later its yellow eyes flashed out at her from the shadows.

Slowly the cat began to creep nearer. . . .

The moon was beginning to drop toward the horizon when Sumi silently slipped through the branches of the tree then darted invisibly through the long shadows of the night. In only a few seconds he was back in the tree next to the Winslows' house and slithering once more through a window. When he leaped onto the bed and snuggled close to the warmth of the body beneath the quilt, his claws were well-sheathed and he was nothing more than a soft and comforting presence. Nothing was left of the golden-eyed demon that had stared accusingly at Laura Cavanaugh, silently demanding that she obey his will.

"Did you do it, Sumi?" the sleepy voice asked. "Did you do what I wanted you to?"

As if in response, Sumi began to purr.

Chapter 26

Jennifer stirred, rolled over, then opened her eyes. The first light of dawn was glimmering outside, and she started to get up when she realized that something was wrong.

This wasn't her room.

And then, slowly, she remembered.

Sometime during the night her father had come in, gently lifted her out of bed, and carried her into her parents' bedroom. Then he'd tucked her in, kissed her, and told her that Eric was going to be sleeping in her room tonight.

Jennifer stayed awake as long as she could, trying to hear everything that was being said downstairs, until at last sleep overtook her.

But she was awake now, with her mother beside her and her father on the other side of the bed. Being careful not to waken her parents, she slipped out of the bed and crept out of the room and down the hall to Cassie's room.

Opening the door, she silently slid inside, then went over to Cassie's bed and gazed curiously at her sleeping halfsister.

She puzzled over the words she'd heard Mr. Chambers saying yesterday evening, and tried to make sense out of them. But they still didn't seem right to her.

Cassie couldn't be a witch, could she? Witches, if they were real at all—and most of her friends thought they were— were old and ugly, with horrid, hooked noses and deep wrinkles all over their faces.

Cassie wasn't like that at all.

In fact Cassie was the nicest person in the whole world. She'd let Jen keep her newly decorated room, and stuck up for her when her mother had gotten mad at her, and hadn't even been angry when Jennifer had followed her that day.

So Mr. Chambers must be wrong.

She poked at Cassie, but nothing happened. She poked at her again, and Cassie rolled over, stretched, then opened her eyes.

"Hi," Cassie said, then frowned uncertainly. "What time is it?"

"Almost six," Jennifer pronounced, climbing onto the bed and regarding Cassie with serious eyes. "Can I tell you something without you thinking I'm a tattletale?"

Cassie nodded solemnly. "What is it?"

"Mr. Chambers was here yesterday, and he said something really bad about you."

Cassie's eyes darkened. "What did he say, Jen?" she asked.

Jennifer hesitated, then looked away. "He—he said you're a witch," she breathed. "He said you're a witch and you're crazy, just like Miranda was, and you ought to be locked up." She fell silent, then finally managed to turn and face Cassie again. "It's not true, is it?" she asked anxiously.

To her surprise, Cassie smiled gently at her. "What do you think?"

"I—I don't know what to think," she said. Then: "After he was gone, I asked Mom."

Cassie's eyes flickered with worry. "And what did she say?"

Jennifer hesitated, and looked away. "She—she didn't say anything," she replied quietly. "But if it wasn't true, why would Mr. Chambers say something like that? Grown-ups don't lie, do they?"

Cassie was silent for a few seconds, and when she finally spoke, she sounded angry to Jennifer. "Sometimes they do," she said. "And Mr. Chambers did because he doesn't like me. In fact he hates me, because of what happened to Lisa."

Jennifer blinked curiously. "But you didn't do anything to Lisa, did you?"

"I—" Cassie began, then shook her head. "It doesn't

matter, Jen. Why don't you just go back to bed?" Turning away, Cassie pulled the covers up and closed her eyes.

Jennifer slid off the bed, but then reached out to pat the spot at the foot of the bed where Sumi always slept.

There was nothing there.

She felt again, then explored the rest of the bed with her hands. "Cassie?" she asked a moment later.

"Huh?" Cassie mumbled.

"Where's Sumi? Why isn't he here?"

Cassie's eyes popped open and she sat up. She quickly scanned the room.

The cat had been there last night. She was sure of it. But this morning he was gone.

"G-go back to bed, Jen," Cassie said.

Jennifer hesitated, but something in Cassie's eyes told her not to argue. She hurried out of the room and a few seconds later was back in bed, snuggled against the warmth of her mother. Soon her breathing evened out into the gentle rhythms of sleep.

For Cassie the night's sleep was over.

It was already ten past seven, but neither Cassie nor Eric had yet come downstairs. Rosemary wondered if maybe she should simply let them sleep in. Certainly they wouldn't be going to school this morning, not after what they'd been through over the weekend.

And what was today going to be like?

She shook her head as she tried to imagine Gene Templeton's response to Cassie's version of what had happened to both Lisa Chambers and Harold Simms. Would he feel the same sense of shocked incredulity she had experienced the previous night when Keith had finally brought both Cassie and Eric home from Miranda's cabin in the marsh?

"I was angry at them," Cassie had explained, her blue eyes looking beseechingly at Rosemary. "I was angry at them, and I wanted to hurt them. But I didn't know what Sumi could do. I didn't know!"

Rosemary had looked at her in confusion. "Sumi? Cassie, what on earth are you talking about?"

"The cat," Keith explained, his voice tight. "There *is*

some kind of communication between Cassie and the cat. The cat understands what's going on in her mind and acts on it."

Slowly Cassie began to tell the story, and as Rosemary listened, her shock grew with each passing minute.

"Sumi went after Lisa because she was going to do something to me," Cassie finished. "When he came back, I saw what happened. It's like I can see whatever he saw." She bit her lip, and her eyes glistened with tears. "Mr. Cavanaugh didn't kill her. But he didn't try to save her either. He just stood there and watched her die."

It had gone on past midnight, and finally Rosemary hadn't been able to deal with it anymore. "I think we'd better call Gene Templeton," she'd said.

But Keith had shaken his head. "Not tonight," he told her. "We've all been through too much, and I won't ask the kids to talk to Gene tonight."

Rosemary had stared at him. What was he saying? Were they all just supposed to go to bed?

"I told Eric he could stay here tonight," he went on. "Tomorrow we'll talk to Gene and Paul Samuels."

Rosemary wanted to argue, but her exhaustion had finally overcome her. "All right," she'd said at last. "I don't know what's happening anymore. I don't know if I believe any of it or not, but I just can't think anymore." Her eyes had gone to Cassie. "I don't think you should expect them to believe any of this," she said. "Even if it's true—"

"Do you believe it?" Cassie had asked. Her voice was low, but her eyes were gazing steadily at Rosemary.

"I—I don't know," Rosemary had replied, even though she was certain that whatever the truth was, Cassie had not yet told all of it. To try to blame it all on a cat . . . "And I'm not going to talk about it anymore tonight."

Nor had she. When Keith had tried to discuss it with her after they were in bed, she'd turned away from him and said nothing. But for hours she'd lain awake, puzzling over it.

Did Keith seriously believe that Gene Templeton would accept Cassie's story? It was impossible. The whole thing. And Gene wouldn't accept it. There was no way he could. It was too strange—too bizarre.

Keith sipped silently on his coffee, warily watching his wife.

This morning Rosemary knew she could no longer put off dealing with it. Sighing, she turned to Jennifer, who was sitting at the table spooning sugar onto her cereal. "See if you can hurry them up, will you, honey?" she said to her daughter.

Jennifer slid off her chair, went to the bottom of the stairs and yelled up to the second floor. When she got no response, she sighed with all the dramatic resignation an eight-year-old can summon and started up the stairs.

"You don't believe Cassie, do you?" Keith asked quietly when Jennifer was gone.

"I—I don't know," Rosemary faltered.

"If you'd been out there yesterday. If you'd seen—"

"No!" Rosemary burst out. Her eyes stung with tears as she turned to face Keith. "I kept waking up all night long thinking about that story of Cassie's, and I just can't accept it! It's just too—too bizarre!" She was about to say more, but abruptly stopped herself as Jennifer reappeared in the kitchen.

"They're not up there," Jennifer said. "They're gone."

"Gone?" Rosemary echoed blankly. "What do you mean, gone?"

"I looked in my room, and I looked in Cassie's room, and—"

Rosemary brushed past her daughter and hurried up the stairs. It wasn't possible. If they'd gotten up, wouldn't she have heard them moving around?

She stopped in front of the closed door to Jennifer's room and rapped loudly. "Eric? Eric, are you awake?" There was no answer. After rapping once more, Rosemary twisted the knob and pushed the door open.

The room looked as it always did, with Jennifer's toys strewn around the floor and a few of her clothes piled on the chair. The bed, unmade, was empty, and there was not a trace of Eric Cavanaugh anywhere in the room.

Frowning, Rosemary pulled the door closed then went to Cassie's room, where she repeated the process.

Cassie's room, too, was empty.

Methodically, knowing it was useless even before she started, Rosemary searched the second floor, and even went up to check the little attic tucked under the roof. When she returned to the landing, Keith was waiting for her, looking at her with questioning eyes. She shook her head.

"They're not here," she whispered, her voice trembling. "But where would they have gone? Why?" Her voice began to rise, cracking dangerously as she tried to stifle a sob. "We hear everything in this house—everything! My God, you can't even breathe without everyone hearing you. And they're gone, Keith! We didn't hear them, we didn't see them. They didn't even speak to us! Why? Why!" She felt herself crumbling, and let her husband gather her into his arms. "I don't understand it," she sobbed. "I just don't understand any of it. . . ."

"Shh," Keith soothed, stroking her hair and leading her into their bedroom. He lowered her gently to the bed. "Just take it easy," he told her. "I'll have a look around. There's got to be some explanation. Just take it easy. . . ." Then, as Rosemary's breathing began to return to normal, he, too, searched the house.

It didn't take him long to figure out what had happened. The window in Cassie's room was wide open and the screen hung loose. Obviously both the kids had gone out the window and down the tree outside. Yet that didn't explain where they might have gone, nor why they felt it necessary to sneak out. He went back to the master bedroom and found Rosemary sitting up, dabbing at her eyes with a Kleenex.

"I'm all right," she said. "I just . . . fell apart for a minute, I guess. But I'm all right now." She listened in silence as he told her what he thought had happened, then numbly followed him back down to the kitchen, slowly and deliberately pouring herself a fresh cup of coffee before she spoke again. At last she turned to face her husband. "I can't stand any more of this," she said quietly. "I know you love Cassie, and I want to love her too. But I can't keep on with this, Keith. How can I be expected to believe what she says when none of it makes sense to me, and she pulls stunts like this? Whatever the truth of all this is, I will not let her destroy my family. I—"

Keith's eyes widened in shock. "Destroy your— Honey, all she's done is take off again!"

But Rosemary shook her head. "She didn't take off, Keith. That's what she did yesterday, after a fight. I saw her go. I heard her go. I even knew why she went. But this morning she just disappeared. Both of them did." Her voice began quavering again, and she could feel her self-control slipping away once more. "I feel like I'm going crazy, Keith. I don't know what's happening, and I don't understand any of it, and . . . and . . ." Her eyes welled with tears, and she cradled her head in her hands as her sobs once more overtook her.

Keith watched helplessly, wishing he knew what to say. But he didn't. All he could do was go out once more and search for his daughter.

"I'm going out," he said tightly. "And when I find her, this time I'll wait till I have her home before I ask her what's going on. This time we'll listen to her together."

Rosemary looked at him beseechingly. "Not now," she pleaded. "Not right now—please. Just stay with me for a little while."

Keith hesitated, then nodded. "Go next door," he told Jennifer. "Get Mrs. Cavanaugh and ask her to come over. Can you do that?"

Jennifer, her eyes wide as saucers, nodded and started toward the door.

"No!" Rosemary suddenly screeched, grabbing Jennifer by the shoulders and pulling her back. "She's not going over there! If Ed came back—"

Keith took a deep breath and nodded. "All right. I'll get Laura myself. Be right back."

He strode across the driveway and knocked loudly at the back door of the Cavanaughs' house. When there was no answer, he pulled the door open and went inside. "Laura? Where are you?"

There was still no answer, and he moved quickly through the kitchen and hall until he was at the bottom of the stairs. Calling out once more, he started up.

He paused to listen when he reached the landing on the second floor, and glanced around. Three bedrooms and a bath opened off the landing. Two of the bedroom doors stood open, as did the bathroom door.

The last door was almost closed, and as he approached it, Keith felt an icy chill of foreboding.

Bracing himself, he pushed the door open with his left foot.

Hanging from the tarnished brass chandelier above the

bed, a sheet knotted around her neck, was Laura Cavanaugh.
Her head was cocked at an unnatural angle, and her legs
hung down nearly to the floor. Her face had turned a mottled
bluish black, and her tongue, swollen and discolored, protruded from the rictus of her lips.

Her cheeks—both of them—bore angry red claw marks.

Keith felt his gorge rise and quickly turned his face
away, trying to block the hideous sight from his memory,
though he already knew he would remember it as long as he
lived. Gagging, and clutching a handkerchief to his mouth in a
futile effort to control his retching, he bolted down the stairs
and out of the house. Falling to his knees, he vomited onto
the back lawn, his stomach contracting violently long after it
had emptied itself of its contents. At last, panting and gasping
for breath, Keith managed to get to his feet and stagger back
toward his own house.

Rosemary looked up at him as he lurched through the
back door, and her face turned ashen as she saw the look of
horror in his eyes.

"Gene," Keith gasped. "Call Gene. It's Laura . . ." His
voice trailed off, and he moved through the kitchen to the
little half bathroom tucked under the stairs. As Rosemary
fumbled with the telephone she could hear Keith vomiting
once more.

"Cut her down," Templeton said grimly.

Photographs had already been taken, and one of his
deputies was dusting the room for fingerprints, but Templeton
didn't think it would make any difference unless they turned
up prints that didn't belong to Ed, Laura, or Eric. Besides,
from what he'd seen, Gene was almost certain about what
happened.

It had to have been Ed.

He could almost picture it.

Ed drunk, coming home and starting one more fight
with his wife. Only this time the beating had gotten out of
hand.

As he stared at the carnage that had been Laura's face,
Gene hoped she'd already lost consciousness by the time Ed
started cutting at her cheeks. If she hadn't—

He winced just thinking about the pain she would have had to endure, and put the thought out of his mind.

Had Ed hanged her before she was dead, or not until he'd discovered he'd actually killed her this time? Not that it made any difference, really, for whether he'd beaten her to death, strangled her, or hanged her, she was still dead, and Ed was still guilty of murder, despite his drunken attempt to make it look as if some kind of animal had attacked her. But animals didn't hang people. If Laura Cavanaugh weren't dead, Templeton would have found the clumsy gesture almost laughable.

The medics cut the twisted sheet and gently lowered Laura's corpse onto a stretcher, covered it, and carried it out of the room. Glancing out the window, Gene saw the knot of people gathered on the front lawn of the Cavanaughs' house. More were drifting down the sidewalk, and Gene could almost hear them murmuring among themselves, passing the rumors from one ear to the next.

"Go pick up Ed," Gene told the deputy who had finished dusting the room. "Unless I miss my guess, he's down on his boat, dead drunk."

The deputy—Tony Vittorio—frowned and shook his head. "Don't think so, Gene. I saw the *Big Ed* goin' out yesterday morning, and it hasn't been back. Slip was still empty when I came up this morning."

"You sure?" Gene asked, though he already knew the answer. Tony lived alone on a sailboat he kept in the last slip of the marina, and made a few extra dollars each month by keeping an eye on things. His heart sank. If it hadn't been Ed then—

Eric?

It was the only other possibility that came readily to mind, but the very idea of it made Gene feel sick. Still, he had to face up to it. "Okay," he sighed. "Cruise around and see if you can spot Eric anywhere, and see if you can get hold of Ed on the radio. I'll go next door and talk to Keith. They must have heard something."

And yet even as he crossed the driveway and let himself into the Winslows' house, Gene had a sinking feeling that no one in the house next door had heard anything the night before.

Chapter 27

Ed Cavanaugh woke up with his head throbbing and his nostrils filled with the familiar odor of stale vomit. For a moment he refused to open his eyes, certain that if he did, he would once more see the gray walls of the False Harbor jail closing in on him. But then the gentle rocking of the boat reassured him, and he let his right eye open a crack to take in the familiar mess of the cabin of the *Big Ed*. Slowly, the previous night came back to him. He'd sat in a bar in Hyannis, putting away boilermakers until finally the bartender had thrown him out. Then a couple of his friends—whose names would come back to him in a minute—helped him back to the boat, and they'd polished off a fifth of bourbon that he'd found tucked away down in the engine room just in case of such an emergency as this. He could even remember when he'd gotten sick, but hadn't bothered to go out on the deck to throw up. After that . . .

He rolled over, pulling the greasy blanket up over his head in a vain effort to shut out the sour smell. No point getting up until his head stopped pounding.

The radio suddenly came to life, and he heard an urgent voice calling to him. He tried to ignore it, but after a few minutes of silence it started in again. Swearing under his breath, he kicked the blanket aside and stumbled out of the bunk to scramble up the companionway to the pilothouse. He fumbled with the microphone for a moment, dropped it, then found the transmit button.

"This is the *Big Ed*." The words were slurred, and his tongue felt thick and cottony.

"That you, Ed?" the voice crackled back.

"Who wants to know?"

"This is Tony Vittorio, Ed. We got a problem, and we need you back here as soon as you can get here."

Ed frowned blearily. "What kinda problem? A man's gotta earn a living, ya know. Can't do that runnin' home all the time."

There was a long silence this time, then the radio crackled to life again. "It's Laura, Ed. She's dead."

Cavanaugh stared at the radio dumbly. What the hell was the deputy talking about? Dead? Laura couldn't be dead— anyway, she hadn't been the last time he'd seen her. His eyes narrowed suspiciously. "Don't you bastards try to blame it on me, Tony. I maybe hit her a few times, but I never killed her."

In the police station Tony Vittorio felt a knot of cold anger form in his belly. Didn't the son of a bitch even care that his wife had died? Taking a deep breath to steady himself, he pressed the key on his own microphone. "We're not saying you did, Ed. But we thought you ought to know. Where are you?"

"Hyannis. Been here all night, and I can prove it."

"Great," Tony Vittorio replied, his eyes rolling upward. "So when can you get back here?"

Ed shrugged in the pilothouse. "Three, maybe four hours."

"You need any help?"

"What for?" Ed spat. "A little hangover never kept me in port before."

"Yeah," Tony replied. "We'll look for you around noon, then. But if you don't show up, we'll come looking for you. Got that?"

"I got it," Ed whined, and shoved the microphone back onto its bracket without bothering to sign off. "And fuck you too." Snotty bastard. Just like all the rest of them. But this time they didn't have anything on him. Anything at all.

His brain still throbbing, his mind still foggy, he started the engine warming and put a pot of coffee on the propane stove.

Numbly, his mind began to accept the fact that Laura

was dead. A strange emotion began to seize him, and at first he couldn't even identify it. Then, dimly, he began to recognize it as grief.

He'd never considered the possibility that Laura might die, never even considered the idea that she might leave him. But now she was gone. She was gone, and he was alone.

What was he supposed to do now? Slowly his grief began to dissolve into a more familiar emotion.

Anger.

"I want to go away," Rosemary said after Templeton had left. He hadn't believed it, hadn't believed any of it. And why should he? She didn't believe it herself, not anymore. "I want to take Jennifer and get away from here." She watched Keith's face, looking for a reaction—any kind of reaction—but for a long time there was none. Then, finally, his head swung around and his haunted eyes met her own.

"I can't go away," he said softly. "She's my daughter, honey. I can't just abandon her."

Rosemary's knuckles whitened as she clenched her hands into fists. "She's crazy! And if she's responsible for what you saw next door, then she's—she's some kind of monster!"

"Yesterday—"

"Things were different yesterday!" Rosemary flared. "Yesterday I wanted to believe her. I didn't want to believe she could have done all this. But this is today, and Laura's dead, and . . . and . . ." Her voice trailed off, but she refused to give in to the sobbing that threatened to overcome her.

"And you believe Cassie did it. Isn't that what you're thinking?"

Rosemary shook her head violently, though his words were true. "I don't know what I'm thinking. I'm trying to be rational, and it isn't working. I just—Keith, I'm scared! I keep telling myself that none of this is true, that there's a reasonable explanation for what's happening. But I can't. All I can think about is that something's going to happen to you next. Or to Jennifer." She looked at him with beseeching eyes. "Why can't we just go away somewhere, and stay away until it's all over?"

Keith's eyes flickered dully around the room. "Just go away," he repeated, as if the words had no meaning. But then he shook his head. "I can't do that, Rosemary. Whatever this is all about, it's partly my fault. Whatever Cassie is—or isn't—she's my daughter. I can't just walk away from that. I have to stay. I have to."

Rosemary's jaw tightened, her lips thinned down to an angry line, and her eyes flashed dangerously. "All right," she said, her voice grating. "We'll stay. But for how long? How long do you want us to stay, Keith? Until we're all dead?"

Keith turned away and went to the window. Looking out into the brightness of the spring morning, everything that had happened seemed unreal. And yet the image of Laura was too deeply burned in his memory to deny.

Had Cassie truly been responsible for that? He didn't want to believe it. And yet—

"I don't know," he said at last, his voice barely audible. "Until I can help her, I guess. Or at least until I can understand."

Cassie faced Eric across the small table in the center of the cabin, her eyes empty, her mind reeling, her body shivering with an unnatural chill.

It wasn't warm and comforting here this morning; would never be comforting again.

She knew what had happened now, knew it from the first moment they had come into the cabin and Sumi leaped into her arms, purring softly.

The images had come quickly, and she'd watched the pictures in her mind with growing horror, watched Eric's mother knot the sheet around her neck, watched her step off the edge of the bed.

Watched as the cat left his telltale marks on her cheeks then slipped back out the window.

She even heard Eric's voice, crooning to Sumi as the cat slipped back into bed with him.

"Did you do it, Sumi? Did you do what I wanted you to do?"

It hadn't been her—hadn't been her at all. From the first moment—the first time they'd been here together—it had been Eric.

It all made sense now.

The day Sumi had attacked Mr. Simms—*Eric* had been holding Sumi that day.

And after Kiska had been shot, Eric had known where to find him.

It wasn't just to her that Miranda had given her gift. It was to Eric too.

"It was you," Cassie whispered. "Right from the beginning, it was you."

Eric nodded, a cold smile playing at the corners of his mouth. His eyes, glittering an icy blue in the morning light that filtered through the scraggly trees outside, were fixed on her with an odd detachment, almost as if he didn't see her.

All the sympathy she'd seen there—all the understanding—were gone.

"But they were our friends," she whispered bleakly. "Miranda never wanted us to—"

"Miranda's dead!" Eric grated, his eyes narrowing to slits. "It doesn't matter what she wanted anymore! She's dead!"

As he spoke the words, Sumi squirmed in Cassie's lap, and another image came into her mind.

Once more she saw Miranda—the quicksand closing around her—a shadowy figure looming over her. But this time she could recognize the face. Eric's face.

"You killed her," she breathed. "You killed them all." Her eyes, glistening with the pain she felt, reached out to Eric, trying to touch him. "Your own mother, Eric. You even killed your own mother. . . ."

Eric's smile twisted into a knife slash of scorn. "Sumi killed my mother, and Sumi killed Lisa. And everyone knows that he does everything *you* want him to do."

Cassie felt numb. He was right—she knew he was right—and already, deep in her heart, she was beginning to understand that there was nothing she could do about it.

"Why?" she asked. "Why did you do it, Eric?"

"They deserved it," Eric rasped. "They hurt me, and so I killed them."

Cassie shook her head as if to dispel the nightmare closing around her. "No. Miranda was your friend—she never hurt you. She loved you."

"Until you came," Eric spat. "She was mine, but you

took her away from me." His eyes were now glimmering with the rage and hatred inside him. "She was just like all the rest of them. She didn't love me—she didn't want me. So I killed her. Just like I'm going to kill my father!"

Cassie gasped. "No! Eric, you can't!"

Eric's eyes glowed with fury. "Why not? No one's going to blame me. No one's even going to know I did it. They're going to blame you, Cassie. They're going to blame you for all of it."

"No!" Cassie shouted. "I won't let you! I'll tell them the truth! I'll tell all of them!"

"Tell them what?" Eric demanded. "You're crazy, remember? No one's going to believe you. You're like Miranda! You're nuts! The little kids all think you're a witch!" An ugly cackle of brittle laughter welled up in his throat. "Didn't Miranda tell you what it was like, having them point at you, and whisper about you, and run away from you? That's what they're going to do to you, too, Cassie. And you won't do anything about it. You'll just let them hurt you." His voice dropped to a bitter whisper. "But not me. I'm done letting people hurt me. I'll kill them all, and they'll all think it was you." His cold smile came back. "And there's nothing you can do about it, Cassie. You're like Kiska and Sumi. You'll do whatever I want you to do. You always have, and you always will."

Sumi stirred restlessly in Cassie's lap, then his whole body stiffened.

Images began to flicker in Cassie's mind.

Images of herself, her face bleeding as Sumi's claws dug deep into her flesh.

Eric.

He was reaching out to the cat with his mind, telling him what to do.

She tried to fight it, tried to calm the cat, but it did no good. He was stronger than she was—too strong.

And then she knew what she had to do.

Her hands closed around Sumi's neck and she began to squeeze her fingers tight.

The cat started to struggle, lashing out with his feet, his claws bared as he tried to twist free of her grip.

She reached out with her mind, tried to soothe the

furious animal, tried to overpower the hatred flowing out of Eric's mind and into the body of the cat.

Sumi's mouth opened and he spat at her, his fangs dripping with saliva.

Cassie could feel herself losing the struggle with Eric now, feel his mind overpowering hers. She squeezed harder, her hands pressing tighter on the cat's larynx. Once more he tried to twist away, but then, slowly, his struggling eased. A minute later Sumi lay still in her lap.

Cassie closed her eyes for a moment, fighting against the tears that threatened to overwhelm her. Then, very gently, she placed the cat in the center of the table and forced herself to look into Eric's cold eyes.

"He's dead," she said. "He's dead, and he'll never hurt anyone again."

But Eric only smiled once more. "I still have Kiska." He rose to his feet, went to the door, then raised his arm and pointed to the sky.

Instantly the pale white form of the hawk rose off the cabin's roof and spiraled upward into the sky. As it started out toward the sea, Eric turned back to Cassie.

"He's going," he said. "He's going to kill my father."

Cassie felt the blood drain from her face, and tried to reach out to the bird.

But once again Eric's power overwhelmed her own, and the great hawk flew on.

There was nothing more she could do. Eric was stronger than she.

She felt her mind slipping, felt a strange gray fog begin to close around her.

Sounds seemed to retreat into the distance, and her eyes began to play tricks on her.

She tried to look at Eric, but he seemed to be a long way away from her now, and as she watched, his image faded away entirely.

She was alone now, and would always be alone.

But it didn't matter; not really. She'd always been alone, except for those few short hours with Miranda.

Now she would live alone, wanting nothing, needing nothing, sitting by herself in the soft gray fog.

In the fog, where nothing—and no one—could ever hurt her again.

Gentle swells rolled under the bow of the *Big Ed*, causing a barely perceptible pitch in the forty-foot trawler. The sky had cleared, and a bright sun warmed the cabin. Ed lounged in the pilot's seat, using his left foot to keep the boat on course while he watched the shore of the cape move by at a steady seven knots. Another hour and he'd be back in False Harbor.

The flat sea and steady throbbing of the diesel engine under the floorboards lulled him, and his mind began to drift. The fog of the hangover was beginning to pass now, and he'd taken a couple of aspirin against the stabbing pain of his headache.

So Laura was gone.

It was something he'd never thought about, really, never planned for. Even when she'd threatened to leave him, he'd never taken her seriously. If she was going to do that, she'd have done it long ago. But she never had, and over the years Ed had come to a dim certainty that she never would. That was the thing about Laura: she didn't have the guts to fight back, and she didn't have the guts to leave. In fact, the way he treated her had been her fault, really. After all, if she let him beat up on her, why shouldn't he?

But now she was gone.

Dead.

Of all the stupid things she could have done—

He checked himself. No point getting mad at her now. And besides, what the hell did it really matter, anyway? Whatever had happened, had happened. He shouldn't even think about it, not yet. When he got home and found out all the details, then he'd think about it.

A flickering movement on the bow caught his eye, and he swung his head idly around to look through the salt-fogged windshield as a snow-white bird hovered in the air for a moment, then settled onto the railing around the foredeck. Ed's lips curled into a cynical smile. "Nothin' today," he said out loud, though he knew that even if the gull could hear him over the roar of the engine, his words would mean nothing to it. "No nets, no fish, not even any bait. You wasted your time."

He half expected the bird to take off then, leaping into the air with a mad fluttering of its wings before it caught the breeze, but it didn't. Instead it stayed where it was, one of its reddish eyes staring at him.

Staring at him almost as if it was accusing him of something.

But that was dumb. He hadn't done anything, and even if he had, what the fuck could a stupid bird know about it?

But as the bird continued to sit on the bow rail, its eyes fixed on him, Ed began to feel nervous.

Why didn't it go away?

Finally, frowning, he opened the window and flung a scrap of the doughnut—which had been too dry for him to force down his throat this morning—at the bird.

The piece of pastry struck the bird on the right wing then fell to the deck.

The bird made no move to go after it—didn't even look at it. Instead its gaze as it stared through the windshield at Ed seemed to intensify.

Ed's frown deepened.

He flipped on the autopilot and adjusted its course, then picked up a wrench and went out on deck. He started forward, the wrench held loosely in his right hand.

He froze as he realized that the bird wasn't a gull at all.

It was the ghostly white hawk that had perched on Miranda Sikes's rooftop for all the years that he could remember.

But it was dead. Gene Templeton had shot it.

And yet there it was, perched calmly on the rail of his boat.

The hawk watched him, cocking its head slightly. Ed tightened his grip on the wrench. He slowed his pace, moving more carefully now, wanting to be sure he was close enough to the bird to hit it with the first swing.

Before he came within range of the hawk, it leaped into the air, its wings beating furiously. But instead of flying away from the boat to hover mockingly just out of reach, it came straight toward Ed.

Its beak opened and a shrill screech burst from its throat, stabbing at Ed's aching head as if someone had jammed an ice pick into his ear. As Ed swung the wrench wildly, the bird's claws slashed at his face, tearing open his right cheek.

Screaming in pain and fury, Ed hurled the wrench at the bird, but with a quick flick of its wings it rose out of the wrench's trajectory and the heavy metal tool fell harmlessly into the sea.

The bird hovered then, and a strange cackling sound, almost like laughter, rattled in its throat.

Suddenly, beneath Ed's feet, the boat pitched violently.

Ed almost lost his balance, then grabbed for the railing to steady himself.

The hawk dove, slashing at him again, and he felt a hot jab of pain in his left cheek, then tasted blood on his lips. Shielding himself with his left arm and hanging on to the railing with his right hand, he started back toward the cabin. The bird attacked once more, its talons ripping across the back of his neck as he ducked inside and slammed the door shut behind him. By the time he got back to the pilot's seat, the bird was once more perched on the bow pulpit, eyeing him malevolently.

Though the sky was still clear, the wind had picked up, and around him the swells were building, their crests topped by frothing whitecaps. But there seemed to be no specific direction from which the sudden squall was coming, and now the boat began to roll in a sickening counterpoint to its pitching. A faint queasiness began to twist at Ed's guts.

As the boat swung wildly off course, Ed grabbed the wheel with both hands and kicked the autopilot off. Now, as the rudder seemed to fight him and he had to struggle to bring the boat around, he forgot the pain from the lacerations on his body. Spray was coming over the bow, and he let go of the wheel with his right hand to reach out and flick the windshield wiper on.

Almost as if it sensed his momentary distraction, the boat slewed around, broaching on a swell, and slid sickeningly into the trough. Twisting the wheel violently, Ed forced the boat around to climb the face of the next swell.

The hawk, its wings folded serenely, still clung to the bow railing, riding the pitching and rolling of the waves as if it were floating on the surface of the water.

Then, as Ed watched, it launched itself into the air once more and hurtled toward the windshield.

He ducked reflexively away from the hawk's threatening

claws, despite the fact that the heavy windshield was protecting him from the creature's fury. But as the bird bounced off the heavy glass then settled once more on the bow, Ed's heart was pounding.

He reached for the radio.

Tony Vittorio recognized Ed Cavanaugh's voice behind the interference on the radio, and reached out to press the transmission switch on the radio that sat on the duty officer's desk. "This is the False Harbor Police Department, Ed. Do you read me?"

A blast of static emerged from the radio, then once again Tony heard Ed's voice. "Something crazy's going on! I'm caught in a squall, and—and there's a bird attacking me!"

Vittorio glanced out the window at the bright morning sun. A maple tree, just beginning to leaf out, showed no signs of anything more than a light breeze. He pushed the switch again, his brows knitting into a frown. "Say again, Ed?"

The message was repeated, but through the static Tony could hear a note of panic coming into Cavanaugh's voice. "I don't know what's going on, but I'm starting to ship water!"

Vittorio picked up a pencil. "Give me your position, Ed."

On board the *Big Ed*, Cavanaugh glanced up at the LORAN suspended above the helm and read off the longitude and latitude as quickly as he could. Outside, the bird was on the windshield again, its flapping wings spreading out over the glass until he could see nothing at all of the sea ahead. To either side the waves continued to grow—enormous gray mountains bearing down on him from every direction. The boat was pitching and rolling wildly now, and the compass was spinning on its axis, giving him no clue at all as to the direction in which he was headed. A huge wave towered over him for a moment, then broke, water cascading over the trawler with a force that made the hull groan in protest. All the windows were covered for a moment, and then the water fell away, washing over the gunnels and draining off the decks.

But the hawk, apparently unaffected by the deluge, still clung to the windshield. As Ed watched with horrified eyes, it slammed its beak against the glass and a crack appeared, moving outward from the point of impact toward the window's teak framing.

"I need help," Ed managed. "I need help, and I need it quick." Then the trawler slewed around, and as the rudder twisted in the heaving waters, the wheel was torn from Ed's grip. He dropped the microphone, grasping the wheel with both hands once more, then shoved forward on the throttle with his elbow.

The diesel roared louder, and Ed felt the trawler surge forward through the sea.

"I don't get it," Tony Vittorio told the off-duty officer he'd called in to relieve him while he went out to look for Ed Cavanaugh. "Sound's like Ed's drunk, but it also sounded like he's scared. I'm going out to take a look." Twenty minutes later he was on his way down the channel in the runabout the marina owner kept on hand for use in emergencies. As he carefully negotiated the narrows near the Cranberry Point light, he tried to explain the situation to Bill Dawson, who had been checking out the runabout when Vittorio had appeared on the dock.

"Sounds nuts to me," Dawson grumbled as he surveyed the nearly flat sea and the cloudless blue sky above. "You ask me, he was drunk again."

"Maybe so," Vittorio replied. "But I'd hate to find out later he wasn't. You got binoculars on this thing?"

"In the forepeak," Dawson said. He disappeared for a moment, then emerged from the tiny double bunk beneath the bow. As Tony brought the boat around to a westerly heading, Dawson scanned the horizon with the glasses. "Something up ahead," he said after a few seconds had slipped by. "About two points off the port bow."

Vittorio adjusted his heading slightly and shoved the throttle to full open. The engine's pitch rose slightly, and the runabout hurtled forward, cutting the water at thirty knots. A rooster tail of foaming spray rose up in their wake. The tiny dot on the horizon quickly began taking shape, and within five minutes was clearly identifiable as a fishing trawler.

A fishing trawler that was violently pitching and rolling in what was otherwise a calm sea.

* * *

Cavanaugh was steering blind. Somehow the hawk had managed to spread itself across the full width of the windshield, and its beak, bloodied now, was still battering at the glass, which was covered with a spiderweb of cracks. Bits of shattered glass were falling from it, and one of them had lodged itself in the corner of Ed's eye. Each time he rubbed at it, the glass dug itself in deeper, until the eye began to bleed and swelled shut.

For a brief second Ed considered opening one of the side windows to poke his head out into the maelstrom that surrounded him and try to get some glimpse of his bearings.

Suddenly the boat pitched once more, and the sliding door on the port side crashed open. Instantly the hawk abandoned its attack on the windshield and burst into the cabin itself. The second it was inside, the boat yawed and the door slammed shut.

Abandoning the wheel, Ed threw his arms over his face to try to protect himself from the bird's fury.

It did no good.

Its beak and talons nothing more than a flashing blur, it tore at Ed's clothes, ripping them away until it had exposed his bare skin. Now it was his flesh the hawk attacked, and Ed began screaming in agony as the sharp beak tore into him, jerking bits of skin and muscle away. The violent pitching of the boat increased, and Ed was hurled across the beam, his head smashing into the bulkhead. He crumpled to the floor for a moment, groaning, then shrieked as the bird renewed its attack. He rolled over, but once again the boat yawed, and Ed's body slammed against a corner of the dinette. He felt a rib crack, and a searing pain slashed through his chest. Then the pain was forgotten as the bird began stripping more flesh from his exposed arms and back.

He tried to roll now, back and forth, frantically seeking escape from the virago that swarmed over him, but there was no escape.

His screams fading to whimpers, he finally could fight no more, and lay still as the bird shredded his flesh. At last the blessed relief of unconsciousness began to overtake him, but at the last instant he opened his good eye.

Just before the bird snatched his eyeball from its socket, Ed thought he recognized a face looming above him.

But it was impossible. It was all impossible. . . .

And then the hawk's curved beak plunged into his eye, and the world, with a last flash of searing white-hot pain, went black.

"What the hell's going on?" Bill Dawson asked as the runabout drew near the fishing trawler. The trawler was still rolling gently, but the violent pitching they had witnessed as they raced out from the harbor had subsided. Still, the sea around the trawler was as calm as it had been when they passed Cranberry Point, and the sun still shone warmly from a cloudless sky. And yet both of them were certain they had seen the boat being tossed around as if it had been caught in a hurricane. Now, with only five yards separating the two vessels, Vittorio slowly circled the trawler.

It was soaking wet, with water still dripping from the cabin roof and running off the gunwales.

The windshield, though still in place, was shattered, and had caved slightly inward. Scattered over its surface was a random pattern of small holes, as if someone had driven nails through it in a misguided effort to gain entry to the boat.

At last Tony picked up the hailer Dawson had brought from the forepeak and called out to the trawler.

There was no response.

Tony brought the runabout alongside the trawler, and Dawson threw a line over its cleats. When two lines had been made fast, both men climbed aboard the *Big Ed*. While Vittorio checked the afterdeck, Dawson moved forward, finally sliding open the port door to the main cabin. A pure white hawk burst out of the pilothouse, spiraled over the trawler for a moment, then settled on the bow pulpit, its head swiveling rapidly as it surveyed its surroundings.

When he'd recovered from the shock of the bird, Bill Dawson stepped into the cabin and yelled for the police officer.

The cabin walls were smeared with the bright crimson of blood that hadn't yet dried, and on the floor, sprawled on its back, was what remained of Ed Cavanaugh's corpse.

The bones of his forearms and hands were completely exposed, the flesh torn away and scattered around the cabin. His chest, punctured and lacerated to little more than a reddish pulp, was covered only by a few remaining shreds of the heavy flannel shirt he'd been wearing.

His face—what was left of it—was a grotesque mask of terror, made even more hideous by the remnants of his left eyeball, which hung from its socket by a thread of torn tissue.

"Christ," Dawson breathed. "I never saw nothin' like this."

"Neither did I," Vittorio agreed, his voice grim as he fought the nausea rising in his gorge. "Get a tow line hooked up while I call in. If the radio still works," he added darkly.

By the time they got back to False Harbor, a small crowd had gathered on the dock. Tony Vittorio was not the only person who had heard Ed Cavanaugh's call for help, and several people had also heard Tony's brief report to the duty officer. As the runabout, laboring hard against the heavy load of the fishing trawler, made its slow way up the channel, a murmur of anticipation ran over the forty-odd people who had been waiting since noon.

In the runabout Tony's expression was one of anger mixed with resignation. "Wouldn't you think they had better things to do?" he asked.

Bill Dawson shook his head. His haunted eyes, still filled with the memory of what he'd seen in the cabin aboard the *Big Ed*, scanned the crowd. "With what's been goin' on around here, you got to expect it. They're scared, and you can bet that after they get a look at Ed, they're gonna be even more scared."

"I'm not giving them a look at Ed," Tony replied. "In fact if there were another place to put in, I'd do it. When we're tied up, make damned sure nobody gets aboard Ed's boat. And I mean *no*body." He pulled back the throttle, gradually slowing the runabout, then prepared to lash it alongside the trawler as inertia brought it even with the smaller boat. Once they were tied together he'd begin working both boats toward the dock.

As the trawler closed, the white hawk that had ridden silently on the bow throughout the long, slow cruise eyed Tony malevolently one more time, then rose into the air, found a thermal, and spiraled upward above the trawler. At last, with an eerie screeching that echoed over the small harbor, it wheeled and soared off in the direction of the marsh.

Every eye in the crowd on the wharf followed it, and every person who saw it recognized it.

It was Miranda's hawk, going home to roost.

Gene Templeton and Keith Winslow approached the cabin slowly. A curl of white smoke drifted up from the chimney, dissipating quickly in the clear spring air.

The hawk perched on the roof, its head swiveling warily as it watched them come. But long before they were close enough for Templeton to get a shot at it, it lifted off, its wings beating powerfully, and sailed off across Cranberry Point and out to sea.

They came to the bottom of the rise, where Templeton paused. "You sure you want to come?" he asked.

Keith nodded. "I have to," he said. "Whoever she is— whatever she is, she's still my daughter. I've loved her since the day she was born, and no matter what she's done, I still love her."

Then, his lungs expanding as he drew in the fresh sea air, he started up the gentle slope, Templeton behind him.

No sound came from within the cabin. All the shutters were closed, as was the door. If it hadn't been for the smoke drifting from the chimney, it would have looked completely deserted.

After pausing on the porch for a moment, Keith reached out and pushed on the door.

It swung slowly open.

Keith stepped inside.

They sat at the table in the center of the room, opposite each other.

Keith could see Eric's face clearly over Cassie's shoulder.

His skin looked pale even in the dim light of the cabin, and his blue eyes seemed to be fixed on Cassie's face. But when Keith stepped across the threshold, Eric's eyes moved slightly. Then he swallowed.

"He's dead, isn't he?" he asked. "My father's dead."

Keith hesitated, then nodded.

"She said he was," Eric said almost tonelessly. "When

we came out here, she told me Kiska had gone to kill my father."

"Why did you come out here?" Keith heard Templeton ask.

Eric frowned slightly, as if he were thinking. "Sumi," he said at last. "He wasn't in the house this morning." He hesitated, then managed an abashed smile. "We knew Mr. Winslow wouldn't let us come back here, so we sneaked out."

"The cat," Templeton said. "Is he here?"

Eric nodded, and glanced down at the tabletop. Keith took a step forward. Then he saw him.

In the middle of the table, his head twisted around in a grotesquely unnatural position, was the gray cat that had been Cassie's pet.

"She killed him," Eric said. His eyes met Keith's and didn't waver. "When we came out here, Sumi was in the cabin, and Cassie picked him up. She held him for a while, and then she told me what she saw." Eric's voice dropped to a whisper. "She saw my mother hanging herself. Sumi was there, and made her do it, and afterward—" He stopped abruptly, shaking his head as if to rid himself of the memory.

"Go on, son," Templeton said quietly. "What else?"

"Sumi clawed my mother's face."

Why is Eric telling it? Keith thought. Why is Cassie just sitting there, letting Eric tell it? But even as the questions came into his mind, a cold knot of fear closed on him as he began to suspect the answer.

"She killed Sumi," Eric went on. "She said there was no reason for my mother to die, but he killed her anyway. She said she'd lost control of him, so she killed him. She—she didn't want him to hurt anyone else."

Keith swallowed, trying to clear the lump out of his throat, but it did no good. Unable to speak, he slowly moved around until he could see Cassie's face.

Her eyes were wide and clear, and though they were staring directly at him, he knew she didn't see him.

Though the pain was finally gone from Cassie's eyes, nothing had replaced it. All that remained was a blank, empty void.

Her mouth hung slightly open, and the muscles in her cheeks had gone slack.

At last, his hand trembling, he reached out to touch her cheek. Her skin felt cool and slightly damp, but she showed no reaction to his touch.

"She wanted to stop Kiska," Eric said. "She wanted to, but she couldn't. . . . She couldn't. . . ."

"It's all right, son," Templeton said gently, laying his hand on the boy's shoulder. "It's over now. It's all over."

A few minutes later Keith lifted Cassie out of the chair and cradled her in his arms.

Her breathing was slow and steady, and he could even feel her heart beating in her breast.

But she herself was gone.

He carried her out of the little cabin and back through the marsh.

Templeton walked beside him, saying nothing.

Eric stayed in the cabin.

"I just want to be by myself for a little while," he said as they left. "I'll be all right. I just—I just have to get used to it, that's all."

Both Keith and the police chief had understood.

Templeton's car was in the parking lot by the beach, and Keith gently eased his daughter into the back seat. They drove across the parking lot toward Cape Drive, but as Templeton paused before pulling out onto the street itself, Cassie suddenly moved, twisting in the seat to look back out over the marsh.

On the porch of the cabin, Eric was barely visible.

Cassie frowned, then slowly raised her hand and pointed.

For a split second nothing happened. Then Kiska spread his wings, found the wind, and rose into the sky. He hovered for a moment, as if searching for his prey, then closed his wings and dove downward.

Eric, relaxed in his moment of triumph and Cassie's defeat, never saw him coming, never had a chance to reach out with his own mind, never had a chance to escape the bird's slashing talons.

Now it's over, Cassie thought silently as she let herself drift back into the cool comfort of the fog.

Now it's truly over.

ENTER THE TERRIFYING WORLD OF JOHN SAUL

A scream shatters the peaceful night of a sleepy town, a mysterious stranger awakens to seek vengeance. . . . Once again, with expert, chillingly demonic skill, John Saul draws the reader into his world of utter fear. The author of nineteen novels of psychological and supernatural suspense—all million copy *New York Times* bestsellers—John Saul is unequaled in his power to weave the haunted past and the troubled present into a web of pure, cold terror.

THE GOD PROJECT

Something is happening to the children of Eastbury, Massachusetts . . . something that strikes at the heart of every parent's darkest fears. For Sally Montgomery, the grief over the sudden death of her infant daughter is only the beginning. For Lucy Corliss, her son Randy is her life. Then one day, Randy doesn't come home. And the terror begins . . .

A horn honked, pulling Randy out of his reverie, and he realized he was alone on the block. He looked at the watch his father had given him for his ninth birthday. It was nearly eight thirty. If he didn't hurry, he was going to be late for school. Then he heard a voice calling to him.

"Randy! Randy Corliss!"

A blue car, a car he didn't recognize, was standing by the

curb. A woman was smiling at him from the driver's seat. He approached the car hesitantly, clutching his lunch box.

"Hi, Randy," the woman said.

"Who are you?" Randy stood back from the car, remembering his mother's warnings about never talking to strangers.

"My name's Miss Bowen. Louise Bowen. I came to get you."

"Get me?" Randy asked. "Why?"

"For your father," the woman said. Randy's heart beat faster. His father? His father had sent this woman? Was it really going to happen, finally? "He wanted me to pick you up at home," he heard the woman say, "but I was late. I'm sorry."

"That's all right," Randy said. He moved closer to the car. "Are you taking me to Daddy's house?"

The woman reached across and pushed the passenger door open. "In a little while," she promised. "Get in."

Randy knew he shouldn't get in the car, knew he should turn around and run to the nearest house, looking for help. It was things like this—strangers offering to give you a ride—that his mother had talked to him about ever since he was a little boy.

But this was different. This was a friend of his father's. Her brown eyes were twinkling at him, and her smile made him feel like she was sharing an adventure with him. He made up his mind and got into the car, pulling the door closed behind him. The car moved away from the curb.

"Where are we going?" Randy asked.

Louise Bowen glanced over at the boy sitting expectantly on the seat beside her. He was every bit as attractive as the pictures she had been shown, his eyes almost green, with dark, wavy hair framing his pugnacious, snub-nosed face. His body was sturdy, and though she was a stranger to him, he didn't seem to be the least bit frightened of her. Instinctively, Louise liked Randy Corliss.

"We're going to your new school."

Randy frowned. New school? If he was going to a new school, why wasn't his father taking him? The woman seemed to hear him, even though he hadn't spoken out loud.

"You'll see your father very soon. But for a few days, until he gets everything worked out with your mother, you'll be staying at the school. You'll like it there," she promised. "It's a special school, just for little boys like you, and you'll have lots of new friends. Doesn't that sound exciting?"

Randy nodded uncertainly, no longer sure he should have

gotten in the car. Still, when he thought about it, it made sense. His father had told him there would be lots of problems when the time came for him to move away from his mother's. And his father had told him he would be going to a new school. And today was the day.

Randy settled down in the seat and glanced out the window. They were heading out of Eastbury on the road toward Langston. That was where his father lived, so everything was all right.

Except that it didn't quite *feel* all right. Deep inside, Randy had a strange sense of something being very wrong.

For two very different families haunted by very similar fears, THE GOD PROJECT has only just begun to work its lethal conspiracy of silence and fear. And for the reader, John Saul has produced a mind-numbing tale of evil unchecked.

NATHANIEL

Prairie Bend: brilliant summers amid golden fields, killing winters of razorlike cold. A peaceful, neighborly village, darkened by legends of death . . . legends of Nathaniel. Some residents say he is simply a folk tale, others swear he is a terrifying spirit. And soon—very soon—some will come to believe that Nathaniel lives . . .

Shivering, Michael set himself a destination now and began walking along the edges of the pastures, the woods on his right, climbing each fence as he came to it. Sooner than he would have expected, the woods curved away to the right, following the course of the river as it deviated from its southeastern flow to curl around the village. Ahead of him he could see the scattered twinkling lights of Prairie Bend. For a moment, he considered going into the village, but then, as he looked off to the southeast, he changed his mind, for there, seeming almost to glow in the moonlight, was the hulking shape of Findley's barn.

That, Michael knew, was where he was going.

He cut diagonally across the field, then darted across the

deserted highway and into another field. He moved quickly now, feeling exposed in the emptiness with the full moon shining down on him. Ten minutes later he had crossed the field and come once more to the highway, this time as it emerged from the village. Across the street, he could see Ben Findley's driveway and, at its end, the little house, and the barn.

He considered trying to go down the driveway and around the house, but quickly abandoned the idea. A light showed dimly from behind a curtained window, and he had a sudden vision of old man Findley, his gun cradled in his arms, standing in silhouette at the front door.

His progress slowed as he plunged into the weed-choked pastures that lay between the house and the river, but he was determined to stay away from the fence separating Findley's property from their own until the old man's barn could conceal him from the same man's prying eyes. It wasn't until he was near the river that he finally felt safe enough to slip between the strands of barbed wire that fenced off the Findley property and begin doubling back toward the barn that had become his goal.

He could feel it now, feel the strange sense of familiarity he had felt that afternoon, only it was stronger here, pulling him forward through the night. He didn't try to resist it, though there was something vaguely frightening about it. Frightening but exciting. There was a sense of discovery, almost a sense of memory. And his headache, the throbbing pain that had been with him all evening, was gone.

He came up to the barn and paused. There should be a door just around the corner, a door with a bar on it. He didn't understand how he knew it was there, for he'd never seen that side of the barn, but he *knew*.

Around the corner, just as he knew it would be, he found the door, held securely shut by a heavy wooden beam resting in a pair of wrought-iron brackets. Without hesitation, Michael lifted the bar out of its brackets and propped it carefully against the wall. As he pulled the door open, no squeaking hinges betrayed his presence. Though the barn was nearly pitch dark inside, it wasn't the kind of eerie darkness the woods by the river had held, at least not for Michael. For Michael, it was an inviting darkness.

He stepped into the barn.

He waited, half expectantly, as the darkness seeped into him, enveloping him within its folds. And then something reached out of the darkness and touched him.

Nathaniel's call to Michael Hall, who has just lost his father in a tragic accident, draws the boy further into the barn and under his spell. There—and beyond—Michael will faithfully follow Nathaniel's voice to the edge of terror.

BRAINCHILD

One hundred years ago in La Paloma a terrible deed was done, and a cry for vengeance pierced the night. Now, that evil still lives, and that vengeance waits . . . waits for Alex Lonsdale, one of the most popular boys in La Paloma. Because horrible things can happen—even to nice kids like Alex . . .

Alex jockeyed the Mustang around Bob Carey's Porsche, then put it in drive and gunned the engine. The rear wheels spun on the loose gravel for a moment, then caught, and the car shot forward, down the Evanses' driveway and into Hacienda Drive.

Alex wasn't sure how long Lisa had been walking—it seemed as though it had taken him forever to get dressed and search the house. She could be almost home by now.

He pressed the accelerator, and the car picked up speed. He hugged the wall of the ravine on the first curve, but the car fishtailed slightly, and he had to steer into the skid to regain control. Then he hit a straight stretch and pushed his speed up to seventy. Coming up fast was an S curve that was posted at thirty miles an hour, but he knew they always left a big margin for safety. He slowed to sixty as he started into the first turn.

And then he saw her.

She was standing on the side of the road, her green dress glowing brightly in his headlights, staring at him with terrified eyes.

Or did he just imagine that? Was he already that close to her?

Time suddenly slowed down, and he slammed his foot on the brake.

Too late. He was going to hit her.

It would have been all right if she'd been on the inside of the curve. He'd have swept around her, and she'd have been safe. But now he was skidding right toward her . . .

Turn into it. He had to turn into it!

Taking his foot off the brake, he steered to the right, and suddenly felt the tires grab the pavement.

Lisa was only a few yards away.

And beyond Lisa, almost lost in the darkness, something else.

A face, old and wrinkled, framed with white hair. And the eyes in the face were glaring at him with an intensity he could almost feel.

It was the face that finally made him lose all control of the car.

An ancient, weathered face, a face filled with an unspeakable loathing, looming in the darkness.

At the last possible moment, he wrenched the wheel to the left, and the Mustang responded, slewing around Lisa, charging across the pavement, leading for the ditch and the wall of the ravine beyond.

Straighten it out!

He spun the wheel the other way.

Too far.

The car burst through the guardrail and hurtled over the edge of the ravine.

"*Lisaaaa . . .*"

Now Alex needs a miracle and thanks to a brilliant doctor, Alex comes back from the brink of death. He seems the same, but in his heart there is a coldness. And if his friends and family could see inside his brain, they would be terrified. . . .

HELLFIRE

Pity the dead . . . one hundred years ago eleven innocent lives were taken in a fire that raged through the mill. That day the iron doors slammed shut—forever. Now, the powerful Sturgiss family of the sleepy town of Westover, Massachusetts is about to unlock those doors to the past. Now comes the time to pray for the living.

The silence of the building seemed to gather around her, and slowly Beth felt the beginnings of fear.

And then she began to feel something else.

Once again, she felt that strange certainty that the mill was not empty.

"D-Daddy?" she called softly, stepping through the door. "Are you here?"

She felt a slight trickle of sweat begin to slide down her spine, and fought a sudden trembling in her knees.

Then, as she listened to the silence, she heard something.

A rustling sound, from up above.

Beth froze, her heart pounding.

And then she heard it again.

She looked up.

With a sudden burst of flapping wings, a pigeon took off from one of the rafters, circled, then soared out through a gap between the boards over one of the windows.

Beth stood still, waiting for her heartbeat to calm. As she looked around, her eyes fixed on the top of a stairwell at the far end of the building.

He was downstairs. That's why he hasn't heard her. He was down in the basement.

Resolutely, she started across the vast emptiness of the building. As she reached the middle of the floor, she felt suddenly exposed, and had an urge to run.

But there was nothing to be afraid of. There was nothing in the mill except herself, and some birds.

And downstairs, her father.

After what seemed like an eternity, she reached the top of the stairs, and peered uncertainly into the darkness below.

Her own shadow preceded her down the steep flight of steps, and only a little spilled over the staircase to illuminate the nearer parts of the vast basement.

"Daddy?" Beth whispered. But the sound was so quiet, even she could barely hear it.

And then there was something else, coming on the heels of her own voice.

Another sound, fainter than the one her own voice had made, coming from below.

Something was moving in the darkness.

Once again Beth's heart began to pound, but she remained where she was, forcing back the panic that threatened to overcome her.

Finally, when she heard nothing more, she moved slowly down the steps, until she could place a foot on the basement floor.

She listened, and after a moment, as the darkness began closing in on her, the sound repeated itself.

Panic surged through her. All her instincts told her to run, to flee back up the stairs and out into the daylight. But when she tried to move, her legs refused to obey her, and she remained where she was, paralyzed.

Once again the sound came. This time, though it was almost inaudible, Beth thought she recognized a word.

"Beeetthh . . ."

Her name. It was as if someone had called her name.

"D-Daddy?" she whispered again. "Daddy, is that you?"

There was another silence, and Beth strained once more to see into the darkness surrounding her.

In the distance, barely visible, she thought she could see a flickering of light.

And then she froze, her voice strangling as the sound came again, like a winter wind sighing in the trees.

"Aaaammmyyyy . . ."

Beth gazed fearfully into the blackness for several long seconds. Then, when the sound was not repeated, her panic began to subside. At last she was able to speak again, though her voice still trembled. "Is someone there?"

In the far distance, the light flickered again, and she heard something else.

Footsteps, approaching out of the darkness.

The seconds crept by, and the light bobbed nearer.

And once more, the whispering voice, barely audible, danced around her.

"Aaaammmyy . . ."

For Beth Rogers, the voice seems like a nightmare, yet not even a little girl's fears can imagine the unearthly fury that awaits her in the old, deserted mill. Soon all of Westover will be prey to the forces of darkness that wait beyond those padlocked doors.

THE UNWANTED

Cassie Winslow, lonely and frightened, has come to False Harbor, Cape Cod to live with her father—whom she barely knows—and his family. For Cassie, the strange, unsettling dreams that come to her suddenly are merely the beginning . . . for very soon, Cassie will come to know the terrifying powers that are her gift.

Cassie awoke in the blackness of the hours before dawn, her heart thumping, her skin damp with a cold sweat that made her shiver. For a moment she didn't know where she was. Then, as she listened to the unfamiliar sound of surf pounding in the distance, the dream began to fade away, and she remembered where she was.

She was in False Harbor, and this was where she lived now. In the room next to her, her stepsister was asleep, and down the hall her father was in bed with her stepmother.

Then why did she feel so alone?

It was the dream, of course.

It had come to her again in the night. Again she had seen the strange woman who should have been her mother but was not.

Again, as Cassie watched in horror, the car burst into flames, and Cassie, vaguely aware that she was in a dream, had expected to wake up, as she had each time the nightmare had come to her.

This time, though she wanted to turn and run, she stood where she was, watching the car burn.

This time there had been no laughter shrieking from the woman's lips, no sound of screams, no noise at all. The flames had risen from the car in an eerie silence, and then, just as Cassie was about to turn away, the stranger had suddenly emerged from the car.

Clad in black, the figure had stood perfectly still, untouched by the flames that raged around her. Slowly, she raised one hand. Her lips moved and a single word drifted over the crowded freeway, came directly to Cassie's ears over the face-less mass of people streaming by in their cars.

"Cassandra . . ."

The silence of the dream was shattered then by the blaring of a horn and the screaming of tires skidding on pavement.

Cassie looked up just in time to see a truck bearing down on her, the enormous grill of its radiator only inches from her face.

As the truck smashed into her she woke up, her own scream of terror choked in her throat.

Her heartbeat began to slow, and her shivering stopped.

Now the room seemed to close in on her, and she found it hard to breathe. Slipping out of bed, she crossed to the window at the far end of the narrow room and lifted it open. As she was about to go back to bed, a movement in the darkness outside caught her eye.

She looked down into the cemetery on the other side of the back fence. At first she saw nothing. Then she sensed the movement again, and a dark figure came into view. Clad in black, perfectly silent, a woman stood in the shadows cast by the headstones.

Time seemed to suspend itself.

And then the figure raised one hand. Once more Cassie heard a single word drift almost inaudibly above the pounding of the surf from the beach a few blocks away.

"Cassandra . . ."

Cassie remained where she was, her eyes closed as she strained to recapture the sound of her name, but now there was only the pulsing drone of the surf. And when she reopened her eyes a few seconds later and looked once more into the grave-yard, she saw nothing.

The strange figure that had stepped out of the shadows was gone.

She went back to her bed and pulled the covers close around her. For a long time she lay still, wondering if perhaps she'd only imagined it all.

Perhaps she hadn't even left the bed, and had only dreamed that she'd seen the woman in the graveyard.

But the woman in the graveyard had been the woman in her dream. But she didn't really exist.

Did she?

Cassie's dreams will alienate her from the other kids, as will her strange bond with crazy old Miranda Sikes—for both feel unwanted. *And in the village of False Harbor, nothing will ever be the same as John Saul spins his supernatural spell.*

THE UNLOVED

The splendid isolation of a picturesque island off the South Carolina coast seems like paradise, but for Kevin Devereaux—

who returns with his family to help care for his aged and ailing mother, Helena—homecoming will mean a frightening descent into his darkest nightmares . . .

"Why are you here?" he heard her demand. "You know I don't want you here!"

He tried to think, tried to remember where he was. He looked around furtively, hoping the woman wouldn't see his eyes flickering about as if he might be searching for a means to escape.

The room around him looked strange—unfinished—the rough wood of its framing exposed under the tattered remains of crumbling tarpaper. He'd been in this place before—he knew that now. Still, he didn't know where the room was, or what it might be.

But he knew the woman was angry with him again, and in the deepest recesses of his mind, he knew what was going to happen next.

The woman was going to kill him.

He wanted to cry out for help, but when he opened his mouth, no scream emerged. His throat constricted, cutting off his breath, and he knew if he couldn't fight the panic growing within him, he would strangle on his own fear.

The woman took a step toward him, and he cowered, huddling back against the wall. A slick sheen of icy sweat chilled his back, then he felt cold droplets creeping down his arms. A shiver passed over him, and a small whimper escaped his lips.

His sister.

Maybe his sister would come and rescue him.

But she was gone—something had happened to her, and he was alone now.

Alone with his mother.

He looked fearfully up.

She seemed to tower above him, her skirt held back as if she were afraid it might brush against him and be soiled. Her hands were hidden in the folds of the skirt, but he knew what they held.

The axe. The axe she would kill him with.

He could see it then—its curved blades glinting in the light from the doorway, its long wooden handle clutched in his mother's hands. She wasn't speaking to him now, only staring at him. But she didn't need to speak, for he knew what she wanted, knew what she'd always wanted.

"Love me," he whispered, his voice so tremulous that he could hear the words wither away as quickly as they left his lips. "Please love me . . ."

His mother didn't hear. She never heard, no matter how many times he begged her, no matter how often he tried to tell her he was sorry for what he'd done. He would apologize for anything—he knew that. If only she would hear him, he'd tell her whatever she wanted to hear. But even as he tried once more, he knew she wasn't hearing, didn't want to hear.

She only wanted to be rid of him.

The axe began to move now, rising above him, quivering slightly, as if the blade itself could anticipate the splitting of his skull, the crushing of his bones as they gave way beneath the weapon's weight. He could see the steel begin its slow descent, and time seemed to stand still.

He had to do something—had to move away, had to ward off the blow. He tried to raise his arms, but even the air around him seemed thick and unyielding now, and the blade was moving much faster than he was. . . .

He opened his mouth and, finally, screamed—

The horror is a dream, only a dream. Or so Kevin thinks. Until Helena, suddenly, horribly, dies inside the locked nursery. And now there is no escape, as tortured spirits from the sinister past rise up to tell the true terror of the unloved.

CREATURE

A terrible secret lurks beneath the wholesome surface of Silverdale, Colorado, where well-behaved students make their parents and teachers proud, and the football team never—ever—loses. But soon, some of the parents in Silverdale will begin to uncover the unimaginable secret that can turn a loving child murderous . . .

"It's two in the morning, Chuck. And Jeff isn't home yet."

Chuck groaned. "And for that you woke me up? Jeez, Char, when I was his age, I was out all night half the time."

"Maybe you were," Charlotte replied tightly. "And maybe

your parents didn't care. But I do, and I'm about to call the police.''

At that, Chuck came completely awake. ''What the hell do you want to do a thing like that for?'' he demanded, switching on the light and staring at Charlotte as if he thought she'd lost her mind.

''Because I'm worried about him,'' Charlotte flared, concern for her son overcoming her fear of her husband's tongue. ''Because I don't like what's been happening with him and I don't like the way he's been acting. And I certainly don't like not knowing where he is at night!''

''Maybe he stayed overnight with a friend,'' Chuck began, but Charlotte shook her head.

''He hasn't done that since he was a little boy. And if he had, he would have called.'' Even as she uttered the words, she knew she didn't believe them. A year ago—a few months ago; even a few weeks ago—she would have trusted Jeff to keep her informed of where he was and what he was doing. But now? She didn't know.

Nor could she explain her worries to Chuck, since he insisted on believing there was nothing wrong; that Jeff was simply growing up and testing his wings.

As she was searching for the right words, the words to express her fears without further rousing her husband's anger, the front door opened and Jeff came in.

He'd already closed the door behind him and started up the stairs when he caught sight of his parents standing in the den in their bathrobes, their eyes fixed on him. He gazed at them stupidly for a second, almost as if he didn't recognize them, and for a split-second Charlotte thought he looked stoned.

''Jeff?'' she said. Then, when he seemed to pay no attention to her, she called out again, louder this time. ''Jeff?''

His eyes hooded, her son turned to gaze at her. ''What?'' he asked, his voice taking on the same sullen tone that had become so familiar to her lately.

''I want an explanation,'' Charlotte went on. ''It's after two A.M., and I want to know where you've been.''

''Out,'' Jeff said, and started to turn away.

''Stop right there, young man!'' Charlotte commanded. She marched into the foyer and stood at the bottom of the stairs, then reached out and switched on the chandelier that hung in the stairwell. A bright flood of light bathed Jeff's face, and Charlotte gasped. His face was streaked with dirt, and on his cheeks there were smears of blood. There were black circles under Jeff's eyes—as if he hadn't slept in days—and he was breathing hard, his chest heaving as he panted.

Then he lifted his right hand to his mouth, and before he began sucking on his wounds, Charlotte could see that the skin was torn away from his knuckles.

"My God," she breathed, her anger suddenly draining away. "Jeff, what's happened to you?"

His eyes narrowed. "Nothing," he mumbled, and once more started to mount the stairs.

"Nothing?" Charlotte repeated. She turned to Chuck, now standing in the door to the den, his eyes, too, fixed on their son. "Chuck, look at him. Just look at him!"

"You'd better tell us what happened, son," Chuck said. "If you're in some kind of trouble—"

Jeff whirled to face them, his eyes now blazing with the same anger that had frightened Linda Harris earlier that evening. "I don't know what's wrong!" he shouted. "Linda broke up with me tonight, okay? And it pissed me off? Okay? So I tried to smash up a tree and I went for a walk. *Okay?* Is that okay with you, Mom?"

"Jeff—" Charlotte began, shrinking away from her son's sudden fury. "I didn't mean . . . we only wanted to—"

But it was too late.

"Can't you just leave me alone?" Jeff shouted.

He came off the bottom of the stairs, towering over the much smaller form of his mother. Then, with an abrupt movement, he reached out and roughly shoved Charlotte aside, as if swatting a fly. She felt a sharp pain in her shoulder as her body struck the wall, and then she collapsed to the floor. For a split-second Jeff stared blankly at his mother, as if he was puzzled about what had happened to her, and then, an anguished wail boiling up from somewhere deep within him, he turned and slammed out the front door.

Secret rituals masked in science . . . hidden cellars where steel cages gleam coldly against the dark . . . a cry of unfathomable rage and pain . . . In Silverdale no one is safe from . . .
Creature.

DARKNESS

The Andersons left the town at the edge of the swamp long ago, meaning never to return. There was something not quite right about the vast cruel lowlands of Villejeune . . . something murky, menacing, hostile . . . an influence too malevolent to be natural.

Darkness wrapped around Amelie Coulton like a funeral shroud, and only the sound of her own heartbeat told her that she was still alive.

She shouldn't have come here—she knew that now, knew it with a certainty that filled her soul with dread. She should have stayed at home, stayed alone in the tiny shack that crouched only a few feet above the dark waters of the swamp. There, at least, she would have been safe.

She would have been safe, and so would the baby that now stirred restlessly within her body, his feet kicking her so hard she winced with pain.

But Amelie hadn't stayed at home. Now, huddled silently in the darkness, she could feel danger all around her, danger she knew her baby could feel, too. . . .

As Amelie watched, the Dark Man held out his arms.

"Give me what is mine!" His voice boomed across the water, the words striking Amelie like hammer blows.

Silently, Tammy-Jo placed her newborn babe in the hands of the Dark Man, who turned and laid the baby on the altar like an offering, unfolding the blanket in which it was wrapped, until its pale body was uncovered in the candlelight.

From the folds of his robes the dark man withdrew an object. Amelie couldn't quite make it out, until the light of the tapers reflected from it as from the blade of a knife.

"Whose child is this?" the Dark Man asked, the blade held high above the baby's naked body.

"Yours," Tammy-Jo replied, her voice flat, her eyes fixed on the Dark Man.

Though his face was invisible, the girl in the canoe shivered as she felt the Dark Man's cold smile.

She wanted to turn away, but knew she couldn't. Fascinated with the black-clad image of the Dark Man, she watched unblinking as he raised the instrument in his hands high, poising it over the tiny infant on the altar. The candlelight flickered, and tiny brilliant stars flashed from the tip of the instrument.

It began to arc downward.

It hovered for a moment, just over the child's breast.

There was a short scream from the infant as the tip of the blade entered its chest, a scream that was cut off almost as quickly as it began.

The glinting metal sank deep into the child's body.

Involuntarily, a shriek rose in Amelie's throat, a small howl of pure horror that she cut off almost as quickly as the Dark Man had cut off the infant's scream.

The Dark Man looked up, gazing out over the fire and the water, and Amelie imagined that his unseeable eyes were boring into her, fixing her image on his mind.

My baby, she thought. *He wants my baby, too.*

Silently she dipped her paddle into the water and backed the canoe away. But even as she moved noiselessly through the black shadows, she could still feel the eyes of the Dark Man following her, reaching out to her, grasping at her.

No.

Not at her.

At the baby within her.

As she turned the canoe, intent on fleeing into the darkness, she heard the Dark Man speak once again.

"George Coulton," the heavy voice uttered. "When will you bring me what is mine?"

There was a moment of silence before Amelie heard her husband reply. When at last he spoke, George's flat, expressionless voice was clear.

"The night he's born. The night he's born, I be bringin' him to you."

Now the Andersons' return has completed a circle of destiny begun long ago. Now they must face a deadly drama of unholy ceremony and secret horror, of ancient greed preying upon young life, of unutterable depravity. For, like the other children of Villejeune—children without mercy or tears—sixteen-year-old Kelly Anderson is about to be drawn into a darkness so terrible it spares no life, no soul.

John Saul is "a writer with the touch for raising gooseflesh," says the *Detroit News*, and bestseller after bestseller has proved over and over his mastery for storytelling and his genius at creating heart-stopping suspense. Enter his chilling world, and prepare to realize your own hidden fears . . .

Available wherever Bantam paperbacks are sold!

*And now, turn the page
for an exciting preview of John Saul's
masterpiece of terror, SHADOWS.*

They call it The Academy.

Housed in a secluded, cliff-top mansion overlooking the rugged and picturesque Pacific coast, it is a school for special children. Children gifted—or cursed—with extraordinary minds. Children soon to come under the influence of an intelligence even more brilliant than their own—and unspeakably evil. For within this mind a dark, ingenious plan is taking form. A hellish experiment meant to probe the ultimate limits of the human brain.

A novel of unrelenting, nerve-jangling suspense, *Shadows* is John Saul's most terrifying tale to date . . . now, here is a chilling glimpse of what awaits you in the . . .

SHADOWS
John Saul

Amy looked up at the clock on the wall. Only five more minutes until her last class of the day ended.

She wished it would go on for the rest of the afternoon, right up until dinnertime, for every minute that went by brought her one minute closer to the experiment.

"But he *said* you don't have to do anything you don't want to do," Josh had insisted when she'd talked to him an hour ago, during the break between history and math. "What are you so scared of?"

Instead of answering his question, Amy had said nothing at all, for the image in her mind was still the one of the cat in the cage, wired to the computer, being subjected to electrical shocks, frightening sounds, and the stinking odor of the skunk.

Her trepidation hadn't been eased at all when Mrs. Wilson, her math teacher, had handed her a note at the beginning of the hour, instructing her to appear at the gym at three-thirty.

The note had been signed by Dr. Engersol.

Why did he want her at the gym? Was that where the experiment was going to be held?

"Amy? Amy, are you listening at all?"

The voice of Enid Wilson, the math teacher, punched through the worries that were churning through the little girl's head. Startled, Amy automatically sat up straight in her chair.

"Haven't you been listening at all, Amy?" Mrs. Wilson, a tall, angular woman whose gray hair was pulled back into a severe bun pinned at the back of her neck, was glaring at her over the rims of her glasses. The stridency in her voice made Amy cringe.

"I—I was thinking about something else," she said, her voice trembling.

"Obviously," Enid Wilson replied, her voice crackling. "But when you're in my classroom, I expect you to pay attention to me." She rapped the pointer in her hand on the chalkboard behind her. "Can you solve this equation, or not?"

Amy stared at the complicated algebraic equation that was written out on the board, knowing that she should be able to solve it in her head. She concentrated, her eyes squinting and her brow furrowing as she began to do the calculations, visualizing the numbers in her mind as clearly as if she were working with a pencil and a scratch pad.

"Come now, Amy, it's not that difficult," Mrs. Wilson prodded. "It's really nothing more than a simple reduction!"

Amy swallowed hard, trying to clear the lump that had suddenly formed in her throat. In her mind, the numbers faded away, and she lost her place in the equation. "I—I can't do it," she breathed.

The teacher's eyes fixed on her, making her want to sink through the floor. "Then perhaps you can do some extra homework this evening," Mrs. Wilson told her while the rest of the class tittered at her discomfort. "If you're not going to pay attention in class, you'll simply have to do the work in your room." Smiling thinly, Mrs. Wilson addressed the rest of the class. "Work out the first fifteen problems at the end of Chapter Three," she told them. "Amy Carlson will do the rest of them for you."

Amy's eyes widened. If Chapter Three were like the first two, there were fifty problems to be solved. And she had a chapter of history to read, and a story to write for Mr. Conners. How would she ever do it? And all because she hadn't been able to solve one stupid equation!

The bell rang. As the rest of the students hurried toward the door, intent on getting out into the afternoon sunshine, Amy lingered where she was. When the room was at last empty save for herself and the teacher, Mrs. Wilson finally gazed questioningly at her.

"Is there something you want to talk to me about, Amy?" she asked.

For a second Amy wondered if it would do any good to tell Mrs. Wilson how much other studying she had to do that night. She decided it wouldn't. Mrs. Wilson wasn't like Mr. Conners, who was always willing to listen to his students' problems. Mrs. Wilson didn't seem to care how much work they had to do for their other classes. "It's simply a matter of planning your time," she'd told Brad Hinshaw last week, when he'd complained that the assignment was too long. "You're all gifted children, and we're here to challenge your intellects, not coddle the habits you developed in public school. I know everything has always been easy for all of you, but life isn't like that. You must learn to do what is asked of you without complaining."

"She's sure a bitch," Brad had muttered as they'd left her room that day. When some of the other kids had giggled, Mrs. Wilson had recalled them to the classroom and demanded to know what they were laughing about.

And then she'd doubled Brad's assignment.

"N-No, Mrs. Wilson," Amy finally said as the teacher's eyes bored into her. "I'm okay. I'm sorry I wasn't paying attention."

Enid Wilson's lips relaxed into a semblance of a smile. "Very well," she said. "Your apology is accepted. As," she added, the smile disappearing, "will your homework be tomorrow. Now I suggest you get about your business. Dr. Engersol doesn't like to be kept waiting, you know."

Nodding quickly, Amy pulled her book bag out from under her desk and left the room. Emerging from the building, she turned left and started toward the gym on the other side of the campus.

She paused in front of the door to the women's locker room, screwing her face into her habitual tight squint of concentration.

What if she changed her mind *right now*?

Was it possible the experiment had already started?

She glanced around. There were a few of the college students lying around under the trees and walking along the sidewalks, but no one seemed to be paying any attention to her.

And she didn't have that creepy feeling on the back of her neck that she always got when she felt like she was being watched.

Sighing, she decided the experiment hadn't begun yet, and walked on into the locker room. It was empty except for Hildie Kramer, who stood up as Amy came into the humid room.

"I was starting to wonder if you were going to show up at all," Hildie said, smiling. "Dr. Engersol wants you to put on a bathing suit and go out by the pool."

Amy's lips pursed. "The pool? Is that where the experiment is?"

Hildie nodded. "Do you have your own bathing suit here?"

Amy shook her head. "It's in my room. Nobody said I should bring it. Should I go get it?"

She had already started toward the door when Hildie stopped her. "It's all right, Amy. We have plenty of bathing suits. I'll bring you one."

Amy went to her locker and started undressing, and a minute later Hildie reappeared, carrying with her one of the shapeless maroon tank suits with which the gym was stocked. "Yuck," Amy said, eyeing the suit with distaste. "I hate those things!"

Hildie chuckled. "Doesn't everyone? But I tried to find one that doesn't look too worn-out."

Amy took the suit from Hildie, then finished stripping off her clothes and pulled it on. Poking her arms through the straps and wriggling, she pulled the piece of material over her body, then looked hopefully up at Hildie. "Is it really awful?"

Hildie cocked her head critically. "Well, I don't suppose you'd win the Little Miss America contest, but it could be a lot worse. At least it fits, and it doesn't have any holes in it. Ready?"

"I guess," Amy agreed. She followed Hildie through the locker room to the showers, then into the foot bath that filled a shallow pan sunk into the concrete in front of the door to the pool. Suddenly Amy's nerves got the best of her. She gazed pleadingly up at Hildie. "Can't you please tell me what the experiment is?" she begged.

Hildie's warm laugh filled the locker room, the sound itself making Amy feel a little bit better. "Why don't you just stop worrying about it?" she asked. "You know I'm not going to tell you anything about it, except that it's not going to hurt you at all. And if you don't want to take part in it, you don't have to. As soon as you know what it is, you can turn around and walk away, if that's what you want to do."

Amy took a deep breath and considered the situation. Should she trust Hildie? Hildie had been on her side over the animal experiments, after all. So whatever this experiment was, it couldn't be too bad. She stepped through the door to the pool.

And stopped, startled by what she saw.

At the far end of the pool, a curtain had been hung, so the diving boards were completely invisible.

Ten feet away from her, sitting near the pool, was a chair. Next to the chair was a table on which sat a computer and what looked like some kind of headset.

There were video cameras in various places around the pool, all of them trained on the empty chair.

Dr. Engersol was sitting in a second chair, facing the computer screen. Seated around him were the other members of the seminar.

Did they all know what was going to happen? Was she the only one who wasn't in on it?

She felt betrayed.

Her first impulse was to turn around and run back through the door, but her friends were already watching her, staring at her as if they were sure she was going to chicken out before it even began.

And it wasn't just her friends.

Her eyes shifted away from the group of children gathered around the computer to the small grandstand that faced the pool from the other side.

Sitting on the benches were at least fifty of the college students, and they were watching her, too.

Amy felt herself burning with embarrassment. Were all these people really here just to watch her? But why? What was going to happen?

Behind her, she heard Hildie's voice. "Are you all right, Amy? Do you want to go ahead?"

What Amy wanted to do was fall through the concrete and have the earth swallow her up. Why were all these people here? Why wasn't it just the kids in the seminar, who were at least people she knew? And what would happen if she turned around and ran back into the locker room?

They would laugh at her.

All of them. They would know she was a coward, and even though they might not laugh out loud, inside they would be laughing at her.

Tonight, in the dining room, she would hear the clucking as all the rest of the kids made chicken sounds.

Even her friends would laugh at her, and she would feel just like she had back in public school, when everyone acted as if she was some kind of freak or something.

No!

She wouldn't let it happen. Somehow, she would get through it.

She took a deep breath, then slowly let it out. "I— I'm okay," she managed to say, but even she could hear the trembling in her voice. "I just didn't—who are all those people?"

Hildie smiled reassuringly at her. "They're from one of the psychology classes. Dr. Engersol invited them to watch the experiment."

"But he didn't *tell* me," Amy wailed.

Sensing what was going through the little girl's

mind, Hildie knelt down and took Amy's hands in her own. "It's all right, Amy. Nothing's going to happen to you. They're just here to watch. They're not going to say anything, or do anything. It's going to be all right."

"Wh-What am I supposed to do?"

"Just go over and sit in the chair," Hildie told her. "Come on. I'll go with you."

Holding Amy's hand, the housemother led her over to the chair, and Amy perched nervously on its edge. Then, at last, Dr. Engersol explained what was going to happen.

"We're going to attach electrodes to you, Amy," he explained. "But they don't do anything except measure your physical responses. I promise you, you won't feel anything at all. All we're going to be doing is recording changes in your heartbeat, and your breathing, and your brain-wave patterns. The cameras will be recording your facial expressions and any movements of your body. So all you have to do is sit there."

"But why me?" Amy asked. "What am I supposed to be doing?"

"You'll see in a minute," Engersol told her. "And remember, you can leave anytime you want to, just like I promised."

And have everyone laugh at me, Amy thought silently.

She sat still on the chair as Dr. Engersol attached the electrodes to her body. Soon she was even more festooned with wires than the cat had been that morning. At last Dr. Engersol placed a helmet over her head, and she felt a mass of tiny points press against her scalp.

"Does that hurt?" Dr. Engersol asked her. "It shouldn't, and if it does, I can make adjustments so it won't. The electrodes should touch your head, but there shouldn't be much pressure."

"I—It's all right," Amy managed to say. Then her eyes met Engersol's, and he could see the fear in them. "Something's going to happen, isn't it?" she asked. "Something awful."

"Nothing awful at all," Engersol reassured her. He checked over the electrodes once more, then went around to the computer screen. On its display, Amy's respiratory rhythm, heartbeat, and brain-wave patterns were clearly visible, reflecting a body under a certain amount of mental stress.

But nothing out of the normal ranges.

"All right," he said. "We're about to begin. All I'm going to do is ask you to make a decision." At the far end of the pool the curtain was suddenly pulled away. Next to the high diving board, a scaffolding had been erected. From the scaffolding hung the knotted rope, the same one she had tried to climb in the gym last week.

Tried to climb, and failed.

"I want you to pick one of them, Amy," Dr. Engersol told her. "Which would you rather do? Climb the rope? Or jump off the high diving board?"

Amy stared at him. Was he kidding? Did she really have to do one of those things?

But he'd said she didn't! He'd said she didn't have to do anything at all! All she had to do was sit here.

Her heart sank.

Already she could hear the laughter that would erupt from her friends when they figured out she was terrified of both the rope and the diving board.

The cat.

He was doing to her what he'd done to the cat this morning.

A double negative.

Make a choice between two things she hated, or let everyone know how terrified she was.

Let them know, and put up with them teasing her.

Scaredy-cat, scaredy-cat, Amy is a scaredy-cat!

Though no one had uttered the words, she could already hear them ringing in her ears.

She tore her eyes away from the rope and the diving board and looked at the faces of her classmates, who were gathered around the computer, some of them watching the screen, some of them watching her.

Jeff Aldrich was grinning, already figuring out how scared she was.

What would he do? Would he just tease her?

Or would it be worse? Maybe he'd hold her out the window, dangling her above the sidewalk, threatening to let her fall.

Her thoughts began to race. What was worse? To have everyone laugh at her and tease her, or to make a choice and try to get through the terror that always seized her when she was more than a few feet off the ground?

But Dr. Engersol had told her she just had to choose! She didn't actually have to do anything!

Except it wouldn't be enough. If she said she'd chosen one or the other, and then didn't go through with it, they'd all know!

Trapped.

Even after all his promises, he'd trapped her.

Which?

The rope?

She remembered freezing up there, terrified that she was going to fall, clinging to the rope until the coach climbed up and got her.

And she hadn't even been able to make herself climb the ladder to the high board.

A ladder and a rope! How could she be afraid of a stupid ladder and a dumb rope!

But what if she fell?

If she fell off the rope, she'd break a leg at least.

But she might not fall off the ladder, not with bars to hang onto and steps for her feet. And when she got to the top, all she had to do was walk out to the end and jump off.

Just the thought of standing on the narrow board three meters above the pool made her stomach feel hollow and her groin tighten with fear.

But it was only ten feet! What could happen to her?

Surely being terrified for a few seconds was better than having everyone laugh at her because she was chicken.

"I—I made up my mind," she whispered. "I'm going to jump off the diving board."

Immediately, Dr. Engersol left his chair and came to remove the helmet from her head while two graduate students detached the electrodes from her body. But the cameras, which had been recording her every facial expression, every movement of her body, were still running.

And everyone was still watching.

She approached the ladder that led to the diving board and gripped the handrails tightly. She put her foot on the bottom step and started climbing.

She was halfway up when she looked down, and froze.

Do it! she told herself. Just climb up, walk out on the board, and jump.

Then, as she stared down at the concrete beneath her, her terror of heights welled up in her and she knew she couldn't do it.

Don't look, she commanded herself.

She forced herself to look up, and there, looming above her, was the board itself.

No!

She couldn't do it, couldn't possibly walk out on it! It was too narrow. She'd fall before she took even a single step.

As she felt the last of her nerve slipping away from her, she began to sob. Tears streaming down her face, she scrambled back down off the ladder and fled toward the locker room, covering her face with her hands, already imagining she could hear the laughter following her. Then she was inside the locker room, scurrying across the empty shower room. By the time she came to her locker, the bathing suit was already half off, and she jerked it the rest of the way, hurling it into a corner and pulling on her clothes as fast as she could. Leaving her locker standing open, sobs of humiliation racking her body, Amy Carlson fled from the gym.

By the time Hildie Kramer came looking for her, the locker room was empty, but Hildie was almost certain she knew where Amy had gone.

As she, too, left the gym, every trace of the warm and kindly expression she habitually wore when she spoke to either the children or their parents was gone from her face, replaced by a look of harsh determination. Before anyone else saw Amy Carlson again, Hildie Kramer intended to find her.

ABOUT THE AUTHOR

JOHN SAUL is the author of nineteen novels, each a million-copy-plus national bestseller: *Suffer the Children, Punish the Sinners, Cry for the Strangers, Comes the Blind Fury, When the Wind Blows, The God Project, Nathaniel, Brainchild, Hellfire, The Unwanted, The Unloved, Creature, Sleepwalk, Second Child, Darkness, Shadows, Guardian, The Homing,* and *Black Lightning.* John Saul lives in Seattle, Washington.